Also by George Packer

THE VILLAGE OF WAITING

THE HALF MAN

GEORGE
PACKER

THE
HALF
MAN

RANDOM HOUSE
NEW YORK

Grateful acknowledgment is made to the following for permission to reprint previously published material: *Frank Music Corp*: Excerpts from "Luck Be a Lady," from *Guys and Dolls,* by Frank Loesser. Copyright 1950 by Frank Music Corp. Copyright renewed 1978 by Frank Music Corp. International copyright secured. All rights reserved. Reprinted by permission. *Edward B. Marks Music Company*: Excerpts from "Total Eclipse of the Heart," by Jim Steinman. Copyright © 1982, 1983 by Lost Boys Music. Administered by Edward B. Marks Music Company for the U.S. and Canada. All rights reserved. Reprinted by permission.

Library of Congress Cataloging-in-Publication Data

Packer, George.
    The half man / George Packer.—1st ed.
      p. cm.
     ISBN 0-394-58192-X
     I. Title.
   PS3566.A317H3   1991
   813' .54—dc20   90-52895

Manufactured in the United States of America

98765432

First Edition

Book design by Lilly Langotsky

FOR MICHELE MILLON

Meanwhile the mind, from pleasure less,
Withdraws into its happiness;
The mind, that ocean where each kind
Does straight its own resemblance find;
Yet it creates, transcending these,
Far other worlds and other seas,
Annihilating all that's made
To a green thought in a green shade.

—ANDREW MARVELL, "THE GARDEN"

ACKNOWLEDGMENTS

I thank my friends Tom Small, who first proposed a trip to Asia; James Fenton and F. Sionil Jose, who housed, fed, and educated me in Manila; Gordon Harvey, who understood the manuscript and gave invaluable literary advice; and Becky Saletan, a discerning and tireless editor.

THE HALF MAN

CHAPTER I

Even in the middle of civil wars, people throw dinner parties.

For years, residents of the capital of Direv Saraun, an island country spilled tear-like off Southeast Asia, were used to thinking of the guerrilla army in the southern mountains as an unlikely rumor: intriguing, with certain comic possibilities; disquieting when given too much thought; on the whole probably ridiculous. But recently the guerrillas had brought the war close to São Sebastião and become an invisible presence in the capital. Bridges were blown, crops burned, and suddenly the markets ran out of charcoal and vegetables, the price of rice doubled; the power failed every evening after the pylons along the valley road were sabotaged; a well-placed bomb left a crater where the national airline office had been; the minister of mines, industry and transport was shot dead in a lunchtime traffic jam. "Transport Min. Misses Bus," ran the headline above the *Daily Nation*'s editorial.

Vulgar in the best of times, São Sebastião began to look gaunt and stricken. Squabbles broke out in food lines. Barside toasts became apocalyptic. Garbage piled up even in the shopping streets and outside the hotels. Tourism dwindled as word spread that Direv Saraun was no longer "safe." But the sex tourists kept coming (a man's *kolau,* said the locals, is the most persuasive travel agent), and two dance girls on Marapang Road fell into a ferocious battle, all knees and teeth and painted nails, over rights to an Australian customer. The thin sun-scorched Saraunese faces creased and tightened, but the people of the capital tried to go about their normal business. A newcomer might not have guessed that a war ringed the city and was pressing in.

On a February afternoon at the end of the typhoon season, Levin was slicing eggplant in his kitchen when the phone rang.

"Shall I get it?" Melanie asked.

"I will. It's obviously for me."

He went into the main room to answer.

"Hello, Mr. Daniel Levin?"

"Speaking." His heartbeat quickened and he lowered his voice. "Who is this?" he said, although he knew.

"This is Connie."

"Connie. Oh, yes. How are you, Connie?"

"Can you meet me in about one hour?"

"Where? At the hospital?"

"Not there." Her voice, which had sounded cheerful by rote, sharpened. "In the place that you know."

"Right. Sorry—Connie. I'll meet you there."

"I can't wait," she told him, going silky. He was taken aback.

"Me too."

Levin hung up. He stood by the phone a moment, calming his breath, then dialed. A landlady answered.

"Ding not here all day," she said. "You the journalist?"

"Yes. Could you just tell him that Dan Levin wants him to come to a dinner party tonight? At eight. It's very important for him to come."

Levin went back into the kitchen, where Melanie was peeling red potatoes.

"Who was it?"

"Feliz. He wants to know if he can bring anything. I told him a case of Temple of Heaven."

"A case! We'll get plastered."

"Well, beer just seems to go down like water here."

Levin came up behind her at the counter and put his hands on her bare shoulders. She was wearing a tank top that said "Penn Law." He kissed her on the knob of her shoulder bone.

"Glad to have me here?" she asked.

"You know I am."

"You'd tell me if you weren't. Wouldn't you?"

"Yes. Going to wear this tonight?"

"Is it dressy enough for your friends?"

"Anything goes. Why don't you wear that green dress you bought yesterday."

"I thought you didn't like it."

"I didn't say that at all. Listen," Levin said, "I have to run some errands. You'll be O.K. here for a couple of hours?"

"I think I can manage." She half turned her cheek to his kiss, but not far enough for him to reach her lips. "Don't forget the fish."

"Right. I'm going by the market anyway."

"Just be careful out there."

He started to leave. "Oh, we might be having someone else. Ding Magkakanaw."

"The names around here."

"Yeah. Even the Saraunese think his is funny."

"Who is he? You haven't mentioned him."

"He's—I don't know. He's not really anyone. Just a free-lance photographer from up in Porto de Coral. It seems like he wants to be friends."

"Not a job?"

"Well, that goes without saying. Everyone here wants a job."

"Except the lucky ones." Melanie was brushing potato shavings into a small pile. "The natives sure must resent you white guys."

Levin stopped in the doorway and gave her a look. But he tried to sound pleasant. "Why do you say that?"

She shrugged. "I feel a little resented here."

"You've been here five days. You don't really know the place."

She returned to her peeling.

In the bedroom Levin put his camera and some newspaper clippings in his black vinyl shoulder bag, and a small blue notebook in his back pocket. He started for the front door: Melanie was watching him from the kitchen.

"See," she said. "You're doing it again."

"Doing what?"

"Touching your wrist. Your pulse."

"Jesus, sweetie. It's a mosquito bite."

"O.K., O.K. Cease fire."

She came forward, a potato in one hand and a paring knife in the other, and draped her blue-veined arms around his neck. She cooed soothingly, and he brought her to him so tight that she gasped, then laughed. Their mouths missed, met, planted, drank, bit. Levin shut his eyes and felt strange tears start in them. He was still a little shaky, so long deprived of human touch. After four chaste months apart the feel of Melanie was sometimes an unbearable pleasure. Every inch of her pressed a memory on his nerves—the strength of her slender frame, the wildflower smell of her shampoo, the thick Midwestern auburn mane. He sucked on her lower lip and kissed it.

"I missed you," he told her.

"Good." She was waiting to meet his eye. "I think," she said slowly, "I can see why you had to come."

"You can?"

"Now that I'm here."

Levin gave her a hug. On his way out, he reminded himself to call Feliz about the beer.

The sky this afternoon was full of melodrama: one minute vivid blue, the next a mass of rising clouds, then almost black, to the west over the harbor, with wind, ragged showers yellowed by the slanting light, and sapphire again, as the pavement steamed and instantly dried under the sun. It was wild pre-typhoon weather; but the storm had already passed. It had swept up from the south, cutting the heads off coconut palms, ripping away thatch roofs, and slashing houses and whole families from the coast. Last night it had blown out to sea, missing São Sebastião entirely.

Levin walked toward Impanang along the edge of downtown and felt his black hair, curly and thinning on top, dance in the humid wind. He pictured himself as a tall white presence among the shorter, thicker brown men and women, a conspicuous figure moving through the city with his long strides, the ubiquitous black bag swinging from his shoulder. He drew looks and sometimes found himself imagining every Saraunese's reaction to him—a harmless tropical solipsism. But after four months here, he no longer thought of himself as a newcomer.

Connie was not the real name of the woman who had called: it was Sylvia Moktil. Ding Magkakanaw had introduced him to her. She was a nurse at a public hospital, and also a member of the illegal Saraunese People's Party—a city cadre of the guerrillas. Although she had never told Levin this, he knew that she knew that he knew. She was as close to them as he had come.

Levin had been waiting a long time for her call.

At the traffic-choked corner of Avenue U Thant and Dag Hammarskjold Boulevard, which ran along the harbor, he passed the hole that until last week had been the offices of Air Saraun. A few street urchins were driving scavenged go-carts over the shattered glass and concrete rubble. The ground floor of the building next door, owned by American Express, had been taken over as temporary quarters by the airline. Outside, a line of well-dressed Saraunese stretched all the way out past the bomb crater and around the corner of the boulevard. They were queueing up for plane tickets. Whenever anyone came out of the office, the people in line glanced up for some clue to their fate. Apparently flights out were booked up, for no one was smiling.

As Levin waited for the light at the avenue to change, a young man approached. He was dressed in the blue slacks and white shirt of a government employee.

"Excuse me," the young man said, "are you a Christian?"

"Nope."

"American military?"

"No."

"But you live in São Sebastião. I see you."

Levin became suspicious, although the young man's smile was benign, ingratiating. It was impossible to stand still for five seconds here without making a friend.

"I'm a basketball player," he said. "I'm the shooting guard on the Rum Direv club."

The young man seemed to realize this was a lie, but there was no offense taken. He launched into a complicated saga involving a church in Akron, Ohio, an uncle in San Diego, a U.S. visa for himself and considerable profit on a small investment for Levin. He repeated the scheme several times but did not succeed in making himself understood.

The light changed and Levin started to cross.

"It is funny," the young man called after him over the traffic.

"What's funny?"

The young man pointed to the line of Saraunese wrapped around the American Express building and the rubbled hole. "You have come to São Sebastião. And São Sebastião wants to leave."

Levin laughed. The young man had a point—one that had occurred to Levin before. In the eyes of the Saraunese, traveling half-way around the globe to see this country disintegrate seemed like sheer perversity. A few of them might even take exception. But Levin was past the point of having to explain himself; he had his reasons for being here.

Impanang was São Sebastião's most famous slum, surrounded by the bay, the Musa River at its point of emptying, and the vast open-air Central Market. It housed untold thousands of squatters on landfill and packed garbage. Levin had been told that it was not a safe place for a white man alone, but he had been coming here for two months without incident to write about the Balatangs. They were an unexceptional squatter family: six children, the father an unemployed laborer at the port, the mother a grade-school graduate who'd once wanted to be a teacher. They came from a fishing village down the coast, to which they'd been resettled by the police numerous times and from which they always returned to Impanang. Levin had met Ani Balatang one day at the vegetable tables in the Central Market and immediately conceived an idea for a series of articles on the life of slum dwellers. She was flattered by his interest and almost desperately open with him. So while other reporters were attending press conferences at the army headquarters or the U.S. embassy, Levin made weekly pilgrimages to Impanang.

Like many of their countrymen, the Balatangs were scavengers. What one scavenged depended on one's circumstances, and since the Balatangs lived across a field of mud from the Temple of Heaven beer bottling plant, they scavenged glass. Their neighborhood, perpetually fogged by the nearby water, was paved with bits of broken glass foraged from the hills of garbage that municipal trucks dumped all over Impanang, making the slum an economic magnet for squatters nationwide. The stuff made its way through a series of middlemen into the beer bottles manufactured across the field. In front of their hovels adults and children were eternally throwing clumps of mud against pieces of screening to sift out the glass, as if it were gold. The children went barefoot without shredding their feet, which had somehow adapted to the habitat.

Levin had made it his special business to know the destitute. He had tried to prepare for Saraunese poverty, but the encounter with it shocked him and defined his sense of the country. So pervasive and so little noticed, it seemed more the truth of the place than all the sensational violence and military intrigue. For him, the poverty never became normal. His colleagues in the foreign press showed condescending interest in the pieces he wrote, but he was envied for his initiative and his empathy. The articles were widely praised in educated Saraunese circles as a significant departure from the usual journalistic gangbangs. Levin, not without ambition, was making a name for himself.

He stepped through the muck in his running shoes and tapped on the Balatangs' plastic sheeting. Neighbors waved in greeting, pleased and amused at his arrival.

"Mr. Dan!" From within Mrs. Balatang removed a drift-plywood section of wall and bade him enter. The ceiling allowed about four feet of headroom; the Balatangs lived underneath another family. The floor of wood and metal scraps was raised a foot off the mud, but Levin saw at once that they had been flooded again.

"It seemed like a light rain," he told Mrs. Balatang.

"Light rain is Noah's flood in Impanang!"

Ani was a thin, intelligent, excitable woman with a chronic stomach complaint. All her children seemed to be sitting in the half-light. Her husband was out: a garbage truck had just arrived.

Levin's dominant impression from his visits to the Balatangs was of wetness. Everything they owned was perpetually rain-damp. The two-year-old with the respiratory infection drooled and sniveled on her T-shirt, her chin, her mother. Even the rice was soggy. Mrs. Balatang once told him that they lived here "like grasshoppers"; but she took care to keep her few dishes stacked, and her prematurely wasted face had touches of eyeliner and lipstick.

"You have lunch already?" she asked.

"Well, I could eat some rice."

Kneeling, he dug his latest article out of his bag and held it up for them to see. The children shrieked with delight—the accompanying photograph showed the whole family standing in front of their house. Actually, they'd posed looking happier than Levin had wanted. The headline read "In Direv Saraun, a Family Lives on Broken Glass and Dreams." Not his choice; he'd have left out "dreams."

"It's about money, how you make a living," he told her. "The middleman's profit, how much per kilo of glass, all that."

Mrs. Balatang laughed and nodded, handing him a bowl of rice and salted fish. Levin felt slightly ashamed about his summary of the article, which none of them would be able to read, because it left out his detailed account of the squalor of their life, the unsanitary latrine, a plague of roaches he'd weaseled Ani into showing him—details that they would consider a disgrace. Differences in culture and class, notions of decency, agenda. His American readers would feel nothing but what he intended—pity and anger.

The family regarded the articles as an honor. At any rate, he and the Balatangs thrived on each other. He always left Impanang feeling his best impulses aroused.

"How's your stomach?" he asked, trying to swallow the mushy rice.

"Not so good." She put a hand to it and mustered her what-can-you-do smile. "No medicine."

"You ran out?"

The smile twitched, affirming it. He reached in his pocket and withdrew the forty *cobas,* about two dollars, that he'd brought for this purpose.

"Oh, Mr. Dan. *Paklan, paklan.* "

"Be sure to get a refill. What about Maria's infection?"

"Still."

"You should probably take her to the doctor."

He took another hundred from his wallet. She bowed and gave the money to her eldest son.

"*Paklan,* Mr. Dan. You are too nice for us."

Levin told her in Saraunese that it was nothing, which made the children scream with laughter. Two of the boys had discovered the camera in his bag and were passing it reverentially back and forth.

"Your sweetheart here?" Mrs. Balatang asked.

"She got here Sunday."

"You are happy man now!"

"You bet."

They had just about exhausted the common topics of conversation. Levin suddenly felt restless, crouched with them in the dank room. The feeling descended on him often here: a need to move on to the next thing. He had a low tolerance for inertia. Even the customary midday nap was beyond his ability. And in Direv Saraun things always threatened to come to a dead stop.

He stroked Maria's head, and she grinned wetly for him.

"Any news in Impanang?"

"Oh, Mr. Dan! Yesterday they kill a policeman over market side."

"Who killed him? Cobra unit?"

Cobra units were the Army of Liberation's urban assassination squads, so called for their quick, lethal strikes. Mrs. Balatang feigned ignorance—the family's politics, which Levin often tried to sound, was of the see-no-evil variety.

"Was he a bad man in Impanang? Corrupt?"

She shrugged, and then nodded. Outside the shack there was a commotion, and when she lifted aside the plywood her husband was standing over the opening in his shorts and rubber boots, clutching the piece of claw-shaped metal that all the glass scavengers used.

Mr. Balatang greeted Levin with shy deference. Levin's relationship with him was less easy than with his wife, and he spoke no English, so she had to translate. It seemed the capital police were about to demolish the neighborhood where their colleague had been gunned down yesterday by guerrillas.

Levin crawled out of the house, and he and the Balatangs hurried through the mud and fog, crunching glass as they went, passing scavengers bent over garbage heaps, to the strip of shanties that faced the Central Market.

The demolition was nearly finished. A dozen uniformed and plain-clothes police had crow-barred and sledge-hammered the dwellings to pieces, and they were busy setting fire to the scraps of wood and plastic. Children cried; their mothers tried to rescue furniture and clothing from the flames. One woman cursed the police so vehemently that she collapsed face first into the mud. A small crowd of squatters had gathered, watching the destruction in silence. An old man among them, seeing a white face, begged Levin to do something. Levin put out his hands. "What can I do?"

He was unzipping his bag for the camera when Mrs. Balatang, mindful of his journalistic needs, pointed out among the spectators a light-skinned woman in clean stonewashed jeans. She was a legal organizer of the squatters in Impanang, Mrs. Balatang explained. Levin asked to be introduced.

The organizer pretended not to notice his approach. At the introduction she nodded curtly and turned back to the wreckage.

Levin brought out his notebook.

"Was there a permit to demolish?"

The organizer didn't answer. When he repeated the question, she told him to ask the police.

"But were the people warned to leave?"

She said that it made no difference.

"If it's an illegal demolition they could file a complaint."

The organizer looked at him and laughed with heavy sarcasm. "And who is going to listen to these people? The mayor?"

"Why do you think they've singled them out?"

By now her face had hardened. "Why don't you ask your embassy? Don't they make the decisions here?" Levin started to contradict her, but she'd switched to Saraunese. He understood that he was being cursed. Mrs. Balatang seemed to defend him, but the organizer would have none of it.

Balked, Levin turned to writing notes.

"Go somewhere else to spy," the organizer told him. And she turned on her heel in the mud and left to join the squatter women.

Mrs. Balatang fell into fervent apologies. "She not polite talking you like that!"

"It's O.K. She's upset about what's happened to these people."

"No good, Mr. Dan! Why you let her talk like that?"

"I'm not—" He knew she wouldn't understand, but he told her anyway, taking care to pick his words so that she wouldn't grasp enough to continue the argument. "It's not my country. It's not my role to tell people how to feel about me. I'm here as an observer." He waved the notebook to demonstrate. "Everyone's very high-strung these days, and people like me are the obvious scapegoat. It's part of the situation—it's not personal."

Mrs. Balatang stared at him in distress.

The cops began returning to their trucks, and Levin realized he was late for his meeting. Saying good-bye to the family, he pressed another twenty *cobas* into Mrs. Balatang's hand. She and her husband waved as he crossed the street, past the smoking debris of the shacks, toward the Central Market. "Don't be stranger!" she called out, a phrase he'd taught her. Mr. Balatang lifted his scavenger's claw in salute.

Halfway across the street, Levin realized that he'd gotten no pictures of the demolition. He swore, and he started to curse the organizer as she'd cursed him, caught himself, and smiled slightly in bemusement. He could hardly blame her for making him forget.

Sylvia Moktil, a.k.a. Connie, was sitting on a stone bench across from the Super City Cinema. Her Chinese-Portuguese mestizo features were neutralized by wire-rimmed glasses and studied nonchalance.

Levin sat down beside her.

"How are you, Sylvia?"

"Fine. You shouldn't have said at the hospital," she told him.

"I know, a mistake."

She wasted no time getting to the point. "Fra Boboy has agreed to the interview you requested."

Levin's heart soared.

Fra Boboy, a.k.a. Simkar Butang, ex-professor of political theory at the University of Direv Saraun, was commander of the Army of Liberation, Southern Region, and almost certainly a leading member of the Saraunese People's Party directorate. He was widely known to be the brains behind the war. "Fra," from the Franciscan order of monks, meaning "brother," was the guerrilla form of address—a touch of Fra Boboy's wit and eclecticism.

"We need your biodata. Bring it to the mountains."

"What should I put in it?"

"The subjects of interest to you. Your political framework. Articles you've written. It's a ten-hour drive to Pulaya, so leave here at night and arrive at dawn. Spend the day in Pulaya, then you will be met after dark to go up Mount Kalanar on foot."

As Sylvia—"Suor Connie"—gave him the details, Levin watched her. She smiled continually and her laugh was staccato, mechanical. She was thirty or so, rigidly single, pretty, perhaps brittle, with the quickness of an educated urban woman. A certain tightness about the eyes and mouth suggested the strain of her double life.

Women passed them with plastic shopping bags balanced on their heads. Some teenage boys were hanging around outside the movie house, smoking and trying to look like Sylvester Stallone.

"Fra Boboy has great confidence in you. He appreciated very much your articles about the proletariat family in Impanang. He was impressed with your analysis of the conditions of the people after so little time with us."

"He gets the *World Press* in the mountains?"

She laughed too hard for the small joke, then broke it cleanly off. "I used our channels."

Levin nodded his debt to her. "But he better not think I'm going to write A. of L. propaganda. I plan on asking some tough questions."

"Who said propaganda? Really, you misunderstand us. You will be free to ask anything you like. Simply he thinks you know the people and the nature of their struggle better than the other foreign press."

Blushing with pleasure, Levin denied it. "I have the four-month mind, still open. But he can't fill it up with just anything. On the biodata sheet I'll put I'm politically a liberal, a statistical liberal. I have what the military call 'simplistic Western ideas.' "

"Mr. Levin—"

"Sylvia, please—"

"It's Connie."

"Call me Dan."

"Fra Boboy has a high regard for you," she said. "Is anything wrong with that?"

As he'd known she would, Connie told him to bring an assistant, a Saraunese; no one traveled alone into guerrilla territory. Ding Magkakanaw had been his first thought, and she approved the choice. But then she asked, offhandedly, "Do you trust him?"

"Why shouldn't I?"

"No, there's no reason. Only"—she looked at Levin with one eye narrowing behind the lens, as if he shouldn't have to be told this most basic thing—"on a trip like this there must be complete trust among everyone."

"Of course. And I can vouch for Ding."

Immediately he realized that this was absurd—who was he to vouch for anyone? Ding had had to vouch for *him*. But Connie waved him off.

"Not necessary. That isn't quite what I meant," and she left it at that.

"Are you going to join the festivities?"

"Yes, I have medical work to do."

"Good."

"Fra Boboy will be available for the next ten days. But you need to specify now."

"Can I leave tomorrow?"

"Impatient!"

"I've been waiting a long time for this."

"We in Direv Saraun," she told him, "are used to waiting a lot longer."

She seemed to have finished with him and he started to rise. "Why did you pick that name—Connie?"

Her smile, caught off guard, flickered but remained in place. "A friend gave me a book by Mr. D. H. Lawrence. Lady Chatterley—I admired her. Because she made herself free, and I through my work in the struggle have also become free."

Levin nodded—his only concession to a fierce urge to giggle.

They parted and he wandered into the market, in search of pula-pula. Pula-pula was the national fish, named for the native chief who killed de Souza, the first European to reach Direv Saraun, in 1519. On behalf of the Portuguese crown, de Souza had come ashore and was invited by Pula-Pula to a banquet, where he was offered the chief's daughter in marriage. When de Souza hesitated, he was impaled. The Portuguese avenged his death by sending several galleons loaded with soldiers and priests to subdue the island. They were received, like de Souza before them, with unctuousness and hostility.

Levin moved slowly among the crates of bright hairy fruit and half-rotted lettuce. He tried to stay out of the sun that brought late-afternoon headaches. Even when he forgot and spent an hour finding his way home from across the river or watching a military parade, the liquid tropical sunlight didn't brown him. Melanie had noticed it immediately. "You've hardly been eating. And you're pale—have you been sick?"

He began to pass fish bins whose contents overflowed onto the ground. Everywhere fish lay in heaps, and the smell about the bins was already going rank. The vegetable women had ignored him, but the fish women plunged hands into their goods and came up waving fish by the tails, shouting, "You buy, Joe! Cheap, Joe!"

They were cheap—less than half the price he was used to hearing. And he seemed to be the only customer around. Behind a bin of corpses that included pula-pula he noticed a nut-brown old woman; alone of the sellers, she was gloomily silent. At his approach she brightened, and her mouth fell open when she saw him take out the notebook from his back pocket. For an instinct already told Levin that a story might lie behind this—perhaps a revelation.

Standing on a slippery mess of corrupted fish guts, a soft-spoken American in an uproarious Asian crowd, he bent to hear the fish woman's answers to his polite questions. Yes, she told him in broken English, all the sellers had lowered their prices. No, they couldn't get rid of their stock. Yes, some of it was starting to rot.

As he listened, the hand with the pen cupped his chin in his thoughtful way, and his soft brown eyes focused on the tiny woman. It was one of his talents, this ability to convey genuine interest. The eyes might gleam skeptically but they didn't stray; the mouth said "I understand" even as an ironic smile formed. This expression unlocked astonishing secrets. Strangers revealed crimes, humiliations, details of income, political schisms, half-formed fears. He found that almost everyone was eager to tell a story. And especially when Levin seemed ready to leave—then, just one word more, as if this would make all the difference and justify or save them.

When he'd arrived in October, an untried foreign correspondent in an obscure, unstable place, Levin had mentally drawn up a balance sheet of his strengths and weaknesses. Against the lack of experience or a shell of protective cynicism he had set this capacity to listen, elicit, disarm: a natural quality, now honed. He deployed it even when his heart was cold. He perfected the false exit. But though his talent unleashed upon him a flood of words, it could not tell him which of them to trust.

"Nobody buy!" cried the old woman, showing blackened lower teeth. She seized a silvery blue fish and shook it in her fist like a doll. "Say fish eat man. The *Esperanza.*"

Levin cried out in surprise. "Well goddammit! The *Esperanza.*"

A ferry that shouldn't have sailed had gone down in typhoon waters a week ago, hopelessly overloaded. Nobody knew how many hundreds were lost, the shipping company gave only the names of registered passengers. Relatives had waited five hours at its waterfront office before starting to heave chunks of concrete through the windows. Levin, over coffee at his usual doughnut shop, had read the papers with their wildly varying figures and reflected that the difference between one hundred and one thousand had lost some significance after four months. Inflation, average temperature, infant mortality, children per capita, cigarettes per annum per capita, registered prostitutes, typhoon-dead, car-dead—the numbers here were always unimaginable. To the readers of the *World Press* the difference between a hundred and a thousand would be page 13 vs. page 1.

The fish woman had given him the sort of thing he was always looking for as a journalist and had a special knack of finding, the detail that would make the numbers imaginable. The boat had gone down in prime waters. People were no longer eating fish because the fish might have eaten people.

"Woman buy pula-pula and cut it, say she find inside—"

The fish woman's wrinkled face colored, her eyes shifted away. Vaguely and rapidly she pointed at the level of Levin's belt.

"Somebody find a man *kolau* inside the fish." The old woman sent the fish slipping across the pile of brother corpses. She held up two fingers six inches apart and stared at Levin in outrage. "Like this! They find. Nobody buy."

In his amusement and haste to scribble notes he almost forgot to buy a couple of the scaly, staring pula-pula. They smelled fresh enough; the old woman shook her head and clapped her hands and swore these fish had not touched human flesh. Look at the eyes— innocent! She wrapped them in newsprint, among the headlines of murders and film stars, rumors of coup.

Before walking home Levin lingered in the market. It was his best time of day. The evening sun at this latitude was a perfect sphere, fiery orange; it sank behind the sea in a fast-motion film, leaving a thin line that highlighted the horizon, contracted to a red point and went out. The heat and smell of the city seemed to die with the sun. After the relentless exposure and hundred momentary panics of the day, Levin found himself suddenly, miraculously calm.

He moved between tables, enjoying the stares of curiosity and humor and approval. To the Saraunese who called out good evening, he called back; and their delight was out of all proportion, as if his very presence was somehow to their benefit. It was an ancient, totemic association, like the passage overhead of iridescent birds. "Ah, journalist! Things here—very bad, very no money." To other Saraunese, like the organizer in Impanang, it now signified the opposite. But at this hour Levin emerged from the sticky web of perception and expression and suspicion that the country had become for him. Scents of garlic and palm oil rose strongly from the tables. Alone, tugged by gestures and exclamations, soothed by evening, he moved along the verge of physical release. It was a feeling of tangible, almost unbearable freedom at the end of the earth—the feeling that had brought him to Direv Saraun and that he'd waited and longed for ever since. But almost always it eluded him.

He was in a downtown street, at a corner next to a Pizza Hut and a Rite Aid drugstore, just closed. The wet bundle of fish was under his arm. He lit a cigarette, the local brand, a habit acquired here by social necessity. On the sidewalk a short, dissipated, apologetic Muslim in a knit skullcap had taken up a permanent position hawking sunglasses by night, in the spot where by day a woman sat or slept on cardboard, with a baby and a wax soda cup for coins. These informal property rights were jealously guarded.

Levin and the Muslim had a ritual, and the ritual was a part of the evening mood of freedom. The Muslim would lift a pair of Ray-Bans for Levin's inspection and hopefully raise his eyebrows (expressive Saraunese eyebrows, signifying five hundred riddles). Levin would put a hand to his chin, as if he were listening to an explanation of the debt problem, and then shake his head no.

"Next time, boss?"

"Next time we'll see."

"Tomorrow, boss?"

Levin broke the catechism. "Tomorrow I'm going away."

"Going away, boss? Where?"

"That's sort of a secret."

"What about your wife?"

Levin looked into the Muslim's ferret eyes. "What about her?"

"Your wife don't like, boss?"

"Don't like what?"

The Muslim laughed. "Ray-Ban!"

Levin's face was going hot. For half an hour he'd forgotten about Melanie. Everything with the Muslim was a game, only this evening the rules, the point, escaped Levin. The Muslim was saying Melanie's presence had been noted and exposed something about Levin, who always maintained his dignity when the vendor added girls to his merchandise. The little brown man went on smiling. Levin felt that he was being mocked.

"She already has a pair."

"A nice pair."

Levin was struck dumb.

"Your wife going with you on your secret, boss?"

"What's it to you, Mohammed?" He shifted the stinking bundle of pula-pula, leaking on his skin. "And she's not my wife."

"And my name not Mohammed, boss. Sister?" The Muslim was just about to give in to laughter again.

"Not that either," Levin said, and then realized he was staying too long for a conversation that had already made him foolish. He walked away, toward his apartment on the coastal boulevard, where Melanie was getting ready for their guests. As he went, Levin touched his back pocket where he kept the notebook and indulged a little mental tic that he'd acquired lately. He began to write an imaginary dispatch.

São Sebastião, Direv Saraun, Feb. 21—In this city's most notorious slum, sledgehammer-wielding policemen destroy the homes of a dozen families. Across the street, an old market woman despairs while her fish stock rots because of a ferry disaster. And a hundred yards away, two-year-old Maria Balatang is enduring her sixth month of respiratory infection. In a country where war stories grab most of the—

"Sonofabitching Muslim," Levin heard himself mutter. "Don't be an ass."

Melanie was writing in her journal when he came in. She put it away and jumped up to kiss him, then took the bundle of fish into the kitchen. Levin showered off the city and changed into his white native shirt, collarless, lightly embroidered on the chest, buttoned at the cuffs. He immediately began to perspire. Sweat was continuous here. A Russian tailor downtown, a flabby-breasted old Georgian with whiskers in the nostrils, whose whole family had been wiped out in the German invasion, had cut the shirt for Levin to wear at official functions. Ministerial press cons, meetings with visiting American businessmen and under secretaries of state who wanted to know how long the country—meaning the small U.S. naval base at Porto Negrais, dating to the last months of World War II, long outmoded, and the Texaco liquefied natural gas plant in the limestone deposits near Tawau, the only American investment in Direv Saraun—would be safe. Levin had come to hate the neutral drone of voices, especially his own, floating like gases over the "Saraunese situation." No one at the embassy or the best restaurants dared to challenge the informality of the native shirt; like pula-pula, it had nationalistic connotations. The Americans were too scared of volatility in the current mood even to mention it. The shirt was his prank.

Levin leaned on the waist-high refrigerator and watched Melanie prepare the fish. Her head, on the long white neck, soft and vulnerable as an inner thigh, bent to the task at an angle that kept him out of her field of vision. Chopping, slicing, squeezing, wiping, pinching, her hands moved like a pair of fierce, methodical creatures. Tiny red spots, broken capillaries, marked the inside of her arms. She was wearing her green dress with thin straps, which followed her contour down to the knees. In the thin garment, on such slight shoulders, her breasts hung surprisingly full. She wanted to make an impression on his friends tonight—the dress, the pula-pula—and she would.

"Come on, talk to me." She wanted no help from him. His job was to stand by and entertain, tell jokes and stories that played over her like a massage.

She slid the knife into the first pula-pula. Fighting bone, she worked the blade the length of its bleeding white belly to the neck, then parted the flaps and plunged her fingers inside, flicking out strings of black gut. But nothing else. Levin, staring in fascination, was slightly disappointed. He remembered a book from childhood, *Charlie and the Chocolate Factory*—the young hero opens a candy bar and out falls a gold dollar, which entitles him to a tour of the factory and a lifetime of trucked-in sweets. Levin was about to tell Melanie the fish woman's story, then changed his mind. Tell it too many times and it dies. He would save it for dinner.

But the untold scrap of his day floated with others between them and violated the kitchen intimacy. Waiting for him to talk, she seemed to sense it.

"Well?" she said. "Tell me who's coming to dinner."

"A pretty interesting crowd. Each of them has a different take. There's John Fraser. I think I wrote you about him, the English guy from the *Financial Times*?"

"I don't remember."

"No, I'm sure I wrote you. Careful, baby, you'll cut yourself. We went to Paranak together when the military killed those peasants and he asked some stupid questions and they threw him in the local clink? John's never quite looked me in the eye since. He doesn't like what I saw there."

"You macho foreign correspondents. Why shouldn't he be scared shitless?"

"His girlfriend is coming too—Rose. She writes for one of the local papers. Great contacts. She translates for him too."

"What does Rose get out of the arrangement?"

"I knew you'd ask that. She lives a lot better than she would otherwise. John has a nicer place than this, on Avenue U Thant."

"And when he's reassigned to Mexico City or New Delhi—"

"He'll leave a lump sum," Levin wisecracked. "Severance pay."

"Funny."

"Maybe he'll marry her."

"But he won't. The brown girls get the short end. He'll just be a journalist heading off to the next story." She was grilling the fillets on the gas stove. They popped and sizzled as she shook the pan, billowing under a ribbon of soy sauce and squirts from green calamansi. "Who else?"

Levin, sweating more heavily now in the close cooking heat, wiped his forehead with a shirt cuff. "Feliz—I've told you about him too."

"I don't know what happened to all these letters—send them by boat?"

Now they were onto a subject Levin would rather have avoided. Melanie's letters had come one or two a week, in her neat looping cursive, words leaning slightly forward with the intensity of her feelings: loving, obscene, funny, then full of longing, then weeping, berating—the recent ones raised to the stunning eloquence of fury. Brief silence. Another storm, quickly subdued; melancholy; and finally a tired determination to travel out and see him. Conversely, over time Levin's anecdotes had dried out, cured into lengthy analyses of the war, the alignments, the killings she called his true passion. She demanded more feeling and got thinner letters, then fewer. After a Christmas card, his January silence. Now, in February, she was here, with an open-return ticket.

Levin knew in exactly which letter he'd mentioned Feliz. And he knew that Melanie knew. Her denial was part of the punishment, meted out in small doses over her week here. When she arrived he'd been caught off guard by his own delight. But lately he felt her probing for some access, some weakness, trying to find him out at the core; and he knew his parries had begun to nettle her and she wouldn't keep quiet much longer, nor would he keep his calm. But now Connie had called and none of it mattered.

"Feliz, sweetie—old slab head. A Portuguese tobacco dealer porked a Malay girl in a nipa stack and they spawned this guy. He wrote for *The New York Times* awhile, edited a whole bunch of local papers—our embassy thinks he's a Communist, the guerrillas think he's C.I.A., nobody can figure him out."

"Can you?"

"Well, he's the only one I really trust—implicitly. He's helped me find my feet. Also he's a *malaka*—likes boys. A famous pederast here. My hairdresser source tells me in this culture certain kinds of ugliness run so deep they come out the other end as beauty."

She laughed, in her rich-throated way; and the sound of it startled him. Her laughter always came as free and sudden as a sob or pleasure gasp. Levin realized that he'd forgotten it; for a long time she was only the dangerous handwriting on airmail envelopes. His early letters had been full of exotica like Feliz the *malaka*—it was what she loved to hear. In one letter she'd written, "I feel like I'm fighting that country for you," but at least she now saw that he hadn't dreamed the whole thing up. And he knew what an aphrodisiac politics could be.

"Feliz will bring Frankie Young along. His 'companion.' Every tenth Chinese is enormous, and Frankie—actually he was born in Burma—Frankie is this hulking man in silk Chinese pants and big bouncing shirts. He spent twenty-five years as a doctor for British Airways, had a couple of nervous breakdowns, skipped around the Pacific Islands a few years, ended up here."

"Frankie Young doesn't sound Chinese."

"It used to be Yung Fan-kee."

"Oh come on."

"I'm not kidding. He anglicized it. He was crazy about everything British for a while. The Mormons do it to the people here—seduce them with success."

"What a crew! And some of them actually come here and get better?"

"Why not? Civil disorder can be terrific therapy if you're a homosexual Chinese-Burmese doctor on lithium. Of course he's permanently damaged. But Frankie has found some peace here."

"At least someone has." Melanie cut him a look and flicked a tongue over her lips. Levin found a bottle opener to twirl on his finger.

"People used to come here for nothing but that. Didn't I tell you Direv Saraun was called 'the cocktail of southern Asia'? Nobody cared about it one way or another." The Portuguese settlers had found nothing to do, with the heat and the forest, and when the island declared itself a republic in 1808 the mother country barely noticed, it was fighting a war somewhere else. The Americans used it as a base in World War II, but since then it had just been an R and R spot. The prime minister spent his time raising orchids and lapdogs, and there were rumors that he was senile or had at some point even died. "Direv Saraun's like a fluke," Levin said.

"But lately it's gotten serious."

"The guerrillas are the only serious people on this island."

She didn't answer; for a while she worked in silence.

"Did Ding call?"

"Ding called. And he's coming.".

"Good," Levin said. "I think you'll like him. He's one of us."

She was cracking eggs on the rim of a bowl, with one quick careless hand, and each egg left a streak of egg white running down the outside of the bowl. Watching her hand, Levin experienced an intense moment of recognition—but her laugh had already prepared him for it. The night she'd invited him to her apartment for the first time he had stood, much as he was standing now, against the wainscoting, while she knocked eggs into a bowl of pasta for spaghetti carbonara. They had spilled as these spilled, on the counter and her fingers. He remembered the effect it had had on him—instant erection. He'd pretended to study the woodwork and willed it down. She had talked about her family, turning now and then to check his face, and every time she turned and smiled he burned. She was from Illinois (Normal, Illinois!), a pharmacist's daughter, a claustrophobic town. She'd had ambitions, come to Pennsylvania to study law, planned never to go back. She was still in law school, he at the start of his third year with the paper. A friend from grad-school days had introduced them at a party.

Melanie would draw people anywhere—Normal, Philadelphia, São Sebastião. It was her heedless, fluid way, quick to anger, quick to laugh. Emotional freedom, Levin had thought that night in her kitchen. She said once it was a sin to sin without enjoying it. She teased him that assimilated Jews like him, who ought to be the least fettered people on earth, turned out to be the most. Abolishing sin, they'd abolished joy.

That night they had made love for the first time, in her bed. She kneeled over him, smiling wryly, hands on her hips, and asked what he wanted. But what he wanted was to do everything for her. In the directness of her gaze and complete assurance of her nakedness he felt a thrilling power—it threw everything wide open and made anything possible. He saw, in her, the promise of gaining himself entirely. No woman had ever excited him like Melanie. And when they finally slept, he who'd always required privacy asleep lay up against the length of her body and held her gratefully from behind. The next morning, making coffee in the kitchen where she'd broken eggs, he became aware of an ancient nerve along his neck from skull to spine at last beginning to relent. He almost told her—but he thought it might sound ridiculous, or frighten her, might expose too much. So he quietly watched the sunlight flame on the reddish hair across her naked shoulders.

She wanted to know everything, all the details of his life.

Early on he framed the thought negatively: There is no reason not to marry this woman. And, as if outracing the chance that a reason would arise, he found himself pressing her. She stalled a long time, saying they were still in their twenties, their lives might diverge, but when she finally assented she told him she'd known it would end this way from day one.

"End" jarred Levin. In the weeks after the engagement they had a series of quarrels that became more contentious than any before. Then he would pick up a book or newspaper, sparking rages in her like none he'd seen. Her anger suddenly had a scraping, desperate sound that made him harden and refuse. Sometimes he raged back. She told him that no one had ever been able to do this to her and he thought the same about himself without telling her. Clothed, they said unforgivable things, and then forgave each other naked.

Late one night, after they'd fought about whether he'd ignored her at a party, and then had reached a truce and Melanie had gone to bed, Levin was sitting in a wired stupor flipping channels with the remote control. A CNN report came on about the growing state of war in Direv Saraun. No American official or academic talking head was on hand to explain the causes, the U.S. position, Direv Saraun's strategic importance. The correspondent—based in New York, using free-lance footage—could say little more than that a lot of people were killing and getting killed. In the postmidnight glow of the TV, Levin experienced a physical sensation of giddiness, as if he'd lost his bearings. At first he took it for fear, but it wasn't only fear. He went to bed so excited that he woke Melanie up to make love.

He talked about the story with his editors, and one of them ventured that the paper should consider devoting resources to look at a post–Cold War revolution. What was America's stake in the realigned world? What was left for people to fight about? Weeks later, when the assignment in Direv Saraun was offered to him, Levin grabbed it. He was tired of studying history or watching it on cable, he wanted to feel it on his skin. He thought of the Jesuits, on whom he'd written his master's thesis—say what you want, but they had made themselves contemporary with the history of their time, had taken on the world. Those who are afraid to do that are afraid of themselves; they become nothing.

He told Melanie that it would give them a little breathing space, a test they both knew they would pass that would solidify their decision to marry. She was studying for the bar—she could use the time away from him. Hadn't both of them complained they were losing touch with their work?

Melanie seemed less than sanguine, and in the waning days she became spiritless. This annoyed Levin even more. But he wouldn't take the assignment without her blessing, and finally she gave it.

"Make yourself like steel tempered in fire," his mother told him, "and you can discover anything you want out there."

"Be flexible," his father told him. "Things might not be what they seem or you expect."

Once he was gone, winging over America toward the Pacific, holding in his mind's eye a picture of palm trees and carbines that thrilled him more than anything since the first weeks with Melanie, Levin knew that he had escaped from her. The next four months brought a slow submergence of this insight. The separation seemed a very long time; it set them apart in ways neither dared to mention. But she'd had the guts, after passing the bar, to postpone a position in the Philly D.A.'s office. And now she was here, in his kitchen, and Levin, watching her cook, wanted to wipe her hand and the bowl and his counter of the filmy mess every egg had left.

"I count seven, including us," Melanie said. "Would you please set the table, please?"

Levin went into the main room. In the picture window that filled half the wall lay the western sea. A Korean freighter was anchored offshore, silver points in the moonlight on black water. A nearly full moon, Levin noted—or just past? No, it was waxing. The Korean sailors would be in town, in the arms of girls, ravenous for three hours of transmitting disease. Three floors below, the taxis on Dag Hammarskjold Boulevard streamed like molten lava along the median. A few families had recently appeared on the grassy strip— refugees from the south. They put up their onion sacks, their plywood and sticks, nervously absorbed like forest animals. Had the typhoon not veered west a few miles, it would have ripped the very clothes off their backs. The capital police might yet. As Levin watched, a group of mothers gathered weeds and scraps of driftwood off the trash-strewn beach to start their evening fire. One woman raised a hand to silence her filthy, bawling child. For Levin's readers these Saraunese were no longer news, and he avoided them when he crossed the boulevard to wave down a taxi.

A debate swirled in São Sebastião about these strays: Were they fakes, guerrillas incognito on assassination missions from the mountains, or were they innocent victims of military operations in the contested areas? It was a war of opinion against perception, Levin had long ago discovered. And amid all the argument and gossip and rumor and euphemism and innuendo—the eloquence of eyebrows— his notebooks filled with scrawl. He was losing the ability to make up his mind about these things. That was a good reason to get out of the capital. São Sebastião generated nothing but heat mist. The truth, everyone said, was "out there."

Levin padded in leather sandals over the hardwood parquet between the table and the cabinet. The dining table was a rectangle of splendid *nara,* rich brown with an orange tint, polished to a waxy brilliance in which he could have made out his features if he'd chosen to look. He didn't. He was thinking about Ding Magkakanaw, who always needed work. Now real work had come. Ding was a year or two older than Levin, but Levin thought of him as younger, since twice he had employed Ding on assignments in the city. Son of gentry, Ding had grown up on a sugar plantation at the conservative northern end of the island—servants, American-style private schools, a pair of Chevrolets—until his father squandered the family capital in oil just when world sugar prices were about to collapse. Oil collapsed not long after. The old man, deep in debt to a big provincial landowner, agreed to put up his second daughter as collateral; he defaulted, fairly warning the girl, who disappeared for the city (where, rumor had it, she married an American officer and took off for the States). Ding's father saved the landowner's men a morning's work by hanging himself in his shower among the beautiful tiles imported from Mexico. Ding's mother continued to live by herself in the enormous hollow house.

Ding dropped out of the university and taught himself to take pictures. Eventually he began to find work as a photojournalist. He had a knack for the kind of photos—sensational, bristling with guns—for which the local and foreign press had an endless appetite. But he lost a job with the AP after missing work several mornings and quarreling with the American bureau chief, a humorless, teetotaling man. Since then he'd gained a reputation as a "committed journalist," a free-lancer with "pro-people" ideas. Levin admired this, though Ding himself—thin, stiff, dark, his black eyes perpetually distracted—seemed too Americanized to be really interesting. But Ding had done him a big favor.

"She's involved in a higher plane of struggle," he'd said one day. They were talking about Sylvia Moktil. Levin took the euphemism as a code. On the higher plane lay guns.

"She works for them?"

Ding had raised his eyebrows and smiled. The fun of undercover had begun then.

Despite all their skill at publicity (perhaps because of it), little was known about the guerrillas. The rhetoric of graffiti and communiqués was too heated and abstract to reveal a coherent ideology. The Americans, of course, assumed they were communists, a growing threat to the rather limited American interests (far more limited than American influence, which had arrived overnight near the end of World War II and by morning transformed the face of Direv Saraun). But no one had been able to trace a shred of aid to China or the Arabs. The guerrillas' guns came from the military, who were as slack and corruptible as fresh fish in the tropics. Some people in the rich north said the Army of Liberation was organizing a regional insurrection; landlords called it an agrarian rebellion, and conscripted their farm workers into private armies; mestizos said it was ethnic strife fomented by Malay Saraunese with a dose of education and gullible tribespeople; European expatriates said that the guerrillas wanted a nationalist revolution, to weed out the English-language dailies, the McDonalds, the tourist brothels, everything foreign; to the nervous merchants in the Chinese quarter they were another wave of the anti-Chinese feeling that washed over the country every few decades. Animists said pro-Catholic, Catholics said anti-Catholic. Some dared to call them democrats. And a few Saraunese declared it nothing more than a personality cult in the sway of some obscure megalomaniac. The trouble was, no one could name him.

The guerrillas had become a political Rorschach test in Direv Saraun; they had become everyone's separate fantasy and fear. It took Levin months to sort out the theories and those who held them, and in the end it was all heat mist. But perhaps a trip out there would clear some of it up.

He had the restless itch to be moving again.

For some days past his heart had been knocking on his ribs, and the blood beat in his temples. He had started grinding his teeth—Melanie had woken him up twice to tell him. Why couldn't he sit still for two minutes?

Something was different with him. And it wasn't recent, either. It had begun almost the day he arrived in Direv Saraun.

At first he'd imagined it was in the air. Hot, sheathing, and unstable, it soured the taste of beer and in minutes dirtied the thighs and seat of his fresh trousers. His skin was always oily, unpleasant to touch, and his six-foot body, normally graceful, became an encumbrance he had to bring with him everywhere, like Gulliver in Lilliput, fold into low-ceilinged buses, stoke with rice and pork fat. For the first time in a decade, his face broke out. He swabbed his ears twice a day. When a mosquito bite on his inner thigh, just above the ball of the knee, reddened and swelled into a festering head, Levin fingered it with a detached curiosity. He squeezed; it burst. His body hardly seemed to belong to him.

There was also this: Between the tendons of his left wrist, his pulse now led an independent life. Without warning it would begin racing: 100, 120 beats per minute. Whimsical and tyrannical, that calibration regulated Levin's mood. Often he found his fingers straying there to locate the quiver of blood, and then he pulled them away with a nauseous dread he couldn't shake.

These things happened to him without volition. It was as if he were accompanied, as if he had a companion in Direv Saraun, less substantial than the scratchy air. At the beginning he found it in the wrist, though sometimes it moved into his chest and managed to stifle his breath with shocking intensity. But over time he became aware of it as nothing more than a disembodied voice. Murmuring, barely audible over the white noise of outside life, came its distinct tone: harsh, irreverent, mocking. It was a dissident voice. It negated, and negated, and negated—always at the worst times. It broke in on an analysis of the land problem he was giving Fraser; on his best effort to get a union official to tell him why a general strike had failed; on remembrances of his parents, his schooldays, Melanie. One hot Sunday

Levin had gone to hear an articulate young priest preach on the subject of human rights violations, when a goat strayed into the back of the provincial church and began to bleat.

That was the sound of the voice.

Levin had always known his own mind and acted on it. People counted on him for opinions, decisions. Now he caught himself hesitating and waiting for signs and directions. With Melanie here he sometimes looked to her for where they would go next, what they would do next—in *his* country. He thought of himself as an active man, morally efficient. Coming to Direv Saraun had been the most decisive act of his life; yet he was balked. A quick study, he found things murkier as he dove deeper into tactics and ideologies and everyday events. And the confusion extended to himself. His feelings were unknown to him for days at a time; then they came clear with riotous, frightening power.

He decided that he was just a little turned around. They'd sent him to figure out this war and its meaning for America, and he was having a hard time of it. Mind and body found it all unfamiliar. He'd hoped that a trip to the guerrilla territory—a dose of out there—would set him right. Now he didn't want to wait another day to go.

Because since Melanie's arrival, the goat voice had given him no peace.

Just yesterday they'd been at Inácio's, the classiest department store in the city, where months ago he'd bought his dining table. Melanie was trying on dresses; she found even her summer ones too heavy for this heat. A salesgirl in the khaki-skirted store uniform (the Saraunese managed to look immaculate even when they began and ended each day in a cardboard slum) helped her pick them out, while Levin hung back, flipping through hangers of Adidas sweat suits. Nothing suited her—too loud, too European, too adventurous, too safe. Levin tried to catch the salesgirl's eye and exchange a knowing smile, seasoned foreigner to native, but she was all commercial blankness, the black bangs falling over her eyes.

"Let's go, sweetie," he finally said. "I've got a tough interview in two hours and I'm not prepared."

"You always say that," Melanie told him as she studied the rack. "And you always do well." She turned her back and retreated into the changing room with the green dress.

Levin was left standing in a sudden squall. He thought: *Filthy—*

But it went no further. The pressure of the astonishing word clogged his chest.

She was here to bring him home; to rescue; to reclaim. And already he was going away again.

He had finished setting the table. He looked at his watch: ten to eight. He went back into the kitchen.

"Melanie," he said.

She looked up from the pot of soup she was stirring. She was flushed in the steamy heat; droplets of sweat beaded above her lip. "It's an interesting cuisine," she said. "Sort of like Thai but a little heavier."

"You're going to knock them out. Listen. I found out this afternoon I've been given an exclusive with one of the A. of L. commanders."

She set the ladle down. "That's great," she said neutrally.

"I know. The thing is, it means I have to leave tomorrow."

He watched for the storm to break. But she just looked at him, as if he hadn't made sense.

"Why?"

"Because that's what they said. That's how it is."

She stirred the soup. "I'm happy for you, Danny." Now he thought she would cry; but she held herself back and the strain made her beautiful. "I feel like a real jerk cooking up this meal so your friends can meet me. I really feel stupid here."

"No, sweetie." He went to her and folded his arms around her shoulders. "They'll love you. And I love you. I'll be gone four days at the most."

The buzzer rang.

"Shall I get it?" he asked.

"Isn't it obviously for you?"

Levin went to let in his guests.

CHAPTER II

Melanie had prepared a feast. From the *nara* slab rose a pungent steam of ginger, soy, and garlic: pink hunks of pula-pula on a mound of saffron rice and egg, ringed with parsley and calamansi; a china bowl of boiled potatoes; moist pale eggplant slices lying like melted dominoes; cups of coconut and bamboo soup; beaded bottles of Temple of Heaven beer from which the labels—a vision of an atypically busty Saraunese girl, crowned with bougainvillea blossoms, rising out of the clouds—were peeling.

"Five days here only? Phenomenal." Feliz spoke between rapid molar chews. "Would one go too far in imagining"—chew, chew—"there is a Malay in your woodpile?" He laughed harder than anyone else at his own joke, tufts of fish fluttering in the corners of his craw. Feliz was barbarically ugly. His head rose neckless from a body that swelled in the middle like seeded fruit. Except for a few erect white hairs, the head was bald, a long slab, flat front and back, peaking in a kind of dromedary mound of skull. He had a flat, tawny face, a sunken chin, jowls like I.V. sacks; the eyes gleamed out of darkened folds of skin with wicked merriment. He seemed to have seen everything, and everything struck him as part of the same scandalous joke from which he alone had been exempted. In his exuberance the sallow skin went crimson.

Tonight he was more exuberant than usual. Frankie Young had gotten sick at the last minute, or so Feliz explained. There was a story behind it, but Levin hadn't asked; it would come out later, with the fifth or sixth beer. Unencumbered tonight, Feliz dominated. His ugliness was a part of his confidence, and it commanded respect. Such a face didn't contain ulterior motives.

"Put some meat on this boy's body," he instructed Melanie.

"I was a little shocked when I saw Danny at the airport. I thought: Hepatitis? But that leaves you yellow, doesn't it."

"Then you wouldn't know him from the porters." Feliz temporarily disappeared again in a riot of laughter.

"I had it once. Rather nasty stuff," said Fraser, in his BBC voice. "Couldn't touch liquor for weeks. I hardly dared touch Rose. It was pretty awful."

Levin had never trusted Fraser, though he drank and sometimes worked with him. He thought that, if it came down to a test of reputations, Fraser would conceal or even steal an important story from him. This selfishness accounted for his vulnerability, the fear Levin had seen in his eyes at Paranak. It was the prospect of failing in front of a colleague, more than having his brains blown out by a drunken soldier, that had undone Fraser in that moment. Beneath his vanity lay emptiness, and left alone with that he was helpless. Fraser played his long knob-knuckled fingers over Rose's small curled brown hand, reflected on the tabletop.

"Daniel does look below the weather," Feliz said. "He hasn't been taking care of himself. He eats in the market, food I wouldn't touch. But what you saw in his pasty Caucasian face"—he turned to Melanie and pointed with a fish-caked knife across the table at Levin—"was shock, not jaundice. The boy is still finding his way."

"You know what he said to me once?" Melanie was still flushed with heat and her kitchen exertions; and now beer was raising her color to the amber of her hair. She was smiling, and the guests leaned toward her. "This was back home, in Philadelphia. Where it's all brotherly love. So this guy we know's girlfriend breaks up with him and Danny and I have to scrape him off the bar floor. We spend half the night telling the guy how attractive he is, thinking of women we know, nice things people have said about him."

If she had looked to the head of the table she would have been met by a fixed smile of warning. But Melanie plunged on.

"We drive him home. And in the car on the way back to my place, Danny says to me he feels different from most of the people he knows. I ask him how. He says, 'I guess I feel at ease in the world as it is.'"

Now she faced him, still smiling. She looked almost tender with the memory.

Levin said, "Thanks for that bit of background."

"I'm not sure what that would feel like," Ding said. "I don't know anyone like that. But I'm wondering why you left if things were that way for you."

"Let's just say," Levin said, "I figured there was something else out there. America specializes in deluding suckers like me into complacency and early death. The thing that did it was when I saw an ad on TV for this new type of TV. It has a little screen inside the main screen so you can watch one thing and flip channels to see what else is on at the same time. Or you can watch the ball game while your wife flips through the shopping channels. That's when I said: I'm out of here."

"I hate these sermons," Melanie said. "Lots of things are happening in America. Two hundred fifty million people live there. Aren't personal lives history too? And if you need to be around people killing—"

"It's not that. Anyway, when they kill here, it's for something. Saraunese can't afford to be neurotic."

"What did you mean," Ding asked, "by the world as it is?"

"Let's skip it," Levin said, glancing at Melanie. He sensed some joke that obscurely included him at the butt end. If so, he didn't want to contribute any more to the fun. "I have a question about Direv Saraun—as it is. If you had the ear of the A. of L. High Command, what would you ask them? At this particular moment. Each of you." He turned first to Ding.

"Which commander? They're not, what do you call it, monolithic."

"Let's say Fra Boboy."

"Well." Ding fingered the sprouts of mustache and goatee around his mouth. He was sitting on Levin's left, across from Melanie, wearing jeans rolled at the cuffs and a Floridian beach shirt that was a badge of iconoclasm in São Sebastião. He'd been eating in a nervous silence, as if his right to be here wasn't certain. When he looked up his close-set eyes were out of focus. "Maybe I would say: 'What made you devote your life to this struggle? Because you were doing pretty well in the world as it is. Was it like a feeling, for a long time? Or something hit you all at once?' " A slice of potato disappeared into his mouth and he looked at Levin, his eyes focusing again. "What would you ask him, Dan?"

"Let's go around the table. John?"

Levin glanced to his right again and saw that Melanie was still watching him. A mischievous smile played on her lips and she started to open them.

"I don't get it, Dan," Fraser said, swallowing beer.

"Oh, just be a sport."

"No, I dislike games of this sort. I can imagine something like this going on at your ambassador's place. He's the one I'd like to talk to. I'd say, 'So what are you buggers up to? What about this American who disappeared in the mountains—Bowers? C.I.A., was he?' I'd ask him how bad things have to get before you intervene."

"Well, you're no fun," Levin said. "And there's not going to be any intervention. We have no interest here."

"That's a bloody good enough reason. Like us with the Falklands, or the French in black Africa. You intervene because you know you're all fagged out as a world power."

"Feliz?" Levin said. "Want to answer?"

"Doesn't Rose get to say?" Melanie protested.

"You go, Feliz," Rose said with a tactful smile. "I am thinking."

Feliz stroked his heavy jowl. "Just this: 'What do you want? The country has a right to know and we don't know. Tell us what you want.' "

"My turn?" Melanie sat up in her chair and reached for a bottle of Temple of Heaven. "I'd ask him why he picked Daniel Levin for his first interview ever with the foreign press. And if he's tough enough for Daniel Levin's clever little manipulations." She cracked the bottle with an opener and filled her glass. "That's what I'd ask this Fra Boboy."

Levin felt her foot on his, and as he kicked it off the words exploded in his head: *Filthy cunt.* Mortified, he couldn't look at her. He felt she must have heard him think it.

"Congrats," Fraser managed to say. The news seemed to have induced a pain behind his eyes.

Ding, too, was stunned.

"When did you hear this?"

"Today."

"From—"

"Sylvia. Connie."

Now Ding had trouble answering Levin's eyes.

"Something wrong?"

"I was just wondering," Ding said, "why she went right to you."

"Maybe that's how they do things."

"Maybe."

Melanie leaned forward with a hand on Levin's forearm. "I get it. I think I figured it out. He wants you to go with him, Ding. Whoops, maybe he wanted you to guess. Since it's games night."

Open-mouthed, Ding looked from Melanie to Levin for confirmation.

Levin whispered to her, "Are you going to steal all my lines?"

"But I don't have any."

Her finger traced a mollifying pattern on his forearm. But a truce at this point would be her victory and he attempted a look of severity. He raised his arm and began to eat. When he met her eyes, he saw that she was miffed. He mocked her pout, and her eyes flashed with an angry film of tears. They looked away from each other.

"It's true, Ding," Levin said. "We'd leave tomorrow night." He waited. "Don't you want to go?"

"Of course!"

Ding's mouth still hung open, the tongue to the lower lip. Surprise had given way to calculation, a sorting out of sudden possibility.

"It might be better," he said, "if it stayed at this table that I'm going. If you journalists can keep a lid on it. I've got an AP gig next week and they might give it to someone else if they think I'm going away for a while. You know how they treat free-lancers."

"But all the same," Levin said, "you don't want to be tied down."

"In a typhoon you do."

Feliz was contemplating Ding with a fond smile. "In the sixties, when I was an editor, with this long hair and clothes they would say you had 'subversive looks.' Now it is quaint almost. Lately I feel so very old."

He was indulging in Saraunese repartee across the age divide, playing lightly on Ding's nerves—the literate and anxious were always his fair game. In any case, it did not sit well with Ding.

"Must be your sight's going," he said at once. "I wouldn't know what that looks like, but you can't be talking about me."

The news had not gone over as Levin had planned. A sort of

hushed unease settled on the table. To his relief, Feliz belched, which indicated he was about to take over the conversation.

"It's a coup, Daniel. Walk softly, your colleagues will want your scalp."

Fraser busied himself extracting a piece of fish from his teeth.

"I think," Levin said, "I've landed their best source."

"Other commanders have been in the field longer."

"But Fra Boboy is the key. If there really is a Middle Way faction, Fra Boboy represents it. He's probably the only alternative to total war."

Feliz smiled and cocked his head with interest. "You think so?"

"When he was legal he was a Social Democrat. And look, he's urban, highly educated, a check on the less discriminate violence of the peasant militias."

"Why do you think they picked you?" Feliz pressed him gently, not wanting to show him up. "Do you have special access?"

"Just ordinary contacts." Levin didn't look at Ding.

"What else do you know about him?"

"Not much. That he went to the mountains after being denied tenure." He smiled. "And I know his dissertation topic. All about primitive sacrifice."

As far as he knew, no other journalist had thought of this bit of sleuthing. Levin had gone one day to the National Library and found, in a dim corner of the basement, a volume called *Dissertation Abstracts.* About two hundred Saraunese had written theses over the years, and under "B" Levin found "*Sacrifice, Impurity, State: Structures of Self and Violence in Modern Primitive Society.* Butang, Simkar, Ph.D. Boston University and the University of Direv Saraun." Fra Boboy's synopsis so amused and captivated Levin that he had photocopied it.

> This study presents a critique of René Girard's theory of sacred violence from a neo-Foucaultian "Third World" perspective. In Girard, primitive society undergoing a "sacrificial crisis" designates a "surrogate victim" in order to restore or perpetuate a stable hierarchical order. Girard terms this sacrifice "pure violence." But his essentialist distinction between "pure" ("sacrificial") and "impure" ("contagious") violence betrays a repression of the historical character of "primitive" society as it has evolved into the "modern primitivism" of the "Third World" state. Appropriating Girardian

discourse to interrogate and undermine it, this discussion develops a theory of the unstable order in which the pure/impure dichotomy of sacrifice is problematized. "Impure" violence in the cycle of political revenge, spilling over Girard's constructed boundaries, is seen as purifying the "impure" state and constituting new transpersonal identities in the process of desubjectifying all identity.

"As an intellectual exercise, it's pretty brilliant," Levin said without going into Fra Boboy's thesis. "He's a brain I'd love to pick."

"You know," Feliz said, "he was a copy boy for my paper when he was an undergraduate. A very bright boy—a little ambitious, a little too sure. The way you see working-class boys when they get to college: the first strong idea that finds them is the last. He borrowed money from me to fix his teeth." A look of mild dismay crossed his face. "He never paid me back."

"Do you think they chose you," Fraser asked, recovering his cool, "because you're fairly new?"

"You mean manipulable?"

"No, don't misinterpret. I mean unidentified with a viewpoint."

"I was told he liked my Impanang series. That's all I know."

"It was a breakthrough," Feliz said. "Not that the idea hadn't occurred to others. They were just too important. It was a model of the engaged style. No false objectivity with Levin."

"But it's so basic. You don't care, your writing won't be worth a damn."

"I don't know," Fraser said. "I personally think there's something pathological in all these slum stories. As if one's got to put oneself through their hell, take it as one's own burden. Because what one really gets from it is a sort of power. You know, the old *piki lan kurat*—the debt in the heart, or whatever. Well, I've got no sins to expiate." Rose rolled her eyes. "I'm here to do a job."

"Everyone," said Feliz, "finds his own justification."

"You think being a journalist gives you a free ride?" Levin said. "You're white—that's all that matters to them."

"And what's wrong with being white?" Melanie said. "Ding, is there something wrong with being white?"

Ding smiled at her across the table. "There's nothing wrong with it, Melanie. Everyone in this country wants to be white."

She said, "Sometimes I wonder what these reporters think they're doing here. Going where the danger is, scavenging around, trying to figure it all out. One guy taking on a whole country. It's just Western arrogance. The whole journalism thing—so neutral, but really so dashing. It seduces these guys. But in his heart of hearts Dan would rather be reading dissertations. If I know him at all."

"Maybe not as well as you think," Levin said.

Feliz grunted at their discord. "Melanie, Daniel—Frankie extends his apologies. He would have liked to be here. He enjoys conversation among intelligent people."

"We're sorry too," said Levin.

"I said he fell ill. That wasn't quite true."

"What's the problem?"

"A little, curious one. Normally he feels better at this time of year, after Christmas. At Christmas there is always a depression. He thinks of the English snow. But I'm afraid a story in the *Daily Nation* set him back. Did you see it? About a black American sailor. Nobody read it? I tried to hide it from him. On the 'human interest' page, his favorite—all that malice and soap bubbles. But now and then it is the genuine thing.

"This sailor had Frankie's very problem, but when the ship anchored at Porto Negrais and the men came into town he left his pills on board. Perhaps the mania had already started at sea—you know, the isolation, the distance from home, confined with other sailors, perhaps racists, this black boy from St. Louis. Six foot four, a beautiful boy! And he got it in his head that his sweetheart was going to meet him here—all the way from St. Louis to the Hotel Pacifica. Just imagine—the power of delusion! She was sending him signals. And everything he saw confirmed it. I have seen Frankie in this state. Later he says, 'It wasn't me.' A shop sign says CLOSED AT SIX—and the boy knows she'll be there at six. So he shows up, in his best clothes (you know the G.I.'s by their shoes) and asks the clerk if anyone has left a message for Anthony Clark. Of course not. Ah! he thinks. How clever of his sweetheart! If she left a message they might try to stop her. So he sits in the lobby and waits."

At that moment all the lights in the house went out. Everyone groaned.

"Oh, bad luck!" Feliz cried in the darkness. While Levin went to get candles he held the conversation. "Goddamn those guys in the mountains. Why don't they just give us one night of peace. I've completely forgotten where I was. Oh, yes."

With the moon behind him in a corner of the picture window above the bay, his voice came to them out of silvery darkness.

"An hour goes by. A local driver comes in, dressed up, the chauffeur's cap. He sees the black American. 'Excuse me, sir,' the driver says, 'are you the South African gentleman who ordered a car?' "

"My God," Fraser mumbled.

"But look how in this state of mind everything is a sign, for you only! 'Yes, I am.' 'The car is waiting outside, sir.' 'Well—the person I'm expecting isn't here yet. Come have a drink with me while we wait.' They go into the bar together."

Levin returned carrying two lit candles.

"After a while the sailor starts playing on the piano. This is a talented boy. He sings, the driver sings. They're having a fine time. A thrilling bond, across cultures. The driver suggests they wait up in his room. 'All right,' says the sailor—but look what a thing the mind is! He tells the driver to get the room key. He is crazy, but sane enough to know they won't give him the key—a foreigner, he has tried before, and anyway they know what the South African looks like and, needless to say, the guy doesn't look like him. He sends the driver after the key—a local, who can get things done. In some corner of his brain, he knows that much. In another, the opposite. He is many people, more than human. With the mania everything works. And they go to the room, they order up champagne and caviar, they watch television, sing, they wait for the sweetheart to arrive.

"Of course the door eventually opens. It is the South African. A Boer, in a horrible safari suit. Just imagine his face, seeing the driver and this two-meter *kaffir* half drunk with their shoes off! He calls the police, they come, arrest the sailor. Now he knows one thing only—he is in trouble. He cries that he is sick, he needs his pills! What do our police know of lithium? It's not on the black market. They take him to jail and lock him up."

"Poor man," Rose said. "They sent him home?"

"Unfortunately not. The end of this story is why Frankie read it in the paper. He stole a guard's pistol and blew his own brains out. From one kind of insane to another. He is Superman or he is nothing. Or do you think," he wondered, "his mind was never clearer—never more human than at that moment?"

"Jesus!" cried Melanie, her mouth vivid against the pallor of her skin. "Too much blowing out of brains in this country." She turned to Levin. "You never told me this kind of thing is a goddamn national pastime."

"You've come at the wrong time." He was slumped back, staring at a candle. Melanie reached for another bottle of Temple of Heaven.

Quickly and with a trace of awkwardness, Feliz changed the subject. He engaged Melanie in talk of tropical flowers. Rose and Ding switched to Saraunese, laughing a great deal, until Fraser got bored and insisted they use English. Levin quietly smoked. He felt that what should have been a celebration had turned against him, and his own mood soured; he felt it was Melanie's fault.

Finally he roused himself and turned to Ding.

"Did you notice what's happened to the price of fish?"

"It's hit the bottom."

They laughed together. For the first time they were two men with a common journey before them.

"But do you know why?"

"They've been overfishing," Fraser said. "Using big net—sweeping the sea. Dynamite too. It's the insatiable Japanese market."

"Now that," said Levin, "is a prime example of simplistic Western analysis. Anybody know the reason? What about the natives here."

Rose said, "People lose their appetites when the hot season is coming."

"Something," Ding mused slowly, "like . . . a taboo of eating our own."

"Exactly! They're afraid of eating the *Esperanza* victims. Things like this are always happening here," Levin said for Melanie's benefit without looking at her. His tone carried an obscure warning. "Strange, impossible things. For example, when I was buying this very fish we're eating, the market woman told me a story about a woman who slit open a pula-pula and found a male organ. A man's pecker."

Rose, mortified, exploded in giggles. The others stared.

"Seriously. Six inches long."

Recovering, Rose said, "I didn't know foreigners were on board."

"Rose!"

"Joking, John."

Feliz passed a tongue over his lips, and the black eyes gazed at Levin out of folds of yellow skin. "But what do you suppose it means, that we won't eat the fish?"

"I think it's a kind of mourning. Solidarity with the dead."

"You are a decent man, Daniel. But personally, I don't think that is the reason. Perhaps as a hybrid I can see it from East and West, both ways—illegitimately, you know! There is the old revulsion of species against eating their own kind. Only on special occasions. The dogs on one of the Antarctic trips, dying of hunger, would not eat their comrades until the explorers had skinned them. Then they were less dog." He paused, without inviting anyone else to speak. "Morality does not come into play. Is a dog moral? But a dog can smell its own death. And it wants to live—like you, like me. Sure! It is the ancient fear. So there would be big trouble from eating this pula-pula. The market people know."

"But they're reminded all the time," Levin reasoned. "Last week that traffic cop who got shot in the face—waving the school kids across, in front of thirty of them. A girl had pieces of brain on her dress. How can people forget about dying?"

"No, they don't forget. It is because they know." Feliz's heavy face had sunk and browned with seriousness. "They know that this country is going to tear itself apart. What can one citizen do? When the typhoon blows in, he prays. In his heart he knows he counts for nothing to the storm. But while the country rips itself, mauls, feeds, swallows, he will not eat this six-inch thing. If I eat this, I will bring the ruin on myself. I know the ruin will come—but I will not call it on myself. It will do fine without my special assistance."

They were all silent, in the sated, boozy stillness after a meal, blood beating in six heads. The table had filled up with smoke.

"But why does it happen?" Levin asked. He leaned over his plate toward Feliz, his dress shirt stained with saffron. "And everyone powerless—all of us? What drives it? I don't think you believe in your own fatalism."

"Well, this is all talk anyway. Nothing we say will matter. To quote Mao: 'A revolution is not a dinner party.' "

"Wasn't it 'picnic'?"

"I don't think so. But I shall ask Frankie if the Chinese have picnics."

Fraser asked Levin, "What do you suppose will become of this place?"

Levin shrugged. "Call it American naïveté, but I'm no catastrophe monger. The majority have a grievance here and I think they'll be heard. It can't go on like this forever."

"American naïveté," Fraser sniped, then pulled in, too fogged to back himself up.

Levin ignored him. "It's pretty clear the army is split now between mid-level hards and top-brass softs. The softs don't want a coup because they're afraid of losing U.S. aid and taking the rap for fucking up the war. The hard-liners, on the other hand, might be thinking coup. As long as the P.M. was just an old man breeding pugs the army tolerated him. He was useful, the world paid no attention. The army could run the war as they liked. But now it's obvious they're losing, and the hards think they need more drastic measures and his government might get in the way."

"The 'Indonesian solution,' " Fraser said.

"That's what the guerrilla symps call it."

"A coup would suit them fine."

"And the 'Indonesian solution'? Thousands killed, on the slightest suspicion killed? What would be left of the symps, or the guerrillas? They're not crazy. No one wants that except a few big landlords and military nuts."

"And don't forget the C.I.A. nuts," Fraser said.

Feliz watched like a great vigilant toad about to leap. "And tell me, Daniel. What are you going to hear from Fra Boboy?"

Levin thought for a moment. "I suppose I'll get a rationale for this urban war. Maybe a new political initiative."

"Ah. A scoop," Fraser said.

"Fra Boboy will give you many things to think about," Feliz told him. "But careful!" He jerked his beer bottle into the air, spilling foam on polished *nara.* He was gripping the neck as if he wanted to squeeze the life out of it. "*In vino veritas!* It is nothing but the old brutality of my country. Rationale! Careful who you drink with, talk with, what you say, what they tell you. They will smile and smile. But they hate! They *hate!*"

The last word burst like a glass in the high-ceilinged room. Ding stared at Feliz, frowned, and briefly shook his head. Levin had paled.

"Feliz, take it easy," he said.

"My God," said Fraser. "*In vino veritas,* indeed."

Melanie slid her hand across the tabletop and touched Ding's with two fingers. "You'll watch out for him. You'll see everything goes O.K. Danny, are you paying Ding well?"

Ding looked from Melanie to Levin and back. "Dan is a sincere guy." He lifted an unopened beer bottle to his mouth, grimaced, and clamped his molars on the cap. Foam spilled over his lips.

"Ding and I'll watch out for each other," Levin said irritably. "I'll let my editor know, but he won't be able to clear full salary on a weekend, so I can only pay you a stringer's per diem out of my pocket. I'll have the paper reimburse for salary and expenses later. The money won't be a problem."

Fraser turned to Melanie. "I've made two trips to the territory."

"And?"

"Lost two of my mates. Cannibals." Rose punched his shoulder. "No, it went perfectly well. The blues are very professional chaps. They're very, sort of, contemporary. Communism with a postmodern face, is what I call it."

"Danny didn't tell me their color is blue."

"Red's a loser these days," Fraser said, "and they know it. And look, they've nothing to gain if harm should come to journalists. It's bad P.R., and they're very keen on P.R. My worry was military— drunk soldiers, sans officers, on the back roads. Military are still doing most of the killing. But they kept clear."

"Tomorrow I'm getting a travel permit," Levin said. "I've got a pal at Camp Pereira who does that kind of thing."

"What?" said Fraser with a friendly sneer. "Safe conduct to the Blue Zone?"

"Salantin Province. Obviously I won't tell him where we're going to end up."

"Do you think your piece of paper from the A.F.D.S. is going to make a bloody bit of difference at three A.M. out in the provinces to some half-starved army guy who's soaked with rice liquor?"

"Will it hurt?"

"That depends," said Ding, showing Levin a quick, conciliatory smile. "Do you really think it's a good idea to score a permit from this 'pal'?"

"I just don't see why not."

"What's all this about?" Melanie had lost control over her voice and her alarm came out as mockery, so that it seemed the whole table had risen up against Levin's judgment.

"No problem, lady," Ding said, thickening his accent, playing the tourist hustler. "Boss no make mistakes."

"You're funny, Ding," Melanie said; and suddenly the others

seemed to be overhearing a private confidence. "I'll bet Saraunese men like to dance. Danny happens to be afflicted with terminal white man's disease. So I won't get to see any of these São Sebastião clubs. Unless Ding takes me. Ding, do you dance?"

"Like a goat, Melanie."

"Like a goat!" she cried. "Ding, show me how a goat dances."

Ding got up from the table, thin, half smiling, and hopped from side to side in a skittish jig, his Florida shirt bouncing.

"Like a goat!" Melanie's voice was high and rich, full-throated. When she got up to join Ding she jumped and stumbled with a thrilling shriek, clutching his arm for support.

"No, really. Dance! *'You must have been sent from up a-bove!'* "

It was a song enjoying great popularity in São Sebastião, heard on radios everywhere. Ding put a hand to his pocket and did a sinuous number with his hips, tossing back his long hair. Melanie tried a bump and grind but tripped, and Ding helped her back to her chair, blushing.

Levin stood up. "I'll go make coffee."

The guests stayed late. Coffee, more beer, rum, cigarettes, the red tips blinking like fat fireflies in the dark. By one o'clock every bottle from Feliz's case stood empty on the foamy table. In the blacked-out street, two men shouted and a man and a woman laughed hysterically. Dag Hammarskjold Boulevard still bled with car lights.

At the door, Ding pumped Levin's hand but seemed to stare past him. "Till tomorrow, partner! Or is it already today?"

Fraser turned to Levin. "So you're finally going out there."

"Guess so."

"Doesn't it make your heart beat fast?"

"As a matter of fact."

"Some of the mountain roads will be just about washed out. Use your high beams. I happen to envy you." Levin, holding a candle, met his eyes and nodded. Fraser returned a lopsided, quizzical smile.

Feliz was still in a state of excitement. His outburst had set something free in him, an energy that hadn't spent itself. Behind the long flame his sunken black eyes danced. "Tell Fra Boboy," he said, his flat yellow face pressed close to Levin's exhaling beery warmth, "that all this killing is a bad mistake. Tell him to stop."

"It's not my country," Levin said.

"Yes, but you see, it's mine. What does he want? Justice? Power? Tell him he is going too far."

"That's not my place, Feliz. I'm an observer here."

"What about your slum family? If you were only observing, then you plagiarized another man's feelings. No—you or I cannot be two people, like that navy boy. We must, I'm sorry, be one."

"Fra Boboy won't care what I say. I'm going there to listen."

"He will listen too. Certainly, he wants someone to talk to. Imagine his isolation, in the mountains. But to change his mind . . . he will try to change yours first!" He lowered his voice. "Keep your eyes and ears open. Be of use by coming back to tell us what you learned."

After the last good-byes, when the door was closed, Melanie went straight to the bedroom and Levin to the kitchen. There would have to be a fight—her silence promised it—but for now the dishes were his to do and he was glad. He stopped the drain, ran water in the sink, and sprinkled the stacked plates with soap powder. The foam rose up around his wrists, water matted the black hair of his forearms. In the dark kitchen he soaked and washed by feel, sponging in rhythmic circles, and the hot radiant water soothed him. He lingered as long as he could, washing the dishes one by one.

When Levin came into the bedroom Melanie was undressing. A candle was lit by the dead reading lamp and the column of glass louvers was open. In this light her lower body, in panties, glowed yellow-orange; above the waist the louvered moonlight sliced her horizontally. The expression on her shadowed face was impossible to make out, but by her silence and her methodical, self-absorbed movements he knew the beer was wearing off. Levin sat on the bed and watched as she arched her back and reached between the wing bones to unclasp her bra. There was no sexual performance tonight, and no shyness either. Melanie undressed as if they'd been married thirty years, as if he wasn't there; except that she moved with a slightly unnatural quickness and avoided his gaze. The hint of self-consciousness embarrassed Levin for her: the deception, and its failure.

As she went by he laid a hand on her hip at the elastic. She stopped.

"You're only interested in me these days," she said, lowering the words to him out of the gray darkness, "when my clothes are off."

"Last night you wanted more sex from me. Tonight you want less." Still he kept his hand on her, and she didn't move away. But now the position of his hand and the way he was forced to look up at her seemed ridiculous.

She said, "You tell me what a turn-on I am, and then you fall asleep. Then in the morning you're fondling me and telling me what you'll do in the evening. At night you fall asleep again. During the day when my clothes are on it's like I'm not there at all."

She moved past his hand and went into the bathroom: he heard her brushing her teeth. Levin never brushed his before bed. He wondered how it was for her to kiss him at the end of the day; he licked a finger, breathed on it, and sniffed. Well, not too pleasant. Hot accumulated sourness plus smoke. The smell of this city: fish, cigarettes, and beer. Quickly Levin took off all his clothes and left them in a pile at the foot of the bed, change slipping out of the trouser pocket. Crawling across the sheets he glanced down at himself: long-limbed, a tuft of black hair in the middle of his chest, a mat around the white belly and the groin below; half erect. The thing wagged foolishly between his thighs as he crawled. Under the sheet he clutched it experimentally and it swelled in response.

Yes, tonight, before a journey, he wanted her. And he began to lose the calm he'd had at the sink.

Melanie stood over the bed and removed her earrings, her watch. Usually by now she was naked, but when she came out she was still in the panties: an ounce of synthetic silk against total revelation; an ounce of mystery and self-possession. But her breasts, which always fascinated Levin, and she knew it well, freckled around the top of the lovely crease, small-nippled and pale at the spreading bottoms, moved about and changed shape as she reached for her earlobes and her wrist. Now, he thought, she was onstage: saying maybe, maybe not.

He patted the empty place on the mattress next to him.

"Not yet. What was the matter with you tonight?"

"Be more specific."

"You weren't very pleasant."

"Nothing was the matter. I was thinking about the trip."

"Are you worried about it?"

He wondered what it would be like to tell her—everything. The sensations of his body. The spot of fear in his wrist. The goat voice. His dreams, so clear, so violent, where he was victim on some nights and perpetrator others. Figments of an overwrought imagination.

Ludicrous! If he laid himself open now, it would have been coerced.

"Not at all."

"Well, Danny, at least one of us isn't."

"You are."

"My God! It's like I don't know you. Of course I am!"

"You can tell me without raising your voice."

"I'm not— All right, I'll be very cool if you want it that way." She was pacing at the side of the bed with her arms folded across her chest—not over the breasts but under them, pushing them together and out, deepening their divide. The hardened nipples seemed to fix Levin with an accusatory look. "All right. What about the way you screamed at that kid yesterday who tried to get money out of you for watching the car while we were at lunch?"

"I didn't scream. That's ridiculous, Melanie. Unfair."

"You did. I've never heard you sound like that. It frightened me."

"Oh, stop acting like I'm some sort of stranger. You should've figured out by now things are different here. Everyone's under pressure. You've got to get angry at those street kids or they'll take advantage every time. Just try the soft liberal stuff."

"Sweetheart, you wanted to brain that kid. And then tonight, you were totally morose."

"Is that why you were ruining my surprises, and coming on to Ding? To punish me?"

"You've got nerve—goddammit, you do!"

She was not at all cool. Her hands planted on her hips, she bent toward him in a fury and the breasts fell forward and changed with the new mood, in the candlelight: the nipples expanded, went from deep red to pink, and the color of her flesh there caught the darker brilliance of her face. Levin lay under the sheet, fully erect, inarticulate, choking.

"You treat me like trash all week. Rushing off here, reading this, going to see so-and-so."

"You know that's not true."

"The only thing you really think about, that interests you, is this fucking country. If it was a woman—but how can I be jealous of Direv Saraun? We haven't had one real talk. I don't know what you're feeling because you don't tell me. Then you spring this trip on me two minutes before everybody arrives. And now you accuse *me*! For four months I thought of nothing but you. At first I thought you did too—like that sailor, pining for me to be here. Too bad you're so sane. Like a fool I'd study at home to get the mail early. Fool!"

The tears began to flow. Melanie wept until her cheeks shone. She sank to the edge of the bed and sobbed and her breasts trembled, huddled between her fragile arms.

"I was stupid enough to think I could come here and fix things."

"Why," Levin said, "does there have to be crying every time?"

"I get angry and then I don't feel angry anymore, just sad. I wish I could bring myself to slug you."

What Levin felt for her was not deep, aching pity, but the memory of pity. It bothered him like a dream, or a flash from childhood, growing only vaguer as he tried to bring it back. This, mixed with the resentment and envy he always felt at women's tears.

He held out his arm. "Here, take a pop."

Melanie managed a half-formed fist that fell into her lap on its way to his arm. "It's only because I care."

"Try not to take responsibility for me."

"For Christ's sake—"

He asked gently, "What do you want me to do?" It was a question she'd never been able to answer—that was why he asked it now. But there'd been a time when he thought an answer might make all the difference between them. "You think I shouldn't take this trip."

She sighed heavily. "What do you think?"

"I think you'd rather have me in a Chestnut Hill town house. Or a subdivision in King of Prussia."

"You don't give me much credit, do you." It wasn't the moment yet; he regretted his little joke. "It's not a trip to take if you're not yourself. Postpone it awhile—give us a chance to know each other again. The guerrillas won't go away."

"I *am* myself. I'm tremendously anxious to do this. It's a fantastic chance and I can't waste it. What am I here for?"

Propped up on an elbow, wiping her face with the back of his hand, Levin created an intimacy in which it was possible for a smile to mean a truce and overture.

"Sweetheart. I wish we didn't fight."

After a while she took his hand and lifted it to her lips. She brushed it back and forth, palm down, palm up; met his eyes; and then deliberately she brought it down to her chest. The brusqueness made him giddy. Clutching the back of his hand she made him squeeze first one then the other breast and knead them in rolling circles, the way he had soaped the plates. He excited her nipples with his palm. Her smile was mock-shy; it was wanton.

"Shall I get the baby oil?" she said.

"No, don't bother tonight."

She threw off the sheet and studied him. "Hmm, very interesting." She gripped his erection and moved it like a driver checking a gear shift. "But maybe you want to sleep now."

"I'm wide awake."

"Wait till morning?"

"You are a tease."

"Tomorrow is another day."

"Time's wingèd chariot."

"Uh-uh, not good enough."

"O.K.—let's fuck right now."

As they spoke their lovers' lines Levin regained his strength and poise. He felt himself disappear from the air into the wet enclosing warmth of her mouth and he gasped.

"Pula-pula," he said.

Her laugh came out stifled. Gently she sank her teeth against his tense skin and nibbled.

"A man may eat of the fish. . . ."

He was in the air again and her hand slithered the length of him, massaging the spittle she'd left. "Will you turn off your brain for one minute? Try to enjoy this. I'll bet the women here don't do it."

"I wouldn't know."

"Saint Daniel."

"I'm the only journalist in this city that hasn't visited Marapang Road. The others think I'm gay, or impotent."

"I wouldn't have cared. As long as you didn't catch something."

"But I was waiting for you."

"Here I am."

"Were you waiting too?"

"Here I am. Right?"

No—he wanted more. Suddenly, the question had to be answered: Had she been with someone else? For a long time he'd told himself that it wouldn't matter. Across an ocean, fidelity and sex should be separate categories—a fool's errand to mix them, asking for trouble.

He had never felt a tremor of jealousy, it was part of his self-sufficiency, but now the possibility was before him and it was intolerable. On his inner eye flashed a vision of Melanie's legs extended in the air the way she liked them, gripping the hard brown laboring hips of—someone. If it were true, then he didn't know what he would do. Perhaps he would weep, rage, dissolve; perhaps he'd say nothing while his heart burst in his chest. On the other side of such a revelation blackness lay thickly like fresh tar; inside the blackness he couldn't see himself. And this nothingness in the face of something easily, easily real—he took it as a danger sign.

Levin pulled Melanie from her ministrations, rolled her over, and entered with a single stab.

Twenty-five minutes later he was still thrusting.

It had become mechanical, not electrical—located in the buttocks and not the groin. It had none of the rising, quickening, tensing rhythm of a climax. His face was buried in the pillow by Melanie's head and wet strands of her hair lay across his mouth. Between their bellies sweat had puddled and on the sheet a circle of damp spread from their groins.

"Are you almost there?"

He grunted.

"I'm getting sore, baby."

He raised his face from the pillow. "Just a little more."

With her forefinger Melanie drew a line across his neck. "Get rid of this."

"A little more." He was nowhere near. And she knew. He had come close early on, waited for her, begun to numb. He lost his erection, pressed pelvic bone to bone, waited, and concentrated on the familiar selection of fantasies, flipping through them like pages in a porn magazine. She came with a shudder, two, three times—a cornucopia of orgasms. He thought about the six-inch penis lying inside the pula-pula and felt it was his own, severed from him and lost, useless, a dead thing inside Melanie. He banished this and thought about Feliz, about the black sailor, the mountain where the guerrillas were waiting, the Toyota's steering column—loose, but too late to fix it. By surprise the erection returned; he was encouraged, thrust, put her hands to his buttocks, panted, drooled into the pillowcase, exhausted himself in the heat. Still he pushed and pushed, and never said a word. When she spoke, he knew it was hopeless.

Melanie was kissing him, a shining snail's trail from his Adam's apple to the hollow of his jaw, his strong chin, his reluctant mouth. Her tongue worked its way between his teeth. He sucked at it, then nibbled at her lower lip. His buttocks had stopped hiking; he was soft again.

Levin bit down, hard, and tasted blood. She cried out—from shock as much as from pain, it seemed. He was shocked too. Yet he had done it; and there was, at last, relief.

"Oh God, sorry. I bit too hard."

"Be more careful. Christ, I'm bleeding." She drew away two red fingertips from the bright wound. Her lip was already swelling.

"I'm sorry. You get me too excited."

She pushed him out and off and he rolled over on his back. Against his thigh the shrunken penis lay like a wet, scolded puppy. He pulled the sheet to his neck.

"Blow out the candle," she said.

"Don't you want a Kleenex?"

"I'll bleed on the pillowcase. The maid will think you knocked me around."

"Par for the course here. I'm sorry, baby."

In the tropical zone couples don't sleep entangled like seaweed; and Levin and Melanie lay, clammy, back to back. Soon he heard from her the deep breathing of a sleeper. The twitches and moans had left her body exhausted. Sleep had always been like a gift for him. Whatever the strain of the day here—even the day he saw his first corpses, the six peasants shot through the head and laid out in the sun at Paranak while villagers kept a sullen, scared distance—at night he fell asleep at once, soundly. His dreams were crowded, complicated, and vivid; he awoke with eyes wide open, already alert.

But tonight he couldn't sleep. The moon was in the west, over the harbor, bathing half the bedroom through the column of louvers. Amid the endless traffic on the boulevard he identified every distinct sound, the engine types, the horns, voices. When he tried to shut his eyelids they flickered as if their nerves scraped his eyeballs. Close air trapped the smell of sex in the bed.

The typhoons were passing; the hot season was ahead. He'd heard about it from the veterans since day one. "You think it's hot today? Just wait." It was part of the apprenticeship. Western reporters tried to keep up the pace of work (what did Philadelphia care about heat?

Philadelphia was snowbound now—though it seemed impossible there could be snow anywhere on earth, on a night like this), fighting inertia and pumping out stories while the country around them went into a kind of equatorial hibernation. They were like men trying to run in water, in a dream.

The night of his arrival, on an impulse, he'd decided against the first-class international hotel near the airport that all arriving journalists booked into. From the start he was going to avoid the gang mentality. Levin recognized that his aversion was based not just on principle but also on fear, the prospect of being unequal to something new. Out of strength and weakness he would go his own way. He told the taximan to take him to a good, cheap place in the middle of town. "Cheap" was his first mistake. The hotel turned out to be a terrible hole, no air conditioner, no hot water. The mattress sank beneath him; his nostrils were stopped with thick air. He lay face up and spread-eagled on the coverlet, breathing quickly through the mouth. In the middle of the night he rose to cup water from the sink into his parched mouth. Two cockroaches the size of baby lizards were startled at the drain and ran up over his hands. He shouted and flung them off. He found himself near tears, horribly lonely, fighting self-pity, and it took thirty quick push-ups at the bedside to restore his self-control. When he finally slept, two or three hours before dawn, he dreamed of the cockroaches: he was in a cobbled town, medieval-like, at night, trying to heave three-foot cockroaches into a casement window lit yellow on the second floor. Someone was waiting to catch them—he didn't know who.

His inner eyelids were dazzled. He opened them to a blaze of yellow light. The ceiling bulb had come on, and the reading lamp too. São Sebastião had power again. The state could count a small victory against the long siege of barbarism. On the boulevard a sarcastic cheer erupted.

He got out of bed, wild with restlessness. Melanie hadn't stirred. He switched off the lights and went into the bathroom and stood under a cold shower for half a minute. When he came out, he was calmer. He walked dripping into the bedroom and caught an unexpected breath of wind through the louvers. The coolness across his chest and thighs felt like strength of purpose. And he did what, in a more fragile mood, he had contemplated but never dared.

He went to his desk and opened the middle drawer, where Melanie kept her journal. It was a clothbound book with a cover of maroon, indigo, and scarlet swirls, feminine colors and shapes, lying among the paperbacks she'd brought along—almost a dozen, as if she expected to find no books here, or to have loads of free time, or to stay indefinitely. He flipped through its pages with the self-accusing, self-forgiving thrill of a guilty act. Heavy cream-colored pages, with rough edges, and blue or black ink. Pages and pages of words! She wrote prodigiously and uncritically, crossing nothing out. Each entry started in a neat small hand and then the loops grew and leaned forward in the increasing urgency of whatever she had to tell her soul that day. A tumult of feeling and expression. It filled Levin with wonder and distaste and fear. He kept no journal, just the spiral pocket-sized notebooks, which he more and more suspected of uselessness. She wrote indoors, alone, for herself; he took notes amid crowds and bins of fish for the benefit of his anonymous readers. Beyond that, he had trouble writing a postcard. He skipped to her last entry and his eyes fell on these words:

> Yesterday almost tripped over a beggar woman with her baby on the sidewalk and she yelled at me. A lot of ambivalence toward Americans here and I feel like someone wrote HASSLE ME across my forehead. It would be O.K. if I were getting unambivalence from him, then I'd feel that I had a reason to be here—it's really such an awful place. Instead all I feel is avoidance. It drives me crazy because if I could just get through to him I know I could help us work through these issues. I don't think there's anything wrong with "us." We're just not communicating well. At all. But sometimes it's enough to make me want to say fuck it. I wish I knew what he wants. I wish I knew what I want. I want

But something had interrupted her. He remembered: she was writing when he came home this afternoon. How little her face betrayed of what she'd been thinking! He looked over at her sleeping, breathing form under the bed sheet. Beneath the fluidity and the woman's ways was this hungry pink-skinned girl, lonely in the world, fighting for her way, crying for comfort. Levin, whose axiom as a reporter was to take people at their word and then go find out, saw concealment everywhere. He thought: We hide and hide, most of all from ourselves. In the end no one but ourselves is fooled.

He was amused, tenderly, and saddened. He dug up a pen and wrote at the end of her entry a single word: *lollipops.*

It was a long time before sleep finally got the better of him. Then he slept with the ache of exhaustion, and at the furthest point of sleep he had a dream in which he was shot through the head by a long-haired Saraunese gunman in Impanang. Curiously, the bullet that entered his mouth came out through his forehead, leaving a small red perfect hole, like the mark a Hindu woman wears. Out of the fog people gathered around, cackling with theories about who had done it and how such a trajectory could have occurred. But for Levin, lying on his back in the glass and mud where he'd been thrown by the force of the shot, the mark was a terrible embarrassment and he tried to put a stop to all the talk. When Mrs. Balatang stooped to offer him water, he refused and said that he would be all right in a minute.

He woke up sweating to a room full of daylight and heat. Melanie had risen, and the morning was almost gone. Levin ate quickly and then packed his bag; at his request she came into the bedroom and watched from his desk.

"Underwear?" she asked.

"Two pairs."

"It's four days, right?"

"I'll try to be back in three."

"And it's the tropics. So pack another."

"All right. Look, I've written some numbers here—John and Rose, Feliz, a doctor, the embassy. You know about the supermarket at Avenue U Thant. *Fatal Weapon 3* is playing at the Super City Cinema."

"Don't worry about me."

Levin went to give her the numbers, and found that he didn't want to relinquish her hand. She looked up at him with mild irony.

"I'm sorry," he told her.

"For what?"

She was a little irritated, but she wanted an answer.

"Leaving."

"But it's what you want to do, isn't it?"

"I don't want—"

"So don't be sorry."

"O.K." Levin realized that he didn't know exactly what he was sorry for; in these small moments he was clumsy and knew himself less than she did. He kissed her good-bye and promised to come back alive. Then he went into the city to run errands and kill the afternoon before his rendezvous with Ding Magkakanaw.

CHAPTER III

Camp Pereira was on the far side of the city, across the Musa River. Levin drove the Toyota through downtown traffic to Avenue U Thant, then turned east and crept among the flimsy taxis and the black exhaust of diesel buses toward Marapang Road. On Marapang he went north along the dead-gray river and through the clubs and guest houses of the red-light district, empty and quiet in their midafternoon anomie, with nothing open but the V.D. clinics. He passed the squatter houses that spilled down the banks of the Musa and the piecemeal shacks raised on piers over the water, which at this time of year floated only a yard under the floorboards, offering back the trash that squatter families had dumped and that no longer flowed out to sea because bilge and filth had dammed the river within the city. After a mile in Marapang he reached Payao Bridge, where the Musa was met by Avenue Peréz de Cuéllar, originally Avenue Trygve Lie (the main thoroughfares had been named in a burst of internationalism during the mid-sixties), briefly renamed Avenue Kurt Waldheim in deference to visiting Chinese officials, who still hadn't forgiven the Norwegian secretary general for supporting South Korea, and finally, after Waldheim's fall from grace, rechristened with the name of his successor, though by then the locals called it Avenue Everyone. He crossed the river and entered a strip of garages that led out of the slums and up to the National Shopping Center and Cinema complex, directly across the avenue from Camp Pereira, headquarters of the Armed Forces of Direv Saraun.

Camp Pereira sat in the lower hills of the Montes Xavieres, where the original Portuguese mission had been established. The hills were mercifully cooler than the swampy city. The Jesuits who had settled became addicted to their breezes, which eventually blew out the flame of the civilizing cause, and for centuries the rest of the island was hardly penetrated. Other Jesuits from Macao, China, the East Indies, and the Philippines took their leaves here, so that São Sebastião had been an R and R spot from the beginning. In World War II, when Porto Negrais became a minor staging point for Allied operations in the southwest Pacific, the top American military brass occupied the plush, airy hillside villas of the mestizo collaborators. After the war the Montes Xavieres had been given back to the elite families, but a number of them had recently emigrated to Australia or the United States. Those who stayed were renting videos instead of going out to private clubs at night; their dinner talk dwindled to terrorism and resale values behind the guard of a private police force, ten-foot concrete walls, and watchdogs whose barks echoed in the hills as Levin got out of his car.

From the vantage point of the camp's parking lot, he could see most of the city he'd just driven through. It glittered without color in the even wash of daylight. Across the river, past the downtown banks and hotels, he made out his own high rise trapped in the haze and heat. Just beyond lay the coast, edged by a calm, silver sea.

In the parking lot he recognized a number of press cars, jeeps, and vans. But except for half a dozen sentries in booths at the head of the path that led into the grounds, the camp seemed deserted. It would be possible, he thought, for a few brave guerrillas to run a truck loaded with explosives past these sentries and blow themselves and the army headquarters into the oyster-colored sky. Instead, they were assassinating traffic cops. For what? To fray everyone's nerves until they fell to pieces like a threadbare coat?

The sentry outside the booth on the left stiffened at Levin's approach. His face was as dark as a South Indian's. He glanced at the press card Levin pulled from his shirt on a chain rusty from sweat.

"O.K., Joe."

"Colonel Siriman?"

The sentry pointed at the annex of the General Staff building. "Press conference."

"Ah. Thanks."

Levin walked quickly along the cinder path that divided the lawn. The camp had the manicured calm of an insane asylum. There was a specific adrenaline to catching a story late, and he temporarily forgot about the travel permit he'd come for.

The annex, single-storied and slate-gray, crouched on the far side of the General Staff building. The complex had been built in the fifties with American money and had the dreary sleekness of the American imperial style. Inside high square windows the annex ceiling gave off a fluorescent glare. Already pulling out his notebook, Levin went in by the side door.

Newsmen were backed up almost to the door. The room was badly overheated, from too many bodies in its small space and from the harsh ceiling lights and the camera spots on the floor. Those in back strained over the heads of the camera crews, who crowded the reporters lucky enough to get seats in front. The pop of flashes revealed photographers kneeling between the front row of chairs and the table where a Saraunese officer was sitting.

Between shoulders and hand-held cameras, Levin recognized the face of Colonel Siriman, the Armed Forces press liaison. A soft, handsome face, with moles that sprouted long black hairs, and the light mustache of Saraunese men. Under the lights he was perspiring heavily and clutching a handkerchief. The Armed Forces uniform of worsted dark khaki, medaled and braided, had circles of sweat under the short sleeves. His amplified voice, muffled in the packed room, carried the cadences of a man with a captive audience.

". . . there will be an investigation into that. All aspects will be thoroughly looked into. We will leave no stone unturned."

"Why can't you give the names of your suspects?" a reporter near the front asked.

"It is due process not to reveal names until their confessions have been completed and confirmed. Yes? The compatriot in the middle."

A Saraunese man began a question in his own language, then switched in mid-sentence to English, with which he had difficulty. At least half the people in the room were foreigners. ". . . that this American was in—was with local gangsters and drug dealers. Can you make comment on that, Colonel?"

"I have nothing for you on that. This is the first I have heard. But I will say that it is very unlikely. It has never been the habit of our gangsters to drag foreigners into their operations."

"Has it been the habit of our guerrillas?" a Saraunese standing near Levin called out, under the cover of anonymity.

Colonel Siriman smiled and squinted into the camera lights. "A question in the back?"

"My question is how you could have the right suspects, Colonel, when no witness has provided any description and the gunmen disappeared into the crowd and even the girl sitting with the American outside the café has given no details?"

The colonel sustained his smile, though he made a motion as if to wipe his face with the crumpled handkerchief. Glancing from his interlocutor, he met Levin's eyes. It seemed that, just before looking away, the colonel raised his eyebrows and nodded.

"The girl was traumatized when she spoke to reporters. But since this morning her mind has cleared. She gave us positive I.D.'s of the two killers—suspected killers. And as I have said several times, they willingly confessed."

"Under torture?"

The colonel answered sharply in Saraunese.

"Where is the girl now?"

The reporters in front had turned around to get a look at this Saraunese who was pressing the colonel beyond common civility, drawing him into a separate dialogue. An ABC correspondent who'd arrived two days ago tried to cut him off: "Somebody else, somebody else, this isn't an interview." Levin spotted Fraser in the third row. He went back to taking notes; when he looked again Fraser had seen him and caught his eye. Fraser raised his eyebrows Saraunese style and rubbed both eyes with his knuckles. He meant: Did you just wake up? Levin shook his head once and turned his attention back to Colonel Siriman.

"She has her work in Marapang," he was saying, "she is a busy girl, but I won't tell you which place because every one of you will be there tonight. Yes, in front. The American gentleman."

"Colonel Siriman, there has been a palpable mood of anxiety in the streets of São Sebastião and it is quite probable that this incident will only heighten it."

Levin knew the bass monotone of Greg Fishelin, the AP bureau chief, Ding's former boss. Fishelin held the floor with a windy mood report. "People are fearful, they are uneasy, they are frightened."

"And scared," the colonel said, drawing laughs.

"There is a sense of random danger. Violence can come from any quarter. Now this sense extends to non-Saraunese. What assurance can you give that this is only an isolated incident and not a sign of growing anti-Americanism in Direv Saraun?"

"None," said the colonel, and this time the laughter was louder. "Are you asking whether you should begin taking precautions, Mr. Fishelin? Everyone in São Sebastião should take precautions. But as far as I know you yourself are on nobody's list. If I hear of any such thing, you will be the first to know—I can give assurance on that. I hope you would return the favor, hmm?"

Fishelin fought through the laughter, cradling his dignity. "There has been a historical love-hate attitude toward Americans here. Do the guerrillas consider them the enemy now?"

"One navy man was shot. Perhaps it is a warning, perhaps it is terror, but only time will tell if it is policy. In the meantime, everyone must make his own decisions about safety."

"It's not my personal safety—"

Fishelin was interrupted by the ABC man. "I'm told it's the second U.S. serviceman to die in a week. Can you comment on that? And I have a follow-up."

"The first had nothing to do with the war," Colonel Siriman said irritably. "It is foolish to confuse the personal and the political. The victim was mentally diseased. All right, from A.F.P."

"Hold on, I had a—"

"Did their orders come from the top echelon?" The Agence France-Presse correspondent was not a Frenchman but a New Zealander. His ability to chase drinks all night and stories all day had already created a small legend in the press corps.

"We have been informed that this action was approved at the highest level of the illegal Saraunese People's Party."

"But no one's claimed responsibility."

"There is often a delay. They want to gauge the popular reaction."

A Saraunese woman asked, "What does it say about the government's ability to handle the peace-and-order situation?"

"The government is taking every necessary measure to safeguard peace and order. But I do not need to remind you that we have a democracy in Direv Saraun."

The Australian cameraman standing next to Levin snorted.

The correspondent from ABC shouted his follow-up. "What are the geopolitical consequences of this incident? Will it impact on Saraunese-American relations?"

An impatient groan erupted.

"Ask your ambassador. I am a soldier, not a statesman." The colonel started to turn his microphone away.

"Then can you tell us if this will precipitate a coup?"

It was Fraser—loud with daring, asking the question on everyone's mind. But the colonel was not going to be caught by brusqueness; he was a careful man. In the lull, before the photographers on the floor realized what they'd heard and replied with a barrage of shutter clicks and flashes, he blinked and his tongue emerged. Then he shook free the handkerchief, neatly folded it into a square, and dabbed at his beaded forehead and nose. The thinning black hair fell away damply, betraying a bald scalp. In the explosion of flashes his skin looked almost white. By the time he spoke, the sting of the question had begun to evaporate, and the colonel was smiling again.

"We are living in a democracy in Direv Saraun. We have our constitutional government. It is a mistake to talk so freely of coups— that is for South America, or Africa. But of course, it is the highest duty of any nation to protect itself from attack. Within the limits of the acceptable we will do what we must to protect the national security."

Several reporters jumped in at once:

"But national security has gone to pieces."

"Suspension of civil liberties?"

"Is the prime minister aware of the situation?"

"What's acceptable? The current policy of restraint is failing, isn't it?"

"Restraint? Fishelin, civilian killings are up every month."

Colonel Siriman sat like a man watching a pack of dogs fight over a slab of beef. "One at a time, gentlemen. We are not in the market."

The Agence France-Presse man managed to make himself heard. "Will this have any effect on the reported split within the A.F.D.S.?"

"I don't know what report is that."

"That certain midlevel officers are dissatisfied with the way the generals are running the counterinsurgency."

"Such reports are totally without basis. The A.F.D.S. is united in its commitment to defeating the enemy in our midst."

The Saraunese near Levin raised his voice above the pandemonium: "Are you saying there is no likelihood of martial law?"

The colonel waited until he had absolute quiet.

"I am saying that depends on everyone in this room. Ladies and gentlemen, today's press conference is finished."

He left the table in a riot of shouts.

Levin slipped between two cameras and fought through the crowd toward the front, desperately trying to catch the colonel's eye. Just when Siriman was about to pass through the door, he turned as if he'd been aware of Levin's presence all the time. He nodded again.

"Colonel, may I see you in your office?" Levin called over the heads of newsmen.

"I want to see you also." The colonel disappeared.

Fraser reached Levin at the door. He was still smiling lopsidedly, as if his face had been locked since last night.

"Nice question, John."

"Somebody had to ask it," Fraser said modestly.

"An American serviceman was killed this morning?"

"Not far from my building. I was showering or I would have heard the shot. Rose heard it and I ran down immediately. I was the first journalist on the scene. They only hit his stomach but that was enough. It's a shame. Freckled chap." The ironic smile twisted his face again. "Did you manage to get all of it?"

"Pretty much." Levin realized that at some point in the growing confusion he'd stopped taking notes. "It'll come in over the wire."

"If you need to have a look at mine—" Levin quickly shook his head. Fraser shrugged. "As you like. So—the long good-bye?"

"Something like that." The crush of egressing newsmen carried them into the fresh air. "What about the girl? Couldn't you get anything from her?"

"What makes you think she wasn't part of the setup?"

Levin felt himself foundering, like a tardy schoolboy trying to find the right page while the teacher fires off questions. "Oh come on, why would they use a bar girl?"

"To make sure the guy's in the right place at the right time. I'm not sure I believe a word the colonel says, are you? That whole performance was a warning aimed at the P.M.'s government. Who's to say the military didn't put this guy away? A pretext for a coup. Or the Americans, for that matter?"

"No way. You've got to assume a basic level of rationality."

"Why?"

Levin cursed himself. Fraser's cynical posture was as reflexive as sentimentality, and as false. Fraser didn't believe the world was a sinkhole. He believed the world was a place where some won and some lost, and he would win. Levin knew all this; but at the moment he wasn't equal to Fraser.

"So it's going to turn into another of those cases—all theory and no truth?"

"With a slightly personal edge. Maybe it's open season on Joes, whoever did it."

"That would be too bad, wouldn't it? As one Joe to another."

"I'm sure we'll both be fine. However, I am glad it's not me taking a trip tonight."

"Maybe it's safer out there."

"Where is Ding, anyway?"

"I don't know—I just woke up, right? We're meeting in a couple of hours."

"Why don't you ask Fra Boboy who did this? Oh, by the way—" Fraser produced a copy of the *Afternoon Express* and opened it to the editorial pages. "Seen this? Hot off the press."

Feliz's column, under the title "My View" and a grainy portrait that suggested a late stage of leprosy, was headlined: "In the Belly of the Fish."

"It's all about last night."

"I'll go get a copy."

"You've got to watch what you tell that guy. You never know where it's going to end up."

Levin started to go. "Well. I'll see you in a few days."

"Thank Melanie for a wonderful dinner. You've got a lovely girl."

"I won't be going back home—errands and all. Look, be sure to call her, will you?"

"Bloody shame you have to leave so soon. Don't worry, Rose and I shall keep her entertained."

The General Staff building was a warren of linoleum corridors and louan hollow-core doors with brass number and name plates. Outside some of the offices, somber, deferential peasants waited to have a petition heard. Colonel Siriman's was as ill lit and shabby as every other bureaucratic office in São Sebastião. A middle-aged, Chinese-looking woman sat behind a metal desk on which several stacks of paper were curling and yellowing, her earlobes weighted with pearls, a roll of fat under her chin and upper arms. She was typing from a carbon copy onto a Royal. Its keys kept sticking, and she'd reach into the machine to unjam them, type a few words, notice that her fingertips were inking up the keys, and dab them on a piece of tissue on the desk. The tissue clung to the inky skin and she'd furtively scrape it off with her teeth and resume typing until the keys jammed again. This routine so absorbed her that she didn't notice Levin until he was standing over the desk.

"Yes?"

"Is Colonel Siriman inside? It's about a travel permit."

"Colonel Siriman is engaged at a press conference."

"I know, I've just come—"

"He won't be back for the rest of the afternoon."

Just then the colonel hurried into the office. He was unexpectedly short, and out of the lights his brown face looked tense; he was frowning.

"Oh, Mr. Levin. Come into my office."

Levin followed him into the next room. After a resentful pause the secretary's clacking started up again.

The colonel's office was lighter and more spacious. A rear window looked down on the end of the parking lot, past a row of quinine trees, to the far distance and a line of shimmering sea.

"So much is happening, I forget about the sea here," Levin said, and the colonel nodded and gestured for him to sit, the overture accepted.

"Yes, we are so introspective on this island. You may notice we have no interest in foreign news. Yet we want the world to acknowledge, approve. We are nothing in our own eyes—like a woman."

A melancholy had settled over the colonel. Levin saw that his performance had drained him. Now he seemed a different man—abstracted. He opened a gold cigarette case, engraved *K.S.*, and extended it. Levin never refused a cigarette from a Saraunese.

"What did you think of my press conference?" the colonel began.

Anyone was likable once you saw things from his point of view, and one of Levin's techniques was to isolate whatever he could bring himself to like in a source and speak to that. Most often it was a weakness, a spot of insecurity. This earned him confidence, it dispelled the natural hostility an interrogator aroused; and when his quarry felt at ease, understood, liked, Levin shot—casually but point-blank—the single question he'd conceived the interview around. It was essential that the subject invite the question himself. The colonel's tension had worried him in the anteroom, but now he knew it was an inroad.

"Very skillfully handled under considerable pressure. But I know you're busy—I've just come for a travel permit to Salantin Province."

"Salantin?" The colonel nodded in obscure assent. "It is one of the hottest areas."

"So they say. If it is, a permit will help."

"Please. The day is almost done. I am curious about your impression."

"I'm afraid I've got to be somewhere shortly."

"Salantin, yes. Just tell me—did the press accept our presentation of the facts?"

The air between them clouded with the smoke of two cigarettes. Colonel Siriman, wincing, inhaled with a short breathy drag.

"By and large. There's always a few skeptics."

"Naturally. Until our suspects make public confessions there will be something short of full belief."

"You were very good with John Fraser's question."

"The Englishman? Did you think so?"

"A Pentagon spokesman would have gotten lost in his own euphemisms."

The colonel leaned back. "I'm glad you thought so. Things seemed to become chaotic toward the end."

"We just can't stand not to get in one last question." Levin started to rise. "Really, I should—"

"Don't you have any questions for me, Mr. Levin?"

"I didn't prepare any. It was really just the permit."

The colonel drummed the fingers that held his cigarette on the tabletop. Without looking at Levin he said, "I wanted to ask you one. People accuse the Armed Forces of being immoral. In one of your articles you suggested the same thing. So I want to ask your opinion. Last week I heard a story of a farmer experiencing a plague of snails in his melon patch. The parasites were eating up his livelihood. Would it be better for this farmer to spend week after week poisoning them with pellets one by one, until at the end of three months he has no more snails and also ruined melons?"

Levin smiled inwardly. He'd known the colonel had a burden to relieve. Was he being asked for absolution?

"Or is it better for him to use the strong insecticide, which kills the snails in two days, and the melons also—but then he can plant again, and in three months he will already have ripe melons to eat? What would you tell this farmer? What would be the moral thing?"

The colonel was pulling meditatively at the strands drooping from the mole on his cheek.

"Won't the snails come back?"

"The insecticide kills their homes in the soil."

"It doesn't kill the nutrients?"

"Melon is one of the hardier crops."

"Is this what you wanted to see me about, Colonel?"

"I wanted to put it," the colonel said, "to a moral man. They are hard to find in our capital."

Levin said, evenly: "If you took power, could the army destroy the guerrillas?"

"Of course! How many are they—five thousand? And how many are we? Fifty thousand. It is ten to one. Only we are afraid of the strong method. We have grown fat and weak. 'The cocktail of Southern Asia'! They have people in this city I know—I *know*—that I cannot lay a finger on. This bureaucracy"—he motioned toward the monotonous clacking in the other room—"it is like handcuffs on our wrists. While they are shooting policemen in the street. Making us into fools!"

"You need stronger methods?"

"Stronger!"

"What about foreign opinion? The U.S."

"The victims are American now! And it is our problem, not theirs. The solution must be ours also. The guerrillas are the only ones with the courage to throw this truth in the world's teeth. We must learn from them—our own generals lack the will to win. The situation must force them either to act or step aside and let others act. It would be better for things to get worse than go on in this status quo."

They sat in silence. Levin felt that the colonel had said what he wanted to say; perhaps more. And he was amazed, again, at the breach that could open in a man.

"I assume this isn't for the record?"

The colonel gazed at Levin closed-mouthed. "Quote without attribution. You are surprised? Consider it an anonymous favor."

Levin shrugged off the word "favor." He took out his notebook and, under his scribbles from the press conference, he summarized the parable of the melons.

The colonel put out his cigarette. It was a signal that the conversation was over. Already he was closing up again.

"What about this travel permit?"

"It's just for— To be safe, say five days."

"What is your purpose in going to Salantin?"

"I'm writing a piece about sugar."

"Not trying to break this Bowers story? The American who disappeared?"

"I didn't even know he was supposed to be in Salantin."

"Our intelligence tells us the Southern Regional Command captured him on Mount Kalanar. Perhaps he and Fra Boboy are sharing a cup of jungle tea even as we speak."

"Does your intelligence have a theory what he was up to?"

The colonel shrugged. Now Levin was having trouble reading his sincerity; he seemed misted with motive. The thought of another American with Fra Boboy—prisoner or not—disappointed Levin. He wasn't going out there for the sound of familiar voices. At any rate, he suddenly found himself with a number of stories to break.

"If that's where Bowers is," he said, "there's not much chance of my breaking it. I'll be spending my time at the sugar plantations around Pulaya."

"The best A.F.D.S. source in Pulaya is Captain Bugan of the Fifth Elite Scouts Battalion. He is making some great tactical innovations down there. Captain Bugan is not in the custom of giving interviews, but if you use my name I think he will accommodate you."

"Thanks. If I have time I will."

"Well—make time. Are you going alone? That would be inadvisable."

"No. The permit should also say Ding Magkakanaw."

A shadow of recognition passed over the colonel's face.

"You know him? Free-lancer."

"He is known to us, yes. But he does not come to Camp Pereira. May!"

The clacking in the front room stopped. The heavy Chinese secretary appeared at the door, her fingertips white with tissue, and received instructions. "Put Levin and Magkakanaw both on the document," the colonel told her. "Five days only." She went out. "For a moment, Mr. Levin."

"Sure, I'll wait."

But the lull embarrassed Levin, for he had nothing else to say and silence now seemed like a waste of the initiative. He was vaguely troubled by the parable of the melons, and the nod he remembered in the annex. He glanced down at the notebook in his lap.

São Sebastião, Direv Saraun, Feb. 22—The body of an American reporter who had been missing for several days has been found in the remote southern mountains of this war-torn country. In a case eerily reminiscent of the 1948 murder of the journalist George Polk during the Greek civil war, the reporter had gone to the mountains in order to interview a guerrilla leader, and questions are now being raised here about the identity and motive of his purported killers.

"Of course," the colonel said slowly, once the typing began again, "if during your travels you learn anything about the Army of Liberation, the positions, movements, it is expected that you will report it back here."

For a moment Levin said nothing. Then he said: "Oh?"

"Do you want to see the other side win?"

"I just want to tell the truth."

"Are you a Christian, Mr. Levin?"

He didn't know where this was leading. "If you were a Westerner, Colonel, my name would tell you I'm Jewish. Personally I'm a nonbeliever."

"A Hebrew? Very good, very successful. Your people had to fight also. Well, it is in the Christian Bible. 'He who is not with me is against me.' We have reached that point here in Direv Saraun."

"What about neutrality of journalists?"

"That space is closing, I am afraid."

"Sorry to hear it. Then we won't be able to work here."

The colonel waved dismissively. "Do you not believe that every act has a consequence?"

"Well, sure."

"And that a man who is free to act must be responsible for it?"

Levin nodded. In fact, they were two of his deepest beliefs, about the only things that amounted to absolutes with him. If absolutes could survive somewhere outside the systems . . .

"It is not a question of working or not working. It is a question of knowing what one is doing and taking responsibility. Just as those who murdered your compatriot this morning must accept the consequence. I will add—this is off the record, please—out there it is more difficult to avoid taking sides than in São Sebastião. And there are some very primitive elements, even on our side, who may not understand your actions as well as you."

Levin smiled tightly. "I'll keep it in mind."

The secretary appeared with the document and a carbon copy. Colonel Siriman removed a pair of bifocals from his breast pocket, scanned the sheet, whispering the words, and signed with a subdued flourish. He gave the original to Levin.

"We have one, you have one."

"Fair enough."

"Don't forget our agreement."

Levin did not know what was meant. But he said, "I won't." Suddenly he wanted to get out of Camp Pereira—out of São Sebastião, with its heat mist and thousand cheap opinions. He longed for the silence of the night drive, the integrity of the forest. He'd thought he had gotten the better of Colonel Siriman. Now he wasn't so sure.

The road curved quietly down from the Montes Xavieres into the furious smoky streets. The five o'clock sun was deep in the west over the sea and its low angle yellowed buildings and signs, cars, utility poles, palm trees. Levin thought the light seemed to come from within the city—like a miasma infecting the atmosphere, a jaundice of human decay, human corruptions, which the septic air sealed in. As São Sebastião flowed past him again and the swampy heat rose around his descent, he had a vision of the city he was about to leave as a great open sore, stung by the salt water, festering with innumerable faces distorted by suffering, deceit, rage—the ancient woman staring from the prison of her Coke stand, a taximan wiping his watery face in the mirror, three girls sashaying in school skirts, a bony news vendor weaving through traffic.

Stalled on the Payao Bridge, Levin closed his window against the exhaust fumes and gazed through the steel webbing of the suspension into the water.

Half-naked men were loading white sacks onto the deck of an ancient barge. Sugar—bound for Western canisters and bowls. The laborers weaved up the ramp, their bowed heads lost under the sacks;

on the way down to shore the younger men jogged and laughed. Amid the gray bilge and orange corrosion, these sacks of whiteness seemed like jewels—the only things in Direv Saraun still clean and pure enough to be sent into the world. In the early seventies the Musa docks had swarmed with men across rows of barges, the sugar sacks rising like wintry hills. But sugar had collapsed at the end of the decade and the industry was now a fraction of its former self. There had been stories of starvation and of landlords making up their losses through graft of international aid. The war had its beginnings then.

Someone knocked on Levin's window. It was the news vendor: a long grinning face. Dark and hollow, a southerner's. Maybe crazy. He held up an armful of newspapers and reeled off their names as if they were one word.

Levin rolled down the window. "*Afternoon Express*?"

The news vendor reached into his fold and pulled out a copy. The traffic wasn't moving. Levin handed him a coin and wrestled the paper open to the editorial page, blocking the windshield. He wanted Feliz's views—a token of clarity to harbor for the trip. He scanned the article and was relieved that his name wasn't used. Feliz wrote in florid Saraunese English:

IN THE BELLY OF THE FISH
At a sumptuous dinner party last night—

"Journalist, Joe?"

The news vendor was lingering at the window, bone wrapped in brown skin. He had noticed the laminated I.D. card Levin had forgotten to tuck away at Camp Pereira. Levin kept it hidden except on official occasions or in places where his status would earn him more safety than suspicion. Sometimes it was a tough call.

"Yes, journalist." He lifted the card inside his shirt, where sweaty hair glued it to his chest.

"Very bad, very—"

"I know, I know, things very bad in São Sebastião. I'm getting the hell out. Bet you wish you could too. Bad as things are down where you come from."

The bridge traffic was starting to unknot and creep forward. Levin put the Toyota in gear and moved up; the news vendor walked alongside with his stiff skeletal stride.

"American very bad trouble."

"The guy who was shot—well, one swallow doesn't a summer make, you know? It's too bad. But how many of your countrymen have gone down that same road?"

Levin was amusing himself and trying to amuse the news vendor— he didn't think the guy understood a word of it. He was having fun with the opacity that descended between him and Saraunese at the most critical moments. The news vendor ambled to keep abreast of the window, looking in with his grinning face, his eyebrows bobbing up and down. Which meant: What the hell are you talking about?

"American here, Joe, Marapang Road!" The news vendor gesticulated wildly to his left, at the street that met the bridge fifty feet ahead.

Now Levin was the one who didn't understand. "What American? Where, where trouble? Show me."

"Marapang Road, Joe, American going to fight!" The news vendor was working himself into a frenzy trying to get Levin to see. "Journalist!" he almost scoffed.

Levin thrust the paper aside and craned his head out the window. Beyond the traffic, among the outdoor tables of the clubs where girls and customers were starting to appear, a few Saraunese men stood in a cluster; someone Levin couldn't see was shouting.

He had to fight across three lanes of clotted traffic to make the left onto Marapang, while the news vendor, suddenly enraged, tried to catch up with a hobble-run, dodging cars, screaming for a gratuity. Levin deftly escaped, wove, came off the bridge, and cut in front of a stampede of oncoming traffic into the red-light district.

In front of the Pink Panther Club Bar, four Saraunese men were casually crowding a white man. The Saraunese were wearing stone-washed designer jeans, American university logo sweatshirts, gold chains—the uniform of pimps and gangsters. The white man, tall, heavy in the belly, collapsed in the chest, was wearing tight velour gym shorts, flip-flops, and a T-shirt that said "Try a Virgin," with "Island" written in tiny letters under the nipple. He was clutching a money belt in both hands. Behind him, two small boys and a girl of about eighteen in a tight tube of a dress that just reached her thighs watched from the door of the club. The boys looked entertained, the prostitute scared. Next door, bouncers, barkers, "receptionists" in the skirts and boots and safari hats of the Australian Club were

setting up for the evening and discreetly looking on. The white man
didn't seem to understand that he was cornered.

"You'd sell your fucking sister, your fucking mother!" he shouted.
"Son of a whore, a deal's a deal—now give me my goddamn money!
Where's my fucking money, son of a fucking whore?"

One of the men said something in Saraunese, another answered
him, and all of them laughed. They were past dialogue, and pretty
soon there wouldn't be words left in any language. They were enjoying his display, but they were coiled with anger.

"What, you think it's open season on Americans, shoot us, rip us
off? We could blow this place to hell—you stinking little Saraunese
wouldn't be shit without our money. You'd be in some stinking
village picking your asses with twigs. I'm a UCSB grad, you don't
rip *me* off—"

"Hey, Joe—" a Saraunese said and started forward, but Levin
jumped out of the Toyota and rushed between them.

"Boss," he began, and located his pidgin Saraunese. "This Joe
know nothing, he no worth trouble, let me have him, my stupid
cousin, he no come back." And as he hustled the American away he
murmured fiercely: "Are you crazy? They're going to kill you."

"Let go of me, brother, I want my money."

"Your money's gone. Get in the car before they come after us."

The Saraunese watched without moving, arms folded across their
sweatshirts. Levin pushed the American into the passenger's seat.
Circling the car, he glanced at a plump young pimp who was gnaw-
ing his lower lip: from the fat-narrowed eyes humor and contempt
answered him.

As they drove away Levin discovered that he was shaking with
fury.

"What's the matter with you? They were going to beat you to a
pulp."

"Let them, sonsofbitches. They took my money."

The American was deep into his thirties, blond, sunburned. There
might once have been a low kind of refinement in his face, but now
the flesh was loose, wasted-looking, and a tic pulsed high in the right
cheek. His bare feet were propped on Levin's bag, and between his
bald red knees his hands played skittishly. The accent was flat West
Coast.

"You work here?" he asked, and Levin nodded. "What, business? Import?"

"Journalism."

"Oh, you mean C.I.A.," said the American, immensely pleased with this piece of cleverness.

"No, I mean journalism. Where the hell do you get your ideas?"

"What's there to cover, for Christ's sake?"

Levin glanced again in disbelief. "You don't know there's a war going on?"

"Oh, that. Shit, it's not a war, it's just Asians killing each other. They've been doing it forever and they'll be doing it forever. I thought you were here the same reason I was, same every Joe is."

A question was obviously expected, and something compelled Levin to comply. "Namely?"

"Sweet kiwi, baby. Asian pussy."

"Rick!"

The American whipped his head out the window. "Hey, sister!" A diminutive prostitute in sunglasses and platform shoes was waving in front of a V.D. clinic. "She wants me to go over. Christ, what's she doing there—she said she was clean! My money's back at the Pacifica anyway, what's left of it. Sonsofbitches. Have to wait till later."

"Haven't you had enough action today?" Levin could not keep his eyes off Rick.

"Action back there? I didn't get shit from her, brother, that's the whole thing. I asked for it doggie-style—the little whore wouldn't do it! Said they didn't do it that way in her hometown. Who cares about her hometown? You pay, and she does what you want—that's the transaction and you don't violate it. Then the fuckers wouldn't give my money back. They'd sell their grandmother and cheat their brother here, they don't give a shit, it's just the almighty dollar. It's worse than the D.R., Turkey, Bombay. They did doggie in Turkey and they're Muslim. Next week I'm going to Thailand. I've heard it's like heaven. It's because they're Buddhist—you can build a pagoda and you're cool again. Hey, the name's Rick. From Sacramento."

Rick from Sacramento reached a hand across the steering wheel. Levin looked at it and then took it. He expected a soggy shake, but the hand was dry and firm.

"Daniel Levin." It was distasteful to give his name, it reduced the distance. "Rick what?"

"Rick what's it to you?"

"O.K." Levin smiled and shook his head. "Your experience seems extensive."

"You heard of the show *Price Is Right,* right? Last year I took second. I'm a whiz with products—detergent, air fresheners. A three-month unlimited ticket on TWA. I did Columbus's route in reverse—the islands, the Med. Then I decided to keep going, follow Marco Polo through Asia. Now I'm on Magellan—just came in from the Philippines. The girls there, oh, very sweet. I've been to four continents total. Skipped Africa, if you know what I mean." Rick winked. "Where we going, brother?"

They were still in Marapang. Levin had been too distracted to give it a thought. "I'm meeting a friend in an hour not too far from here. I'll let you off there. It's a few blocks from your hotel."

"She got a friend?"

"Unless you go both ways, Rick—" Christ, Levin thought. He's already gotten to me.

"Oh, a guy? Uh-uh, not for me. But let me buy you a drink while you wait—it's hard to find an intelligent conversation around here. So you're really a journalist? I think you'll want to hear my theory about how America can get international respect back. I've seen a lot on this trip."

Rick's smile pulled the loose skin into doglike folds around his jaws. The guy was repellent, but he was a curiosity—they tended to turn up in the warmer places of the world. He would help pass the time until the rendezvous with Ding.

Outside Happy's Grill, a guard armed with an M-14 sat on a stool. Inside was all frosted lamps, vinyl-upholstered booths, a jukebox with Sinatra and Def Leppard. Foreigners and fashionable Saraunese came here to be seen.

A girl rendered shapeless by brown polyester, her long black ponytail sprouting from a baseball cap, took their order. Rick made no linguistic adjustments for the Saraunese.

"Got Temple of Heaven, sweetheart? One here. What are you drinking, brother?"

Levin was just having coffee.

"Oh come on, have a real one. No? All right, coffee for my buddy. Staying up late or something?" Levin nodded. "Suit yourself."

Levin sat back. "So you've got a theory?"

Rick leaned forward with a look of unwholesome earnestness.

"I've made friends all across this earth, Dan, and you know what? People are the same everywhere. Know what else? They all love Americans. They *love* us, goddammit."

"Like your friends back there?"

"If you would have let me handle them my way. Because this is the thing: why were those guys pissed? What do people really want? Do they want to make decisions, responsibility? What does a kid want? He doesn't know what he wants. He wants to be *told*. And he loves the one who tells him. Very few people ever get beyond this early stage. I'm one—I could tell right off you're one."

"Let's leave me out of this," Levin said.

Rick didn't seem to hear him. "Now, this is the thing. The same is true for countries. They want to be told too. Just a few get past that to the telling stage. France, England, Germany—you notice it's always Caucasian. Now it's our turn."

The waitress brought their drinks. Rick was too worked up even to glance at her. The tic in his cheek had begun a rhythmic *mezzo-mezzo* dance.

"And everyone knows it—that's why everywhere I've gone I get treated well. The people are *dying* to be told. But, hold everything! The *governments* don't know it anymore. Every day at the U.N. Joe Blow from the Democratic Republic of Upyourass scores points off us."

"For not telling—"

"Our embassies get trashed, the flag gets burned, Americans shot—look what happened this morning. The people still know it, but the governments forgot. And now the whole world's a fucking mess. I hope you take good mental notes, brother, you might want to use this."

Levin finally voided the laughter pooling in his chest. It carried the taste of the anger in which it had washed up.

"What they know," he said, "is that you've got money. Those guys were calling you *banyi-banya*. That's clown in Saraunese."

Rick smiled with pity and disgust.

"Now, you're the type of American that's brought us to our knees. I saw that in you right away, sucking up to those pimps. You don't know your own mind, brother. That's why the world's pissed off at us. Not because we tell—it's because they want to be told and we *don't*."

"Let me see if I get this. You have Turkish girls do it doggie style to restore the world order? Every girl from Jamaica to Manila wants to go down on you because the Pax Americana makes them horny?"

Rick pointed at Levin's face. "You have the money, but you do the bending over. Just put it right in there, little brown brother. Since the Pharaohs there's never been anything like it."

Levin thought: Why am I sitting still for this? But Rick had worked a cheesy fascination on him—the kind that kept him from turning the channel from a weepy evangelist or a big-time wrestler. He'd always had a special susceptibility to these narcotizing fast-talkers, typhoons of energy with their thirty-second *Weltanschauungen,* explicators of the universe, fantasists of omnipotence. It had something to do with his readiness to listen, to take the other's point of view; he could end up with nothing to offer against. In the end, the Ricks gave him a half-hour's idle amusement and a mild dose of depression. As a journalist he'd learned to check them before they filled his notebook with sodden inanities. Yet he'd listened to this one.

São Sebastião, Direv Saraun, Feb. 22—Pox Americana, a dick-borne plague, seeped through the fish that ate Rick from Sacramento and may have infected this reporter—

But here was his rescuer.

Ding was standing on the sidewalk next to the armed guard, a slight figure with a duffel bag, peering in at the glass with a hand to his eyes so that his face was hidden.

Levin was halfway to the door before Rick could yell after him: "Hey, asshole, wait a minute!" There was terror in the voice.

On the street Levin seized Ding by the hand.

"Glad to see you, partner."

"Me too. Who was that sitting with you?"

"A nobody. Come on, the car's around the corner." It was night: the sun had set while Levin was inside with Rick.

"No one is nobody."

"This guy is. He's nothing."

"Let's not start with secrets, partner."

"You want to know? A piece of rot. Empire in decay. Let's go."

Levin flashed a smile, and Ding returned it uncertainly. It would be too much to explain. As they got into the car, Levin in the driver's seat for the first leg, their eyes met again and Levin thought how strange it was to be about to travel so far and spend every waking hour with a man he hardly knew.

They began the drive in darkness, going south.

CHAPTER IV

Once they were past the hotels on the edge of downtown, and then the southern slums; past the abandoned ice factory, industrial warehouses, masonry blockhouses in scrub fields where the stevedores were quartered, the banana and pineapple plantations, and the packing plants: once past these, the sea came into view again and they joined the coast road.

Immediately Porto Negrais appeared: the ghostly rigging of ships on dark water against black sky, the long projections of the docks. The highway veered away from the ocean and made a wide arc around the base, with its patches of floodlights and heavy-engine sounds. Tonight the traffic into the base was light and Porto Negrais was free from human voices. No laughing of hookers on a mission to lure sailors into town, no whooping of sailors in the frenzy of shore leave. An order had been issued: no one was to leave the base without "essential need" until the "security situation in Direv Saraun" had been "clarified." Marapang would be empty tonight and several kinds of essential need would go unfulfilled. A lone radio reached the highway with the defiant howling of the Rolling Stones, fading as Levin and Ding left the base behind them. Off to the right, the full moon hung like bruised fruit over the slick black face of the ocean. The air seemed to smother its radiance.

After a few miles the sign for the North-South Highway came into the headlights. They turned left into the interior, and at once everything was behind them.

Levin had never been south of the naval base. He felt as if his tour was beginning now, the months in the capital only a prelude to his real work. He remembered the shock of humidity at the airport, the cabbie's brown face, hand-rolled cigarette, strange accent offering (he'd finally deduced) a female escort, and the palm trees along the highway, and the cane-juice sellers with their hand presses in the throbbing streets. Only four months, yet at moments like this his time here seemed as unanchored to the rest of his life as a dream.

The highway took them deeper into the country. He had caught the sense of adventure again, and he was elated.

"Dark," he said, trying out the sound of his voice.

"Very hot, very dark night here in Direv Saraun," Ding answered in mock-pidgin. Conversation made the night seem human, familiar again.

Levin turned off the headlights. A blackness engulfed them so totally that, though the road had been clear a second ago, they were certain to crash. He dared himself to leave them off for five, six seconds, until the blindness became unbearable. "Christ."

"You see, it's dark. Without electricity there's only the moon."

"Of course. I've just never driven like this. Not a streetlight from here to—God knows where. Pulaya."

"There are towns. But between—"

"I didn't expect São Sebastião to end so fast. Ten miles outside, then nothing. Not even villages along here."

They were driving through a wilderness where the land was flat but lightless. These were fallow fields, not rice paddies of the monsoon.

The North-South Highway had been built with USAID money in the fifties, along with most of the administrative and military buildings in São Sebastião. It had cost a minute fraction of the vast cargo of cash that America was beginning to sink into this part of the world, but the road did its part in the American mutation of Direv Saraun. The population of the capital immediately doubled. The road workers whose careers ended at the terminus of the highway on the southern coast returned to São Sebastião to form urban gangs with names like Kings of the Road and Highwaymen. The rural economy exploded, and then it caramelized. Every tenant farmer with five hectares of rice "went sugar" as the expense of getting the stuff to the capital and out of the country was halved, and the loss of the Cuban supply to communism temporarily raised the price it fetched in the United States. Later, with the advent of saccharine, OPEC, and a European sugar cartel, the boom in the Saraunese countryside imploded. For every thousand Americans who switched to NutraSweet a Saraunese lost his job, and São Sebastião swelled to the bursting point. Since no one was growing anything but cane stalks, Direv Saraun had begun to import rice. In the south, rashes of starvation broke out. And then, at the end of the seventies, twenty years after the first bulldozers had rolled off the cargo ships at Porto Negrais, the first reports surfaced of guerrillas in the mountains. By then the North-South Highway, pocked and eroded by trucks and typhoons, lay half ruined. The guerrillas were finishing off the job. They now employed roughly the same number of Saraunese as had the American road contractor, a Mr. Phelps, who had since gone into Florida real estate.

But here, in the northwest valley of the Musa, the road was still good. It stretched on before the headlights until they lost it, a stripe of black asphalt without lines, edged by high green grass.

A pair of headlights appeared on the bank of a curve and suddenly a taxi-van flew past, sounding its horn and flashing its brights. Then it was behind them, like São Sebastião, without a trace.

"We don't have much company," Levin said. "Everyone's going the other way."

"Then we're going in the right direction."

Both of them laughed. It was time to begin a conversation, make a formal gesture of companionship. Levin turned on the high beams and began to accelerate. The salty breeze whipped through his hair and riffled the pages of the *Afternoon Express* on the dash. "Why don't you read what Feliz has to say in there?"

Ding had to fight the newspaper open against the crosswind. It folded clumsily on itself and he stamped the middle down against the dash.

"Turn on the light if you need to."

The interior light illuminated Ding's features: the flatness of the nose, the dark handsome watchful eyes, the tense poise of the mouth. It was a face dominated by eyes, as appealing and opaque as Buster Keaton's. He began to read silently.

"No, I mean out loud. I haven't read it yet."

" 'In the Belly of the Fish,' " Ding read, his enunciation halting. "Pula-pula, no? 'At a sumptuous dinner party last night a foreign visitor recalled to mind a Saraunese folk story. Long ago another foreigner named Jonah had the misfortune to be involved in a shipwreck during typhoon season. He was most unexpectedly swallowed by a pula-pula. (This was no market-stock, but one of the monster sizes from deep waters.)' It's from the Bible?"

"Of course!" cried Levin, slightly impatient. "Keep reading."

" 'It happens that Jonah had given God the frosty shoulder and then (incredibly!) slept through the typhoon in the ship's hold. For this, he was chucked overboard. According to survivors, he asked to be chucked overboard, being a conscientious chap at heart and feeling guilty about his role in the situation. God, being God, saved him by sending the pula-pula to eat him in the weedy'—*weedy*?"

"Weedy. Full of weeds—you know, like seaweed."

"—'bottom of the sea. He spent three days and nights down there, not the best of his life if however the most unusual! When the pula-pula finally puked him up on our shore, he made straight for São Sebastião with a message from God. Because of your evil and violent ways, he told the population, in forty days this city will be overthrown. Well, they took him seriously. They settled their differences and God made up his mind to spare them as he'd spared Jonah.

" 'Only then did Jonah realize that during his sojourn in the pula-pula his reproductive member—organ—*kolau*—the thing with many names—had been eaten off. It was gone.' "

Ding giggled. Levin shouted with laughter. "He went home last night and thought this up?"

" 'Consequently, Jonah sulked. Better to be dead, he reasoned, than live like this. God, however, pointed out to him: I've just spared a city of half a million—you can live without six inches of yourself. And Jonah, being conscientious, agreed.

" 'Now it seems that God has turned away from our tormented land. And this time we are doing the job for him. Instead of Jonah's sacrifice, we are haunted by that other creature who has lost half himself, the ogre our Jola people call Ngot. What will be left in forty days? I have waited all my life for a revolution to clean this rotten country, but what is happening in the streets and mountains makes me want to spend the days I have left in a pula-pula's belly. Compatriots, we have become the sweet, sweet fruit without a core. We had all better wake up before it is too late. Saraunese, come to your senses! Find out the part of you that wants blood—the pride, hate, fear, dogma, revenge, greed, lust—and cut it off. Then you might survive to say: The waters compassed me about, even to the soul. The earth with her bars was about me for ever: yet hast thou brought up my life from corruption!' "

As the last word left Ding's mouth Levin lifted his hands from the steering wheel and clapped.

"Wow! It won't make a bit of difference, but it's a brilliant piece."

Ding was scanning the article, mouthing words. "He is comparing himself to Jonah?"

"Jonah? I don't think so. That's the last six inches Feliz would part with. If anything, he sees himself as God. I have this image of him sweeping the city into the sea—a great slab-headed god."

Ding's eyes narrowed with stubborn dissatisfaction. "The meaning isn't clear to me. Sometimes I don't know why that guy says some things he says." He looked up from the paper. "There were stories about him, you know."

"What do you mean, stories?" A slight nod of Ding's head spelled them out. "That C.I.A. nonsense? You don't believe that."

"No?"

In the dim light, Levin searched Ding's face for a trace of irony, but his eyes and mouth were humorless and hard.

"There's stories thrown around about everyone. And it's all such crap. Where's the evidence on Feliz?"

"When he worked for *The New York Times,* people said—"

"People said, people said. That's what I'm talking about. It gets repeated enough, pretty soon it's a fact. Feliz is the last person to be on their payroll. He's too independent. And he's on the left."

"They find their way even to so-called revolutionaries." Ding rubbed his thumb and index finger together. But Levin felt that he didn't believe his own case.

"Look, it's a mistake people here make to give them credit for everything in the world. Even God could be a mole, is the idea. If they were half that effective America would be on the up and up, not the down and down. Look at Vietnam, Central America, the Middle East. I mean, it's understandable—it's a distortion the weak are prone to."

"And we are weak," Ding said, staring out the windshield, folding his arms. "We are practically nothing."

"But I'm surprised to hear someone like you fall for that rumor."

Levin too looked out the windshield, becoming the driver again, giving himself a task. He had trouble making out the road.

"You know us. Even when we try to be Western—hotheads, sentimental. We've been fooled so many times we don't even trust ourselves."

Levin disliked the tone: self-pitying, self-dramatizing. He'd come to know it as a Saraunese tone, a coward's sniping. He said simply: "I trust Feliz."

"How can you know?"

"Because of the way he talks, because of the look in his eye, the way he eats. Because he's never given me a reason not to."

"Around here that's no reason to trust anyone but yourself."

"You trust me, Ding, or we wouldn't be in this car together. If you follow this suspicion thing to the end, you can't even get a haircut. I trust Feliz because I choose to, I have to—"

"Huh." It was a syllable of contempt, like the articulation of a snicker. Levin was deeply annoyed. He concentrated on driving.

"Turn off the light, will you."

As soon as the light was out, the straight black road reappeared and a group of cement dwellings fronted by a Coca-Cola billboard came into view a hundred feet ahead. They had been passing through a banana plantation; the trees spread away from the highway in orderly rows.

"Something to eat?" Levin asked. He tried to sound neutral, unappeasing. But they were going to have to spend a lot of time together out there. And in his heart, he wanted to appease. Ding had told Melanie that Levin was sincere: it was an elusive status for a white man in Direv Saraun, and he didn't want Ding to change his mind. If Ding went on thinking him sincere, it would be easier to think it himself.

"Sure," Ding said. "Let's eat."

The restaurant was a humid, boxlike affair. Two plantation hands in filthy overalls were drinking moonshine at the bar. Levin and Ding sat at an oilcloth-covered table and a tiny girl of almost black complexion came to take their order. No one showed any surprise or interest at their arrival. Ding ordered something called *sukindo*.

"It's native food," he said.

"I'll have the same. And a Coke with that, please. Order a beer if you want, Ding. I'll drive a couple more hours."

"Coke for me," Ding told the girl.

When she had gone into the kitchen, Levin asked, "Jola?"

Ding nodded indifferently.

The Jola were the southern mountain people among whom Fra Boboy had his headquarters. They were the island's oldest inhabitants, historically wary of the ethnic Malays who ran the country. Their position in the war was uncertain. They had not actively rebelled but they now appeared to be supporting the guerrillas, though opinion in São Sebastião differed over whether their hospitality was willing or coerced. In Levin's imagination the Jola occupied the difficult neutral space that Colonel Siriman had said was closing.

Someone in the kitchen turned on a radio for the diners' entertainment. The restaurant filled with the helium-high voice of Madonna, distorted by speakers so far gone that it sounded like Burmese love music.

Levin took his wallet out. As he extracted a few bills he had an image of Mrs. Balatang and her children waiting in the dark hovel.

"Here's your per diem for today and tomorrow. There shouldn't be too many expenses after Pulaya."

Ding fingered the bills, trying to count without seeming to.

"It's two hundred *cobas*," Levin told him. The money amounted to a little over ten dollars. Ding folded the bills and stuffed them away in his shirt pocket.

"Will that be enough?"

"Sure. That's fine."

"Obviously that's on top of basic expenses, which I'll cover. It's spending money."

Ding was watching the plantation hands at the counter. "Thanks."

"If for some reason you go over, let me know and I'll give you more. But we should try to keep it down, since we don't have the full-salary O.K." He hustled the wallet back in his pocket, aware of Ding's tight smile. The two hundred figure had been a careful medium between appearing tightfisted and manipulable. "What's so amusing?"

Ding shook his head. "It's just funny."

"What?"

Ding was still looking at the bar. The smile disappeared.

"Our Saraunese custom is to pay for the guest. You're a guest in my country."

"Don't worry about it."

"It just feels funny for you to pay for me."

Levin knew that there was nothing funny about this for Ding, but he said, "Well, we have a traditional saying in America—'Money talks.' The Japanese are buying everything in sight. There's not a thing we can do."

"But most of your immigrants are poor, right? In Direv Saraun the foreigners have the money. Some Saraunese are even squatters—in their own country, squatters. It's funny." Ding gave a dry laugh.

"Ah. I see what you're saying. Yes."

"I think money is a pain."

"I completely agree."

The girl returned with their dinners. *Sukindo* turned out to be chunks of meat drowned in a thick red-brown sauce. Levin took a forkful. It tasted like something he knew but couldn't place.

"Pork," Ding said, chewing briskly. "In school we called it 'chaos.' They cook the meat in the pig's own blood." He watched Levin take a forkful. "You like our cooking?"

"Very much." The blood Levin had been holding in his mouth drooled over his lip.

"The school where I went as a boy, they served meat every lunch. That was very rare."

Levin tasted the pun, and swallowed it with his pork and blood.

"I knew what having money is all about," Ding went on. "Now I know the other side. I'm lucky, that way."

"But remember what you said at dinner, about being tied down in a typhoon?" Levin had been turning this over in his mind. "Did that mean you don't like being free-lance?"

"You have to understand something," Ding said. "People in Direv Saraun don't admire doing your own thing. It's not cool to be off on your own trip here. When I said I was going to be a photojournalist my family thought I was crazy. Some of my mestizo friends dropped me. Because that's not something a Saraunese elite does. When I quit AP to go free-lance, they thought that was even crazier."

Levin had heard that Ding was fired for intemperance and absenteeism, but he didn't interrupt.

"My mother said I was trying to kill her. You know what she said to me? 'Son, other families lose their money and they can still be respectable. But the Magkakanaws are not so lucky. If you make this mistake our name is finished.' " He looked across the table at Levin. "Do you know what she meant?"

Levin shook his head. Ding held up his arm and pinched the skin. His mother meant that the Magkakanaws were too dark for leeway.

They finished their *sukindo* in silence.

After paying the bill Levin realized that he should have given Ding another hundred *cobas*. But, of course, he couldn't do that to him now.

It wasn't much of a roadblock—a metal barrel placed in the middle of the highway—but Levin had to brake hard, and for a moment the wheels glided to the right and the headlights flashed on a bank of grassy earth and trees. He turned into the skid, feeling the looseness of the steering column, but the car righted itself just at the broken edge of the asphalt.

His elation was returning. He hadn't panicked; he'd done exactly what he should have.

He slowed to the barrel, keeping it on the left. There was enough room to pass without going off the asphalt. But beyond the barrel a pair of mongrels blocked the road. They'd gotten stuck in coitus and had tried to pull apart, and they stood rump to rump, joined at the genitals, panting and dumbly blinking in the headlights.

A clapboard guardhouse stood off the road, half hidden by trees. Out of the shadows a soldier appeared, with a carbine on his back and something in his hand. He flicked two fingers at the road.

Ding said quietly, "Keep going, Dan."

"He's telling us to stop."

"Just go slow and wave, smile. He'll wave you on when he sees you're white."

"I don't think he cares if I'm blue. He wants us to stop."

"Keep going."

Levin smiled, waved, and coasted to a stop in front of the barrel. He didn't look at Ding, but watched the soldier walk toward them on the asphalt. The soldier was very young, skinny and tense. His teenager's mustache hadn't yet been shaved and his brown cheeks were smooth. The object in his hand was an open can of Hunt's franks and beans, with a fork sticking out. He was still chewing, and the corners of his mouth were flecked with tomato sauce. He halted ten feet from Levin's window.

Levin said, "Boss."

The soldier stopped chewing and stared. "Boss," he echoed. He was terror-struck.

No one moved. Suddenly Levin understood that he'd driven into a vacuum where words and movements were unstable. Someone had to break it, with air, authority. And he knew that he would be the one—he, the foreigner.

He turned off the ignition, leaving the lights on. The engine kicked and died, and for a moment the night silence was total. Then came the din of katydids in the trees, sudden masses of them trilling to a climax. He imagined them as big as rats.

He reached across Ding, opened the glove compartment, and among a pile of tapes found the envelope with Colonel Siriman's letter. Ding opened his mouth; every human sound reverberated.

Levin got out of the car. His shirt was wringing wet, matted to his back. Now that they'd stopped the air was hot and dense, smelling of mud and gasoline. He approached the soldier with his head tilted at a disarming angle, trying to make himself a little shorter.

"Boss," Levin repeated.

This time the soldier didn't answer.

"Is your sergeant here? Your superior?"

The soldier's eyebrows twitched up and down.

"We're journalists. Journalist," and he reached in his shirt for the plastic I.D. and held it up for inspection. The soldier barely glanced, without leaning forward. Levin maintained a respectful distance of a few feet.

"I have a letter from Camp Pereira. Colonel Siriman, the press liaison. It's a permit to travel to Salantin Province." Could it be the soldier was illiterate—didn't understand any English? It was a possibility Levin hadn't even considered. "Salantin, you understand?"

"No."

"No?"

"Not Salantin."

Levin started to protest that his permission was official, then he realized the soldier meant this province was not Salantin but another one. They'd been driving almost three hours, so perhaps this was Balaga, though since they'd lost the coastline and moved into the forested interior Levin had been driving blindly, with no mental picture of where they were. This checkpoint was so lonely there might be nothing for a hundred miles in any direction. The loss of geographical equilibrium made him almost dizzy on his feet.

"*Going* to Salantin. We go to Salantin. Understand?" Levin waved vaguely past the barrel, into the void of the road where the dogs were stuck. He opened the envelope and pulled out the letter. "Look, I don't know if this is going to— Here's my permit from the A.F.D.S. It says right here—Daniel Levin, Ding Magkakanaw. That's this gentleman, my photographer. We're going to Salantin Province, we'll be there three days, then we're coming back. My paper is the *World Press,* American." This barrage of information produced no discernible effect. He shook his I.D. at the soldier. "Journalist."

The boy's fear made him unreachable. Levin felt Ding's eyes in his shoulder blades.

Suddenly the soldier answered. "O.K., boss."

Levin didn't know which piece of persuasion had worked.

"O.K.? O.K. We're going. See you when we come back." He retreated to the Toyota. Ding was staring straight ahead at the locked curs.

"Boss!"

Levin turned around.

"Road is bad." The soldier waved in the direction they were going.

"Washed out, huh? Typhoon?"

"A. of L."

"Ah. Wouldn't that be ironic," Levin murmured. He started the car and eased it forward. The copulating dogs stared and seemed unable to move, threatening his small victory. He honked three times in the silence of the night before they finally broke apart and hobbled into the trees on either side.

As Levin drove away he leaned out to wave. The soldier was eating his pork and beans again. He seemed to lift his fork in the barest shadow of a wave back.

Ding sat rigidly in his seat. His elbow was propped on the window-sill and his face against his fist, turned from Levin.

"He thinks we're crazy to be going this way," Levin said.

There was no answer.

"Direv Saraun's finest. No wonder you're losing this war."

Ding snapped a look as if Levin had cursed him. "Who, me? I'm losing this war?"

"I mean the government. Of course you're neutralist."

"How do I know what you mean? I'm very ignorant!"

"Ding, don't start that again."

Ding sat back in his seat and stared out the windshield. Without looking at Levin, he said: "Why did you stop when I told you not to?"

"Because he flagged us down. What if he'd shot out the tires?"

"He would not."

"It's a foolish risk."

"It's foolish to stop. He might have detained us. It's foolish not to obey a native-born Saraunese in this situation."

"What—are you the boss of this trip?"

Immediately Levin regretted the word. Its pin pulled, it was a word to be thrown as far away as possible before it went off.

"Not me. It's you, the boss. You have the money."

"The money doesn't matter. It's one ingredient. You bring others. We're partners."

"There's always a boss. Nothing happens without a boss. In your country maybe it's different, but in Direv Saraun, the one with money is the boss."

Levin resolved to say nothing, not to be goaded.

"And it was foolish to bring this thing." Ding lifted the colonel's letter from the dashboard and read it. "It's got our names. We have five days—that's nothing! They kept a copy at Camp Pereira?" Levin nodded. Ding threw the sheet against the windshield. "I thought we agreed you wouldn't get it."

"At the party? I never said that. Look, it's already been useful."

"That bastard couldn't read it!"

"But it impressed him—I could see. Official stationery."

"It was a serious mistake to bring it. Get rid of it before we see Fra Boboy. He won't appreciate it at all."

"Explain why to an ignorant foreigner."

"They have our names, they know where we're going, when we're supposed to come back! They could follow." Ding looked away again. "Fra Boboy doesn't even know who you are."

Levin couldn't restrain the urge to check the rearview mirror. No lights pricked the screen of darkness.

"Why are you angry, Ding?"

But Levin knew the answer. Because, back at the roadblock, Ding had lost face, and part of losing face, what drove embarrassment deep into humiliation, was being unable to say so. The grievance stayed silent within and it scoured. Losing face was a complicated business in this country. Somehow he'd never thought of Ding as the type to be vulnerable to it.

Ding said, "I'm not angry."

Levin drove for a while without speaking.

"If that blows out the window," he said, as gently as possible, "we'll have the worst of both worlds."

Ding stuffed the letter and envelope into the glove compartment. Then he rummaged through Levin's tapes and fumbled one into the cassette player. Suddenly the car filled with the thumping bass of The Police, Sting's slurry voice.

Levin leaned back and drove, singing under his breath. *Every move you make, every bond you break.* Absurdly, his eyes were filling.

Ding said, "I used to love this song."

It wasn't just the emotion that surprised Levin. He hadn't known when he would be addressed as a friend again.

"I played it in a rock band."

"You had a band?"

"In college. I had two Yamaha guitars. I dressed in black."

Ding's voice had changed—softer, detached, like a man speaking into a tape recorder.

"After my father died the family's affairs were all helter-skelter. And it was up to me to straighten it out. My mother was in bed all day."

"She had a—breakdown?"

"All day, in bed. My father, see, he was a great man. Just ask anyone in Porto de Coral and they'll tell you: Magkakanaw treated his workers fair. When the union came, he said: 'O.K. If a woman wants to leave a man, is he going to tie her to the bed?' But if my father said no, the workers wouldn't have sabotaged or left him. They loved him and the land. The plantation was their life. That place is in me—I can't preach this class warfare. And when my father died they waited five hours outside the house to view the body."

"I believe it."

"Then the plantation shut down." Levin became aware that Ding wasn't speaking to him. The reminiscence involved him in some obscure way, but Ding released the words like a worm spinning itself into a cocoon of silk. "I came back from college and spent eight months with lawyers, signing, selling, all that. It was like putting powder on a corpse. I put the house in order—it was my mother's tomb."

"I'm sure she knew it was necessary."

"She never appreciated what I did. She was like a child, and I was the father. Then I had to get out, something terrible was going to happen to me if I stayed, I didn't know what but something. I left my guitars behind, my tapes—I knew that was finished. School too. Everything. Finished.

"In São Sebastião it's easy to lose yourself. So I became the guy with the camera. I learned the city, I learned to study people. When you're behind a lens, you have the upper hand on anyone. I slept with the damn thing around my neck."

Levin thought: Like sunglasses, a cigarette, a new name. It let you hide. He looked over: the moon shone white on Ding's head; the close-set eyes were full of raw sorrow. They drew Levin so powerfully to this stranger that the feeling was almost erotic. And his gratitude for the strong human feeling, mixed with the relief of finding that they were still friends, with a common purpose, that he wasn't alone out here—these began to alarm him.

Ding said, "I saw a book of Robert Capa's pictures and I knew that's what I wanted to do. Notice all our heroes are American? It's too bad. We don't have any of our own."

"Capa was Hungarian," Levin said.

"Capa?"

Levin nodded. Ding stared at him and then looked out the window. Levin hadn't meant to break the flow; he wanted Ding to tell his story.

"Go on."

It was some time before Ding would start again.

"Video is making still photography obsolete and it's a damn shame. Because still does something video can't. It finds the image that tells more about the story than a film of the whole story does. More than a written report too. It finds the face, the human element. That's what war is—the human element."

Levin thought of Ding's photographs and realized that what he remembered about them was not faces but guns.

"The thing Capa did was he didn't pretend he was objective. He participated. In Spain he just shot the Loyalists. He didn't want the Fascist point of view."

"Engagé," Levin said. "Committed."

"Just labels. It doesn't matter what you call it."

"Doesn't it? I consider myself committed, but there're some things I won't do. I won't write propaganda, consciously. I won't consciously elevate my sympathies above the truth as I see it."

"As you see it."

"That's all there ever is."

"So you're never objective."

"No. It's not that simple."

Levin looked into the road. They were beginning a long slow ascent, but he only knew this from the strain of the engine. He tried to locate the thread of conversation that had recently been pleasant, collegial.

"You're committed, too. It's something I admire in you. But you wouldn't doctor your pictures, right?"

"The premise is off key," Ding told him. "Slants happen in every little choice you make. People shoot color film—that's a choice. It means what you see is sky and grass and blood. Not people. I did some color work once for *Far Eastern Economic Review* and they ended up like pictures to please businessmen in Hong Kong and Singapore. That's not who I'm taking pictures for. They pay top dollar and so it's cost me something, but I don't do color anymore."

"Well, we'll need some color stuff for this story."

Ding shook his head. "I said I don't do color anymore."

Levin watched the odometer turn and waited until he knew he wouldn't sound pushy.

"I don't like color much either, but practically every paper in the U.S. uses it. They'll expect some from us. And what if we get a magazine article?"

Ding shrugged. "That's their problem."

"I think we have to work out some compromise on this. We're going to have to have some color pictures."

"You don't think I'm serious? I'm telling you, this is my rule. I'm not going to compromise myself when I'm getting paid a hundred *cobas* a day for professional work."

"Ding." In the interior darkness Ding was staring at him. "The paper's going to pay you and I'll make damn sure it's a handsome sum."

"What if they don't want the story. Huh? What if they decide Direv Saraun isn't worth five minutes at breakfast."

"They won't. Trust me."

Ding folded his arms and settled back against the door. Levin reached across him to open the glove compartment and found a pack of cigarettes. He pushed in the lighter and offered the pack to Ding, who took one wordlessly.

Before long Ding's voice came out of the darkness.

"Why did you come here anyway?"

Levin lit his cigarette and casually passed the lighter to Ding.

"First of all, it's an assignment. But frankly I had my own reasons. I wanted to see what a war looked like. I wanted to be a part of something bigger than my own life. It must have been something like why you became a photojournalist."

Ding exhaled smoke impatiently. "You think it's the same?"

"I'm not saying that."

"It's not. It's not the same at all, you and me. You were free to come, a reporting gig. The American is more welcome here than the Saraunese. Fifty thousand squatters in the capital. How can you squat in your own country?"

"Well, *you* can't. I mean, in a peasant's eyes you're still an elite."

"You think so, Dan? That's very naïve. Nothing like that matters now. Everything's gone helter-skelter."

The American of the far-flung, a decade and more out of sync— picked up from TV and radio, relatives who'd been to the States, his old private-school crowd. But Levin had been badly mistaken about Ding. Ding was Saraunese to the marrow. Levin had imagined simple companionship—instead everything was going to be complicated. He flicked his cigarette into the road and drove on, listening to the music and the sibilance of tires on tar.

Gauging their whereabouts by mileage, he turned off the North-South Highway at a dark Mobil station, as Connie had instructed, and followed a narrower road up into the central plateau. For miles there were ruts in the dips between rises, where water collected. Levin slowed to a dead stop for these and then eased the wheels in, down, up, out, to reduce the stress on the shocks and axles. Even so, the steering seemed to loosen with every hole. And he was beginning to feel the strain of the drive himself. The back of his neck had stiffened.

A week before leaving the States he had gone to New York to look up the free-lance cameraman who had shot the footage CNN used in its report. A light-skinned black man with an Afro, short, heavy in the buttocks, laconic, George Pendergast sat among video screens and digital control knobs and sound levers in a converted Chelsea warehouse. Over and over he played back footage of an A.F.D.S. helicopter gunship attacking a soccer field near Paranak where guerrillas had assembled to recruit fighters. With Levin, who had come for advice and whatever contacts might be forthcoming, Pendergast was all street smarts and business tough.

"Man, they don't like you, they'll blow you away if you don't watch out. I blended in, I looked like them. You'll stick out like a sore thumb." Pendergast took his eyes from his own work long enough to look Levin up and down.

His next project would be Peru—he planned to film a "doc" on U.S. anti-drug operations there, which, Pendergast said with apparent satisfaction, were going to turn into another Vietnam. He was a video cowboy, slipping in and out of hot spots without passport or companion, counting on the help of the local peasantry. He didn't trouble to hide his contempt for Levin's mainstream brand of reporting. But Levin was not going to be intimidated.

"What you going to do over there anyway?" Pendergast had asked.

"Same as you. I'm going to see what that war looks like," Levin had told him. "I'm going to find out what it's about."

Pendergast had looked at him a long moment, and then nodded at the three video screens where soccer dirt was being chewed up by aerial strafing and young men were running into the bushes.

"That's what it's about, man."

They passed through a village, then another. The shacks were massed at the road's edge—even in the bush they built their houses on top of one another. Here and there an oil lamp shone; a solitary figure watched from a mud alley. But it was past eleven and these places still obeyed the rule of the earth's rotation. No enterprising headman had bribed electricity out of a province chief to put his village on the map and serve cold drinks to travelers. What did the fighting mean to these people? Whole areas were being drained of youth, to the Armed Forces, the Army of Liberation, the city, to hiding like quarry in the hills. The lucky few got out altogether, but that had become most difficult of all. It was possible that the only people left in these villages were women, the very young, and the old. You needed silence, exile, cunning. In these places, mostly silence.

The tape had ended. Levin knew he was being watched. And when Ding finally spoke, the only surprise was the sound of the human voice itself, so specific and close in the encompassing emptiness. His question came in a flawed spurt, as if he'd been getting ready to ask it for a long time.

"What do you think of—about the revolution?"

Levin's mind pursued the possible replies like a finger tracing a map of streams. He could say that it was difficult enough for a Saraunese, let alone a foreigner, to know exactly who the guerrillas were and what they would bring to Direv Saraun. He could mention his, or anyone's, moral objections to some of their tactics, while conceding the overall injustice under which so many islanders labored, including, it was safe to assume, the people in the villages they'd just passed, and then express the hope that it was for people like them that Fra Boboy was sending his men on ambushes and raids—though armed struggles all too easily lost sight of the initial goal of justice and violence itself became their goal, ensuring that the necessary harshness of guerrilla life became a permanent feature of the new society. He could quote Mao on power growing from the barrel of a gun, Lord Acton on absolute power corrupting absolutely, Orwell on the Party seeking power for its own sake. He could say that he was taking this trip precisely to answer the question.

In the silence of the night, in the heart of the country, his thoughts clanked deafeningly. But the hours in the car with this other being, beside him yet outside the floodlight of his understanding, to whom he might as well be handcuffed for four days, were forcing him to answer to something else. His reply came out of a place he'd needed three decades to discover, through a change of scenery, the spot in his wrist, the goat voice that would howl if he let it.

"What I think of it," Levin said, "is totally irrelevant."

Now the highway was a ruin, hardly a road at all. Driving had become a matter of gauging the exact span of the front wheels. After a jolt shook the Toyota's entire frame, Levin learned to navigate the watery holes with respect. Between bad spots he sped to make up the lost time, but his lights, even with the brights on, hardly picked up the next trouble before he was on top of it, braking, swerving and swerving again, downshifting and going off the road. A privileged eye, from a helicopter at two thousand feet, would have guessed him a drunk or a madman.

Levin leaned over the wheel to ease his back and give himself a few more milliseconds of reaction time. His neck felt paralyzed, rock-hard. When he thought to look at his watch, it was past one o'clock, yet they'd barely covered seventy miles since the checkpoint. Over time Ding disappeared, the music, the interior, the trees or fields or whatever lay outside the car, the moon, until everything was reduced to steering wheel, front wheels, headlights, twenty feet of road, and him, and he was down to eyes, hands, and feet.

But the intensity of the drive set his thoughts free. In the rhythm of swerve and brake and jolt, Levin was thinking about his parents.

He tried to guess what they were doing this very moment, but the effort of working out the time difference was too much. Anyway, he knew where his father would be, whatever the hour in Philadelphia: in the big chair in the living room, the blue-upholstered, maple-framed, thick-cushioned relic of the fifties, before furniture went sleek; his long legs, black-socked, would be up on the companion footrest, crossed at the ankles; and Trollope, any Trollope, propped on his lap. Back in October he'd been two novels short of finishing Dickens, and Trollope came next, and Trollope was prolific. On the stereo, either Mozart or Haydn. His father's taste in music had been ground down over his adult life to these two. The grinding had accelerated a few years ago, when he'd taken early retirement from the chemical company where he'd been a products engineer for thirty-six years. In rapid order he'd found he could no longer stand Debussy, Mahler, Liszt, Schumann, and even, finally, Beethoven.

"It's just random, chaotic noise—nothing pure, nothing ordered. With the Romantics the aesthetic dignity went all to hell."

His mother, of course, would be upstairs, at her computer or on the phone, selling real estate—a late-life career begun as suddenly as the quiet of her daytimes had been invaded by the tall, stooped, silent form of her husband.

At twenty-five, brash and intellectual, Levin's father might have risked the life of a composer, a music critic, a professor at least. Nothing had ever really made him happy except music, and the occasional book. Now, after decades filled with seven-thirty commutes and business luncheons with men who spent Saturday on the links and Sunday in church, he'd stripped his life down to these original loves—no longer loved but joylessly used.

"I put art on the chopping block of sound finances," his father once said. And sound they were, enough to pay for a Media Line mortgage and two Saabs, with plenty left over for large annual checks to Save the Children and the Southern Poverty Law Center. But his father's spirit had turned small and hard and dry as a sand pebble—even as he argued cogently against Edwin Meese's fitness for office and figured out how to reroute a downspout that flooded the basement every spring.

"I'm damned if he's going to ruin what's left of my life," his mother had said. "You shouldn't either."

Levin, living in Philadelphia through these years, took the brunt of his parents' state of divorce. He played mute backgammon with his father, he listened to his mother mock, rage, laugh, weep, make plans. Jonathan, the oldest son, and his father's favorite, taught contract law at Northwestern. Eric, the middle, and his mother's, had graduated from ashrams to computers in northern California. They'd missed the fission of the nuclear family that sent their father to his armchair and their mother to work. So that when the sons came home one Christmas—a secular feast at the Levins', gifts, no tree, no maxims, no caroling nonsense, a celebration of the clay in man's feet, the capacity for human sympathy and heavy shopping— it was as though in their absence the house had burned to its foundation. But the house still stood, gray invincible Pennsylvania stone, and the marriage was unbreakable as the pebble in his father's chest.

On an August evening Levin and Melanie drove out for dinner. Two days before, he'd been offered his assignment overseas. It was a hot, dense night and they barbecued on the back lawn. The summer smells of freshly cut lawn and juniper, the leafy chlorine of the pool, and the smoky odor of chicken grilling with the rosemary twigs that his father had cut from the bush by the fence, were the smell of Levin's boyhood. Though the decision hadn't been made yet, the evening was sweet and sad with the air of leave-taking, like the days before a graduation.

Melanie stood by his father over the hissing grill; Levin and his mother sat at the picnic table of two-by-six teak. Smoke divided him from Melanie, but from time to time when it cleared she held him with her look—her questioning, lips-parted, half-smiling, un-ashamed look that established intimacy across fifteen feet of lawn. It was strange to see how she'd already claimed a place here, where he'd spent millions of minutes without her. Her presence changed every-thing. His father was attentive and charming, his mother was ironic; he was an adult, at a safer distance from his parents, proud and confused. They were engaged; the engagement fights had begun, they'd both drawn blood. But that night Direv Saraun was still an exciting name to both of them, abstract and lush.

"It's a real vote of confidence from the paper," his mother had said when they were all busy with the chicken and corn. Melanie ate with a methodical speed unusual in women, her pretty mouth busy at the bone or cob. She polished off the corn like a Midwestern pro, moving horizontally across the kernels and tearing them out by their roots.

"You don't want to get tagged their Third-World-backwater guy," his father said. "Why not wait till there's an opening in London or Paris, or better yet Eastern Europe."

"What's wrong with the Third World?" his mother demanded. "That's where it's happening. Not Europe. Europe is dead."

"They've been saying that since Rousseau and Diderot at least. And Europe still turns out the novels, the playwright-presidents. You'd be intellectually isolated in a place like Direv Saraun. Fine minds rot in that sun."

"If I were young," his mother said to Melanie with a confidential smile, enlisting her support, woman to woman, "if I were twenty-eight, I'd go to Direv Saraun at the drop of a hat. I'd go as a reporter, a nurse—hell, I'd pick up a gun if they wanted me to, fight for the people. *Barricadas!* But I'd find a way to go."

His father was working a piece of corn from his molars. "If you do go," he told his son, producing the yellow slip on his tongue and blowing it onto the lawn, "let it be with considerably more sophisti-cation and circumspection than your mother is displaying. People get killed in those places. The headlines are quite real. If you need to test your guts, go to the meatpacking plants in North Philly."

Later, he and Melanie lay upstairs in his boyhood bed, the bed where he'd once held his knees against his chest for fear of snakes at the other end, been brought milkshakes when he was sick, learned to masturbate.

"Your mother's funny," Melanie said.

"How do you mean?"

"She kind of scares me. She already assumes you're going."

"She's had to put up with a lot. I think she holds my father personally responsible that she *didn't* go to Direv Saraun when she was twenty-eight. She got married instead."

The window was open, letting in warm, fragrant night air. With her finger Melanie was tracing the outline of his face. "Would you hold me personally responsible in thirty years?"

"Of course not. It's my decision."

"Not *ours*?"

"I mean ours. But I'm ultimately responsible for what I do, right? Everyone does what he really wants."

She took him up on the abstract and returned it in the immediate. "And what do you really want to do?"

Levin never answered. Instead he made love to her with all the intensity of their first time. He'd already made up his mind to go, he felt it in his fingertips and the small of his back as a need to be moving, almost to writhe out of his skin, with the sense of such power and possibility conferred on brain, heart, and stomach by a war-wasted island that he pitied Melanie and loved her and kissed her with gratitude that she would lie under him like this, her hands cupping his hot face, her eyes full of sadness—for she knew, she knew, and in his chest he experienced the first sharp inhalation, like a stifled sob, of being gone.

And then—what? He'd forgotten her. It seemed like simple ab-sentmindedness, but in Direv Saraun he couldn't sustain a thought about Melanie. She vanished for hours at a time—days. And when the thought of her did come, or one of her letters, Levin had to wonder if he would ever find any woman as compelling a companion as the world had turned out to be.

He breathed with the memory of that night. He hadn't meant for his thoughts to end up here. Tonight, on this road that reduced his knowledge to twenty feet, longing and regret were gathering close with other presences. He'd been holding them back ever since the music came on.

"You know that Police song?" Out of the long silence his voice sounded strange again. Next to him, Ding stirred. "It's interesting you played it in college. I remember dancing to it at a party when I was in grad school. A woman named Sara Markoff was there. She had these eyes, Jewish girl's eyes, deep—like some women here. Did I have a thing for her that night. And when this came on we slow-danced and this electricity went through us because we both knew it was a great song. When it was over we even kissed and it was pretty intense. But after that night nothing happened. It was like we needed the song to have the feelings. I never called her. I saw her about two months later and she was very chilly. But whenever this . . ."

He didn't finish; he looked into the black, green, spotlit road and tried to understand why he'd made up the Jewish girl. For she didn't exist—she was Melanie.

He moved his head and body to the right, so that he could see his face in the rearview mirror. He met his own eyes and waited for an old sensation to come over him.

As a boy, he used to stare in the bathroom mirror until he looked like someone else, someone he'd never known, or an animal—until he couldn't stand it, feeling a thrill and a horror that this face he'd always possessed, seen a million times, and taken for granted, could look back and suddenly seem not to be his face. Then he had to stop. He'd never gone near a mirror then without sensing its power to make him a stranger and feeling obscurely flawed.

Ding sat up.

"Jesus."

The road ahead, twisting downhill through forest, gave out onto an opening that the moonlight clarified as a chasm of air—a drop into something wide and deep and green, vertiginous. A gorge.

They slowed to the edge. The drop fell at least two hundred feet down, to a silver flash of river. It was the Musa again, which bent to the interior in the central plateau, toward its source in the mountains, and met the road here at Pala. But what had caught Ding's attention was the bridge, a narrow causeway of concrete perched on skinny steel and concrete legs—for most of the bridge was gone. The middle legs had disappeared. On either side of the span the road simply ended in twisted steel.

They left the car on the road and walked out to the edge. There was no barrier; Levin craned his neck and looked down. It was all shadowy, deep green above, black in the depth. Wild mahogany grew out of the far wall of rock; at the bottom the snake of water gleamed. He leaned a little farther over and spat.

There was always this suspicion, on ocean bluffs or in skyscrapers, church towers, that if he leaped out he would stay aloft. He could feel what it would be to float above this chasm. A thought, silly and risky, like the thought that he in all the generations of testimonial bones might be spared death.

His palms moistened, his fingers tingled lightly, and then a shudder of blood went through his face. He waited for faith in his existence as a solid object of gravity to return, and when it didn't the gorge struck him with terror. He imagined the crash of his soft bones against unyielding rock. This depth had nothing to do with his six-foot proportions. Suddenly the sabotage seemed an act of immense hubris, a towering defiance like Prometheus'. To blow the bridge over this abyss, send the great steel girders collapsing in a cloud of concrete dust—it was like giving the finger to galaxies.

Levin stepped back.

"I could have told you it's deep." Ding's voice was startling. He had hung behind a few feet.

"I wanted to see for myself."

"Maybe it's better not to see. Especially at night. You don't know where the hell you are. Then you're down there."

"I just didn't know they were doing things on this scale. That they had the engineers—the explosives."

They faced each other, Levin's back to the gorge.

Ding asked, "So what do we do?"

Connie had said nothing about the bridge. Levin felt incapable of any decision—even whether to scratch the itch that was crawling over the rim of a nostril.

Ding looked vaguely around. "There must be some way across."

"Do you see any?"

"If they gave us this route there's a way across."

"At night, on this ridiculous road? Washboard dirt would've been better."

"Only one checkpoint—not ten. And they know the roads they've mined. Have we hit any mines?"

"Just a canyon."

Levin had no ideas. But turning around seemed unthinkable.

Ding walked back to the car. In the trees katydids were shrilling their forest lust.

"Hey, what's this?" Ding was poking in the shrubs at the road's edge. "Dan, come here, this is it."

"It" was a piece of plywood nailed to a mahogany stake that had been driven into the ground. A black spray-painted arrow pointed left.

"Isn't that the fucking army for you." Ding was shaking his head. "Put it where you can't see it and paint it black."

"They don't count on anyone driving at night."

"Come on, let's go."

"Where?"

"Where the thing says. And look: it means there's soldiers over there. And that means no stopping, no piece of paper, you just smile and wave. The town is on the other side and they'll be so drunk they're going to be shooting their damn Armalites like firecrackers."

"Then how will they know I'm white?"

Ding eyed him suspiciously. "What difference does that make?"

"Back at the last—"

It was no use. Levin, tired in the depths of night, and a little dizzy, couldn't remember what Ding had said or how it would fit into whatever point he wanted to make or how that was going to persuade Ding of anything in the irritable mood settling over him again. Ding was electing himself leader, and Levin was ready to yield. The blind black heat pricked his skin, sweat flowed in his ears and crotch. A few yards away the earth opened wide. He thought: Ding doesn't like me much, and I don't know why, but at least he's on my scale. A few inches shorter, as a matter of fact. At least he has a human voice.

Such thoughts failed to summon confidence.

They bounced over stones and grass along the northern edge of the gorge, keeping ten feet of berth. The path took a sharp turn backward, and when they were around the bend they found themselves face-to-face through the windshield with three soldiers who were squatting on M-16s—Saraunese still called the weapons "Armalites," though the American brand name was thirty years out of date. In the light of a hurricane lamp the soldiers were passing a clear unlabeled bottle. Directly beyond them a temporary bridge, a bulky complicated metal extension, sagged to the far side, where, up on a ridge, isolated lights suggested a town. It had all been just around the corner.

The soldiers watched the Toyota approach. They were sitting in the middle of tire tracks, where the grass was flattened, and to go by on the safe side Levin would have to drive into underbrush. He veered to the right, where the way was narrower. It wasn't much of a choice—a soldier or the gorge. He was aware of smiling, taking his hand off the wheel to wave.

He squeezed through, passing within a foot of the soldier whose back was closest to him; even so, he had less than a yard on the gorge. The two soldiers facing him, the third turning around to look, stared without waving. Levin remembered the pimps on Marapang Road.

"That's it," Ding muttered.

But just as the front wheels hit the ramp of the extension bridge one of the soldiers shouted: "Hey, Joe!"

Levin braked. He looked at Ding, and Ding hesitated.

"Go."

The Toyota eased onto the ramp with a deep hum of rubber on metal.

"Hey, Joe!"

Levin pressed the brake again. He glanced in the mirror. The soldier whose back had been turned was on his feet with the automatic rifle in one hand—not yet pointed at them, but headed that way. Standing in front of the lamp he was shadowed, but the faces of the others glowed in the white phosphorescent wick. One of them, shirtless and flabby breasted, set the bottle down.

Levin said, "I think they want to talk to us."

"O.K." Ding reached for the door handle. "I'll go. Keep the motor running."

Ding got out of the car and walked back. Levin gave the parking brake a jerk of vindication and watched the scene in the mirror. Ding did a good deal of the talking, and it was astonishing how fast he became the wheedling, deferential Saraunese and allowed the soldier to play his boss, like a taxi driver stopped by a cop in São Sebastião, a laborer in an employment office. Bowing, flattering, laughing, hands behind his back. Ding fell easily into the manner that defined one side of every relationship in Direv Saraun—he made himself powerless.

He came back to Levin's window and said, "They want money."

"How much?"

"They want fifty, American." Levin didn't answer. "Did you bring American dollars?"

"Yes."

"Good thinking, partner."

"That seems like a lot. That's really a lot."

"It's what they said."

"Didn't you try to bargain?"

"This isn't the Central Market!"

"But maybe if you told him we'll only pay twenty-five—"

"Look, rice liquor makes these guys crazy. There's no guerrillas to shoot at and, believe me, they want to shoot at something. So what's the point?"

Levin unzipped his shoulder bag and found the wad of dollars he'd tucked inside a sock. Three twenties, a ten, and ten ones.

"Here's forty. I only have twenties, no tens."

"You'd better give me another twenty."

"Goddammit—sixty dollars for these drunk sonsofbitches."

"Shh."

"They think all Americans are stupid or rich enough to just—"

"Shh. This way they won't shoot each other over who gets stuck with the ten."

Levin said, "I wouldn't cry if they did."

"Now you're talking like one of us."

"American money's spoiled this place."

Levin was not yet able to release the bills. And now he'd out-smarted himself.

"What if we try the permit to travel, just try and see—"

Ding cut him off sternly. "It's too late for that. Throw it off the bridge."

Somehow this gave Ding the high ground. Levin had to let his money go.

In the mirror he saw the soldier hold up the bills Ding presented him, crumple them, and watch them open in his palm: it was a test for counterfeit exchange. The others were interested enough to get off their guns and stumble over. The American green brightened everyone's mood, like the totemic effect of white skin on peasants, market people. Tens would have had the same effect; maybe ones. Dammit, Levin thought, Ding should have bargained. Refusing had been nothing but a petty display of power. Ding didn't know what he was doing any more than he—and with this thought his confidence revived a little.

Good-byes were exchanged amid much Saraunese laughter and handshaking. Now Ding didn't have to wheedle; he was their brother, because he was the one with a white partner. When he got back in the Toyota he said, "Let's go. That sure as hell worked." His leg was jiggling on the seat. "Good thing you thought ahead. Look, they're happy as babies." Ding seemed happy too. He was almost manic with relief. Levin looked in the mirror. The flabby soldier was kissing the face of Andrew Jackson.

"This army is idiots," Ding said.

They were high over the gorge, humming on metal without railings, the tires sliding sideways in the grooves of the fretwork, sloping into the sag. Levin didn't dare look to either side. Ding was whistling "Every Breath You Take."

In Pala they got lost.

It was a slum town of narrow, mostly blind streets and few electric lights at 2:30 A.M. The road by which they entered dead-ended at a Catholic church. The sudden stucco facade, niched and arched, seemed as funny at this hour in this place as the onion dome of a Russian Orthodox church. It looked unpainted and derelict.

As they turned aimlessly through back streets in search of the road from the demolished bridge, they passed cinder-block houses and shuttered shops with hand-painted signs that bore no trace of decoration. Fancy had been wiped off the town's face. There was a pervasive sickish smell. Levin wondered how people lived here.

After fifteen minutes of circling through the same streets, they saw a light burning in a narrow shop. A basket-weaver was working on a bench in a room sparsely stocked with sacks of rice, local brown pastries wrapped in plastic, and cans of Quaker Oats, powdered milk, and pilchards in tomato sauce. She was perhaps forty and already enormous, the muscle and fat straining every stitch of her aging cotton dress. An electric tube on the wall shone murky blue, and along with the two journalists it had attracted every insect on the ridge—great insects with legs, wings, colors, teeth—creatures Levin didn't know existed in nature. They crawled thickly over the hot light like ants feeding on a snake's guts. The woman was sitting with her back to the wall under the light, threading strands of nipa grass with her heavy bare thighs spread apart. At their arrival she burst out laughing.

Levin said good evening in Saraunese. She laughed again. She had most of her teeth but they were wet and brown with rot. He wondered if she was simple, or a lunatic. The crazy moved among the sane in Direv Saraun—the expats had jokes about how to tell them apart. Also, he'd identified the smell of Pala. It was the heavy, burnt, drenching sweetness of a sugar mill. The regional central must be on the other side of the ridge. He was amazed it still operated a twenty-four-hour shift, no doubt under armed guard—or maybe this was the after-smell of a closed mill, clinging for years like the pulpy stink of certain paper towns in New England.

"She doesn't speak Saraunese," Ding told him. "They have a different dialect in Batak Province."

"Can you talk to her?"

Ding shrugged, greeted the basket woman, and she answered. There followed a brief exchange, with Ding stumbling through bits of questions, to which he got long laughing open-mawed replies. She wasn't surprised or afraid or put out, just vastly amused by these characters who had walked into the shop in the small hours.

"What does she say?"

"Left at the house where her daughter-in-law lives, down to the third tree, right, right again at the 'ugly carpenter shop,' continue till we see the big road—unless she meant the 'hidden carpenter shop'—"

"For God's sake."

Ding turned to the woman. He spoke and passed his hand over his face, and she threw back her head and roared until the fat fluttering in her neck seemed to press on her trachea and choke off air.

"It's the 'ugly carpenter shop.'"

Levin waited for Ding to decide if this avenue was worth pursuing.

A door at the back of the shop opened and a little boy appeared. Naked, he tugged at his penis and rubbed an eye in the bluish glow. He called for his mother. She answered curtly and nodded him over.

He was seven or eight, with a dirty lifeless face and an underfed look to his upper arms and belly. He stood between his mother's knees and whined with sleepiness. Levin noticed that the hand rubbing the eye was black and wet at the tips of the third and fourth fingers, like the decay in the mother's mouth. And then he saw that the fingers were stumps—cut off at the second knuckle, plastered over with black mulch, raw and inflamed in places underneath. The boy held the fingers stiffly apart, and when he stopped rubbing he cradled the whole hand in his other.

"This boy is hurt," Levin said. "Look at his hand."

"Ah, his fingers are cut. It's a shame."

"It's more than a shame, that infection's going to kill him. Here, let me see."

Levin reached for the hand, and the boy, seeing that he was white, stared open-mouthed but let him hold it. Levin steeled himself to examine the wounds. The joints had been severed roughly and the open gashes badly sewn, an uneven suture along the tips, crumpled like a pulled seam. Red swelling bulged down the fingers. The stumps were going septic.

"What's this stuff?" The mother had stopped weaving. Levin noticed that her baskets were sewn with far more care than her boy's fingers. She was looking on with a smile of mild concern.

"They chew tobacco and put it on the wound to stop infection. It's their traditional medicine."

"Well, it hasn't worked. The whole hand's going to be infected."

Levin looked at the amputation for a long time. Then he touched the wounds lightly. He scraped aside a bit of tobacco pulp and exposed a mass of red flesh. Levin thought the little boy was very brave and he tried to linger on the agony of the stitching but this much he couldn't manage.

"I'll be right back."

They hadn't moved when he returned from the car with the medical kit Melanie had prepared for him in Philadelphia. He instructed Ding to have the boy wipe off the disinfectant that was going to kill him, because he didn't think he could do it himself without inflicting pain. The mother produced a rag and water and performed the task herself, cooing to calm her son, who moaned and sobbed and pulled his uncircumcised penis by the tip but allowed his circumcised hand to be held and cleaned.

"How did it happen?"

"He says he was chopping sugar cane with his friends and the blade slipped. It happens sometimes."

"They were fooling around?"

"This boy works in the fields." Ding smiled at Levin's surprise. "How much do you think he's paid?"

There was no need to answer. He coated the stitched stumps with bacitracin. The mother and the boy were looking at him hopefully, with a trace of awe, and as he worked the yellow gel over the worst places he understood the power a doctor feels, the thrill of competence and doing good and being completely accepted, maybe even loved for it; he felt it in the mother's willingness to have her work erased and in the boy's suffering his hand to be touched by a stranger. Reverence for a doctor's hands—white, magician's hands. This geometry of trust locked Ding out. It consigned him to the role of translator.

"Didn't she know it's infected?"

Ding shrugged. "These are poor, illiterate people."

"But there's at least a clinic in this town."

In the neon blue Ding smirked. "You think they have health insurance? You think there's any doctor around here? The state shits on these people."

"Ask her."

Ding stared at Levin for a long time. In the immobile features Levin was certain he read hatred, but it couldn't undermine him. When Ding finally asked, he used the English word "clinic." Was the thing so new to Batak that it hadn't found a place in the local vocabulary? American beneficence, post–World War II.

The answer seemed to be affirmative. Levin, taping gauze around the middle finger, did an inward jig of triumph.

"At the clinic they sewed him up but she didn't have enough money for medicine."

"O.K. When I get through I'll give her a few *cobas* for penicillin. What, twenty?"

"Thirty."

"All right, thirty. And I'll leave some fresh gauze. Tell her to change the bandages every few days. Maybe this boy won't have to lose the rest of his hand." A thought came. "Her money must be drying up because of the bridge. No one getting into town—look at the shop. Ask her if the bridge has affected her."

"These people understand the necessities of the war."

"I'd like to hear what she thinks."

"She's not going to criticize one side or the other in front of you."

"Look, we've got to get something straight. To do interviews on this trip I need to get it from the source. That means I need you to translate, not surmise."

Ding was stung, so much that he had to look away. With the slightest of smiles he recovered himself. "O.K., boss." He spoke to the woman, who shook her head. "She says it hasn't affected her." The woman laughed a few words. "She says such inconveniences are part of the people's own path to liberation, boss."

Levin finished bandaging the fingers. He felt strong, calm, purposeful, alive. Let the guerrillas show him anything. Let Ding learn to get along. He felt, even, a peculiar sort of gratitude toward the mother and her boy—for needing his help. If you looked long enough you might find some perversion in this, Fraser would have been glad to point out, but Levin had no desire to do so. Looking long enough did you no good in Direv Saraun. It called attention, it marked you, it put you off guard. Look long enough and you'd fall in.

The woman took the gauze and *cobas* in both hands and instantly clapped them overhead with a deep bow at the neck—an extreme gesture of self-effacement. *"Paklan, paklan,"* she kept muttering with her face in her great untethered bosom, as though thanks required her to disappear from existence altogether.

"She's yours now," Ding said sourly. "She can't ever work off a debt like this even if she spends her whole life trying. That is our peasant mentality."

"Tell her it's canceled—we're even."

"Oh, no, I won't tell her that. She won't understand, she'll laugh in your face, she's yours forever."

"I see. *Piki lan kurat* rears its ugly head."

The woman said something and pushed the boy toward Levin.

"Ah ha! She wants you to take him to America, to be educated. She's giving him to you. Look, some Joes come all the way to Direv Saraun for this chance."

Levin felt slightly sick. He looked away from the naked bandaged boy who stood offered to him. "That's really funny, Ding. Tell her to forget it."

"She's not going to forget it. You can't just walk away from our customs, that's arrogance. This isn't New York. She won't let you leave without taking something, or the rest of her life she'll be ashamed."

Levin didn't know whether to believe Ding or not. It sounded like pious bullshit. By his own calculation he'd be forgotten by noon; the beggars in São Sebastião had won him to this point of view. Besides, he'd done what he had because it was the decent thing to do, not to become a lifelong creditor. Creditors have bigger headaches than debtors. They want their money back and they don't get it. Yet he knew it was fatuous to imagine himself and this creature on equal terms.

"O.K. Tell her I'll buy one of her baskets for my girlfriend."

"Take one, don't buy."

"I'm not going to take her livelihood without paying something."

The woman had grasped the word "basket." She reached behind and held up a stack five feet high. Was she offering the whole pile?

"I'll buy this one off the top." It was an unremarkable thing, no dyed pattern, no oil finish, just a plain nipa hemisphere big enough to hold fruit. He'd seen much nicer ones in the native craft shops in São Sebastião. He guessed that forty *cobas,* around two dollars, would be right. Melanie would laugh and maybe use it as a waste basket.

"What are you doing? That's way too much!" Ding cried.

"How much, then?"

"You'll ruin the local economy. You have to follow customs. Give her the money and tell her it's up to her. Here, let me."

Levin released a thick wad of *cobas* into Ding's hand. He was embarrassed to have so much cash flashing around the bare shop. Ding turned his back and stooped to the woman's face. At first she refused—simply turned her chin away. Levin couldn't blame her. "It's up to you"—he remembered the innumerable times it had been up to him, when any answer, any sum, seemed either paltry or extravagant, and someone was taking advantage of someone else. "It's up to you" guaranteed that the deal would end in bad feelings. But now courtesy seemed to leave no choice.

At last the basket woman took Levin's *cobas* into her taut lap and stripped away a single bill. It was a ten. She crumpled it into her bosom and wouldn't look at her benefactor.

Ding pressed the wad into Levin's hand. "Now let's go."

"She only took a ten. It's worth twice that, at least."

"The debt is unpayable." A trace of solemnity had stiffened Ding's voice. "She takes something to save face—because you insist."

"So it's my fault." Of course! He'd walked into a social situation fraught with nuances that were centuries old, as highly developed as the human eye, evolved for purposes of survival among people jammed together on this island; and he felt as clumsy as Gulliver. He'd been heroic, and he was leaving a mess. "All right, the hell with it. We're going to miss our date in Pulaya."

He almost forgot to take Melanie's basket. The woman and the boy stood waving in the door of the shop. The boy gazed at Levin with terrible longing, and the woman didn't look at him at all.

At the Toyota Levin said, "All that and we still don't know how to get the hell out of here." The street was the gray of spoiled fish. It was past three o'clock.

"But you did the boy a good deed. And you learned about our national behavior. Nothing is wasted in a foreign country." Ding looked at Levin. "You're tired. Let me drive the rest. I think I know how to find the road again."

Levin wondered briefly about insurance, Ding's driving skill, checkpoints. But he didn't believe he could keep his eyes open; he was exhausted.

He settled into the unfamiliar passenger's seat and watched Ding start up and put the car in gear. He drove well enough, and by some miracle, or perhaps the woman had had a store of wisdom invisible to the foreign eye, in two minutes they'd regained the highway and put the town behind them and were gliding, then bouncing, down the far side of the ridge into a sugarcane valley that danced with moonlight and even at this hour looked wonderfully lush.

Levin sat back and closed his eyes. At once, sleep threatened. After a few seconds he opened them and reached in his front pocket to transfer the *cobas* to his wallet.

Something was wrong. Before leaving his apartment he'd put 3,000 *cobas* in his bag and 1,000 *cobas* in his wallet. He counted the bills from his pocket twice: 150 *cobas*. He opened his wallet and counted what was left there, then counted again: 100 *cobas*. Once more he counted the wad he'd taken out in Pala: 150 *cobas*. The woman had taken a 10. The meal at the banana plantation had cost 35, and then he'd given Ding 200. He'd bought a paper on the Payao Bridge—2 more. Gas in São Sebastião—160. He'd spent 407 out of the 1,000 *cobas* today. Why was he down almost 350?

He grabbed the bag and fumbled inside for the notebook with his dollars and *cobas*, and spent three minutes counting and recounting. All there—3,000 *cobas*. He patted his front pockets, his back, he looked on the floor, he wondered if they'd fallen in the shop, or at the first checkpoint, or in São Sebastião, on the bridge, with Rick, at Happy's Grill—where?

Ding finally noticed the stir. "You lose something?"

"I'm not sure. Maybe three hundred fifty *cobas.*" He'd packed 3,000 in the bag, stuck 1,000 in the wallet. He remembered: 3,000, 1,000. It wasn't exhaustion. He was becoming frantic.

"Where?"

"If I knew, there wouldn't be a problem."

"Anyway, it's what, less than twenty dollars U.S.? Does that buy dinner in New York these days?"

"That's not the point. It's the principle. And we're not in New York. It would be enough to support that woman for a month at least."

Levin drove the heels of his hands into his eye sockets. Was that it? Was it? *Of course!*

He said, "Son of a fucking whore." The words didn't sound like his. He knew where they came from: Rick.

"What?"

"That—" Levin literally spluttered. But then black rage made him articulate. "—bitch, that fucking bitch took it. Of course! What an act, the groveling! After I fixed up her filthy little runt of a—"

"Take it easy, partner. Are you positive?"

"Positive as I can be about anything in this fucking country."

"You're sounding pretty engagé."

"Stop the car, Ding. I said stop the fucking car."

Ding shrugged and complied. Levin was dizzy with fury. He wanted to repay her repayment by going back to tie her son's arm down and whack off the whole dirty hand that he'd saved—*he*! It wasn't inconceivable, was it, that she kept the boy in that degraded state for just this purpose—was this very moment undoing Levin's fresh bandages and cramming her rotten mouth with tobacco leaves. Levin had played the white-father part to a T. A T! She'd spotted him right off—got the boy up in the middle of the night for this fat white prize. Taken this charitable sucker for a ride. His cheeks burned and he couldn't keep his eyes from brimming.

"You want to go back?"

Levin didn't answer.

"Let's go back."

His voice broke. "To let her know I know she made a fool of me?"

"Maybe she'll confess."

"Maybe she'll laugh in my face. Spit tobacco in my face. I'd like to kill her, is what I'd like to do."

"That's a big word."

"I would."

"So quit talking and let's go back."

"Don't be stupid. What am I going to do?"

"Then don't talk about killing if you don't mean killing."

Levin sat back, deflated, humiliated by his rage. He felt dangerously exposed to Ding. "The hell with the whole thing."

"Whatever you say."

"At this rate I'll be broke before we get to Fra Boboy. We'll have to watch our expenses in Pulaya."

"Whatever you say. The money is yours."

"That's what I thought too."

It seemed unwise to sleep with Ding at the wheel. It seemed that as soon as he fell asleep they would crash. But he drifted off soon enough: he gave in to sleep like a man downing a drink set on his table hours ago. He dreamed, fitfully, retaining little: there was the stone of the house outside Philadelphia, Melanie in her green summer dress, fish—the boy sticking blackened finger stumps in the fishmouth. Everyone else ate; Levin refused to eat.

When he woke the night had almost burned itself out. Ding was playing a tape—the Brahms. Its quiet passages were lost to the Toyota's engine and wheels on rough road. Levin thought: The Romantics didn't take car travel into account. Baroque is better for a Third World drive. At the start of the trip he might have shared this notion with Ding. He wondered how they'd managed the drive so badly. Only yesterday, in São Sebastião . . . was it yesterday? He slept again, and counted endless money, never counting right, and when he woke up it was with the feeling that his companion had somehow made the woman's theft possible. Outside Ding's window, above hills, the sky was pencil-lined red with dawn. They were climbing. They passed coffee terraces and groves of coconut palms whose high fronds had been slashed to the ground by typhoon or hung limp like hanged men. In a field, six electrical towers stood broken with their tops bent harmlessly down to the grass in a tangle of wires. Legs apart, they resembled grazing giraffe. The car took switchbacks uphill, crashed into road flaws, passed through a village.

The sky was paling in a great arc from left to right, and the villagers were waking up in public. They stretched, washed their brown bodies at pumps, dressed on the roadside. Some of them waved at Levin, who stared out, sleep-drugged. He drifted off again, for something like an hour.

The light woke him up. The sun had risen. Pulaya spread out before him, and behind the town green mountains receded into sunshine; among them stood Mount Kalanar, the volcano where Fra Boboy was hidden. In every day's first moment of consciousness here, sunrise exposed a dread. This morning it attached itself to something particular. Levin looked at Ding.

He thought: Ding took the money.

But he didn't say anything.

CHAPTER V

Las Encantadas, on a street near the main park, was the only decent hotel left in Pulaya. Its three stories were painted robin's-egg blue and designed according to some Asian fantasy of a Venetian palazzo. The room had been reserved under the name Henry Wong, a Chinese businessman who had ties to the movement, according to Connie. Local cadres had even ordered breakfast and newspapers for their arrival. At nightfall they would meet their contacts and make the last leg of the trip into the mountains. Ding said that it would not be safe, as strangers in Pulaya, to leave the hotel until then.

They slept a few hours, on twin beds separated by a night table with a phone and a Bible. The air conditioner made more noise than cold air, but after an hour the room was chilled. For Levin it was an exhausted but inadequate sleep at the wrong time of day; open or shut, his eyes burned. Fully clothed save his shoes, lying under the corduroy bedspread, he wound slowly downward along minutes of rambling semiwakefulness toward a place where everything was extinguished. No sooner settled there than he plunged upward again into the cold, darkened room. The windows were fringed with sunlight around the heavy drawn curtains.

He felt leaden. He seemed to be drowning in air. Across the table Ding was sleeping open-mouthed, a snore escaping from time to time. With his frown and clenched eyes he looked like a corpse still warm after violent death.

Levin's blood raced around his body and his thoughts laid claim to everything they touched, without limit, like de Souza the explorer before Pula-Pula slew him—sea-bounded rocks and coconut groves and fragments of memory and ancient history. But in another moment he felt as small as a Jola peasant under the corduroy bedspread, buffeted by typhoon.

His confidence rose and fell so many times he felt nauseated.

"Ding?"

For a long moment, no answer. Then: "Mm?" A snort and a gulp.

"I'd like to think you and I can be friends."

Again no answer.

"Do you think we can?"

"Mm . . . I don't know."

Levin waited, but there was no elaboration. Ding had turned his face into the pillow.

"Look, the story won't be any good if we work at cross purposes. We have a job to do—let's just do it."

Ding turned to look. "Who's not doing their job?"

"I just mean we should work together."

Ding seemed to consider how to take this proposal. "Sure, I'm a professional," he said, and Levin allowed this to signify an entente.

Ding picked up the phone and spoke rapidly in Saraunese, before signing off in English. "Twenty minutes. O.K. Put it on the bill."

"Who was that?"

"Room service." Ding sat on the edge of the bed, cleaning his fingernails with a toothpick. "Anyway," he said, "what is the story?"

"What do you mean?"

" 'A Western diplomat observed that many Saraunese feel . . .' Is that the truth as you see it? The world as it is? See—everything gets fucked up."

So much for working together, Levin thought. If you want a fight, you'll get one.

Brave words!

He was lying back on the pillow when someone knocked at the door. A trim squinting bellhop wordlessly set a tray on the writing table by the door. From where he lay, peering into the hall light, Levin couldn't make out what it held, but Ding motioned the bellhop to Levin's bedside with the bill. Filet mignon, fries, two *balimbim* (fertilized duck eggs, boiled and served hot inside the shell), and a bottle of Rum Direv: the total was 185 *cobas*, plus service.

"Christ, Ding—"

"One of the *balimbim* is for you. Time to teach you to eat our food. Help yourself to fries and rum."

Ding was already pulling up a chair to the writing table. He began cutting the steak into neat pieces.

"Please sign, boss," said the bellhop.

Levin signed. The bellhop remained standing by the bed, clutching the bill and looking stupidly at Levin.

"Excuse."

"What?"

"No . . . tip, boss?"

"It says service on the bill!"

"For kitchen and management, boss."

Levin snatched the bill and scanned it. He plunged a hand in his pocket and came up with five *cobas.* That was all the bellhop was getting out of him.

On his way out the bellhop exchanged a word with Ding. Ding twisted in the chair, his mouth crammed and juicy with red meat. "Do you want any receptionist sent?"

"Meaning?"

"Girls. The guy wants to know if you want to order a girl."

"Of course not." Levin was annoyed that the suggestion aroused him. "So room service offers that too?"

"Why not? If you wanted it."

"I don't. Do you?"

Ding dispatched the bellhop with a wave and returned to his food.

Knife and fork clinked on the glass plate. Ding chewed noisily with an open mouth and swallowed the meat in large chunks, washing it down with rum. Then he addressed himself to the fries.

"No ketchup," he muttered.

Levin was on his feet, groping for shoes. He retrieved his money from the duffel bag and stuffed it, dollars and *cobas,* in his pockets, together with the little notebook. He started for the door.

"Where are you going?"

"Out."

"You can't go out."

"Says who?"

Without another word he left the room.

. . .

The concierge chatting on the phone lifted her eyebrows in acknowledgment as Levin came downstairs. She was a small-boned young woman, her hair in a braid, formal and neat and pleasant-looking in a belted dress.

"Going out, Mr. Levin?"

"Just for a walk."

"Do you need a guide?"

It might have been a joke; but he saw that the concierge was not the type to banter with guests. He smiled and shook his head.

On the terrace, white sunlight struck him full in the face. He reached in his shirt pocket for the Ray-Bans that he'd brought along in anticipation of the strong southern sun. Through his shades the light appeared amber, like weak ale, and the driveway, the gate, the bed of frangipani were flat, without texture. It was high noon and the sun, in a coruscating blue sky stripped clean by the recent typhoon, uniformly bleached everything. The coconut palm's shadow fell only three feet.

A man was sweeping the canopied tables where no one sat. His features were unmistakably southern, somehow purer down here than on the southerners in the capital—no fleshy, yellow, European or Chinese trace. Gaunt cheeks, tight browned skin, a patience in the bone-narrowed eyes that could look like wisdom or animal passivity. The man stood and raised his nipa broom in greeting.

"Afternoon, sir."

"Afternoon."

It carried no trace of smartness or innuendo: the simple humility of a hotel employee and a provincial. The man had twenty years on Levin.

"Is anything open at this hour?" Levin asked.

"Not in siesta, sir. Three o'clock."

"So they do siesta here. In São Sebastião things are open straight through the day, even this time of year. It's more like an American city, you know."

The sweeper smiled and nodded and Levin felt foolish for saying more than the encounter required.

"Well, I think I'll go for a walk anyway."

The sweeper looked distressed. "This time no good for walking, sir. Better sleep now. Or swim."

There was a kidney-shaped pool behind the hotel, where Levin had seen a blond, German-looking couple floating on inner tubes. But he was set on going out. The only thing seemed to be movement—just to get away from Ding and the room.

"I'll be all right," he said cheerfully.

The sweeper smiled once more, as if the problem had been solved. He bade Levin take care and bent again to his labor.

It was as though the light had cleared and immobilized the streets. On a pole in the center of the park the Saraunese flag slumped. Levin crossed the well-watered green on a dirt path between flowering jacaranda and stunted pines, aware that he was the only thing astir.

Hilly Pulaya, by some divine dispensation, was clean, ordered, lovely, and deserted. Houses had wrought-iron balconies off the second story and cornices at the roof line. The shops around the square, shuttered and locked at this hour, carried conviction with their signs proclaiming hardware or fresh vegetables. The asphalt emanated no stench. On one street off the square there was a nightclub, next to it a casino, and two blocks down a parlor claimed to offer traditional Saraunese massage. At the head of the square stood a four-story glass structure, reflecting the azure of the sky. A sign over the double glass doors said NATIONAL SUGAR GROWERS BANK with a logo of a cane stalk clutched rifle-like by a fist.

Away from the square, Levin saw a few solitary people. From a shadowed chair in a doorway, an old man watched him walk the length of a block. A man in a polo shirt and stonewashed jeans, plump and light-skinned, rounded a corner, came toward him—younger, Levin guessed—veered to pass, smiled, and was gone. A pleasant-looking fellow in a pleasant town, a town like a hill resort in the off-season, light- instead of snow-bound.

Levin had no destination, but the empty streets quickened his pace.

A marquee hawked a Saraunese action film called *No Mercy.* Against the wall of the cinema a woman sat with a metal bucket, selling *balimbim.* Suddenly hungry, Levin bought one, blew to cool it, and cracked open the top of the shell on the wall. He pressed a finger to puncture the placenta and sipped the warm amniotic juices that Saraunese said were the delight of aborted duck. Within, a tiny but recognizable creature with an oversized head was curled fetally. Though he'd learned to eat *balimbim,* Levin had to close his eyes when he popped it in his mouth. Opening them again, he noticed a splotch of black paint on the wall where he'd cracked the egg.

It was part of a mural. He stepped back to see better.

The scene stretched thirty feet, rendered by several earnest, untutored hands. It showed Saraunese figures in various situations: a nurse holding a stethoscope to a baby's chest with the mother looking on; a man lying dead on the ground, bleeding gruesomely from the head; three workers hacking at a wall of sugarcane with machetes, guarded by men with guns; a family eating fresh fruit off an outdoor table; a group of men in overalls with their fists raised.

There were bright colors of orange fruit, rich velvety blood, a sky as blue as the one overhead. The moods, too, were primary ones—chiefly sorrow and joy. It was a clumsy piece of social realism, Diego Rivera third- or fourth-hand, with overlarge heads on bodies crushed or resplendent. Obviously the mural was meant to show Direv Saraun at extremes: as it was, and as it would be, after the liberation. A protest and a daydream.

Yet the overall effect was both funny and sinister—for a vandal had blacked out the head of every figure. It was against the nurse's face that Levin had opened his *balimbim*. Over the scene of sugar workers a message was scrawled in the same black paint. COMUNISM IS AN ALIEN IDEALOGY, it read. WE WILL CUT THEIR THROATS.

His stomach clenched and he turned from the wall to look behind him. Except for the *balimbim* woman, who seemed to be sleeping, the street was empty. He walked toward the corner, hurrying a little to get around it and out of sight. But the emptiness felt like a mirage. He imagined Saraunese peering out behind shutters up and down the street, their black eyes following him, and it occurred to him that he had felt watched from the moment he left Las Encantadas.

Rounding the corner, he nearly collided with the young man in the polo shirt and stonewashed jeans.

Recoiling, Levin found that his fists were closing for a scuffle. But the look he got was smiling, frank, intimate, with a hint of boyish mirth in the eyes.

"Hello," the young man said, extending his hand.

"Excuse me." Levin started around him.

"But I was looking for you."

Levin stopped and checked the face again. "I don't know you."

"Of course not, you are a stranger, I can see that. But I thought you were in trouble."

Levin tried to appraise him. The whole face was arranged for a smile, soft cheeks, swollen lips, merry eyes, yet Levin couldn't shake the suspicion that this man meant him harm, and the sooner he put distance between them the better.

"There's no trouble. I'm just going back to my hotel."

"Las Encantadas."

Levin nodded. He didn't want to give the stranger the satisfaction of his surprise.

"I was interested," the young man said, "because it is unwise to walk the city alone in this time without knowing where you are going. Especially a foreigner. So you interested me."

"I know where I'm going. I told you, back to my hotel." Levin made to leave again, but the stranger put up a hand.

"Please. You have no allies in Pulaya, isn't it?"

Levin wondered if he was being threatened. There was no obvious menace in the tone, only benevolent concern, yet the insistence was slightly alarming. "Allies" worried him, too. It made him a player when every instinct told him to stand by and watch.

"Look," Levin said, as evenly as he could manage, "I went for a stroll, I wanted to check out the town, now I'm going back. There's no cause for distress."

"Maybe not—but why take risks? Here"—the young man touched Levin's elbow and guided him gently toward the cloth canopy of a shop—"let's move out of the sun." When they were under the canopy he lowered his voice, even though no one was in sight. "Don't you know there have been killings in this city every day for two weeks? Some of them in broad daylight like this?"

This time Levin couldn't disguise his reaction. "God no, I didn't."

"Yesterday a union official from one of the plantations. The day before a health worker was cut a few blocks from where we are standing—a woman."

"Cut."

Lightly and slowly, the stranger drew a line under Levin's jaw from ear to ear, just as Melanie had done two nights ago in bed. "That is the method. They take the body away and leave the head in the street. You saw their sign?"

Levin shuddered. "Yeah. So the victims . . . A. of L.?"

The stranger shrugged in a way that suggested the futility of thinking about just deserts—it might as well have been either of them.

"Who's doing it?"

The man shrugged again. He was smiling as if they were in cahoots about something. Whatever this guy wanted from him, Levin decided that he would take the sweeper's suggestion and go back to Las Encantadas for a swim.

"Thanks for the information."

"Look, my friend. Don't be worried. I know who you are."

"Hey—just cut out this gaslighting shit."

"Daniel Levin? Isn't it? Because you see, I know Mr. Feliz. And Mr. Feliz has telephoned that you were coming down here to write about sugar. He wanted me to make sure everything went O.K. So I am making sure everything goes O.K."

The young man watched as Levin weighed the probabilities.

"Serge Cruz—*Pulaya Standard and Broadcasting*. Formerly I worked for the *Afternoon Express* in São Sebastião."

Levin decided to offer his hand.

"I saw you leave Las Encantadas." Serge leaned forward. "I think you haven't noticed the military have already taken an interest in you?"

"No." By now Levin had nothing to say for himself.

"A jeep is parked behind your hotel. Anyone not known in Pulaya draws attention. Especially . . ." Serge indicated Levin's skin.

"I guess it's a good thing you found me."

"But you are not here to cover the killings?"

"We never heard about them in São Sebastião."

"São Sebastião knows nothing of the war. When it finds out—too late!"

"It knows a little. But I figured there was something more out here."

"When did you come in?"

"Last night—this morning."

"You drove all night from São Sebastião?"

Serge registered Levin's nod with some unspoken insight. He looked too young to be much of a reporter, but he sounded a good deal shrewder than he looked. His English, less sure than Ding's, placed him in the lower-middle class, street-smart rather than well educated. "You have a car? Do you want to drive with me to a sugar plantation a few kilometers from here?"

"Now?"

"Why not? I have something to give the landlord of Fazenda

Maria Luísa. The visit may interest you. This man is out of the common."

"Do you mind if I ask how you got your name?"

Serge sighed unhappily. "They always ask. My father worked for the U.S. Navy. His favorite music was jazz—Satchmo, Duke Ellington. The time the news about me came from the hospital he was listening to 'Blue Serge' on the radio. Blue was my nickname at home."

Levin felt his spirits rise. He was beginning to like Serge Cruz; and the mention of Feliz had worked a calming effect. Anyway, he'd had no idea of his next move. The thought of returning to the hotel had actually made him sick.

They retrieved the Toyota from Las Encantadas, where Levin left a note with the concierge for Ding, saying that he would be back by six o'clock. It would give them an hour and a half before checkout time.

"Going out for the afternoon, Mr. Levin?" The concierge was reading the Far East edition of *Elle*. Levin nodded. "If your companion should inquire where you've gone?"

Levin glanced at Serge. "You can tell him Fazenda Maria Luísa."

"Very good, sir."

When they were out on the terrace Serge said, "Maybe it is better not to tell strangers your movements."

"The receptionist?"

"Maybe it is better."

Behind the hotel, the German-looking couple had disappeared from the pool.

The *Pulaya Standard and Broadcasting* occupied two floors of an old commercial building in a street behind the square. On the sidewalk in front of the door, rice sacks filled with sand were stacked like a barricade. Inside was a battery of oversized antique Underwoods and Royals, filing cabinets crammed with clippings, and a half-dozen Saraunese asleep at desks or playing mah-jongg. The paper itself looked like an American college rag, but its headlines clamored about vigilantes and mutilated bodies.

"Siesta," Serge apologized. He added whimsically: "I try to fight it."

He took a photographer's vest and a bag holding camera equipment. As they skirted the sandbags on the way out he said, "A conversation piece. Also a statement. Last week a letter to the editor came in: 'Your days are numbered.' "

When they were on the road, winding out of town through highland pine forest toward the east, Levin said, "You from Pulaya? You don't look southern."

"São Sebastião. I came down last year."

"What made you do that?"

"I wanted to be a provincial reporter. Provincial journalism is where things are happening. The front line." The bravado sounded uncharacteristic, perhaps ironic or self-mocking. "In Pulaya there are two kinds of faces," he went on. "You have the southern look—what you were talking about. We call it 'ethnic.' And then you have another—we call it 'Mediterranean.' It is like two different countries here. The man we are going to see—he is king of the Mediterraneans."

"Some character out of Homer."

"Wait until you hear the name people must call him: Dom Hipolito de Oliveira."

"A Portuguese feudal lord?"

"He is a throwback, for sure," Serge said. "But he is the biggest landowner in the province. He is crazy, but very strong." He paused. "He even has his own army. So people respect him."

"I'll be sure to call him the right thing."

Levin turned on the radio and got a local AM station that was playing a Whitney Houston anthem to self-love. Sentimental Stateside pop was greatly favored in Direv Saraun.

"I came," Serge said, "because I always envied the foreign journalists like you, who could see both sides. Here I am almost a foreigner."

"In São Sebastião a man told me that it's impossible not to choose sides now, especially for a Saraunese—especially out here. You disagree?"

"Who told you that?"

Levin hesitated. "Another journalist."

"He is clever. No, I agree. You cannot avoid choosing."

Levin ventured to ask which side Serge had chosen.

"Both." Serge's laugh-prone face remained straight.

"How do you pull that off?"

"Gymnastics." This time he laughed. "But you have to score ten every time."

"I thought that broke the oldest rule. The friend of my enemy is my enemy."

"But the enemy of my enemy is my friend, isn't it? So I must be everyone's enemy, and everyone's friend."

They were descending out of the pines toward what seemed a soft grassy valley. The hillsides were terraced with lustrous coffee, and the blossoms of great flamboyants glittered orange in the afternoon light. Mount Kalanar stayed on their right, to the south, a nearly perfect blue cone.

"My paper is pro-people. We are not liked by Dom Hipolito and some others."

"Committed journalism."

"Personally, I don't like the word—it sounds too final. But we need news from the other side too. We have to keep a liaison. And then, we want to survive. So as a northerner they chose me. I have no reputation here."

They passed a Texaco station and a chicken shack. The smell of roast fowl, for which the region was renowned, reached Levin and he felt a stab of hunger. At each bend the road gave a glimpse of the valley below: a vast floor of cane fields extended to the far hills.

"Sounds like a dangerous act," Levin said.

"Dom Hipolito likes me—that is the main thing. And when he is unhappy, I write things . . ."

From the canvas bag Serge fished out a fresh newspaper clipping with the headline "Landlord Decides to Fight Back."

"The other side sabotaged the rail lines from his plantation to the central, and burned a carload of cut cane. And they were trying to recruit from his workers. That was when Dom Hipolito began organizing the Cavaleiros de Aviz."

"What—crusaders?"

"Vigilantes. The ones who ruined the painting. Who are doing the killings."

Levin absorbed this news, and then struggled to phrase a question. "How do you deal with the problem of writing about him at a time like this? Finding anything good to say?"

Serge looked out the window. When he answered it was with the weariness of experience, not anger. "At a time like this, you don't take a stand if you're not covered. This is basic. You have to be like two people—or you get nothing. Having one reality is like having none. But in myself I know who I am. I have no doubt."

"That must be a comfort," Levin said without irony. But this time Serge looked at him with a shade of irritation; he had misunderstood.

"It was a mistake to walk by yourself," he told Levin. "You see how we are different. I keep good relations with everyone, but you move alone. I prefer my situation."

"Well, it's my method. I find it works. In the end you're alone too."

"I try to postpone the end."

Serge had put him on the defensive. "It's not as though I've come down alone. I'm with a photographer."

"Saraunese?" Levin nodded. "How is it?"

"Well, he's one of the top free-lancers."

"But—between you?"

"Between us? A few problems. Nothing big."

By now Levin would not have been amazed if Serge asked whether he was experiencing a few difficulties with his fiancée too. He looked into the plump, yellow, affable face by the window, so different from Ding's narrow features, and was tempted to unburden himself. He knew there would be a cost. He was becoming Serge's subject, a role in which so many others had made themselves vulnerable to him.

"I might as well tell you it's been very bad. I don't know how it happened but we were at each other's throat all night. Honestly, I felt he was at *mine.*" Levin struggled to keep a firm dry voice.

"Where is he now?"

"At the hotel. Asleep. Or eating filet mignon on my tab."

"It has shaken you."

To his horror Levin felt tears in his eyes. He swallowed them back. "You don't seem surprised."

"Some Saraunese cannot work for Americans."

"He's not working *for* me—"

Serge paid him no heed. "Especially professionals. They begin to feel small."

"This one," Levin said, "is as small as a leopard waiting to pounce. He stole money too."

"Stole? Why haven't you told him to go to hell?"

"At one point I wanted to kill him."

"No, I can see you are no killer. You want to please. But why have you let him do this to you?"

The conversation had drawn Levin much further out than he intended. "I didn't know what else to do. We're sort of stuck with each other. I don't know, it seemed dangerous to be fighting out here. And then I wondered—" Levin stopped himself. It was possible Ding was a sympathizer, if not actually one of them—but he still possessed enough judgment and restraint not to say such a thing on suspicion, even about Ding. At this moment his own motives were obscure, and in that darkness he sensed things would not go well for him. He'd crossed a line and he didn't know what he was doing out there.

"I don't have any allies," he finished.

"I would have told him to go to hell."

"You're Saraunese. I have some precedents to live down."

"Allow me to say that you should not let this guy beat you, because he will try. Soft feelings are traps. Hardness he will understand."

The road was leveling, the trees clearing, and they were coming to the entrance of Fazenda Maria Luísa.

A private road turned off through open gates into a dirt area ringed by trees where a dozen antique iron railcars stood bristling with cut cane. The head car, a steam engine with a wrought-iron cowcatcher, made Levin think of the Wild West. The tracks trailed off through the cane fields in the direction of a complex of buildings a half mile away, whose chimneys were smoking white. A hot breeze blew the smell of unrefined sugar across the fields.

As they drove through the gates, Levin put an end to the conversation. "We'll be fine," he said, "Ding and I."

"Ding Magkakanaw?"

"You know him?" Levin thought: You know everything, don't you? You know far more than I do. I hope it's a good thing Feliz called you.

"Last year we covered a few stories in the capital together." Serge put two fingers to his lips as if an appraisal was required. "He is . . . his own type. Unusual for us."

By the railcars three figures with Armalites slung on their backs emerged from the shade of a mango tree. Two of them looked barely old enough to fire the weapons. The third was an old man (though he might have been only in his forties—Saraunese shrank up in the years Americans called their prime), with a graying ponytail and suspicious illiterate eyes under a green baseball cap that was embroidered in red with a shield over crossed staves. All three wore green T-shirts with the same insignia on the breast pocket.

Serge waved out the window.

"Cavaleiros de Aviz," he told Levin.

"Three gallants."

Serge bellowed a question. One of the boys shook his head.

"Dom Hipolito's not home yet. Let's drive up to the house and wait."

"No bribe required," Levin muttered to himself, intending to be overheard.

"I am known to them."

They drove on a quarter mile, straddling the narrow railroad tracks, and all along the way a green wall of sugarcane ran ten feet high on either side of the car. It was like driving through an alley. Above the cane they could see only the sapphire sky, streaked with harmless cloud in the south. The feathery white wisps at the stalk tops bent slightly in a breeze that was intangible on human skin.

"How much does he own?"

"Dom Hipolito has one thousand five hundred hectares. And he owns the milling central at the end of these tracks. The other planters pay him a fee to use it."

"A good businessman."

"He is no businessman," Serge said quickly. "By profession he is a warlord. This was all passed down through his family during the century we have had sugar here. However, Dom Hipolito is a different bird."

"How's that?"

"Well—because there is some opposition now. People say he's insane. From inbreeding. The de Oliveiras hate a brown skin."

Around a bend a railcar appeared on the tracks with cane stacked well above the sides, and behind it, linked at the bottom, was another car, ancient as the rest. This one was half full, and a two-by-eight plank without cleats stood pitched up the side at forty degrees. Levin braked to a stop and considered the width of the passage between the cars and the green wall of sugar.

Serge suggested they get out to see the work.

Beyond the railcars, on the loading side, the high cane yielded abruptly to a field of dirt and cut stalk with dead brown leaves. A few hundred feet away workers were dwarfed against green where the uncut cane began again. Hacking with machetes, they looked to be clearing a jungle. And yet they had already harvested an area nearly the size of a football field. Two workers were making their way across the field under loads of gathered stalks that nearly concealed them, and for a moment the stalks appeared to be moving toward the railcars under their own power.

Levin and Serge walked in the furrow between mounds where the old cane had grown. Sliced stumps shot up like clusters of knives. The field smelled of hot dirt and dry leaf. In the heat and stillness, they heard the machetes from halfway across: the sound came as a rustle and a thrash, punctuated by a man's grunt as he hacked the stalks off at the root, another softer thrash at the top, then another rustle—the cane thrown on a bundle behind. In an unbroken motion the sequence started over: rustle, thrash, grunt, thrash, rustle. Out of the implacable wall of green, the men had created orderly rows of bundled cane.

At one end of the field a little boy rode a grazing ox, its massive horned head bowed to the grass.

The two cane bearers approached along the journalists' furrow under bundles of at least forty cut stalks, seven or eight feet long. They were gloveless and barefoot; their feet were black with grime. They wore jeans, long-sleeved shirts buttoned up against nettles and slicing leaves, and rags wrapped around their heads and mouths like women in purdah. Baseball caps, John Deere, and Pepsi instead of the insignia of the Cavaleiros, held the rags in place—apparently these two had not been admitted into the order. Of their clothing, there was more gap than material. It was as if a cloud of moths had set on them and spent five minutes furiously chewing. What remained was literally falling to pieces, and a sudden move, a cane stalk's pointed tip, a brush of the machete, could leave them naked in the eye of the sun.

They were barely men, young as the guards at the gate, and stalk-thin.

Before Levin and Serge could move aside, the workers stepped up on the ridge to pass. Serge was fumbling with the camera in his canvas bag—too late.

When they were abreast, Levin looked into their faces. The men gazed back—and straight through him. They gave no greeting, no sign of recognition. Just before they passed him, Levin glimpsed in their black eyes and their bony, leather-dark faces a look of such hopelessness as he'd never seen. It was not human despair but something animal, insentient, dull, like a flogged mule he'd once seen hauling a plow in the north.

"The loaders," Serge explained superfluously. "Some load, some cut. Other days, they switch."

The journalists continued along the furrow toward the cutters at the cane-face.

"They go that far with every bundle? Then walk back?"

"In three weeks the trip will be half a mile." Levin had no answer. "They call the walk back the 'Sunday' because it feels so easy."

Even this much human fancy seemed unthinkable in the loaders.

"What do they call the walk there?"

"They have no name for it."

"Why not use that?" Levin directed Serge's gaze across the field where the ox was browsing, oblivious to the boy's whip. "Get it to haul the cane in a cart?"

"Dom Hipolito's overseer would never allow it."

"Why the hell not?"

"These men are paid *tek-tek,* piecework. With an oxcart the work would go faster, and they would make too much too soon."

"So this walk—it's a cost-effective measure."

"In the American way of speaking." With the back of his hand Serge wiped his forehead. "Dom Hipolito does not love Americans too much."

"I guess they're not unionized, these guys."

Serge laughed a laugh of long native experience.

It occurred to Levin that the situation called for a moral response, and he waited for it to rise in his blood. But the sun and the field overpowered him and his tongue stuck to his palate.

They reached the group of cutters. The noise of their labors seemed amplified in the heat. They were dressed more or less like the loaders, but when they turned from the cane-face to throw down the deracinated, decapitated stalks, the cutters turned out to be mature men. One wore a head rag from which black hair spilled in curls. Wide-eyed, sun-cured, he had an expression of fierce intensity entirely self-contained—the mute determination exacted by the work. Like the loaders, they took no notice of the visitors.

Serge now had two cameras slung around his neck. He screwed a 35-mm. lens onto the Nikon and began snapping pictures. The shutter opened and closed in rapid clicks. Serge crouched, held the camera vertically, moved closer, focused, snapped. He walked around to the edge of the sugarcane and snapped from alongside to catch their faces. He backed up five feet, then fifteen, snapped, approached so close that the arc of eighteen inches of sharpened metal passed within a foot of his lens, focused, and snapped. Levin stood watching, the sweat running off his eyebrows.

As he took pictures, Serge played guide for Levin; his tone was flat and factual.

"These guys make nineteen *cobas* for every ton of cane they cut and load. That's, let's see . . . about a dollar U.S. On a good day they can make twenty-eight *cobas* each. But you see, they never get out of debt, because they are not paid until the end of the season—the 'crushing' season it's called, the mills crush the cane. So they live on an advance and pay interest on it and buy overpriced provisions at Dom Hipolito's store and by May they have earned maybe fifteen dollars U.S. Then they go home and wait for the crushing season to start again in October." Serge lowered the camera from his eye. "The wait is worse than the work."

If the cutters knew that they were being discussed, they betrayed nothing of it.

"Of course, these guys are the lucky ones. Most sugar workers are unemployed now."

"They don't live on the plantation?"

"These are migrants, from Batak Province. Their families live in barracks by the milling central. Dom Hipolito won't let you go there, but I got in once because the guard is an uncle of a printer at the *Standard.* Fifty families in three rooms. The babies crying. It is like a place to keep pigs before slaughter."

When the Nikon ran out of film, Serge transferred the lens to his Canon. One cutter, whose T-shirt said "I Am a Celebrity," glanced up when the camera was three feet from his face, and went on chopping.

Belatedly, Levin took out his notebook and wrote down the figures Serge had given him. It occurred to him that it would also be important to have descriptions of the work and the workers.

Across the field, the loaders were climbing the plank onto the railcar. One swayed under his burden, stepped back, then leaned into the last few feet. Standing in the car on the loaded cane, they were framed above the far field against the blue volcanic slope of Mount Kalanar, the guerrilla base. The sun had begun its descent to the west over Pulaya, and the loaders' shadows slanted over the side of the car. From this distance, solitary and upright above the fields, they appeared almost heroic. The possibility occurred to Levin that he had been looking at the Saraunese poor in the wrong way from the start, without imagination.

He turned his gaze back to the cutters, dwarfed under dense green. *Rustle-thrash-grunt-thrash-rustle-grunt.* It went on and on, as regular as machinery. Thousands of strokes a day, every day for months, season after crushing season, in this prison house of sun and dirt and stalks.

"They work all day on a few handfuls of salted rice." Serge, as methodical as the cutters, went on with his labors.

In his mind's eye, Levin saw the framed prints of Serge's film at the photo gallery on the Upper East Side where he'd gone one bright winter day to see a Capa retrospective. Top-lit, light-gray, the walls would be covered with sugar workers. This afternoon's yellow, ocher, and green turned to silverchrome black-and-white. He knew these pictures. They were as familiar as wedding shots, in Direv Saraun and all over the world. They were the kind Ding took—a shout of protest, a raised fist, the before-and-after mural on the wall in Pulaya. Stock footage; they took themselves.

The pictures were designed to evoke a moral response.

Sun and sweat fused in Levin's eyes and he swayed dizzily in the furrow. He had been too long in the sun already. He wiped his eyes on his shirt sleeve and allowed a moment's hope that his own tears were blinding him. He was still clutching the notebook; he'd written nothing more than a few numbers.

Pulaya, Direv Saraun, Feb. 23—In a gallery in Manhattan, Robert Capa's brave fighters and bleak refugees moved this reporter to tears. But in a sugarcane field on this Asian island he only felt the futility of all eyes—his, and the camera's and the sun's. The cutters were as strange as lizards. The loaders were mute as fish. In the gallery in Manhattan, all their faces would be painted over black.

Across the field a car horn sounded, then again and again.

"It must be Dom Hipolito," Serge said. "We are blocking the way."

The two loaders came running through the furrow and arrived panting, their expressions as close to panic as their features allowed. The cutters paused at their task.

"We'd better hurry," Serge told Levin.

They began jogging toward the road, leaving the cutters and loaders behind. The horn honked them all the way across the field.

The old Cavaleiro de Aviz with the ponytail stood next to the chauffeur of the black Mercedes, his hand on the horn. Two more knights waited nearby, elbows resting on the Armalites dangling from their shoulders. Another man, toward whom the Cavaleiros were angled attentively, was standing with his back turned, arms crossed, giving short hard flicks to a cigarette lighter. In Jordache jeans and a sport shirt and tasseled leather shoes, his black hair youthfully long over his neck, his build trim and powerful, he would have suggested an Italian playboy were it not for the .45 stuck in the back of his waistband. When he turned around, still flicking the lighter, the mustached face, though light-skinned and coolly Continental, showed no trace of decadence. It was square, ravaged all through the cheeks and neck with acne scars, and the eyes stared hard as opal. Levin guessed him to be thirty-five. The pitted flesh ruined a handsome face.

Dom Hipolito de Oliveira nodded at Serge and got in the passenger's seat behind smoked windows. The two knights jumped in back on either side, revealing a girl sitting in the middle of the seat.

The Mercedes pursued them the last quarter mile to the house. Dom Hipolito lived behind a ten-foot concrete wall on which broken glass and barbed wire were set. A half dozen Cavaleiros de Aviz patrolled the grounds with dogs, and at each corner a machine gun was in place over the ramparts. The wall made it impossible for anyone outside to appreciate the splendor of the landlord's quarters. Beds of frangipani, a colonnaded porch, French windows in the second story, Spanish tiles in the front hall, lofty walls painted red, mahogany balustrade on the winding stair, imposing oil paintings of de Oliveiras past—every one square-faced from inbreeding, with blemishes hidden by beards or a portraitist's tact. The central portrait showed a grande dame of the twenties, presumably Dona Maria Luísa de Oliveira. Hanging from a hall mirror was something Levin had never seen in a Saraunese home—a crucifix.

Dom Hipolito showed his guests to a mahogany table twenty-five feet long in the dining room. Immediately a maid brought plates of pork, rice, and stewed tomatoes. Serge introduced Levin to Dom Hipolito, who bowed graciously at the head of the table and begged his visitors to sit. The girl they'd seen in the car was seated across from Levin and Serge, but she wasn't introduced. She looked eighteen, dark and doe-eyed, and she said not a word.

The landlord recited grace. He addressed Serge in Saraunese, then apologized to Levin for his rudeness and switched to English.

"A courtesy visit?"

"Courtesy, and also. . . ." Serge brought out his clipping and passed it down the table. He watched eagerly as Dom Hipolito read, and when a smile appeared on the landlord's face Serge matched it.

"Very good," Dom Hipolito said, folding the article and tucking it in his shirt pocket. "I didn't like what the *Standard* wrote about that union guy—but this, this is very good."

Serge brought a slice of pork to his pleased mouth.

" 'Democracy has its risks—that is the beauty of democracy.' I said that?"

"Words to that effect."

Dom Hipolito smiled and shook his head over the folly of human utterance. He cut with firm, decisive strokes and chewed quickly, the hinges of his muscular jaw creaking.

"Do you like the end?" Serge asked. " 'I will not rest until the last communist . . .'?"

"Very good. Overstatement has its place." Dom Hipolito looked at Levin. "Do they know about the Cavaleiros de Aviz in the U.S.?"

"They don't even know in São Sebastião. But they'll find out soon."

"Help yourself to more meat. Nila!"

The maid appeared at the kitchen door. "Senhor?"

Without looking, Dom Hipolito gave her orders, and she came back with four brandy glasses and a bottle of coconut rum liqueur.

"No, none for the girl." The maid removed one glass, and Dom Hipolito filled three with the spirit, while the girl kept her head bowed. He raised his glass. "We are," he announced, "the most significant incidence in this country in years. You can be the one to break the story, Mr.— I have forgotten. What are you down here for?"

"Levin. I want to write a few articles about sugar."

"About sugar." Dom Hipolito stared blankly, and then he gave vent to vacant laughter. It was as if Levin had proposed an article on sand to a Berber. "What the hell does sugar have to do with anything?"

"Maybe the whole war is based on sugar," Levin heard himself say. His voice sounded far-off and provoking. Dom Hipolito sipped, and Levin, following his lead, downed the whole glass. The liqueur was light and fine, like sweetened coconut milk with an alcohol after-vapor. Dom Hipolito poured him another.

"That analysis," he said, "is too much like this Marxism. Is that what you learned from watching my workers?" Levin smiled through a sip and shrugged. "Did those workers look to you like fighters? No. You cannot build a war on sugar. Sugar is soft, and sweet. But you can build a war on boredom. And that is what these terrorists are doing. Boredom empties the head, then they fill it with other things. Disrespect, Marxism, unnatural desires. I know my people, I am like a father to them. They are simple and these things can destroy them easily. The terrorists don't care about their well-being as I do. So the solution is to give them something to do. Self-respect. This is the genius of the Cavaleiros de Aviz. You would not imagine how they change when they receive their first gun."

Dom Hipolito's heavy black mustache glistened with liqueur. The handsome, pocked face had settled into a sated confidence. Coconut rum liqueur misted between Levin's sun-weakened brain and eyes. He tried to will the girl to look at him but she kept her eyes on the table.

"Do you consider yourself a Marxist, Mr. Levin?"

"I'm a Caramelite."

The landlord looked at him with new interest. "A—Catholic?"

"I believe in the ultimate vindication of a despised American sect known as humanists."

"I see. Then you have no bible," Dom Hipolito pursued, "no book of truth."

Levin realized that this was so and it seemed somehow to disadvantage him. On an impulse, he pulled out the notebook from his back pocket and flipped its scribbled pages before the landlord's eyes. "This is as close as I can get."

"Not a Christian, then?" Dom Hipolito was suddenly angry; Levin's gesture seemed to disgust him. "Nor a Marxist? In my country, you are standing on the most dangerous ground."

Levin gazed at the high colonial blood-red walls and told himself to be careful, to sober his tongue. He returned the notebook to its hiding place.

"But, Dom Hipolito," Serge said mildly, "many Saraunese are not Christians and few are Marxists."

"Let them choose. Between the religion of my fathers and the false faith of this girl there can be nowhere to hide your head."

They all looked at her. She hadn't understood the English, but she bowed her head deeper. On exhibit, she was trembling visibly, goose bumps raised all along her bare upper arms.

"The military arrested this one yesterday at the bus station. But they handed her over to me—my men pinpointed her. At first, I admit, I was tempted to kill her. But she has valuable information for us, sure. And I give even the worst of them a chance to repent."

The girl summoned the courage to look up at her captor's guests. Levin waited till he had her eye, then he mustered what he hoped was a reassuring smile. In response a smile of gratitude, or entreaty, flickered nervously over her brown lips.

With elaborate formality Dom Hipolito poured another round.

"These Marxists say: 'Let the people be the sea in which the fish swim.' In Vietnam the Americans thought they could drain the sea, and then the fish would die. It was a typical error of these modern thinkers who don't know how to fuck, even. Any peasant here can tell you the sea is too vast to drain. You cannot disappear the sea." He shot Levin a look of rebuke. "But you can stock it with your own fish. So that the other fish don't know what is what. Which fish are harmless, and which are the barracuda kind? Nobody knows. And this is also the genius of the Cavaleiros. We have made everyone afraid of everyone in Pulaya."

Levin said, "I'm too young to know much about Vietnam."

The maid came in to take away their plates. Levin was looking at the girl again. Dom Hipolito produced a pack of local cigars and tossed it with his lighter down to Serge and Levin. When the lighter was back in his hands he began striking the flint-wheel on the edge of the table.

"Suspicion, informing—you see how we have turned the terrorists' weapons against them. And if these gutless politicians and generals in São Sebastião cooperate, we can win the war inside six months."

"I see. The Indonesian solution?"

"The righteous anger of the people. They hate these terrorists. Our peasants want to preserve their traditional culture in the *fazenda* system."

Knowing he'd provoked a scowl, Levin drew on his cigar and retreated behind a cloud of hot smoke. All the elements of the air seemed to be unstably humming. The rhetoric and posturing and zeal had acted on him like intoxicants, and he felt giddy and reckless. Moreover, through a rummy, leafy haze, he was distressed to discover that the captive girl had managed to stir his sympathetic lust. He'd been imagining a scenario in which Dom Hipolito would release her to his temporary care. Without looking, he felt her desperate eyes on him and a vision came of his futile buttocks hiking over Melanie. His face burned; pushing away his glass, he tried to muster some self-righteousness.

"Look, excuse me—doesn't terror play a role on your side?"

"We are not terrorists. No one can say we are."

"I understand people have been decapitated in Pulaya."

"They were A. of L. I am one hundred ten percent sure."

"Your information came from vigilantes—Cavaleiros?"

Dom Hipolito, staring, gave a small nod.

"I can think of reasons why a Cavaleiro would imagine he was seeing infidels."

Dom Hipolito's square jaw tightened. "It was not imagination, Mr. Levin. I issued personal invitations for these people to join us. They refused. Why refuse unless you are one of them?"

"Anyway, even if you got your man, don't you think you'll lose support? The guerrillas didn't win anyone over by killing that serviceman yesterday."

"Perhaps we will lose the support of humanists. Perhaps we never had it. In either case, it doesn't matter."

There was a silence, in which Serge worried his cigar. Levin recovered his glass and drained it. Dom Hipolito was still flicking the lighter on the table. The girl was looking at Levin; when he noticed, he looked away.

"How long are you staying with us?" Dom Hipolito asked.

"Unfortunately I have interviews tomorrow on the coast."

Serge's eyebrows went up.

"I think," Dom Hipolito said slowly, "you will want to stay in Salantin a little longer."

Levin looked up. Was he being threatened? "Oh?"

"You are skeptical of our sources. You think I'm lying. O.K. What do you say if I tell you we are close to pinpointing the headquarters of Fra Boboy? You know Fra Boboy?"

"I've heard of him, of course."

He extended his glass, and Dom Hipolito tipped the bottle over it. Serge leaned forward. Dom Hipolito was smiling again; he was about to turn up his ace in the hole.

"In the next week there could be some kind of operation in the mountains. The objective is very limited, simply to steal their computer—what do you call this?—the floppy disks. The entire strategy of the Army of Liberation would fall into our hands. As a journalist it could be of interest to you. Perhaps we could arrange an exclusive. It might also cause you to reconsider the Cavaleiros de Aviz."

Serge's mouth hung open in shock. Levin could hardly believe what he'd extracted in his intemperance.

"Ah. Well, it's my bad luck."

The maid appeared gesturing toward the front hall. Dom Hipolito pointed angrily at the table and cursed her. She hurried away.

"My best friends arrive and this idiot asks should she bring them in."

The front door closed, and after a moment two Saraunese men strolled into the dining room. One of them was middle-aged, of Dom Hipolito's high color. He had the apologetic smile and wide girth of a pleasure-seeker, and his drinker's eyes were encased in folds of darkened flesh. The other was a military man, young, southern, serious, his dark-khaki A.F.D.S. sleeves rolled up over lean biceps. The name on the shirt was Bugan. He and Levin exchanged a wordless look.

"Johnny was expected," Dom Hipolito told the soldier. "But this is a pleasant surprise."

"Just to say hello," Captain Bugan answered. "We happened to arrive at the same time."

Despite hue and rank, he plainly enjoyed favored status with Dom Hipolito. They embraced, and as their cheeks grazed Levin noticed the captain whisper something in the landlord's ear. Dom Hipolito's gaze fell to the terra-cotta floor tiles; his hard opal eyes had suddenly gone weak.

In his distraction he failed to introduce his guests, and it was left to Serge to do the honors.

Johnny Ochoa, chief executive of the Regional Association of Sugar Planters, was as blandly loquacious as the captain was guarded and intense. "You know, Danny," he said, at once familiar with Levin in the Stateside way, "I was at Berkeley in the fifties. Thanks, Serge, just half a glass. My friends and I lived across the bridge on Nob Hill. Every weekend, we were at the clubs in North Beach—oh, Christ, those places! Do you suppose they're still around?"

Levin said that he didn't know the West Coast.

"Well—what times we had, I'm telling you. Of course, that was before Berkeley got serious."

"Radicals," Serge explained to Dom Hipolito. Dom Hipolito was paying enough attention now to grunt.

"You've got to hand it to the Americans, though," Johnny Ochoa continued. "They knew the meaning of work. I'm sure those same radicals are making a buck or two today." Levin agreed that they probably were. "I've spent my life trying to get that spirit going here in my own little country. Our peasants live for today. I tell them: No work no money, no money no honey. Pulaya used to be soaked in money, did you know that, Danny? Champagne every Saturday night! Then sugar went bad."

"The war came first," said the captain. "The war has damaged us more."

"No question, until we beat these boys there won't be prosperity. That's the captain's department. But after the war we'll have to get away from sugar—bring in factories, industry, computers. You know, the American model. Bootstraps!"

"The American model," said Dom Hipolito, "is to betray your friends. Nobody counts on them to lift a finger for us. I hear Americans in this country insulting their homeland. To a Saraunese, that is like letting another man fuck your wife." He sucked through a nostril in disgust.

"We can't run the world anymore," Levin said, "if that's what you mean."

Serge said, "The A. of L. has said you are getting ready to intervene."

"On whose side?" asked Captain Bugan, and he enjoyed a strained laugh with Dom Hipolito.

"I would say that's a misperception. Possibly a useful one."

The bottle of liqueur was emptied around the table.

"Captain," Levin said. "Colonel Siriman of the A.F.D.S. Press Office spoke highly of you."

"Yes?" The captain seemed not at all interested. "He is a good friend. We see eye to eye."

"I'd have liked to talk to you about the situation here if I had time."

"Ah. The situation."

Dom Hipolito said, "But he is going down to the coast."

"Really? The coast?"

"Because he is going to write about sugar."

"Ah. Well, we have sugar in Salantin too." Captain Bugan looked at Levin; he still hadn't smiled.

"He says the war is about sugar."

"Really? That is interesting. Well, perhaps another time."

"Another time," Levin said.

In the silence he reached for his glass but found it empty.

Dom Hipolito knocked his back and loudly set it down. "I'm tired of this politics," he announced. "I prefer living."

"Dom Hipolito owns Pulaya's number one club," Serge told Levin.

"And I insist on adjourning there. Have you experienced our Saraunese entertainment?"

Slowed by alcohol, Levin failed to answer.

"Not me," said the captain. "Back to work. Shall I . . ." He gestured to the girl.

"Not yet. We haven't had our dialogue. What about these Dutch?"

"I don't know yet. So many foreigners in Pulaya these days."

"Me," Dom Hipolito said, "I've never liked the Dutch. They make good beer—the rest is windmills and pornography."

The others went outside; Dom Hipolito and Captain Bugan lingered briefly in the dining room.

A military jeep with five soldiers inside was waiting at the gate. The driver was bizarrely coiffed: he wore his hair fashionably long in back and short on top, with the sideburns shaved to the temples. There seemed to be streaks of purple all through the black. He and the others watched Levin and Serge walk to the Toyota.

"You've got a funny country," Levin said.

Johnny Ochoa left his car behind and rode with Dom Hipolito in the chauffeured black Mercedes; Captain Bugan went in the jeep. The captive girl was left at the gate in the care of the ponytailed Cavaleiro de Aviz. Levin didn't look back at her as he pulled out.

Across the field, the cutters toiled at the wall of cane in what seemed the exact same spot; but the loaders had filled the railcar almost to the top.

When the house, the sugarcane fields, the workers, and the vigilantes at the entrance road were all behind them, and the journalists were snaking up the hill toward Pulaya in the lengthening shade, Serge asked, "So what can you say about Dom Hipolito de Oliveira?"

"I say he deserves whatever Fra Boboy has planned for him."

To his own ears it sounded false. As always, his high surprised him. He'd been drinking nervously, the riskiest way.

"But there is an appeal just the same?"

"He knows what he believes. I suppose that has its attractions."

"His Euro-dignity—" Serge chuckled. "It touches me. There is nothing in Direv Saraun like it. We Saraunese wear our hearts on our sleeve. Our feelings are strong and simple, like children."

Levin was beginning to hate the self-generalizations of Saraunese.

"What about those cutters and loaders?" he asked. "Do you know how they feel about their master?"

"I will tell you a story on Dom Hipolito. Once, he saw an ox plowing one of his fields. The ox was limping. Dom Hipolito called to the ox-driver and said: Why is that beast limping? And the ox-driver, who was old and tired, said: Sure, if the animal has to drag the plow up and down every day he will be injured. Dom Hipolito kicked the ox-driver in the chest—so hard that before Dom Hipolito's driver reached the hospital in Pulaya, the old man died. Dom Hipolito paid the family for funeral expenses and compensation. They received one thousand *cobas.* Everyone on the *fazenda* talked about Dom Hipolito's generosity."

Levin glanced past Serge over the road's edge and saw below the great fields of cane, richly green in the lowering sun as the tops danced like whitecaps. Their loveliness beguiled him. The workers were now invisible.

"How long till they turn their machetes on him?"

"They do not have the mentality. And the guerrillas do not know how to reach them. Dom Hipolito has hurt the A. of L. with these Cavaleiros—believe it. But the other one—Captain Bugan—he is doing the most harm."

"How?"

"This girl has no information to give. She is probably a cultural worker. The Cavaleiros are cutthroats, not intelligence gatherers. But the military—they have infiltrated into the mountains. They have these so-called deep-penetration agents—elite guys, Bugan trains them, who go as guerrillas. And they are bringing chaos. No one knows who to trust up there. Some of Fra Boboy's units are eating themselves up like sharks."

Levin's heart pounded. Through his boozy screen, he was trying to keep the jeep and the Mercedes in view around the curves. "So they really are getting close to him."

Serge confirmed it with silence.

"So things are going worse than the guerrillas say."

"It is dangerous up there. A cornered snake is very dangerous."

"Well, it's pretty academic to me. No such dangers on the southern coast."

"Just take care in Pulaya," Serge told him. "Captain Bugan is interested in you. That jeep was the one behind Las Encantadas."

By now Levin felt stunned but not sobered, as if he'd been jabbed by a dental instrument in an anesthetized place on his gum. The pain would come later, but the knowledge now was almost like the pain.

As he watched the electrical lines, shaggy with creepers above the roadside, Levin had a flash of Colonel Siriman's nod under the camera lights. He didn't try to summon the clarity to understand why this should come to him now.

"Too bad you're going to the coast," Serge was saying. "This is where the story is. You've found it. Anyone else would get away, but to a journalist it would be like good luck."

"It doesn't seem to matter whether one's a journalist. One hardly feels like a journalist."

"There are still distinctions. But you have to be flexible."

Levin nodded, without knowing what Serge meant. "What do you think's going to happen to that girl?"

"The guerrilla there?" Serge touched Levin's hand on the wheel. "It's better not to know every answer. In our work we have to keep our spirits up."

Levin wondered how Serge achieved this, and he badly wanted to ask. At the moment, it seemed an extraordinary feat of juggling, courage, willful blindness—or some precious fluid that was draining out of himself.

"It's like this at first for every Joe who comes down here," Serge said sympathetically. "Don't worry, this club where we're going will cheer you up. You have never seen such girls, my friend. Ding Magkakanaw will envy you."

But Ding was already there, sitting with some boisterous locals and the couple from the hotel pool. And he was already drunker than Levin.

CHAPTER VI

The Casa Amor went by the slogan "Where every man is king." This was painted in gold-leaf script under the hot pink neon sign, already lit above the door outside, and again inside on a placard behind the bar. In the flash of white strobe lights from the ceiling, pink and gold stained the entire club—the colors of the floor tiles, the spray-painted tables and chairs, the uniforms of waitresses and bartenders, the costumes of dancers. Pink and gold limelight showered the platform where the dancers performed. Gold was for wealth, pink for the secret inmost heart of love.

Dom Hipolito's taste ran to colonial soap-dreams. The dance stage was framed by a trellis of latticework on which hung an artificial bougainvillea vine. In the middle of the stage a metal lolly column that supported an I beam in the ceiling was dressed up as a fluted Doric shaft. On either side of the floor, an arcade of plywood arches and gleaming plastic columns bounced from the front of the room to the back, walling off lavatories and offices. And hanging behind the stage, a pink Christ was nailed to a cross of gold—mortified, it seemed, by the view.

This decor only partially offset what brought in the business—the bathing suits that crawled well up the girls' hips, and the music, one throbbing American disco number after another.

It was early; more than half the tables were empty. Johnny Ochoa had joined two men in sport shirts and Hush Puppies near the stage. Dom Hipolito had disappeared. The long table where Ding and his companions were drinking ran perpendicular to the stage halfway back. Besides the waitresses and dancers, there were only three women in the room: near the back two bejeweled, bored Saraunese going to fat and the white woman in Ding's group.

When Levin pulled up a chair Ding said to the others, "This is the guy I'm talking about."

Ding's companions looked at Levin.

"Hello, Ding," Levin said. "So you decided to go out."

"Where were you?"

"Just snooping around."

"Snooping?" From across the table, Ding looked askance. Drink had unfocused and inflamed his eyes. He turned from Levin to the others. "You see?"

"Sure." Levin allowed himself to be on display. "That's our business, isn't it, Ding?"

"It's not mine."

Serge materialized behind Ding. "We went out to the proprietor's fifteen hundred hectares," he said, "where we learned many interesting facts." He put a hand on Ding's shoulder. "You remember me?" Ding turned his gaze on Serge, cried out and embraced him, spouting a stream of hearty nationalistic Saraunese. Serge looked uncomfortable.

Of the three other Saraunese at the table, two wore photographer's vests like Serge's. They were reporters on the *Pulaya Standard* whom Ding had found at their office. One was an unusually big Saraunese named Siolao, whose smile revealed a gold front tooth; the other brooded and before long was asleep. The third man, named Lubis, spoke poor English and laughed at everything the others said. Possibly he was an imbecile.

The white couple, as Levin suspected, were not German but the Dutch Dom Hipolito had mentioned. They alone weren't smoking and they alone were still sober. Erich Veeder had a mossy reddish beard and the hollow-eyed exhaustion of a northern European new to the tropics. His wife, Renée, was either much younger or much older, for her skin had taken the sun better. In the blinking strobe she looked alternately glowing and preserved in bronze.

Seated, Levin addressed himself to Veeder. "What's your excuse?"

The Dutchman was confused, and he allowed himself to seem scandalized. "Please, my excuse for what?"

"Being here. *In partibus infidelium.*" Veeder and his wife exchanged a glance. "You disapprove of me?"

"My friend, I have no opinion of you."

"You look like tourists." Veeder's sallow face tightened with displeasure. "No, forgive me. That isn't fair. It's just that—you know, I haven't seen a white face in twenty-four hours. One forgets how to be."

"Of course," said Renée, with only a nuance of sarcasm. "We too forget."

"Let me buy you good people a drink."

Veeder was already full of mistrust for Levin. "No thank you. I'm having only soda water—the heat, you know."

"I absolutely insist. You don't refuse a drink in this country. I bet I've been here longer than you."

Over the Veeders' objections Levin ordered a round of beers for the table. From the Saraunese end rose smoke and hilarity.

"Sobriety," he told the Dutch couple, lowering his voice, "can be taken as an affront here. You don't want to be pissing anyone off."

"I think that is your interpretation," Erich Veeder said.

"I didn't say it was anyone else's."

"Maybe," Renée said, "you are looking through American eyes. For us, we never have problems when we drink with Saraunese."

The beers arrived and Levin raised his glass.

"To harmony in mixed drinking."

He struggled in his pocket among the pack of bills he'd stowed there, and came up with the wrong currency, then *cobas* in too high denominations. What he laid on the waitress's tray amounted to a staggering tip. She giggled and leaned down to kiss his cheek, automatically—not even a real kiss, just a brush of the lips and a click in the back of her throat. She left an overpowering smell of perfume on his face.

From the end of the table, Siolao, the gold-toothed journalist, raised his glass to Levin. "You've made a friend, sir."

Lubis broke into staccato laughter.

"Ah, well, friends . . . you never know about them."

"To friendship," Siolao insisted, and everyone's glass was raised. Ding was now drinking with both hands. Levin thirsted down half his beer at one swallow. Siolao said, "You are a journalist."

"Yes indeed."

"American."

Levin nodded; he saw no reason to deny it.

"Good."

"Really?"

"Of course. It is better for your people to be informed than not informed."

"I agree. That's what I'm here for."

Siolao saluted with his glass.

"What do you think of our beer?"

"The best. Ours is just piss by comparison."

"And our women?"

"Well . . . it's unfair to generalize. I'd say for the most part they're very kind and charming."

"Would you marry one?" Siolao was smiling pleasantly. Levin decided it was all in fun.

"In theory. There would be no objection in principle."

"But in practice?"

"In practice . . . cultural differences, you know. There could be misunderstandings."

"Betrayal?"

Levin had meant nothing so strong, and he shrugged.

"So many foreigners here are not sincere. And we Saraunese are very open to them." Siolao lifted his chin and pointed. "But you, I think, are sincere."

Levin put up his hands. "That's up to you. I've got some clippings back in my hotel room. You can read them if you want."

"No, don't worry. We can read your character."

Levin smiled and signed off from the exchange. It wasn't auspicious that his character had become a subject of discussion, and in the very bonhomie of the table he felt a possibility of things turning bad. So he waited for the Dutchman to lose interest in Ding's mumblings, then caught his blue eye.

"No kidding," he asked, "what are you doing in Pulaya?"

Renée answered. "We are working on appropriate technology. To study the practicality of a cooperative among the workers, using the sugar waste to produce ethanol. Also to encourage them in foods production, growing macrobiotic foods with natural fertilizer."

For a moment the complexity of this left Levin speechless.

"You approve?" Veeder asked ironically.

"I don't think that matters."

Among the others a conversation had begun in Saraunese. Ding scowled and snapped in his cups.

"We came to Pulaya yesterday only," Renée said. "To Direv Saraun three weeks ago."

"And you're staying at Las Encantadas. Who sent you?"

The question affronted Veeder, and he answered in his scandalized Pays-Bas voice. "We are with the World Council of Churches."

"Missionaries."

"No," Veeder said, "not missionaries."

"Just a minute. I studied this stuff and they were a tougher bunch than us. Anyway, missionaries have a pretty good track record here, not like the Philippines or Timor. They never got very far—hard to get any work done here. Generally they were well received."

"We have a big difference from the missionaries," Veeder said.

"They came with their ideas to impose on the population," Renée told Levin. "But we come to listen only and to help. It is the people knows best their wishes."

"And the people wishes cooperatives," Levin said. "And ethanol, and macrobiotics."

Veeder nodded tightly. The head of his beer was undisturbed.

"This is what you've picked up in your three weeks?"

"What you see in the plantation structure," Veeder explained wearily, "is the result of many years of landlord-sponsored division. It is every man for himself under this structure, which accounts for the failure of government-run cooperatives."

Renée added, "To make work the cooperatives it is necessary to interface the workers with the traditions of their village life, which they have lost. Such as diet. The wage worker docs not notice the phases of the moon. He has lost his soul."

"The traditions of the Saraunese people," Veeder finished for her, "is caring and nurturing. Not killing. This the landlords have destroyed. Our project is founded in social structures that are many centuries older than your country, for example. The American way of life is a violent aberration here. Their authentic life is much closer to socialism."

On the last word the disco medley ended. The Saraunese journalists had heard and they looked across the table. Levin leaned over his glass toward the Dutch couple. In a series of wire photos he was imagining unspeakable deaths for Erich Veeder—the blond head sawn off where the beard ended, the body recycled into ethanol. His face flushed, but he let the images linger.

"May I offer a bit of paranoid Yankee advice? Keep such thoughts closer to your chest."

"There is nothing the matter if—"

"Don't be a fucking sentimental idiot. If you want my opinion, go back to São Sebastião tomorrow," Levin said. "You've already been noticed."

Beneath her desiccated tan Renée Veeder colored, and she glanced at her husband. Veeder took his first sip from the beer and shrugged.

"I don't mean to scare you folks." Levin was smiling. "But in their traditions, our type has been known to get knocked off now and then. Just yesterday . . ."

He reached across the table and drew a line across Veeder's throat. Veeder pulled away, then carefully licked foam from his mustache and put his glass down.

"We are not your type."

The girls in swimsuits cleared the stage. A P.A. system announced that the floor show was about to start, and the strobe lights went out. A happy murmur rippled across the tables. Siolao ordered another round of drinks on the tab. He asked Levin and the Veeders if they had had the opportunity to enjoy Saraunese nightlife.

"It is interesting. As interesting as our politics."

"We are not here for nightlife," Renée said, and her husband seconded her with a nod over his glass of beer, which was beginning to occupy him.

"In our situation," Siolao told them wanly, "you find amusement where you can."

Dom Hipolito had reappeared in one of the deep wicker sofa-booths by the arcade, wearing a linen jacket and a pair of leather gloves, smoking one of his natural-leaf cigars. People from nearby tables came over to greet him, shake hands, indulge in exaggerated laughter. When he sat back in the shadow of the booth, nothing could be seen of him but his designer jeans and Italian shoes and the gloved hand holding the cigar.

Sound filled the room again, a lovelorn a cappella female voice:

> "Once upon a time I was falling in love
> Now I'm only falling apart
> Nothing I can do
> A total eclipse of the heart"

The instruments cued a showgirl from backstage. She danced on lip-synching with the verve and grin of a performer paid specialty fees. Bathed in pink and gold lights, she looked no older than twenty. She wore a miniskirt and sweat jacket, and under makeup she was perspiring on her upper lip, where there was a mole. Her face was what Levin thought of as singularly Saraunese, dark, hollow-cheeked, pretty, obscure, without Chinese or Iberian reference points. Lipstick and rouge and mascara only deepened the impression.

She climbed the trellis (metal, it turned out) and dangled by her hands and knees. Her hair dropped, her neck arched, and she gazed upside down at the tables, trying to form a cleavage with her upper arms. Unquestionably, she was looking straight at Levin and smiling. He joined in the scattered applause. She suspended herself by her arms and fell to the floor in an imperfect split. Springing to her feet, she seized the column and wrapped herself around it. As the song rose toward a climax of self-pity she whirled about the pole with her black hair flying, her skirt ballooning out, her face flashing by in a grin of astonishing calm.

The unaccompanied voice returned. She spun away from the pole, collapsed to her knees at the edge of the platform, clutched her breasts in her hands, and mouthed the despairing words of the final chorus with such fervor that the audience actually leaned forward to hear. She hurried off amid claps and cheers.

"That was brilliant," Levin said.

"Wait," Serge told him, "the next act is better."

"She's very innocent, in a way." The showgirl had put him in mind of the young woman at Dom Hipolito's house. "Charmingly vulnerable."

Ding turned from the stage. "You like her?"

"Do you?"

"She's dancing for you, boss, not me."

"Ah. So you share the moral response of our Dutch friends."

Ding's face dropped like a fighter dropping his hands into fists. "I hate that word. It smells American."

Serge said something mollifying in Saraunese but Ding shook him off.

"In São Sebastião they start at ten, eleven years. That's the taste of our visitors. The girls get hooked on smack to face the fucking.

Then they fuck for their smack. You heard about the one last month up in Porto de Coral—fourteen-year-old died when a vibrator snapped off inside her?" Renée exclaimed in Dutch. "That's my hometown and people are saying it was a sex tourist that did it. The family's trying to find him and sue him for everything he has."

Sections of the press had focused speculation on Bowers, the American who had recently disappeared in the mountains. Levin was wondering about Rick.

Veeder said, "And I have heard that the Americans buy brides from the peasant families by post."

"Oh, wise up," Levin told him. "Saraunese prey on suckers like you."

Siolao said, "To me it's understandable. We have a Saraunese saying that sex is like puppets, better when you believe there are no strings. A foreign girl, a Saraunese—one string is gone. A whore— another. A child—and now you are really free."

In his flat, amiable way Serge told the group a story.

"An Englishman once corresponded with a Saraunese girl from the catalog for many months. Half his age. She was virgin, she had finished secondary school, she cooked chicken and sewed and liked children, a member of the São Sebastião Beautification Society. As for her picture—well. So he decided to marry her. He arrived at the airport and she was there to meet him—and she was more beautiful than his dreams. They took a taxi directly to the Pacifica. You can imagine the passion in this guy, after so long. In the room she said she would take a shower first, because of the humidity. She was shy—she told him to wait outside. But this guy was on fire and he spied on her from the door. When she came out of the shower, he was the one to have a big surprise—because his beautiful future bride was a boy."

Siolao and Lubis laughed at once, as if they'd already known the end.

Levin said, "What a shock."

"The way I heard it," Ding said, "the guy was American."

The second act was starting and everyone retreated to his beer.

This time it was a reggae number, the sweet rhythm mounting lazily through the rise and fall of an organ. The same showgirl came out, with another girl and a young man. Fairly soon the girls had shed their sweat jackets; underneath, they wore black lace bras. The

young man was in characteristic Saraunese stonewashed jeans and
T-shirt, but he had built his muscles to an unusual bulk, and when
the showgirls stripped his shirt off and he posed and flexed, there
were gasps of appreciation across the floor. The three performers
swayed their hips lasciviously to the Caribbean beat. Then, with a
single motion, the man seized the girls' skirts and tore them away.
In panties they sandwiched him, grinding him front and back; he
wheeled around and they were reversed. He looked at the audience
and shrugged: the embarrassment of riches.

"Yah, mon!" somebody called out in high Asian mimicry.

The number ended with the young man doing pull-ups from the
trellis and the girls beneath, bra straps off their shoulders, stroking
the length of his thighs to the V of his crotch.

Lusty applause trailed them offstage, tinged with anticipation.

The journalists ordered another bottle of Rum Direv.

Meanwhile, Dom Hipolito, leaning back in shadow, had been
joined by two of the dancers in swimsuits. Levin watched as they
perched on either knee, sipping colorful drinks through straws, and
stared out at the crowd with bland contentment. When Dom
Hipolito's gloved hand slipped under the arm of one, lifted the tight
nylon, and disappeared over the roundness of her breast, rolling it
under his palm, her expression didn't change. His other hand was
splayed across the second dancer's thigh. Levin could see him turn
his wrist and plant his fingers against the material between her legs.
She looked down and closed her eyes and sipped her drink. Impatiently, he wrested aside the swimsuit and then his glove was buried
deep between her thighs, working hard against the resistance of
clothing and position until it found what it was after and relaxed into
gentle digging, his arm pulsing along her thigh like a snake. She
leaned her head on his shoulder, sipping hard.

Levin found himself unable not to look. Just as he'd read Melanie's
journal—a guilty fascination. And why not look? This was the way
of things. Why should it be up to him to judge?

Renée Veeder stood up.

"I am going to the hotel."

Her husband said he would accompany her, but she insisted that
he stay. It was only a short walk, after all.

"It is not a place for ladies," Serge murmured when she had gone.

"Or for gentleman," said Erich Veeder, but he accepted a glass of rum.

"Every man in this room wants to be Dom Hipolito," Siolao said, "don't you think?"

"No. I don't think."

Levin clinked Veeder's glass. "You're a man of moral courage."

Ding muttered, "I'm telling you I don't like that word, boss."

"Yeah, I heard you."

"I don't like the company it hangs with. You look up and they're gone and that's when the real evil shit is about to go."

"You're absolutely right. We should just get out of places like this. Then you wouldn't have any excuses for fucking up."

Ding uttered a Saraunese word that Levin didn't know, and Lubis whooped. Serge and Siolao put their hands on Ding's arm and whispered to him, but he said, "Don't tell me to take it easy. This Joe's been running me around since São Sebastião."

"Settle your differences," Siolao told Levin. "You cannot work like this."

"You tell him that. As far as I'm concerned we don't have any."

Prodded, Ding spoke rapidly to the others in Saraunese. Veeder was looking at Levin coldly, and Levin met him with a drunken glare. By the arcade one of the dancers was gone from Dom Hipolito's booth and the other was rising and sinking on his knee.

Siolao turned to Levin. "You suspect him with your girlfriend?"

"He said that?" Now Ding wouldn't look at Levin. "You're crazier than I thought."

"Who's crazy? The chick was coming on to me," Ding told the others. "Is that my fault? And the guy just sits and watches."

Levin's cheeks burned and he waved angrily. "She doesn't have anything to do with what's between us, Ding."

"Then why don't you pay me fair? Why did you give them my name at Camp Pereira? Why did you go out today when I told you not to?"

"You know the answer to all of those."

"I know shit."

"What is it about fair pay?" Veeder wanted to know. "Why don't you pay this man fair?"

Levin spent his animus on the Calvinist revolutionary. "Shut up, Veeder. Shut the fuck up. He ought to be paying me. This guy's been draining my pocket."

In an instant Ding was on his feet. He plunged his hands into his pockets and turned them inside out. He shouted for anyone to search him for money, and then he took a step toward Levin's chair. Lubis egged him on, but before Ding could get his fists up Serge and Siolao had risen to hold him back.

"Why did you say that?" Siolao was easing Ding back into his seat, Serge talked him down in Saraunese. "An American should not say that to any Saraunese ever."

Levin agreed. "I apologize." He swallowed the last of his rum and looked up for the waitress, but she was not to be found.

"Some things are too strong for apologies."

"In that case I withdraw it."

"In Saraunese we say it is *impang kurat*, the badness in the heart." Siolao tapped his chest. "It doesn't go away."

"Impang kurat," Lubis repeated for Levin's benefit.

"I know the expression." It was roughly the opposite of *piki lan kurat;* it carried the same taste of abject permanence.

"You know the words, but not the feeling." Siolao shook his head. "You seemed sincere to me."

"Don't set guys up and they won't let you down."

"The only thing you can do is try to lift the humiliation from him."

"Debase myself?"

"Debase yourself," Lubis said.

"Sorry. You won't have that pleasure this evening."

Across the table Ding had settled into a black sulk. By now the third and final act was under way.

The showgirls started where they had left off. This time it was their bras that quickly found the floor. They had danced on with transparent black scarves over their heads, incongruous modesty, and now they used them with considerable skill, whirling and fluttering, to veil and half reveal the brown nipples of their small breasts. They stripped the young man to his jockstrap and then the three pantomimed a scene to the skittish, keyed-up beat of "Dancing in the Dark."

The man begged first one and then the other to dance with him. Coquettes, they refused behind their veils, mocking his pleas, affording only glimpses. He disappeared offstage, and when he came back he had a whip. Then he chased them down, cracking the whip in half-time to the drums, and when he cornered each girl she fell at his feet and hugged his ankles. As he let the whip hang limp she crawled up his sculpted body like the artificial vine on the trellis overhead, pocking him with kisses. He tossed the whip aside, but by now the girls had grown enamored of it. They forced it back on him and threw away their veils, finally giving their breasts full view, and in the song's fading bars they stood facing the trellis with their hands against the metal latticework and threw their heads back dreamily to the snap of leather.

This number drew loud and sustained applause.

The showgirls skipped off the platform and circulated among the tables. The second showgirl ended up in Johnny Ochoa's paternal lap. Dom Hipolito had stood up in the wicker booth and at a word from him the first showgirl, the acrobat of the opening number, came over. With a hand on her shoulder he spoke to her and then disappeared behind the plywood arcade. Stopping here and there for tips, the showgirl began making an indirect course toward the table of journalists. Again her eyes met Levin's: it seemed accidental, but their blackness, so frank and so opaque, spoke of availability, and this time her eyebrows posed an unmistakable question. Levin had the poise to acknowledge it, and she smiled and gave him a wink. He blushed to his scalp. Saliva filled his mouth and he swallowed.

The disco medley was pounding away again, signaling the end of Casa Amor's afternoon show. A few customers were getting up to leave. Johnny Ochoa was laughing at the pleas of the showgirl in his lap.

Erich Veeder cleared his throat. "Poverty is very degrading, I think."

Siolao began a long slow laugh, a silent shaking of the shoulders that turned into a chuckle at the back of his throat.

"You miss the point of this thing. Did you never sleep with a prostitute? In Holland?"

Taken aback, Veeder quickly shook his head.

"What about you?" Siolao was speaking to Levin. "Never?" Levin didn't answer for a time. Finally he said that he hadn't. Lubis was amused to the point of outrage, as if they'd confessed to virginity.

The showgirl reached their table. Her black panties were bulky with *cobas*. She smelled of sweat from her efforts and the blue around her eyes was smeared.

The sudden presence of a half-naked girl sent a jolt of electricity across the table. The men stirred and sat up in their chairs. Even the reporter who'd been sleeping roused himself, as if he'd scented her arrival.

Beneath her makeup she looked even younger. She was chunkier than most southerners, high-hipped, but very brown. Her body was a peasant's, compact and firm. Offstage, among clothed men, it had tensed a little. She moved past the whites to Siolao, Serge, and Lubis, whom she greeted in Saraunese. Serge tucked a few bills inside her underpants and complimented her talent. Flattered, the girl thanked him.

As she moved around the table, Siolao edified the white visitors.

"We know the economics," he said, "better than you. The pressures, the reasons, the results. All of that. But don't judge us so easy. There's some kind of beauty in this thing too—maybe you don't see it. In your culture, it's shameful. But for the right man, this girl would—hmm. Some things are too sacred to say. But once the economics is arranged, she is *yours*. She'll give and give. Anything. If you don't know, that is a beautiful thing to see, and without the paying it cannot happen. Cannot."

She was above Ding now. But Ding's head was clutched in his hands and he didn't move. She passed on.

"A woman whose name you don't even know but she wants all your wants? If you've never known it, try to imagine this kind of happiness. Don't make your wishes clear and she's insulted. Ask about her unhappy childhood and she laughs at you. It is really a beautiful incredible thing. You love the money in your pocket for making it happen. It's sacred too—the money. If you're hard up, in a hole, like this guy—"

Here Siolao indicated Lubis, who was pretending to swipe a bill out of the girl's waist. She slapped his hand and let out a playful yelp.

"—you cannot guess how much you hate yourself. He won't tell us, because he is ashamed, but right now he is calling himself some terrible names. In fact, he's wishing he is your color."

The girl had reached the white men. She laid her hand on Veeder's bony shoulder. "Hello, Joe."

Overwhelmed, Veeder looked at his hands.

"Don't think this guy hates you," Siolao went on, pointing at Lubis again. "Maybe he hates you a little. But really he understands that the white guy is going to win every time because he has the biggest pocket. Every Saraunese knows that. What he wants is to change places with you—so how can he really permit himself to hate *you*? He keeps it for himself."

The girl was rubbing Veeder's neck. His whole face was strained to translucence and in his forehead the blue veins bulged. He glanced up and smiled painfully. "No thank you."

Lubis found this extremely funny. He raised his index finger and flicked it rigidly. "Saraunese cock," he said. Then he took a soiled handkerchief from his pocket and twirled it round itself and waved it limply. "White cock."

Siolao was suddenly angry. "You think we'll curse you if you take her? White *kolau* imperialism? You underestimate our sense of self-respect. We'll curse you if you don't."

She left the motionless Dutchman and came to Levin's side. Ding had lifted his head.

"Hello, Joe."

Ding said, "Jackpot."

She sat on Levin's knee and carelessly let her hand brush his crotch. Her effrontery got an answer. Encouraged, with her other hand she stroked the bristled back of his neck. She pressed herself clumsily against his shoulder. "You like me?"

Levin looked at the Saraunese men across the table.

"She's yours," Siolao informed him.

Ding said, "Take up the White Man's Burden."

Sweat broke on Levin's forehead. He was breathing with difficulty, in the smoke, constrained by too much drink, with her half-naked body and her smell on him. In his temple blood beat like a piston puddled in oil. He looked at his watch: just before six. The hookup was set for seven-thirty. He tried to will himself into sobriety and made some rapid calculations.

"Well, it seems like a cultural duty," he said. "I don't want to let down our side." Somehow the girl understood, for he felt her weight lighten. Then he was brought up short. "How much?"

"Discuss with her later," Siolao said with a businesslike wave.

"Up to you." Ding had locked his rum-poisoned eyes on Levin's.

Levin stood; the girl's hand was in his. "You pay bar fine?" she asked him.

"Ah. There's always a catch with you people."

The girl disappeared to change. For an employee to be released from her official duties, Dom Hipolito's establishment charged a customer two hundred *cobas*. As he reached in his pocket Levin recalled the fury with which Ding had turned out his own. For now he felt immune to it. Ding was holding his head in his hands again; Veeder alone was watching Levin with disgust—and Veeder mattered least of all.

In a few minutes the girl came back, wearing a denim dress with a bib. Levin gave the bar fine to the waitress, who showed him the afternoon's tab. It wasn't possible to know how many of the drinks in the three-page list belonged to Ding, nor was it possible under the circumstances to ask. He dug for more money; he seemed to be carrying innumerable bills, and at the same time the sensation swept over him that his money was no longer under his control. He hurried to settle, didn't wait for change, and had already led the girl to the door by the time Ding called after him to be quick at it.

Her English hardly existed but Levin made it known that he wanted both of them to shower. Horniness made him clumsy with his buttons, his laces, the soap. In the stall his whole sudsy body was melting slackly under the hot spray except for two furious heartbeats, in his chest and below. His hands could not stay off her, but it was the burning in his belly and thighs more than the swells and rubbery tautness of her skin that thrilled him. The taste was entirely within. A head lower, her face was vague in the rising steam—the mole over her lip, the dun eyes. When she refused his soapy hand between her legs, a blue flame of anger leaped in him, and for the first time he felt afraid.

He gave her the towel and told her to dry him. In the quick rough motions of her hands he saw the village girl at her chores, washing clothes or a baby brother. Her immodesty was a peasant's, not a geisha's.

"You like this job?" he asked, and from where she was kneeling, rubbing his calves, she glanced up and shook her head once firmly.

Then she knew what was happening to her? He wondered what had made him think she didn't. And how to set in motion a process by which an exception would be made for him.

They went into the bedroom. She took up his pile of clothes from the floor, folded them, and set them on a chair by the bathroom door.

"Does Dom Hipolito mistreat the girls at Casa Amor? Take advantage, cheat them?"

She smiled. "Dom Hipolito say you his friend, I treat you nice."

"I'm not his friend. Not at all." They were sitting on the bed, naked strangers side by side. "Your family are farmers?"

She didn't get it.

"When you come to Pulaya?"

"I born Pulaya."

It was a lie, Levin knew. And he gave up the effort and closed his heart to pity and imagination. They had no business here.

The girl—Baby, she'd told him, and he was glad for the falsehood, felt freed by it—tried twice to switch off the light but he turned it back on and she had to relent. He wanted her face, her eyes. Ding had left the air conditioner running and they huddled for a few moments under the corduroy bedspread against the chill.

He was thinking: I'm not going to be first. She has to move, she has to come for it.

But—his, entirely—she didn't move. Anger ran out to his fingertips, where lust teased him, and he lumbered on top and opened her like the parted flaps of the pula-pula. "You like it?" he said and she didn't answer. He told her to hold still, and then he rolled her on top of him, then pulled her underneath again. She complied with everything and yet she stayed free of him.

"What you want?" Baby asked.

To obliterate the beating of this third heart. But first you have to laugh, moan, cry.

It was the goat voice talking.

He stared down into her black pupils and saw reflected light, his own shadowed face. The eyes that had offered everything in the club now gave him nothing. He shut his own, for without his will it had begun to happen. The inflammation he'd become as she lay inert reddened and ripened and he was lost, lashed by it, gave himself up with a torn sob and clutched her as his arms shook. She had escaped him; he'd never had her. His shouts came without benefit of tears—the clotted heart below burst loose its veins but the one above, pulled hard, tightened to a small unyielding knot and he knew in the moment before release the dreadful emptiness that awaited him the instant after.

It was as though she'd tricked him. And Siolao, and Ding. All of them.

While he was still quivering the girl pushed him off and went into the bathroom. He heard the water running.

Levin tried to lie still but fear was stopping his lungs. His fingers found his wrist. The heart was there now, crouched like a gecko, pulsing monstrously.

He counted a hundred a minute. Every thought was turning dull and ugly. He looked for comfort to his innermost self, the silver gleam at his depth, and it was like looking for the point in the center of her eyes that looked back. Nothing. It was painted over black. He stared down too long and became afraid and shrank away.

His eyes searched the room. The remains of Ding's meal sat on the writing table. On the table next to the bed, there was the Bible. An address label was pasted on the back cover: Pacific Palisades, Calif. It was a trashy illustrated version, shipped out in bulk to desperate souls all over the iron-roofed world, who'd taught themselves enough English to be kept in a state of hope by the good news from the Global Fellowship of Christ.

Nonetheless, its solidity calmed him a little. He skimmed the onionskin pages and paused over the pictures, smiling for an instant outside himself at the thought of reaching for this book at this moment. Something in it had been playing over his thoughts. Not Jonah, Feliz's Jonah, but something in Genesis that Jonah had put him in mind of. Genesis sprang from simpler, hardier stock, before Jonah's Hebrew melancholy, the fatal self-consciousness, appeared.

It was the story of Jacob and the Angel of God. In a lonely place the Angel jumped Jacob and wrestled him till dawn. But he couldn't throw Jacob, though he managed to dislocate his thigh. Two figures grappled on the banks of the Jabbok, casting shadows on the desert floor in the blue-black moonlight. Jacob, who had thought he was all alone out there, caught completely by surprise. Where did the stranger come from? Why did he want a fight? "You have striven with God and with men," the Angel told him, "and have prevailed." And Jacob got God's blessing, though he never learned the stranger's name.

The moment came, Jacob acted and was rewarded. To those who become nothing—nothing is given.

Levin set the book down on the table. He touched his own thigh, where the old mosquito bite above the knee had been infected. It was hardening into crimson tissue.

He was, as Serge had said, alone, without allies. He couldn't even count himself.

He thought of Melanie, her cool body, her bright voice. She loved him—she'd said it a thousand times and it was such a simple thing that not once had he considered what it could mean for him. Whenever he echoed her words he heard himself from outside, as if on tape. Flushed with shame, he thought: When did I stop knowing how?

Someone knocked on the door.

Levin drew a breath and sat up. The knocking came again, insistent.

"All right, all right."

He went to the door wrapped in a sheet and opened it to find Ding standing in the doorway with his arms folded. He was grateful that Ding didn't look at him.

"Seven-fifteen," Ding said.

"O.K. Give me five minutes."

The girl had come out of the bathroom dressed and she was picking up his trousers from the chair where she'd laid them.

"Hey," he said. "I'll get those."

There was no time to wash, though he was wet and matted and badly wanted a scrub. His nakedness now embarrassed him and he hustled on his trousers. Baby sat beside him on the bed while he buttoned his shirt and she tickled the back of his neck until he told her to stop.

There remained the question of her payment. He thought that two hundred *cobas,* equal to the bar fine, would be enough—certainly in a provincial town. He figured in a 15 percent tip. He told her that if he could have it his way the whole 430 *cobas* would go to her, that the bar fine was a bit of bondage, really, and that he hated for her labors to line Dom Hipolito's pocket—but there it was. He didn't know if she understood what he was saying. She seemed disappointed with the amount he gave her. She looked from the money to him and opened her mouth to say something, and then she closed it. There was really nothing she could do. Somehow things had worked out so that he was the boss of his own money again and he would try to keep it that way.

They passed Ding in the hall. He and the girl exchanged a word in Saraunese. Levin was fairly certain it was only good evening.

In the lobby of Las Encantadas, Serge was waiting. He greeted Levin heartily and patted the girl on the bottom as she left to go back to work. Then he asked Levin to come out by the pool.

"I'll meet you in a minute," Levin told him, and he set down his bag.

The concierge behind the desk was on the phone again. Levin motioned that he wanted to use it.

"Could you put a call through to São Sebastião?"

"Certainly, Mr. Levin. In a moment."

"Look, it's important."

"Very well, Mr. Levin. Please write the number."

He wrote down his own. The concierge called the operator and spoke in Saraunese. After a pause, she handed the phone to Levin.

It had become essential to hear Melanie's voice. He found himself desperate for a word from her to take up the mountain. Instead, he had to wait through an interminable ringing and then listen to the sound of himself on the tape. There was nobody home. He'd so completely expected to hear her that he panicked. About to leave a message, at the beep he lost faith in his ability to say anything reassuring and hung up.

"Try again later," the concierge suggested.

"No phones where I'm going."

He caught himself but it was too late. He looked at the young woman. She was smiling; she seemed neither curious nor surprised. Levin tried to understand what this meant but he had no energy for the effort.

"Come back to see us soon, Mr. Levin."

"I hope not," he muttered on his way out. He was fighting a downward crush on his spirit. If the concierge hadn't been there he might have called back and had the answering machine ask Melanie how she could be gone in his moment of extremity. He felt as though, drowning, he'd grasped a line and found that no one held the other end.

It was long past sunset, and the floodlights were on around the pool and at its bottom. Serge's polo shirt swam aquamarine. Levin crouched with him by the edge, and reflexively each put a hand in the water. It was deliciously warm, limpid, clearer than anything could naturally be in Direv Saraun. Behind the pool a lawn spread out to a stone wall that was smothered by jacaranda trees; a few violet blossoms floated in the water.

Levin said, "It's not so humid at night as São Sebastião."

Serge nodded at the shoulder bag. "Leaving already?"

"We decided to drive to the coast tonight."

Levin's hand lapped at the water.

"Take care on the road," Serge said.

"Of course. The trickiest part's still ahead."

Except for the sound of water there was absolute silence in the yard. Serge was smiling.

"You know where we're going, don't you?"

Serge nodded and looked serious.

"How?" It came to him. "Feliz told you."

Serge shook his head. "Magkakanaw told us, after you left." Levin started to protest. "But I knew before that from what you were saying. You didn't sound like a man who is going to the beach."

They both murmured laughter.

"You're a better journalist than me, Serge. I mean that."

Serge brushed it off and splashed a palmful of water to his forehead. "Did you know he was planning to stay up there after you leave?"

"Ding? He said that?"

"He was very drunk and careless."

"Christ—no wonder he's such a raw nerve."

"He was very boastful with us. He wants to take pictures of them for a book—pro-people pictures. If they will have him. I don't know if they will have him or not."

Levin looked at their shadows on the bottom of the pool. He saw Ding as he imagined Ding saw himself, a romantic outcast getting closer to the face of the revolution than anyone else in order to help the revolution win. In this picture there was excitement and self-deception and dangers that were probably no more real to Ding than to him. Ding's recklessness was beyond anything he'd prepared for.

"I sometimes asked myself if I was traveling with one of them."

"He doesn't trust you."

"That I know."

"Listen," Serge said, and Levin was moved to look at him. "He told us you were not who you say you are."

In his mild face, lit by the pool, Serge's eyes gleamed.

"What does that mean?"

"Perhaps . . . you are working for your government."

"As—"

Serge shrugged. "Information gathering."

"A spy. A spook. Is that it?" Levin's mouth tightened. He was suddenly dizzy in his crouch and put a hand to the smooth concrete. "I guess it doesn't matter if I say he's wrong. Once you're called that it sticks. I've seen it happen."

"I don't tell you this to find out if it's true."

"Then why?"

"Watch out what you say. Under these circumstances your position in the mountains will be delicate. Think about what Dom Hipolito told us could happen any day."

The shadows swam vaguely at the bottom of the pool. Levin leaned back to remove his.

"You think I shouldn't go?"

"How can I answer that? I only warn you to be careful if you go."

Serge rose and Levin stood with him. Through the glass doors he saw Ding coming downstairs with his bag.

"I'm sure we will meet."

Serge was already shaking hands and turning to leave.

"Serge—" The Saraunese stopped and cocked his head politely. "You have to believe me. It's very important to me that you do."

Serge smiled and winked. Tonight everyone was winking at Levin. And now that he was losing Serge, his loneliness grew deeper. Yet this man who made such a specialty of delicate positions was no sharer. He knew, and knew more, and kept himself back. It was a way Levin had once thought himself to be.

Ding was watching through the doors as they returned.

"What do you think we'll find up there?" Levin asked.

"I think," said the other journalist, "you will find a hell of a story."

CHAPTER VII

Everything happened quickly, in just the way Connie had described. They drove several blocks away from the town center, and as they passed behind the hotel Levin was relieved to see that Captain Bugan's jeep hadn't returned. They left the Toyota on a dark street, outside a closed Chinese restaurant, then walked back to a hardware store off the main park. There a tall young man, elegant, self-assured, was waiting for them. A type from São Sebastião clubs—but he was a cadre. Fra Simone drove them in a pickup out of Pulaya on a narrow south-bound road, but after half a mile they stopped at a traffic circle, where they were met by a girl who materialized out of the roadside darkness. A small smiling creature named Suor Pin-Pin, she squeezed in between Levin and Fra Simone, with whom she exchanged a few terse remarks in Saraunese.

"Your car is in good hands," he told Levin soothingly. "Our Pulaya cadres will safeguard it while you're with Fra Boboy." He waited, then held out his hand. "You have the keys?"

Unwillingly Levin surrendered them. "Where will they—"

"We can use the restaurant owner's garage."

"Ah. The restaurant owner." Everyone was turning out to be a cadre. The country was swarming with them. "Look, there are people in Pulaya who know the car's mine. The concierge at Las Encantadas knows. Are you sure—"

"There is no problem."

"I'm just saying you might attract attention. I'm supposed to be going to Karoep tomorrow." Fra Simone gave a dismissive nod.

"And the steering's coming loose. I had trouble with it on the way down. Your Pulaya cadres should keep their joyriding to a minimum."

Fra Simone laughed elaborately. "Oh, yes! Well, a revolution is not a joyride." Levin decided that Fra Simone was a new recruit.

They sped along the night road, ascending, taking turns fast. On a long straight stretch Fra Simone glanced in the rearview mirror and, barely letting up on the gas, swerved into a sharp right turn where there was a dirt track and an illuminated cement house. The road left behind, he braked into the first holes of a downhill slope. He checked the rearview again and exchanged a look with Suor Pin-Pin.

"Here, here," she said.

Within a hundred feet of the main road, a man appeared alongside the track with a flashlight and another object that he clutched to his head. As they approached Levin saw that it was a two-way radio, and that around his neck a blue bandanna was tied scout-fashion. Behind him a few children were staring from the windows of a bamboo and nipa house in the forest. Like Fra Simone and Suor Pin-Pin, he seemed impossibly fresh for the work of the war. He had dark peasant features, and Levin decided that this guy wasn't a city cadre, did not have, as Connie did, a double self; he didn't move back and forth across the invisible shifting lines that overran Direv Saraun like a network of sinews in a body at work. One such line they had just crossed. The moment, the point, was unknowable—but Levin knew that for the first time he was in the Blue Zone. It did not look much different.

The cadre greeted Fra Simone. They didn't seem to know each other well; on the lookout's part there was a careful reserve, on Fra Simone's what seemed like excessive camaraderie. The lookout switched on his radio, and Fra Simone put the truck in gear. Another three hundred yards of rugged descent and climbing, and they leveled off into a patch of high grass lit yellow in the headlights. The track seemed to have ended. Fra Simone looked confused and Suor Pin-Pin questioned him.

They had missed their contacts. Fra Simone backed up against the grass and pulled a Y-turn into the direction they'd come from. He smiled apologetically as he drove. "No problem. It is the normal uncertainty of guerrilla life."

Levin had the impression of being a tourist with the sort of guide who chatters while he screws things up. He guessed that Fra Simone was providing the revolution with his father's truck and cash, useful but inessential. There was a bravado about him, an unnatural pleasure in the dangers and secrecy, that would keep him from achieving any importance. And Suor Pin-Pin—more sober, but a child. Levin struggled to demystify these people now that he was on their ground. He'd lost track of Mount Kalanar but it could be just on the other side of that canopy of trees.

They met their contacts halfway back to the main road, at a cluster of huts where a light now flashed. Fra Simone told Levin that the lookout had been unable to find the contacts on his radio. These new men, also wearing blue neckerchiefs, had the quiet, fierce faces of peasants—fighters. Faces without much English. One wore sideburns that spread down his cheeks into a mustache; his camouflage cap said "Rambo." Armalites were slung from their shoulders. These ones, Levin thought, had certainly killed.

Everything happened without comment, by plan. Levin and Ding were given water by a woman from one of the huts—who might have been a cadre herself, or might have been a friend to cadres, or simply might have happened to be here, on this side of the invisible line where it was drawn tonight, which required of her water. The journalists, cottonmouthed, drank so deep they spilled down their shirt-fronts, and Ding stumbled when he tried to stand. The fighters exchanged a look; the one in the Rambo cap discreetly sniffed the air. They'd realized that their charges up Mount Kalanar weren't completely sober. It seemed to amuse rather than annoy them—dirt on the dignity of the professional, citified, and foreign. Aware, Ding busied himself with slinging his Leica around his neck.

With no word of good-bye to Fra Simone and Suor Pin-Pin, the guerrillas started off on an imaginary path into the trees. The journalists, hefting their bags over their shoulders, fell in behind. The truck receded along the dirt road.

They hiked uphill for a very long time. The guerrillas' route traversed coconut groves along gentle slopes and then crossed a stream on the massive trunk of a teak gone slippery with rot. Rain had recently fallen up here. After the stream, the forest closed around them and the real climb began. The guerrillas used no lamps or flashlights, and although the moon was just beginning to wane they

lost its brightness as they penetrated the high woods. Levin labored
as he hiked. From time to time wet branches brushed his face and
he had to convince himself that they couldn't be snakes.

As they climbed, a sound from another part of the mountain
pursued them. It was too distant and unvarying to be distinguished
as anything besides man-made, machine-made. From the sideburned
guerrilla Levin gathered that the Armed Forces of Direv Saraun was
using its Pulaya units to guard loggers chain-sawing the big teak in
these mountains and make a hefty profit off the illegal hardwood
trade.

Teak was their picnic table. Unbearably sweet—the smoothness,
the dry-wood smell. The charcoal-grill smell. And mowed grass,
junipers, fireflies.

Fatigue overtook him. He was walking in a spell of dizziness that
involved his head more than his legs. The body pushed upward on
its own, but in the wild dark his mind had sprung loose and was
wheeling through intricate arabesques of song, fragments of talk
from the long drive, from Dom Hipolito, the face of the showgirl,
memory again. This forest smell, heavy and green, brought frog
quests with his eight-year-old pals, the reek of the amber pond where
trees decayed, the plop of a peeper from mud to water. Frogs and
caterpillars and pill bugs and wounded birds had filled those years.
Then came a long animal-less stretch, with few smells. Melanie's
hair. This mountain was so dark it could just as well be the hillock
beyond the pond where deer sometimes wandered out of the birch
trees.

Sweating was fine, it purged the drink through his skin. And he
had three changes of underwear in the bag, thanks to Melanie. The
pair he had on were already messed up, of course. Showerless back
there, her odor on him. It's never what it seems like it will be. Past
reason hunted, and no sooner had . . . You didn't do it, a wiseass in
a bar once told him—your dick did it. You didn't tell her that—your
dick did. Sorry, but that was me. Being a damn fool, with liquor,
cultural pressures, other mitigations involved. And Melanie—why
not home? Wherefore? With whom?

No—that way madness lies. Ding would be happy to hear this and
he wasn't going to satisfy Ding. He'd go on trust now. That was the
thing about trust—you never knew. And not a single step was taking
him any closer.

The group had become separated: Ding and one fighter were fifty feet ahead. Levin trailed with the sideburns, watching the silhouetted barrel of his M-16, singing to himself against the distant whine of the chain saw—Police, Dylan, entire sides of records he knew. Whenever he stumbled on the trail the arm fell off the record and he had to right it before the music was lost completely.

Every step was like an act of trust. But there was no trusting them—any of them. Up ahead Ding and his friend could be leading him to a drop, another gorge, some pit studded with bamboo stakes. So it was himself that he tried to concentrate on. You wanted to go alone into the world—you got it. Now what? Did you know who you were going with, out there? You don't know till you go.

Something from Plato—how do you know you've found the answer if you didn't know what it was when you went looking.

A pox on paradox. Unhelpful in the establishment of links to oneself in the jungle. No one knows who he travels with, but that's the thing about trust. After all, you're who you think you are. Aren't you? But who ever is who he thinks he is? On a night like this—on a mountain like this.

Levin patted the back pocket where he kept his notebook. Instantly a cold shudder passed over him—for his pocket was empty. The notebook wasn't there.

"Oh shit," he said aloud.

He didn't know when he'd last had it. He'd taken off his trousers in the hotel room—but he felt sure it wasn't there. With another shudder it came to him that his notebook was in the possession of the man hiking up ahead. There was no need for proof. He had to learn to drop that old business. While you're out looking for independent confirmation someone is setting a trip wire across your door. Nor did he know why—something to do with Ding's plan to stay on the mountain. It would be a merit badge with the boys, proof of his seriousness. Levin would be Ding's ride into the ranks. He tried to think of names written down and thoughts that could compromise him, but the entire notebook had become a blank. Mostly quotes, he recalled hopefully, descriptions—he was not in the habit of recording private reflections. He didn't keep a journal like Melanie's. Still, his empty pocket felt like death's weightlessness. It left him dizzy on his feet.

Somewhere on Mount Kalanar, Direv Saraun, Feb. 23—High on

this mountain, a revolution is being waged by a guerrilla army which, until recently, few people in the West had ever heard of. Now that one of the chief architects of the war has granted his first foreign interview, the question on everyone's mind is whether this reporter is who he says he is. If he isn't, the outcome of his meeting with the Army of Liberation is very much in doubt. Privately, Western diplomats predict severe repercussions.

One thing seems certain: the reporter is an American. The full significance of this unexpected discovery is yet to be determined.

Suddenly Levin had a terrific itch around the groin. Fastening his feet in shallow toeholds up a sharp climb, grasping at branches, he had to stop and bury a hand in his pants to put out the fire. A few minutes later it was there again. His skin was alive and moving. He kept hiking, one hand tugging and clawing at his abdomen through the khakis. It was difficult to walk this way, especially when you hadn't exercised in months. Or really slept in days. He fell farther behind Ding.

His guide was laconic about location and time. The hike seemed to last half the night. At a leveling the forest cleared, and they emerged on a ridge that afforded a view of the entire eastern slope, dim in the blue moonlight. But they couldn't have climbed more than fifteen hundred feet.

Ding and the other fighter were resting on a rock. A cluster of white orchids flowered from its base. Ding fiddled with the camera around his neck and talked to the fighter in hard, throwaway chunks. Guerrilla-cultivating, Levin thought as he came up panting and sweating. The fighter watched Levin and made no sign of acknowledging Ding.

Ding raised the camera and the flash went off in a white burst that was blinding in the darkness.

"Hey," Levin said. He had been absently scratching his crotch.

"Smile," Ding said. "Candid camera."

"You're supposed to ask permission before you do that."

"You don't give your questions in advance."

"I know the rules here. That's stealing my soul and it's not cool. Technically I could demand the film."

Ding was adjusting the lens. "I didn't have the right aperture anyway." His mildness seemed like preoccupation—or perhaps he didn't want another quarrel just now. Perhaps, entering the camp, he even wanted Levin on his side. Yes, there it was, dancing in his eyes: on this mountain, in this company, Ding was scared. So he would have to learn to seduce. A whiff of Ding's weakness gave Levin a moment of angry confidence and he fed it with the thought of his notebook.

"This guy says the camp is another twenty-five minutes," Ding said. "Is this still Direv Saraun?"

"I think it's Africa by now."

"Well, let's get it over with."

They pushed on, and shortly they were in pairs again. Levin could not make the itching go away. He tried to endure until it passed but it lingered, intolerably. His very skin crawled. When he scratched inside his trousers the hair was dried stiff. It would have taken two minutes to shower.

He heard voices up ahead. The trail had flattened for a while and now it led out to a rice paddy. Ding and the other fighter were at the far end of the paddy as Levin approached the first dike. He had to keep his eyes on the ridge of mud made for smaller feet than his, so when the first flash came it might have been heat lightning in the sky. He looked up in time to see another flash, the soft white burst of Ding's camera, and at the same time he felt his shoe sink into warm collapsing mud as water rose around his ankle. His companion said something and Levin answered "Sorry." But it wasn't the broken dike that had the fighter's attention. On the far side the voices had fallen silent.

White popped again; then a red-blue light flared and a shot exploded across the paddy. Men were shouting in tones of command, and the camera flashed once more. Levin froze in the water where he'd been struggling. He was sinking calf-deep among the reeds of mature rice. He thought he should lie flat but the water dissuaded him. He waited for another shot—it didn't come, only men shouting, and then his companion broke into a trot toward the end of the field and Levin sloshed out of the water to run after him.

When he reached the group on the ridge of earth above the paddy the first thing Levin noticed was Ding's face. In the watery moonlight he looked shocked, scared, defensive, defiant. He was clutching his camera to his belly as if if he'd stolen something he knew he shouldn't have but wasn't going to give it back.

"It happened like *that,*" he murmured to Levin. "I saw them."

There were two other guerrillas on the ridge, and the guides seemed extremely angry with them. At their feet was a dead man. The short dark squarish body lay face-down in the grassy mud, the face twisted sideways against the earth and grimacing, as if still in anticipation of the shot. The blow had been to the base of the skull, which in the darkness looked black with blood. He was shirtless, in tight-fitting jeans; his rubber sandals and a white golfer's cap had fallen off. The cap looked like the inspiration of some sadistic wit. He appeared to have been unarmed; the execution weapon, an automatic pistol, was in the hand of one of the guerrillas whom the guides were excoriating.

"I didn't know what I was seeing," Ding said. "I just shot, then . . ."

Levin said, "It was instinct. That's what we're here for." He didn't know what he meant.

The dead man was a Jola—short, mocha-colored, bushy-haired. He had probably been a rice farmer two minutes ago. And possibly an informer. Though he felt embarrassed, ashamed for the corpse, Levin couldn't tear his eyes from its face. It was like the face of a man ejaculating, like Ding sleeping—yet, already sunken in the eyes. A thought came that came often here: At least I'm seeing this. Levin stared with shameful fascination at the face that couldn't look back, until he felt sick and had to walk across the ridge to spit bile.

By the time he returned Ding had composed himself enough to say, "I guess this is what a war looks like, huh?"

The youth who had fired the shots told them to proceed into the camp a hundred yards ahead. He was subdued, somewhat chastened, but unrelenting. He could kill and walk away—Direv Saraun gave him the right. He didn't have the face of a killer.

It was almost midnight when they entered the clearing between nipa huts. It was a mountain farming village, spread out across a saddle between the main slope of Mount Kalanar and a lower peak that appeared black and deep green in the full moonlight. The rice fields around the dwellings were terraced for lack of level ground; the huts themselves nestled under a high canopy of lichened hardwoods. Silent, except for a couple of goats poking in the grass and murmurs from within the huts; dark, except for the flashlight a watchman switched on when they approached, and a lamp inside one of the dwellings.

Dogs somewhere greeted their arrival with suspicious barks. The watchman greeted them with no ceremony at all and led them to the hut where the light was shining.

The man at the desk didn't seem to hear the bamboo door open. He had full black hair peppered gray on a large head. His body, bent to his task, was trim and strong. Levin had time to take in everything about the room: it was spare to the point of severity. On the bamboo floor, a woven sleeping mat, and beside it a Tec-9 automatic pistol like the one that had killed the man on the dike, with a perforated black barrel and a long magazine clip. A poster was tacked to the wall slats: "Revolutions Begin in Quiet Places," it said, over a picture of a man sitting reading in a study. Levin had seen it elsewhere in Direv Saraun, but here the poster gave him a jolt of association: it seemed to be a poster of this very room.

The man wasn't reading, though; there were no books to be seen anywhere. He was typing at a laptop computer. The furious muted clicking of keys scattered across the silence like small animals over a wood floor.

"For a moment," the man said without looking. He peered into the blue brilliance of the screen and typed with tremendous speed. Where not much else seemed to be moving, the scuttle of his fingers was like a delirium of energy.

He typed his last commands, and a printer at the end of the desk suddenly zinged to life.

The man turned around.

"Well well well," said Fra Boboy.

He was smiling. No one had taken a picture of this face in five years, but Levin recognized it. It was still the ambitious young professor's. Guerrilla life had thinned it and drawn lines around the eyes and mouth, but none of its ironic confidence was lost. It hung large and loose and intense. But the intensity was benign and intimate; it found its focus directly on another face. Levin's.

"Dan, isn't it—Daniel Levin? I am so very, very glad." A hand reached for his. "Simkar Butang."

His head dominated the short body; the features were handsome but the size was out of proportion. In gym shorts, the brown thighs looked undernourished; the torso was square and stocky, stump-necked. With his high Asian voice, Fra Boboy slightly resembled an attractive dwarf.

"Fra Boboy," Levin corrected him.

"Well." Fra Boboy gave a dismissive smile. "Names, you know. They have their uses. To some of the older peasants here I'm the Professor. Our veteran fighters can't help calling me Commander— old habits die hard, don't they? My military code—well, leaving that aside. In extreme times everyone has plenty of names, and rightly so. It reflects a certain fluidity of identity. Fra Boboy if you like—I don't insist," he said. "I think you've had a hard journey."

"It was fine."

Fra Boboy narrowed his eyes and leaned in. Levin found himself stepping back. The commander seemed to be weighing some terrible revelation he'd just made. The little smile, head cocked, claimed to know more about him than Levin himself knew. Unnerved and irritated by a half-remembered feeling, Levin thought: Keep some distance. He'll have you telling your dreams.

"Perhaps you would like to sleep now?"

"What I'd really like is a shower."

"Easily arranged." For the first time, Fra Boboy took note of Ding. "And it's Mr.—"

"This is Ding Magkakanaw, my—the photographer."

Ding was hanging back in the doorway, the Leica slung around his neck. He was poised like a suitor between anguish and desire.

"I'd forgotten you were coming. Welcome, welcome both."

Ding stepped forward and grasped Fra Boboy's hand.

"I've waited a long time, Fra Boboy."

"Well, we are all in Direv Saraun waiting, Mr. Mag—how is it?"

"Fra Ding," he said solemnly.

Fra Boboy's throat quivered with laughter. "Hey, slowly, my friend! You just arrived. Oh, these names!"

Levin stripped in a stick shower stall down a trail from Fra Boboy's hut. A cadre brought him a bucket of water from a stream he could hear through the trees, and left him with a fresh bar of soap and a kerosene lamp. Before sponging water over his sticky body he held the light to his groin. Baby had given him a rash, bright red from all his scratching. A rash of brown spots no bigger than freckles, sprinkled from his navel down into the tangle of black hair, and more, he knew, for he felt the itch, in his scrotum. He looked for a long time, touching the spots on his white belly flesh.

That's what you get, he thought.

He tried to scratch a spot off with his fingernail, and it came. He picked another. This one stayed on his fingertip. It was just a fleck, like a detachable freckle. But it seemed to be moving.

He held it to the lamp.

White hairs, like cilia, writhed in the light. They were legs. The creature lay on its back grasping for the flesh it had been torn from. The brown spot was its shell, round and slightly curved. The legs wriggled desperately.

A crab.

He watched it for a few moments against the light, and then with his thumbnail he cut the thing in two. Interest lingered, the kind that makes you touch a nasty open wound on your own body. Yet this nest of lice didn't feel like his body, and he was abstracted again.

When disgust finally set in, it shortly heated to rage, burning through the last of his liquor high. And with the rage came absolute lucidity—he saw it like printed words. Ding, Siolao, the other drunks. They infested him; the whore was their instrument. Take her, they said, she's yours. And now, at last, she was his: she'd left him with these.

He played the kerosene lamp over the length of his body and noticed all his defects—folds, moles, hairs, wrinkles, scars, pimples. Crabs. Exposed thus, he was gross with corruption. His anger had ingrown piquantly, with a sense of just deserts. The crawling in his hair and scrotum finally led him to the bar of soap. He worked up a lather in his hands and scrubbed furiously. He soaped his groin until it was rubbed raw and every spot was gone.

"I thought you lost the way," Fra Boboy said when Levin returned.

He was standing next to the guide with sideburns; the latter had stopped talking when Levin came in and was now staring straight at the floor. Both men looked unhappy. Between Fra Boboy's thick eyebrows the flesh was creased in thought.

"I apologize for the nature of your arrival," he said to Levin. "It was extremely unfortunate and unpleasant for you. I hope you understand it was a dreadful mistake."

Levin wondered if he meant the timing or the deed itself. He hadn't the presence or courage of mind to ask.

"I understand."

"Good."

Levin and Ding were taken to a hut across the clearing, where mats and native cloth were spread over the floor slats. Their guides slept in the room with them. The pariah dogs barked all through the night, the guerrillas snored on their rifles, Ding muttered in his sleep as he clutched the camera bag to his chest. Levin was woken more than once by his own scratching.

In the morning his cheek was printed with the weave of the mat. Fragile-headed from rum, sore with lying on bamboo, exhausted after three nights without good sleep, he didn't realize at first that he was alone in the room. Just outside, Fra Boboy was talking to someone. He was speaking gently, full of pauses, patiently persuading. Words started to become clear; a few were in English. "Film" and "photos" emerged, and then a distinct sentence: "Just to keep within the movement." A pause followed. Fra Boboy said, "Think it over, Ding," and Ding answered, "O.K." Then Fra Boboy's tone became more natural.

Levin sat up. He was alert. He would have only a few seconds but he was moving automatically now, self-surprised. Ding's bag was clumsily hidden under his sleeping cloth. The Leica was there with the other cameras. He checked the number of exposures—five. He rewound Ding's film and removed it from the camera. Fuji, black-and-white, of course, 100 ASA, 24 exposures. Levin stuffed it in his trouser pocket. Then he looked in Ding's bag for a fresh roll of the same film; but all the rest was 36 exposures or 400 ASA. Still going on blessed instinct, he chose a 36 at 100 and hoped that Ding had loaded the camera in his inebriation. He tried to advance the film. A lull in the conversation outside the door made his fingers inept, and he nearly broke a sprocket as he forced the film leader down over the gear. It advanced. He took five rapid pictures with the lens cap on; then he replaced everything as it had been.

The whole time he'd been half searching for his notebook, but it didn't matter that he couldn't find it—enough to be revenged. He stood up, yawned, and went out into the fresh mountain sunlight.

Fra Boboy's hand lay on Ding's shoulder; Ding was looking off into a grove of coconut palms. When Levin appeared, he and Ding exchanged a glance and in that moment it seemed that all the menace had drained from Ding's unshaven, tormented face.

"Good morning, Dan," Fra Boboy said. "If I may?"

"Of course."

"Our accommodations are a little primitive."

"They're fine."

"But you're not fully rested." Fra Boboy smiled wanly. "It takes some time up here before you feel the good effects."

In a nearby hut a young Jola wife served them rice with egg and pork sauce in honor of the visitors. Midway through the meal they were joined by Connie, who had arrived yesterday. She smiled very little and seemed even less at ease up here, where there was no alternative identity, than in the city. Whenever she spoke her look shifted to Fra Boboy; he seldom returned it. Most of her comments merely echoed and amplified his remarks, but when she suggested that right-wing extremists might have blown up the Pala bridge, he contradicted her sharply. Though they hadn't claimed responsibility yet, it was the Army of Liberation's job. Dishonesty served no purpose, he said. A blown bridge was an inevitable part of the struggle. There was nothing to apologize for. Connie hastened to agree. She seemed strung between reverence and anxiety, like an impressionable grad student with a star professor.

"Shall we?" Fra Boboy said to Levin when their plates were empty. Connie had patients to see among the peasants and guerrillas. Ding, Fra Boboy said, should feel free to photograph anything in the camp. If he requested, the guerrillas might be willing to pose in armed formation.

"Something wrong, Ding?" Fra Boboy asked.

"Oh, no. I'd just like to take your picture sometime if I can."

"Normally I don't permit that," the guerrilla commander said, "because I don't like this cult of personality in revolutionary movements. The American readers could think I am a celebrity here, even some kind of self-promotionist. When in fact I'm not even first among equals."

"It might help them," Levin said, "to have a face to go along with the story. Since Direv Saraun is so little known. It might clarify your case."

"That's true," Ding said.

"A color portrait might be best of all."

"I'll take it under consideration." Fra Boboy started off.

Ding, a spurned suitor, was still unwilling to let them go. "I can't just shoot a portrait cold, Fra Boboy. I would need to spend some time with you. I'd have to get familiar with you."

"This isn't Stieglitz. It's news photography, no? So let's keep it simple."

Ding was left standing in the semidarkness of the Jola woman's hut. He seemed to be staring at his camera.

Fra Boboy took Levin on a guided tour of the camp. It was a mountain village, bordered on two sides by rice terraces, on a third by a grove of coconut palms, and directly uphill, across a hundred yards of fallow field, by dense rain forest ascending to the peak of Mount Kalanar. The village occupied an outsized glade, a patch of level clearing on the mountainside. Fra Boboy pointed out the virtues of the setting for a guerrilla army headquarters: food and shelter were willingly provided in communal fashion by what he called the "mass base"; there was plenty of natural cover for maneuvers, munitions storage (Levin was shown ample stockpiles of automatic weapons and explosives), or cadre assemblies; the place was barely accessible on foot, and from a helicopter it was indistinguishable from any other Jola village nestled in the southern range. No one could reach it without the prior knowledge of the Southern Regional Command. And yet, with radio and computer, communication with the other commands was almost instant.

"I was kind of surprised to see it," Levin said.

"The computer? Well, it's only a Toshiba 1000. I would prefer to have a 1200 but one makes do. What kind is yours?"

"Oh, it's an old Kaypro."

Fra Boboy didn't trouble to hide his disdain. "A fax would revolutionize our operations, but we have to wait for these Motorola satellite cellular phones to be developed." He smiled apologetically. "On the whole, things are still a little rustic."

"No one's written about all this technology. How does it go over in a village like this? They're not even living in the twentieth century."

"A state of cultural confusion is normal in Direv Saraun. And a revolution must deal with norms of history."

"Modernism isn't going to corrupt these people?"

"You see, that's just Western sentimentality, Dan. America may be corrupt, weak, null, but its inventions haven't made it so. The inventions are neutral things—we invest them with meaning."

Fra Boboy was walking quickly through the market, a narrow maze of wooden stalls. Behind the shacks livestock, mainly pigs, was penned in muck, and several buffalo were tied to poles. Apart from a few women selling prepared food—rice dishes, corn paste wrapped in leaves—the market was empty today. It was pervaded by a sharp odor that might have been dead animal.

Outside the market, among the bamboo huts that surrounded the open place at the village center, a few guerrillas were repairing peasants' roofs blown off by typhoon. Jola men—shorter than their Saraunese guests, with skin and hair midway toward aboriginal—squatted on the ground, weaving nipa grass into patches for the roofs; the guerrillas stood on wobbly ladders, nailing down crude rafter poles or lashing thatch the Jola men handed up. A few kids were playing with stray nails and bits of nipa. One of them saw Levin and called out something he didn't catch.

"Civic action," the commander explained.

"Hearts and minds?"

"Not really." Fra Boboy didn't acknowledge the allusion. "We have hearts and minds. As you can see, relations between the movement and the mass base are very harmonious."

"Do you think the mass base are up to the work of revolution?"

"They know where their interests lie. And the revolutionary forces are the natural defenders of their interests."

"It just looks awfully peaceful up here. You know—static."

Large numbers of naked children wandered about the open place, seemingly parentless. Some of the villagers idled around the dwellings; others had disappeared out into the flooded paddies. Some of the men and all of the women wore sun-faded, washed-out sarongs. The guerrillas, identifiable even out of uniform by their Malay features and their M-16s, kept to the huts and the shade of the palms or the forest trees with their towering, perfectly straight trunks.

"I will tell you something, Dan." Fra Boboy was leading him across the open place in full view of Jola and guerrilla alike. "We can learn valuable things from these people. It is taking our propaganda cadres some time to understand this, but these Jola are more ready for the work of revolution than the urban Saraunese. They are open to the grander vision precisely because of this timelessness you refer to. They are free from petty distractions, personal ambitions, ego trips. They do not have the Saraunese cynicism about the future."

He stopped in his tracks and turned to point at the civic action in progress among the huts.

"Typhoon can change their lives in two minutes. Nature is the god up here, Dan. Not God the merciful Father. Certainly not the god of the Enlightenment. They already know all about larger forces. There is a certain smallness, even emptiness to human affairs here that I find salutary—freed from all sorts of illusions. Why does that bother you?"

Fra Boboy was giving him the look of last night—confidential, supremely knowing. This time Levin remembered. It was the way Melanie watched him in bed, as she traced his face. Her finger wandered across his cheek and nose like a fly. It scanned his skin for the deepest contour of feeling beneath. He could never bring himself to throw her hand off, so he lay immobilized, enduring the unendurable, while every inch of his body cried out in protest.

He looked around: peasants, hogs, guns. It was real now—this was no place to fall to pieces in someone else's hands. He told himself that he had business here: he was a journalist.

"It doesn't," he said. Something more seemed required. "I wonder if your analysis squares with anthropology, for instance."

Fra Boboy shrugged, and they continued toward the huts on the far side. There, a young Jola man in a disintegrating shirt and trousers leaned against a papaya tree, smoking a cigarette. He watched their approach; his eyes seemed to look everywhere at once. When he had Levin's eye he took the cigarette out of his mouth and smiled. Under a nest of hair the dark face was all eyeballs and teeth. It seemed ancient—the face of the first man as if he'd been leaning on that tree for millennia. When Fra Boboy noticed him, the cigarette went back into his mouth and the young man turned his head away.

Nausea rose in Levin's throat. *Why does that bother you?* Because the cutters and loaders, the showgirl in Pulaya, felt like kin compared with this. What did these people do all day, what did they think? Idleness and timelessness and early-hominid stares were not going to free him from any illusions he wanted to part with. He had planned to interview members of the peasantry, but now it appeared a hopeless conceit.

Everything floated slowly in the sunlight, and everyone seemed subdued in the high air, except Fra Boboy. He talked and moved with a speed of purpose, a core of intelligence and vitality that put him at odds with all around him. In this silent Jola place, with its smell of waste and mud, he was the only person who could tell Levin that he was going to be all right. And that disturbed Levin more than anything else.

"You can see, Dan, that it is a perfectly functioning base." They were passing the hut where last night Fra Boboy had been busy at the Toshiba. "You saw the extent of our weaponry—all of it from the domestic market. We are fully prepared to step up activities in the south. It is important for the military to understand this."

Offhandedly, he indicated the hut next to his. Armed guerrillas were sitting outside.

"We have the American in there."

"Bowers."

"Bowers." Fra Boboy glanced at Levin. "Can you wait until this evening? We have a nice little cultural presentation planned and there will be some time before that to talk."

"First things first. I'm up here to interview you."

"Good." Fra Boboy patted his back and gave him a warm look. "The most comfortable place to talk is the river."

On their way through the eastern part of the village Levin saw more peasants and more guerrillas. Studying the Jola faces, he felt like a reader confronted with a new alphabet; to his eyes, they betrayed no attitude at all toward their armed guests. The guerrillas, some of them female, many teenagers with prematurely hard looks, cleaned their rifles and talked among themselves. The two groups seemed to have nothing to do with each other.

He tried to gauge a reaction to his own presence, but aside from the amazed cries of the children—always the same unintelligible syllable—he elicited nothing from the Jola. The guerrillas registered him with sidelong looks that stirred his anxiety. He tried to will it down.

The river ran below a grove of coconut palms that sloped steeply downhill. Levin and Fra Boboy sat side by side on a great trunk that had been felled to make a bridge, the hollow barkless wood going to rot. The river was narrow but fairly deep, and its clear bottom swam with rocks. On the near bank, by a clump of bamboo, a tiny Jola woman was washing clothes. The slow water, the woman's white blouse, the green crowns of the palms were charged with highland light. Birdsong spun and whirled in the pleasant air.

"Ask me questions," Fra Boboy said with smooth good humor.

CHAPTER VIII

Levin turned on the little Sanyo tape recorder.

"This is the first interview with the Commander of the Army of Liberation, Southern Region, February 24. Fra Boboy, you were telling me a few minutes ago about the Jola worldview. I'm wondering if you could go into that a little more."

"You don't use a notebook?"

"I—this lets me pay better attention. It'll catch everything."

"The technique has changed since my days. To me a notebook gave the reporter a degree of control. He is the one to decide what is recorded."

Levin never felt at ease with a tape recorder; he always overheard a strain of formality in his voice. Fra Boboy sounded completely relaxed, expansive yet calm.

"What about my question?"

"Yes, well, it's a complicated subject, full of misconceptions. The Jola people say: There is a time for the mountain, and a time for the city. Their view of time is of long stasis punctuated with disruptions. They believe there is a man on this mountain who disappeared during the Japanese occupation and went into the volcano crater to gain power through contemplation. When the time comes, they say he will return to rid this country of its corruption."

"Has the time come?"

"In fact I hear many of them talking about him."

" 'A time for the city' is an interesting phrase. It suggests the A. of L.'s recent operations in São Sebastião."

"If we are following a deep Saraunese pattern, so much the better!"

"Has this been your 'time for the mountain'?"

"I have learned patience here. I have unlearned the Western obses-sion with time and continual activity. In a paradoxical way, these are incompatible with revolutionary work."

Levin noticed what was strange about Fra Boboy's English. The vocabulary was almost unknown in Direv Saraun, but he spoke with a heavy Saraunese rhythm, a taxi driver's, accenting the last syllable of all his sophisticated words. At first it was the vocabulary that had sounded unreal, parroted. Now the distorted cadence seemed willful.

"But your manner, your style, sets you apart, even from your own fighters. Aren't you intellectually isolated?"

"Of course, there is some loneliness. The human factor is always present."

"Someone I spoke with said it was one reason for giving an inter-view."

"That sounds like my old employer Feliz."

"You're right. It was Feliz."

"He is a shrewd old guy. A great amateur psychologist. It's too bad he has nothing to offer his country at this hour of decision except sagacity."

"Was he right about you?"

"There were several reasons for the interview."

"What are they?"

"Not just yet. Let's finish this topic."

Levin knew that it was his own role to guide the interview, choose topics and shift them as he needed. But he found himself without a plan, and he was hearing manipulation in every word—to what end? Just anti-imperialist mind-fucking? To ease him into a nasty trap of Ding's making, toward an end among these Jola faces, on the paddy dike like that farmer last night, a round red hole in the middle of his forehead? The loss of his notebook seemed a catastrophe. It was as if he'd lost control over the tone of his own voice, unable to disguise anything.

Then he remembered a piece of paper he'd folded into his shirt pocket in São Sebastião. A small thing, but the feel of it reassured him slightly.

"I didn't notice any books in your hut. Don't you read up here?"

"No. That surprises you—formerly, you know, I was so much in the word, the text. The Jolas' thinking seems clearer than that of my old colleagues at the University of Direv Saraun. And I find a great lucidity in myself up here. Particularly at night. When night falls there is no real light and your thoughts can be really limitless. It is a better intellectual setting than any university."

Levin took out the paper.

"I xeroxed your dissertation abstract when I was in the National Library. I'd like to ask you about it."

Fra Boboy snatched the sheet from his hand. He balled it up and, with a dramatic pause and a merry flourish, dropped it into the slow water below their tree trunk.

"A slice of nothing. I was playing with fire and I didn't even know it burns."

Levin watched the crumpled photocopy float downstream in the sunlight like a dead bird, white glitter on blue. He'd thought it would surprise, please, impress Fra Boboy. He'd been counting on it to make them equals.

"You don't believe in it anymore?"

"No . . . I wouldn't say that. In my own cock-of-the-walk way I was fumbling with the truth. It made some significant theoretical points. It is the spirit, the manner of the thing, that life, which seems so remote now."

"Maybe America seems remote—your grad-school days."

"I'll tell you something about America," Fra Boboy said with sudden vehemence. "It has more to fear from Direv Saraun than from Iran or the Arabs. And the reason why is this: Our war has nothing to do with America. It is not an anti-American war. The expressions of anti-Americanism you still find here are obsolete. And if I were American, that would disturb me more than one hundred thousand demonstrators chanting 'Yankee go home!' Then you could at least feel you were indispensable. It is far worse to be irrelevant." Fra Boboy poked him lightly in the chest. "Do you feel irrelevant here?"

The touch of the finger infuriated Levin. He was not going to be bullied away from his interview. "You don't anticipate an American involvement?"

Fra Boboy didn't answer at once; and the little delay told Levin that Fra Boboy wasn't surrendering his own question. "I hope and think she has better sense. It would be a tragedy for everybody, a futile one for America. As for the Army of Liberation, we have no ideological quarrel with the U.S. Nothing that happens here should matter there."

"Then why talk to the American press?"

"Well, it is just this—we want no misunderstandings. Americans do not yet appreciate the reasons for our revolution. But an informed public would keep your government from doing something ill advised, acting out of nostalgia for Third World adventures or to exercise the atrophying muscles of the military. That in turn would serve the moral purpose of sparing our people and yours a senseless destruction. This Bowers whom we captured—to me he is a perfect instance of America in its late-imperial stage. Politics reduced to personality, private trauma acted out publicly. Nonetheless, a threat."

"What are you going to do with him?"

"What do you think we should do?"

Levin thought: *It's up to you.* But of course it wasn't up to him. Then why ask? Because there was no answer he could win with. He imagined himself forced to carry out the sentence, in some bit of guerrilla justice. He imagined the sentence he suggested carried out on himself.

"Well, it would depend on what he did."

"If he is working for your C.I.A.? Or even the A.F.D.S., in counterinsurgency?"

"I suppose there would have to be a punishment."

"A severe one."

"That's not my call. Look, let's go back to the urban war." Levin decided to escape into deep water. "What moral purpose does it serve?"

"It is the only way left to bring the military to the negotiating table. It is the only alternative to a protracted war of attrition, total war."

"No one seems to be taking it that way. In São Sebastião it looks like chaos."

"We did not imagine it would be welcomed with parades. But the people understand. We feel their support."

"But it's not having the desired effect, is it? It's driving the A.F.D.S. to a harder line."

"Ah. Now we have come to the main reason for this interview, Dan. The war is entering a crucial moment and there are opportunities we might not have again. For a settlement. I want to get a message out, and in you I think I find a clear-sighted messenger. As you yourself have seen, we could go on fighting for a long time if the message is ignored."

Levin didn't have to feel his wrist to know his pulse was racing. Somehow, everything had come out his way. In the deep water he'd found a scoop. But the scoop didn't thrill him as much as his relief to be out of the glare of Fra Boboy's eye—a journalist again. A clear-sighted messenger.

As coolly as possible, he said: "What kind of message are we talking about?"

From his own shirt pocket Fra Boboy took out a piece of paper with a neat block of dot-matrix print. Above the text was a title: PRELUDE TO ANY NATIONAL RECONSTRUCTION: A PROPOSAL AND A MANIFESTO. He handed it to Levin with the smile of a benefactor.

It was a seven-point peace plan. It called for integration of the two armies, prosecution of human rights abuses by the military, genuine land reform, equitable industrialization, neutral foreign policy, closing of Porto Negrais, nationalization of the natural gas plant and banana exports.

Levin read it over three times, trying to find something that he might have missed. Though the language was conciliatory, there were no surprises. It was hardly different, in fact, from a plan proposed and rejected fifteen months ago. Vague enough to be unobjectionable to anyone outside the Saraunese military and ruling class, the multinationals, and the U.S. State Department. Therefore, doomed to fail.

Levin stalled, unsure how to go on.

"It doesn't read much like your earlier writing."

"Monographs aren't my line. What can you say about this?"

"Is there another page?"

"What more needs to be said?"

"I'm just not sure I see the breakthrough you do."

"This! This is the breakthrough. Any journalist can look at it and know he's been given a scoop."

"Well, of course, any proposal is newsworthy."

Levin had counted on hearing some kind of peace plan, some overture from Fra Boboy. He had assumed it was the reason they'd summoned him. But he knew with certainty that this paper was worthless. Even the print looked flimsy and transparent. He'd been expecting the subtlest of traps, but the manipulation had turned out to be utterly banal: a politician trying to snowjob a young reporter.

He could hardly bear his disappointment. It meant he would have to go it alone, after all.

He said, "I don't think the government will look at it twice."

Fra Boboy leaned back. "Well," he said tightly. "I'm very sorry to hear you say that."

"I'd like to see it your way. Show me what's in this proposal that's new, that hasn't been talked about fifty times before."

"The timing is new. We are saying: Let's stop and consider. Let's stop before everything goes up in smoke."

"Everything has. In São Sebastião you hear a car backfire and expect to be blown sky-high. And people aren't saying it's just the military anymore."

"The Army of Liberation reserves the right to defend itself against the A.F.D.S. And the people expect us to protect them, and avenge blood debts. It gives us our credibility."

"Do traffic cops have blood debts? Did that farmer last night? And the American serviceman—"

"Every army shoots informers. He risked the lives of a hundred people. But we never claimed responsibility for the American." For the first time Fra Boboy's voice was edged with irritation.

"The A. of L. didn't kill him?"

"I cannot speak for our associates in the capital. It isn't my region of authority. But I have reasons for believing it was an act of military terrorism. A pretext for crackdown and increased U.S. aid."

"Do you expect a crackdown?"

"I hope this can avert one." He pointed to the sheet of paper on the log, then delicately folded it and returned it to his pocket, as if it would be more tempting there. "With your help, Dan. If you are willing."

"I'm a reporter, not a courier. Anyway, I don't know how you're going to get your message across with vigilantes killing people in the towns, military abuses all over the countryside, urban terror by your Capital Command. And I've heard the Southern Region is having its own troubles."

"What kind of troubles?"

"That there's been a lot of internal violence here. Infiltration, denunciations, purges. So why would the A.F.D.S. come to the table for last year's news?"

"You may be a reporter but you are badly informed. The small level of infiltration has been eliminated. Who told you this?"

"There was talk in Pulaya."

"A lot of fatuous gossip."

"Well, I don't know. But the point is, it's probably too late."

"Too late for peace?"

"Maybe. If the hard-liners do what they're saying. If they can swing the pendulum away from the prime minister and the generals and justify a coup. The blood would really flow. A lot of innocent people would die. That's not—"

Fra Boboy's face had assumed a look of deep suspicion, like a room suddenly losing sunlight. "I don't follow. Who said this?"

"It's just a rumor. I don't know."

"What do you know?"

"I'll ask the questions, Fra Boboy."

Levin was watching the old woman kneading her wash in the sudsy shallows. The ends of her fingers were raw and swollen with the work; he thought of the fingers of the boy in Pala. She was singing to herself in a tone devoid of melody; the strange music seemed designed to arouse fear.

"You know a lot, Dan. Your information seems privileged."

"Only by luck."

"You knew we have Bowers. I noticed you were not surprised back there when I told you. So you've gained excellent contacts. Siriman is certainly a well-placed source."

Before Levin could answer Fra Boboy reached into the shirt pocket where he'd tucked away the peace proposal. But what he unfolded on the log was Levin's well-worn permit to travel, with the bold letterhead of the Armed Forces. Ding had decided to make use of it, after all.

"What does that prove? It's common sense these days."

"Your companion said some amazing things about you. Do you want to hear them?"

"Not really."

Dizziness enfolded him and Levin gripped the slick surface of the log. By now disbelief seemed ridiculous, yet it was the only thing he could feel. He told himself, very distinctly: Ding is serious. Everything is serious now. He looked into Fra Boboy's brown, heavy, creased face. It had softened and it invited confidence.

"What did he say?"

"That he had it from you that you do intelligence work. 'Snooping,' as he put it."

"And you believe him?"

It was weak, contemptible, suspect to ask—but he felt himself to be all of these.

"I have to weigh the available information, Dan. But you are, as they say, on the horns of a dilemma. It is something like the case of someone who is asked by the A.F.D.S. to do X. If he does X, from our point of view he has crossed the line of neutrality. But—if he does not do X, then the A.F.D.S. would have to question his motives. And in an emergency—martial law, for example—wouldn't the A.F.D.S. have to act on its suspicions? Isn't this more or less the dilemma?"

"I wasn't asked to do anything."

The conversation in Siriman's office came back to him, all at once and in its entirety.

"You were given a message to deliver, about the possibility of a coup and killings on a large scale. They expected you to write it—but you delivered it in person, like a courier. Still, it's a scoop. You think they want nothing in return?"

"I didn't think I was doing that. I was doing what journalists do. Anyway, why would they want it known?"

"Haven't you thought about that?"

"No!" In fact, Levin had forced himself to forget the colonel's unwanted confidences. He tried once more to take control over what the recorder was taping. "Look, we were talking about your proposal. And I'm saying it's a ruse and every objective Saraunese would know it. It's just a sheet of paper at this stage."

"Show me this objective Saraunese. Objectivity is a foreign import. Very few Saraunese can afford it—none, really. Can you?"

"It's my stock-in-trade."

"Don't you ever get tired, man? From experience I know it's a terrific effort."

"It's not my country. That makes it easier."

"What you need in Direv Saraun," said Fra Boboy, "is a buddy, and an enemy, and a gun. These three things make life just tolerable."

Across the water a screen of dense foliage rose eighty or a hundred feet into the jewel-blue sky. Somewhere in it a pair of sex-crazed birds went chasing and shrieking through the leaves. Levin was suddenly aware of the lice in his groin.

"So the idea is for me to prove my good faith by writing about the new guerrilla peace plan. To keep the Americans out of your war when the shit starts to fly. Fra Boboy and the Middle Way—"

"There is no Middle Way, Dan. I know it and you have found out." Fra Boboy, two fingers to his lips, shook his head and smiled sadly. The washerwoman was laying out her clothes on the rocks, flat wet oblongs of color.

"I thought it was you."

"It couldn't be me."

Levin said, "Well, I'll tell you something. I'm sick of proving my good faith. When you make someone prove it too often it just naturally goes bad."

"Yes. I knew this about you, Dan. I knew we could really talk. I'm seldom wrong on a hunch."

"We got off the track back there—I don't remember where."

Levin looked at his tape recorder, breathing on the log as if it were a sentient being—mocking him. From far down the mountain a noise started up. It was the growl of a chain saw.

"Is there logging going on here?"

"That would seem to be the case."

"Then the mountain isn't entirely yours."

"No?"

"We must have passed through a White Zone last night."

"I can tell you Mount Kalanar is a total Blue Zone. No one can penetrate it without our knowledge."

"Then it's you doing the logging."

"Call it a joint venture. Don't look so shocked, Dan. What is a tree? It can have any number of meanings—in itself it has none. To that Jola woman it could be sacred, the house of her mother's grandfather. To an international lumber concern it can mean a lot of money. And for a guerrilla army it can keep five units supplied. The military pays us to let them bring in pirate loggers and they take their percentage, which is spent on drink and carnality in Pulaya. The money buys us weaponry on the domestic market, most of it A.F.D.S. Sometimes they even pay us in guns—for use against them, when they are unconscious from liquor and whoring. This is how you win a flea war, Dan."

Levin was watching Fra Boboy's face, waiting for a terrible transformation. But it remained intimate, almost comforting, merely shaded with irony.

Levin said, "You do business with the enemy."

"When two people are trying to destroy each other they are as intimate as lovers! Anyway—"

"You can't make an omelette without breaking eggs."

"It's a vulgar cliché, I know. But vulgar clichés may be our best approximation of the truth."

"Would it be vulgar to ask if the Jola know their protectors are deforesting their ancestral land?"

"Again, you realize how easy it would be to lie and say we have drawn a cordon sanitaire around their sacred forest. But you and I are in the truth now, Dan, and that is a great pleasure for me. No, they accept because that is what they do, what they have always done. And when the angry mood comes over them—we channel it outward. Of course they don't imagine this is our policy. The misdoings of a few bad apples."

"Was that farmer last night a bad apple?"

"He was an informer. It was one hundred ten percent certain."

"I've heard that figure before. I had my doubts then and I do now. Mistakes just get made too often. Someone gets labeled and the wheel starts to turn. The more he denies it, the faster it turns."

"He confessed. Last market day in Pulaya he gave names to a certain captain there at the military HQ."

"Maybe the captain tortured him."

"Well, this is possible. But we could have helped the guy. Remember the three things I said you need—he tried to go without them. A Saraunese would think he was careless at best, maybe insane."

Rising heat held the water dead still. But in the canopy on the other side a large bird was flapping among the branches, cawing from time to time. The only other moving thing in the nonhuman world was the colony under Levin's scrotum.

"What these peasants are born knowing is—they are nothing." Fra Boboy's voice was close in the green stillness. "Fecal—dregs. One of them puts on airs and the others mock. They have no mirrors here. Why should they? To make sure they exist? They don't ask ontological questions. To know what they look like? They look like everyone else. Every blade of grass looks like every other blade. If every Saraunese accepted this, our country would have been liberated two hundred years ago. And with our fighters, the same. It has to be. Because when you think that you yourself matter, you just cannot help resenting death. That's a heavy weight for anyone, let alone an army."

Fra Boboy had begun to sound a little sad.

"It will amaze you, but men and women come here begging us to take the weight. They don't want to live their own lives. Here, they say, I lay down the burden of my life. Take it! Give me a gun and show me the enemy. And then, Dan, these poor children of cane cutters flower like jacaranda."

Levin thought of the Cavaleiros de Aviz. Green and red were the colors of that flowering. The question seemed to be who got to you first.

As for the interview at hand, it was much too late for rescue. He surveyed the wreckage and was bewildered, like a drunk sobering in the red lights of tow trucks and police cars.

"You're saying individuals don't matter to a revolution."

"No. I'm not talking about ends and means and that Marxist detritus. I'm saying individuals are a very pernicious illusion. I hate to talk this way, but the point is the philosophical subject predicates the political subject. Look: subjectivity—subjection—subjugation." Fra Boboy tapped the words on the log. "How can one person carry the load of a life without being crushed? Can one person develop a wireless telephone hookup that sends faxes by satellite? Or build a bridge? Or blow one up? Or fight a company of men? Can you—with your stock-in-trade?"

Fra Boboy took a breath and gestured at the washerwoman down the bank.

"When I went to Boston, I learned what she's known all her life. They gave me a lot of money to do graduate work at B.U., as a so-called Third World scholar, person of color, doing the latest things from France with a Saraunese accent. Oh, I was a catch. Like an exotic bird. And they made a very big deal over me. The literature and philosophy departments held an all-day conference on Saraunese culture. They called it 'In the I'—vertical pronoun, Dan—'of the Modern Primitive World.' In my honor. And I felt so honored.

"About fifteen people showed up. There were a dozen white schol-
ars and three members of the Boston Saraunese community—a nurse
I happened to have gone to grammar school with here and an old
couple, the man was a retired dentistry teacher. His wife had her hair
done up in a formidable beehive. Of course they had very little
interest in neo-Foucaultian revenge cycles. And the radical profes-
soriate must have been pretty disappointed to see what modern
primitives looked like in the flesh. Afterward I had to talk with them;
we spoke Saraunese, but all the same when the nurse began a story
about how I was scolded for wearing shorts the first day of school
because my parents did not buy me trousers, and they were all
gesturing and laughing in that way of ours that seemed so vulgar, I
felt humiliated. I cursed them to myself for ruining my day. They
invited me to dinner at a Saraunese restaurant in Chelsea, but I
begged off and went to have hamburgers with my colleagues.

"But after the conference, things changed. I began to turn down
the invitations that kept coming—dinners, parties. I realized the
flattery was a satisfaction of my colleagues' vanity. They didn't
respect me at all; they coddled me and despised me. And I couldn't
forgive the shame of my behavior at the conference. I embraced my
loneliness and began spending a lot of time by myself, usually eating
at a certain bar in Kenmore Square. There was a waitress who would
greet me in Saraunese—I taught her. And the sound of those words
made me so sad, I wanted to hear them just to get a tender feeling
again. I had lost my tender feelings in Boston. I even considered
inviting her to the room I rented, but I didn't because there was no
help for it and in the morning it would be worse.

"One evening—it was about this time of year, February, so bitter—I had a seminar. There was a student, Jewish, like you, very
smart. I was proclaiming something and he turned to me and said,
'Look. If you're not very familiar with Adorno it's not a crime.
Nobody here was born knowing the *Dialectic.*' Just like that. A
minor slight. But I tell you I held the table so hard the edge drew
blood in my hand. Because I wanted to tear his throat out. I almost
fainted and the blackness frightened me. Afterward I went for comfort to the bar and my waitress served me bourbon after bourbon,
she didn't even keep track of the bill, but the comfort didn't come.
It was night, and once I looked up from the table and saw the whole
room reflected in the window, lit orange, and yellow. And there I

was—the only eyes looking back. I was the only unreal thing. The thing I couldn't stand being I had to be. Me, Butang. And then . . . I don't know how to describe, but I—sort of—I disappeared. I watched myself disappear from the window. I don't know if I can explain to you."

The washerwoman had stopped humming, as if she sensed Fra Boboy's emotion.

"I knew I was not living my life—my real life. And I can say that from that moment I became Saraunese. Six weeks later I was back in São Sebastião. To save myself. I took a job at U.D.S., but my colleagues sounded like talking sticks. They were appalled that I threw away my American scholarship. They really believed that knowledge sets you free—and they were less free than any Jola farmer. As for me, I was elated. I would walk through the Central Market and weep. I wanted to kiss the slimy pavement. I almost forced them to deny me tenure. And the day the word reached me that it was refused, I knew where I belonged. I knew."

Levin began to wonder if Fra Boboy might be mad. It wasn't just the words, but the glad triumphant roll of his voice. Over Levin he had plainly triumphed, and so perhaps it didn't matter whether he was mad or not. Without knowing the what or how of it, Levin had lost and there would be consequences. High up the other bank the green-breasted bird squawked.

He tried to gather the shards of his interview.

"Will the A. of L. respond to what I told you?"

"You mean from Siriman?"

Levin nodded.

"There will be some action. You see now why they wanted us to know? One side acts, the other reacts—this is the stage we're in. It makes me think of the Jola creation myth—are you interested? In the beginning there is only sea and sky and an eagle, and the eagle is tired of flying around with no place to land. He goes up and tells the sky that the sea has plans to drown it in water; the sky says that if the sea tries this, it will rain down huge boulders and mountains of dirt to stop it. Then the eagle flies down and reports to the sea that the sky is going to rain down huge boulders and mountains of dirt. The sea is enraged and rises up to flood the sky, and the sky sees it coming and buries the sea in rocks and dirt. So Direv Saraun is born. It was a clever eagle, to think of that."

The green bird had ceased squawking. It perched, as if waiting.

Levin said, "But now it's the world's end. Sea and sky wiping out the earth and all the people on it. I keep hearing the middle's the most dangerous ground."

"For now. But it's necessary, you understand, really necessary to eliminate that ground because Direv Saraun is a clod of earth where eagles shit. We are a historical absurdity. The Saraunese people are by nature hedonists: they must be made to choose where hedonism is no longer a question. You are not in a position to blame us. To give our people something like an identity, a sense of purpose and greatness, what other nations take for granted—we have to make them choose between sea and sky. Yes, there are unfortunate short-term consequences. But peace would be worse now than for the sea to rise and the sky to fall. A second creation. No birth without blood."

Levin felt sun-drained, fighting off his crabs and his fatigue. In their utter indifference the bird, the trees, the Jola washerwoman all oppressed him. He was unable to meet Fra Boboy's gaze.

"I guess I don't understand why you've told me these things. Some of it won't be attractive to people at home. My parents, for example, would be quite disturbed—though my mother would enjoy having you to dinner. They're the ones who brought me up on the Middle Way. We were too tough for Santa, the Tooth Fairy, even the Supreme Deity. But at least there had to be a chance for earthly salvation. So they'd be very disappointed."

"Then why tell?"

That it was his job to tell sounded so droll in his inner ear that Levin didn't answer.

"And do you think I would come up here with the ticks and leeches and dirty rice and a price on my head if I did not believe in earthly salvation? Those tenured parrots, Feliz, journalists talking about the 'Saraunese situation' over Temple of Heavens—they're the ones who do not believe. I tell you, there is nothing like armed conflict to make your lungs work again."

Levin had to draw air and found he couldn't. It was as if Fra Boboy had bewitched his lungs shut. He gasped, and as he started to panic his shoulders rose and fell until suddenly the air rushed in. Their eyes met, and Fra Boboy glanced away. It must be embarrassing, Levin thought, to see another human creature so susceptible.

"Just not your way, Dan. Not the way your experience has allowed you to imagine it. History has finally reached us in Direv Saraun, and all this nothingness is going to rise up into something great, but not your way. So then, one learns to let go of what is no longer tenable. As I have done."

Fra Boboy's cheeks had darkened and the large head seemed to bear down on him. Levin had an instant's vision of Melanie standing over him in his bedroom, naked, odorous, and reddening.

"But some of it you already knew? I didn't have to tell you?"

"In some sense . . . I guess."

"When you arrived last night, Dan, I said: Here comes one looking for something, and it is killing him. Here comes one who might seek the truth. Without any mirrors you have to take my word for it, but I think you would be quite struck by your face."

Fra Boboy's eyes fell to the little Sanyo. It whirred on heedlessly, recording everything. He looked up at Levin and with a lift of the eyebrows—inquiry, victory, irony, sympathy?—he shut the machine off. A pain was breaking just behind Levin's eyes—nettling, malarial.

"That bird," Fra Boboy said, "has hung around too long. This afternoon you and I will go hunting. Did you hunt in the States?"

"We weren't that kind of family." Levin looked into the trees, sun-dazzled, and imagined an explosion of blood and green feathers.

"Journalism is so cerebral. Are you feeling all right?"

"Maybe the sun."

"But your body is in some discomfort."

"Oh. I've got some kind of rash."

"Suor Connie should look at it."

"No. It's not a big deal."

They climbed off the log and stood on the bank. An itch flared in Levin's groin so intensely that he had to ball up his hand to keep it from going below the belt.

"Better to have it treated. In the tropics one never knows."

"O.K. I suppose she's seen worse things."

"I will tell you about Suor Connie—at heart she is a middle-class girl."

"Is it going to be just you and me hunting?"

"You mean not Magkakanaw? No." Fra Boboy put his hand on Levin's shoulder and gave a little pat. "I don't think he would be much good. His eyes—you have to be able to focus."

Fra Boboy turned and started along the bank. Levin couldn't keep from asking, "Do you have a hunch about him?"

Fra Boboy stopped to face him. "I know the type. Very passionate, but since they are from the monied classes it is all abstract. In a way they are very dangerous animals." Levin barely nodded. "Very persuasive with these peasants, who still have the old inferior mentality. But this type cannot get over the feeling that they, individually, matter. They will try like hell, but they cannot. And that feeling has no place here. So you have certain contradictions to deal with. And if they are disappointed, because it is so abstract they can switch sides like cigarettes. This is the real danger."

"You're a quick study."

"This guy may be different. The desperation is rather shocking. Inside, he is burning. But people's actions reveal them, Dan. The truth about everybody comes out much faster up here."

Levin tried to catch his eye to read what this meant for himself. However it was intended, he heard it as a threat. From his pocket, Fra Boboy took out the sheet with dot-matrix print again; this time, he threw it in the river, where his graduate studies had gone.

They made their way among the rocks toward the path, passing within a few yards of the washerwoman, who had finished laying out clothing and was now soaping her calves in the shallows. Fra Boboy didn't acknowledge her. She bent in greeting and said something to Levin.

"What's that she said?" Levin asked. "I kept hearing it in the village."

" *'Ngot'*—what they call white people. They see so few."

"What does it mean?"

"It has to do with a little story of theirs, a spirit story." Fra Boboy swallowed a belch and sighed. "It means half man."

Levin looked back at the Jola woman. Her calves were browned and tough, like a forest animal's.

"Why do they call us that?"

"It is like a joke. When you leave the village at night and go into the woods, they say you meet a guy there who has one eye, one arm, one leg and so on—half a man. This guy will challenge you to fight. If you win, he buys you off with secrets of wisdom."

"Ah. So it's flattering. What if he wins?"

"What they say is: You return to the village never more. I like the ambiguity."

"I won't be starting any fights."

They were passing through the palm grove. At the crest of the hill the Jola's bamboo and nipa huts came into view. Levin walked behind, scratching like a dog.

"Maybe we'll run into him this afternoon. On our hunt."

"I don't think so, Dan."

"Ngot stays out of the Blue Zone?"

"Put it like this. If he is on Mount Kalanar, even Ngot is a guerrilla."

Connie attended to him in the medical hut, mercifully dark. Yellow light, cut by the shutter slats, striped his naked hairy thighs; his trousers were around his ankles.

She shone a penlight on his groin.

"It's not so bad. It's in the early stage."

Levin spoke for the first time since she'd asked him to uncover his lousy privates. "I'll bet you don't see this up here much. The fras and suors behave themselves?"

Once he had asked a guerrilla turned taxi driver how sex was managed in the mountains. The man had circled his hand around an imaginary penis and slid it up and down.

"Not up here," Connie said. "But I worked two months at a clinic in Marapang Road. And believe me, this is nothing."

The comparison did not ease Levin's mortification. At least there was no danger of embarrassing himself with tumescence.

"Are they also under the testes?" she asked.

"I'm afraid so."

"I have to shave you," she said. "It will grow back in three to four months."

Levin sat back in the chair. He felt sordid, found out, undone. Melanie was going to think it pretty strange. Worse if she found a crab on herself. He remembered the feel of the shaved fur around his dog's groin after they'd had him fixed, and how the animal had hung his head, as if he too recognized the disgrace.

Connie was snipping with surgical scissors at his pubic hair. She twisted tufts about her fingers and pulled to cut close to the roots. Tiny black curls sprang from the tip of the scissors onto his belly and thighs. Levin's manhood had receded further than he'd ever seen it.

"Did I hurt you?"

"It's just . . . very humiliating."

Connie clucked with nursely reproval. "Don't flatter yourself. This has been done one million times."

"Was it the sight of all those syphilitic white cocks in Marapang that made you a revolutionary?"

Hard as she tried, she couldn't help laughing. "One doesn't join out of disgust."

"But you were disgusted. You're disgusted now." The only remedy for such exposure was to call attention to it. Connie snipped without answer. "Anyway, why not out of disgust? It's a powerful emotion. It's a lot stronger than historical determinism." He looked down at her head; the hair was tied back with a rubber band. "You are disgusted, aren't you?"

For a reply he got a belittling nasal huff; a revolutions-don't-have-room-for-your-self-abasement answer. It strongly irritated him. She was self-righteous and evasive, and in these circumstances he felt he deserved straightforward treatment.

"I mean, there's kids out there with respiratory infections and you name it, bullet wounds. And here I am, a parable of white *kolau* imperialism. Wouldn't you rather stick me with those?"

She finished with the scissors and laid them aside. She drew up her tub of soapy water and lathered Levin vigorously, then produced a razor from her kit, a peach-colored disposable Lady Gillette. Quick half-strokes bared his pubis.

"You should try to keep your self-discipline here," Connie told him. "Maybe there's something about the Blue Zone, but you seem not the same as before. It's happened to others I've seen. Calm, calm."

The hot sudsy water and the pressure of her fingers soothed him. He entertained a brief fantasy of Connie as geisha at his knees but it didn't help and he did away with it. Among the nubs his evil guests were coming into view. He was freckled everywhere with the lice. He looked away.

"What about Ding? Does he seem the same?" She missed a stroke but didn't look up from her work. "Because he's been difficult. To say the least."

"I'm sorry, I've cut you." And indeed a nick in the white of his lower abdomen was filling with blood.

"Didn't feel a thing. So what do you think?"

"I think," she said, "that Ding is not your biggest worry."

"What is?"

"You are."

She scraped a crab loose and held it up on a fingertip to her penlight. Levin knew what he would see there. Legs, wriggling. Identical hundreds.

"You take care," she told him. "You watch out about yourself, not Ding."

"You mean the crabs?"

"The crabs are your own business, and I'm going to keep it that way. Your reputation here would certainly suffer."

She lifted his penis aside and inspected his scrotum. Then she set her razor in the tub and toweled his groin dry. When she looked at him a blade of sunlight caught her across the glasses; her brittle mouth was unsmiling. Levin decided that the Blue Zone made Connie a very nervous woman.

"Your reputation has already suffered," she said.

She opened the bottle of delousing agent, a local market brand from the People's Republic of China, and an ammoniac odor rose between them. When she laved his skin it stung a little in the place where she'd nicked him.

"He's spreading lies about me. He's crazy. I don't care."

"You'd better care."

When the reflected sun left Connie's lenses, he saw behind them that she was frightened. The intimate treatment made her his accomplice. It was as though he were seeing her real face for the first time, and he wondered what she had to be afraid of.

"How did your interview with Fra Boboy go?"

His belly muscles tightened as the cool burning hand of the agent covered his testicles.

"He's not the interview I expected."

"What did you expect?"

"I expected that the war would have made him uninteresting. From the human point of view."

"Is that what a war does?"

"Of course, if you're any good at it. It's done it to you."

Connie laughed her staccato laugh. But she didn't stop her ministrations; with a fine-tooth comb she was scraping his skin clean.

"You've lost your charm up here. You're all wires and armor."

He wondered if Connie had any female vanity in her—if that could be a way of finding her out as she'd found him.

"My best friend in São Sebastião envies me," she said. "She tells me my life is so fulfilled—that I always know the next thing to do."

"Do you dream here in the mountains?"

There was a silence, broken by the light scrape of comb on skin.

"Of course. Everybody dreams."

"Will people dream after the liberation?" The nursely cluck again. "What did you dream last night?" She shrugged; and again the evasion angered him. "I dream a lot in this country. Most of them involve violence."

"You're not habituated to it."

"What about you? Are you habituated to it?"

"I accept the necessity of armed struggle."

"That guy they shot last night—did he accept it?"

"The first violence is the state's. Revolution is the people's self-defense."

"Looks to me like educated people beating up on peasants again." That one found her.

"You've learned very little here."

"Executing peasants—that doesn't bother your conscience? As a medical person at least."

She put the comb down and brought up the basin of water. She began to wash him rather roughly. "Maybe before. But it was the hypocrisy of a bourgeoise. I wanted to squeeze every drop of it out of me. I volunteered for difficult things." She looked up at him squarely. "Once I asked to carry out a sentence—one that I had voted against. Fra Boboy wouldn't let me, but after that no one looked at me the same."

Levin shuddered and leaned back. As she dried him in silence even Connie seemed overwhelmed by what she'd told him.

Her labors were finished. Levin was shorn, deloused, rinsed, dried; clean, bare, and raw. She gave him the bottle of agent and told him to repeat the treatment in a week, when the eggs left by the crabs eliminated today could be wiped out too.

Across the open place, Ding was sitting on a bench next to one of the guerrillas, engaged in earnest talk. When Levin and Connie emerged in the sunlight, the two men looked up and the guerrilla stared at them with rapidly blinking eyes.

"It would be a good time for you to catch up on sleep," she said.

"You look like you could use a nap too."

"Do you know," Connie asked, "what rich Saraunese do when a

political crisis is coming? They check into the best hospital until it passes. I would like to do it for just a day. It's the bourgeoise in me, Dan." She smiled. "But I am needed here, so I go on."

In his hut Levin managed to sleep a little, but a mosquito that he'd killed a dozen times in his ear woke him up. He came out of obscure dreams with a weight of sadness on him; he felt it had something to do with Connie. Sadness was all right; he would take it. It wasn't bottomless, a bridgeless gorge—it might leave him with himself again. Sadness could be something like love. He could be in love with a woman like Connie.

It had to do with passion and commitment. She had these things, but they left her bereft. They didn't do it for her, she was still unhappy here under the wires and armor. That opened some space for him; but passion and commitment were his enemies, and she was faithful. So the space was closed off. What she required, he thought, was what Melanie had in abundance. Freedom of limb and tongue; devotion to basic needs. An ideology of the personal. Melanie knew more about herself than Connie ever would. And more about him too—that was the trouble. When she lay in bed tracing the outline of his face, she was declaring dominion in every aspect of his life. She would always get his number. But Connie had her own drama, her own sadness to hold her in her inward soul. It was part of her attraction for him. He could stay unknown—even when she shaved his genitals. For a while he pursued the fantasy of a hot-country affair, fine and light as the rum liqueur Dom Hipolito had served. In other circumstances, where there was plenty of freedom to go around. Connie. Connie Chatterley . . . It dissolved in the hard light of his present situation.

He dropped a line down to gauge his feelings for Melanie but could not get a read. The sadness didn't linger; the goat voice broke in and it sounded like murder. If he had a bond with Connie that was partly love, it was also partly murder. The situation came to him in a rush of clarity: she was in trouble and he was her trouble. If he was not what he made himself out to be—a thing that he, for one, was well past certain of—then she, his contact with the movement, was possibly not what she made herself to be. It was far-fetched, but Serge had said units were tearing themselves to pieces like sharks. Paranoia seemed to be the operating mood here. And if you sketched the likely profile of a deep-penetration agent, it would be someone who spent time above ground in São Sebastião, who had access to the highest level of authority, who was educated and "bourgeoise," who was unhappy in her own life. So Connie's eyes and mouth were tense with the fear that her fate depended on a man whose private parts she'd just restored to cleanliness.

If he was her trouble, then wasn't he also Ding's? But Ding was a thought he wanted to go away. Ding was trying to kill him.

Levin touched his fingers to his groin. The raw shaven feel of it burned his face with an overpowering memory of shame and fear. The skin hadn't been so bare in sixteen years.

At the time he'd been alone with his parents, and he mostly kept to his room. His brothers were gone: the oldest in law school, the middle at Hampshire College, where he was studying Cosmology with a minor in Fornication, according to their father. His parents ate dinner to the clink of silverware—his mother did Latin vocabulary cards with him to fill the silence. His father sometimes joined in, recalling the Latin of his Brooklyn boyhood: *horum, harum, horum, puella on the floorum.* It was a way of being a family together.

At the end of a week his mother had spent visiting Eric in Massachusetts, his father left the kitchen right after dinner. But later he was not to be found in the living room; he'd gone straight up to bed. Levin's room was separated from his parents' by the empty bedroom of his oldest brother, but he still managed to hear, as he did his math homework, their angry voices through the dead space. Then came a different sound, louder and heavier. Someone was crying: it was his father.

The noise, muffled by two walls, was like an animal in terrible pain—some great wailing bear caught in a steel trap. At intervals he heard his mother, soft and urgent.

The boy sat frozen at his desk, mortified.

Then she was in his doorway, lips blood-drained and thinning. "Your father needs to go to the hospital. You stay here. If I have to be overnight, can you take care of yourself?"

"Yeah, I can."

"Good boy."

"Is he going to be O.K.?"

"Of course."

She came over and kissed him on the head. He heard the water running in his parents' bathroom.

His father spent eight days in the hospital. Once the boy spoke to him on the phone. His father, on some kind of sedative, slurred and sounded oceans away, and when it was time to hang up he answered his son's good-bye with another, and another, and another. Finally in alarm the boy hung up on him.

He was given to understand that his father had experienced a nervous breakdown complicated by mild alcoholism. It turned out that during the week the mother spent at Hampshire the father had been on a bender without his twelve-year-old son's noticing.

On the day she brought her husband home from the hospital, Levin's mother spoke to her son in the kitchen.

"Things won't be the same around here," she told him. Behind the dishwasher steam he saw in her eyes focus, resolution.

There was no longer the glass of wine at dinner. Home again, his father seemed relaxed and relieved. Levin tried not to be in a room alone with him for fear that the incident would be mentioned. At times his mother referred to "your father's illness," but in general the threesome conspired to banish the memory. With a kind of grim stoic purposiveness his mother took on responsibilities—she called the plumber, she paid the taxes. And it gave her an unchallenged authority in the house. His father, dried out now to desiccation, grew docile with sporadic fits of childish pique. Side by side on the sofa arguing quarterbacks' calls on Monday Night Football, Levin and his mother wrote a tacit pact into which his father could never enter. And things were not the same again. The wail echoed through the stony house, threatening disintegration, and his mother, steel tempered in fire, was their only line of defense.

Levin, under native cloth in a Jola hut, experienced the shock in his chest. The wail was the goat voice set free.

CHAPTER IX

At altitude the ferocity of the sun deceived; under a calm blue sky the noon air was tolerably warm. Levin crossed the patch of empty dirt at the center of the hamlet to the cluster of nipa huts backed by the fallow field; beyond was the steep green rise to the crater. Outside the hut next to Fra Boboy's, a quartet of young guerrillas in various states of paramilitary dress, one female, were cleaning their automatic weapons. A fifth—Levin's guide up the mountain—strummed a guitar missing a string. Beneath the Rambo cap, his battered peasant face with the elaborate sideburns looked older and better humored than the others. He seemed to be attempting the chords for "Puff the Magic Dragon."

Levin walked by, determined not to be stared down, and smiled in a way he hoped was neither fatuous nor fearful nor aloof.

"Will you give that goddamn song a rest?"

The voice from the hut was shockingly American. Somewhere north of New Rochelle; deep, maybe cultivated; suggestive of drink and smoke and suspicion.

"Your compatriot," one of the rifle cleaners told Levin. It was Fra Timo, Ding's new friend, the cadre in charge of propaganda and community relations. He had a facial tic that amounted to a hard and constant blinking, like a recurrent wince.

"Bowers is in there?"

"Bowers," echoed the guitarist, ceasing his strumming.

"You cannot see him now," said Fra Timo.

"I don't want to. But thanks for the information."

The voice inside—it seemed to be prone—begrudged a "Thank you." The guitarist took up his chords again; from the hut came a long groan, appended with "*Shit.*"

As he passed into Fra Boboy's hut, Levin felt the stares of the guerrillas on the back of his head.

Someone was bent over the computer. When Levin stepped up onto the slatted bamboo floor, the man started violently. Ding was standing in the blue glow of the Toshiba.

"It was on," Ding said.

Levin came into the room.

"It was on when I came in."

"I believe you," Levin said. "Maybe it was meant to be seen."

Adjusting to the semidarkness, he looked into Ding's face. The eyes were wide open, as if stunned by the screen's phosphorescence. He waited, but Ding said nothing, a hand still on the commander's desk. If Levin had said "Boo," Ding would have jumped again.

"Were you looking for something?" Levin asked.

"Sort of . . . yeah."

"Something you lost?" Staring, Ding nodded. "Was it money?"

"No. Not money." He was too tightly wound to catch the joke. "Notebook?"

Ding looked bewildered. He shook his head.

"But you think Fra Boboy might have it."

"Why do you say that?"

"Well, seeing that you're in here." It was so easy to do. Like a face that follows every movement of an open hand until it gets the hard slap. "I guess it's important, whatever it is."

"It's not that important."

"Is it bigger than a bread basket? No, never mind. We'll respect each other's privacy."

Levin went to the desk and peered at the computer screen. Ding moved away and watched him with moist black fearful eyes.

The words on the screen were these:

> They ask our ideology. There is none. Mind has kept the green world in its grip. No more! They say History has ended. Lie! East and West are dead and History is born in bastard lands. Saraunization will proceed from Shadow to Act, from Absence to Presence, from Silence to Speech, from Halfness to Wholeness, from Dark-

ness to Light, from Subject to Object, from Non-Existence of Force to Existence of Force to Use of Force, from Shame to Victory, from Zero to Infinity, from Nothingness to Power. The Will to Identity shall be made concrete in Structures, Institutions, Languages, Codes, Modes of Being, which will behold the emergence of the Saraunese People in the History at the end of all histories.

Levin stepped back. "My."

"Heavy," said Ding, "isn't it?"

The capitalized nouns gave Levin a feeling of vertigo—for an instant he was peering over the Musa gorge. "What does it mean?"

"It's the genuine revolutionary article. This is the pure uncut stuff. It's all right here in this room where we're standing."

Levin looked from the swimming screen to the eyes of the man beside him and saw that Ding was not merely frightened. Within his fright crouched a creature whose eyes were not the black of fear but the yellow of—something Levin didn't know. Ready, trembling, for release. Levin understood fear, but with this other thing he was at a loss. It was, perhaps, a thing that responded to sun and stars, ocean trenches, massacres of thousands, scores of centuries and sudden obliteration. The universal mind and an exploding head. Nothingness, power. Animal eyes.

"That may be," Levin said, "but what does it mean?"

Ding laughed, sounding suddenly like the man with whom he'd shared a car the length of the country. "Shit. What you make of it, is what it means. The words are there for you to do something with."

"You'd be making a serious mistake to go on that reading."

Ding's expression became hurt and worried. "Why?"

"I don't know." Levin scratched his ear. It had been days since he'd swabbed it and the hole felt dirty and wax-clotted. "I don't think these boys are interested in subjectivity."

Ding seemed not to hear. "I knew it was going to be like this. Some of them are calling me Fra Ding." His eyes tried to focus on Levin again. "You were talking to him?" Levin understood that Ding meant Fra Boboy, and he nodded. "Did he mention me?"

"You?" He pondered Ding as a creature delivered accidentally into his hands. "Yeah. He said you were a very dangerous animal."

Terror passed over Ding's face, but it quickly flamed into aggrieved outrage.

"Bullshit! He may talk to you but he trusts me."

"Why would anyone trust you?" The flare of confrontation was making Levin dizzy again.

"You're the liar. Not me. Did you tell him you want to change the fucking attitude of the fucking American public about wars of national liberation?"

Levin recognized the phrasing of the biodata sheet he'd prepared for the guerrillas with a view to gaining entry and trust. It had seemed like a passable version of the truth at the time. The paper was in his shoulder bag, back in the hut.

"You're a sneak, Ding," he said. "See? No one can trust you. You've been going through my things."

"To find something you stole from me. Don't pretend you don't know what I'm talking about."

"I don't," Levin said. "Between us two you're the thief. A thief and a sneak and a very dangerous animal."

Ding moved toward him, until Levin's greater height made him look fiercely upward. "I don't come to your country and cheat you out of pay. I don't humiliate you in front of your friends. You say you believe in the fucking 'justice of the people's cause,' but that's not what you're about. You despise us."

Levin started for the door. "There's no point in this. You and I have nothing to say."

"You told me to keep expenses down. Then you went and bought yourself a whore." Ding was roused, pursuing him. "Did you tell her you were a statistical liberal before you put it in?"

Levin wheeled in the doorway. "How I spend my money's my business." He thrust a finger at Ding. "Just keep your fucking hands off it."

Ding came alongside him. "I know who you are."

"What are you trying to do to me?"

Levin was shouting. He moved blindly for the door, but Ding blocked the way. Levin elbowed past and suddenly they were tangled, stumbling out into the silent light in a furious embrace. It seemed absurd to him the way they grappled, exposed, in a melodramatic slow motion; he had the sense that Ding, for all his rage, was performing.

One of the guerrillas separated them, and Fra Timo pulled Levin away.

"You should concentrate on keeping friends up here," he said through a triple wince, "instead of losing them."

Midday had emptied the open place of all but a few villagers. Several women were shelling a heap of nuts under the papaya tree. The smoking Jola in his wrecked city clothes sat with them. A few stray hens were scavenging nearby and here and there a rooster crowed. The sun stared down so directly at this latitude that the huts and poles and fowl cast no shadow.

Fra Timo announced that he had details to see to for the night's events, and with Ding he crossed the open place and disappeared into a hut by the market.

It was not an hour for the human animal to be about. Midday and midnight, Levin had heard somewhere, were the dangerous times in Direv Saraun. You were alone in the sun or moon, the eye of the world.

Outside the hut where Bowers was kept, the guerrillas were carrying on in the cult of the Armalite. Bolts, pins, rings, magazines, trigger housings lay across greasy cloths. The guitarist was thrusting a wire brush up the barrel of his gun and drawing a light shower of carbon dust.

"Cleaning," he explained when Levin sat down beside him.

The siesta mood hung over the little band of gun cleaners. Levin recalled Dom Hipolito's theory of boredom as the mother of revolution. Revolution, it turned out, was no antidote. And at some point perhaps boredom mothered counterrevolution, too, betrayal and murder. Outside his bedroom window in São Sebastião a wind chime was ringing aimlessly in the hot ocean breeze—making the music without melody that always brought him the empty, far-off, castaway sadness of midday. Already his scuffle with Ding seemed unreal, soaked up by sunlight. Like Jacob's apparition jumping him in the desert night on the Jabbok. But Ding was real, demanding to be acknowledged, confronted.

"Do you ever use that thing?"

The guerrilla smiled slyly and looked at the pieces of his gun. "If I have to. But this not combat unit, Joe. This propaganda unit."

Levin had him placed: the capital's tin slums, rum with the boys in the afternoons, acquired city manner but a lingering peasant rawness. A neighborhood roundup, a beating in jail, another guerrilla was made and brought back to the deadly green silence of his fathers.

"Who do you propaganda?"

"Them." The guerrilla gestured at the empty village, the women shelling nuts, and the young man squatting with them who now noticed Levin. "Jola."

"But I don't see you people talking to them."

"Tonight. We talk."

"What will you talk about?"

"The liberation, Joe."

It was the old catechism, meaningless with repetition, hollow and irritating. Yet there was no taint of the perfunctory or ironic. He believed. And Levin remembered the time when his own stomach would have clenched in a fist of secret solidarity.

The young Jola was crossing the open place toward them. From what was left of his shirt pocket he took a pack of Marlboros.

"Cigarette?"

The guerrilla declined and went back to his cleaning. For the first time in Direv Saraun, Levin refused too.

"You don't smoke?" the Jola asked.

It seemed incredible that English should come out of his mouth, under the wilderness of hair.

"No. Where did you get those Marlboros?"

The question surprised the Jola. "In São Sebastião."

"That's where you picked up English?"

The Jola nodded, and bent toward Levin. The closeness of his grin was a little unnerving, and Levin leaned back. The Jola murmured, "I wish to talk to you."

"Well, I'm engaged right now. Maybe tonight or something."

The young man stiffened and nodded. "Tonight." He returned to the shade of the papaya tree, as if he would wait there all day for Levin.

"Unemployed," the guerrilla said, blowing carbon off his hands.

"The idleness here is really something."

Levin avoided looking toward the papaya tree, for he knew the Jola was watching him.

"So tell me," he said. "What's it going to be like, after the liberation?"

The guerrilla put down the rifle and the brush and took off his cap to wipe his forehead. His leathery features tightened to a squint, as if he could just make out a liberated Direv Saraun over the hillside beyond the huts.

"After the liberation . . ." He was searching for the words. "Free and equal, you me them. No boss. My kids eat every day, my little boy diarrhea cure. His papa don't got to live in the mountain." The guerrilla shrugged. The recitation had embarrassed him, and he began reassembling the Armalite's operating parts. "You going to come and see, Joe?"

"The liberation? I'll do my best. Sure."

Levin was thinking of the Balatangs. He reflected that, as much as he liked this guerrilla, he would like him even better, all of them, without guns. Guns came between him and them, guns made it difficult to think of them as victims. However, he could hardly expect them to disarm.

The guerrilla pointed at an undernourished hen pecking the dirt and grinned, expanding his fantastic sideburns and showing the black space between his lips. "Her husband going to fight tonight."

Levin didn't understand at once. "You mean . . . a cockfight?"

The guerrilla nodded. "The Jola—" He made a face suggestive of some mad obsession. "Yow!"

"They'll be gambling? Drinking?"

"Gamble. Drink. Cultural Night—yow!"

The guerrilla spoke as between civilized men faced with an unfathomable barbarism. He had completed his ministrations and he hinged his weapon shut.

"Who is that man, do you think? The American in there?"

"Spy, Joe." The guerrilla said it the way he'd said "the liberation," as if it were common knowledge.

"Do you think all Joes are spies?"

"Oh, no, Joe." He looked at Levin quizzically and touched him on the hand. "Not all. Like you—journalist."

Levin was sorry to have broken the thread of simple belief by which the whiskered guerrilla seemed held. In another mood, at another time, it might have been enough to sew up the fragments of his notion of justice. Instead of a notion, he now had an enemy. No wonder he didn't feel like a journalist.

Somewhere on Mount Kalanar, Direv Saraun, Feb. 24—As a believer in the inevitability of ultimate justice for the Saraunese poor, this reporter staked his hopes and in some sense his reputation on the existence of a guerrilla Middle Way. His hopes dashed and his reputation jeopardized, he is led to wonder whether the emergence of the Saraunese People in the History at the end of all histories will look anything like his private vision of justice; whether, if it won't, he has any right to regret that fact; whether such visions are not part of his fundamental irrelevance. Justice, little bird, has shown herself no match for blood and razors. She lies in the dirt sliced, gored, shredded, her feathers matted. And after all, she was always a vain thing, preening, too delicate, incapable of feeding herself in the world as it is—only able to survive caged. A fighting cock, unseen enemy, did her the favor of showing this. When they let her out, innocence provoked him—maddened his blood. He said: You want a picture of justice? And answered with hard blind furious kicking spurs.

It was a long moment before Levin became aware of someone standing over him. The figure was shadowless in the noon sun and faceless against the light, but each hand held a rifle and one of them was thrust at him. An instant later the figure turned into Fra Boboy, binoculars dangling from his neck. It was only posture and light, playing a sinister trick. Levin took the offered gun, a lever-action Winchester .30-.30 with a battered walnut stock.

"Have you eaten?" Fra Boboy asked. Levin shook his head. "No one hunts on an empty stomach, unless he has to. Otherwise he wants his prey too much."

They had a plate of Chinese macaroni and pepper sauce in the house of the village headman. Then Levin and Fra Boboy left the village and crossed the field toward the steep green volcanic mass of Mount Kalanar.

From the field the forest had glistened, every leaf shone wet and trembled. Inside it was like dusk, nightfall at the height of day. The half-light condensed into a kind of mist on the forest floor. Trees, furry lianas, saplings, shrubs, fallen leaves, rotten logs whirled about—Levin had no names for them. The sigh of his own feet on the earth was swallowed by the encompassing green, then reappeared somewhere else. The forest's noise rose around him. Noonday cicadas vibrated their belly membranes in the frantic hunt for a mate before death—their trill rose to the pitch of a buzz saw and fell away again. Frogs pulsed in a low shaded place where water stood; higher up, birds stuttered and shrieked. The noises ceased to be distinct, to originate anywhere. The forest seethed with sound.

Within two minutes Levin didn't know whether the village was behind them or in front.

Fra Boboy led, making his way through the lichened trees. He carried his gun loosely at his side as if there would be some hiking before the hunt began.

It changed things, having a rifle in one's hand. Levin's body was electric and so was the immediate air. Fra Boboy seemed not to care that his back was turned to an armed man he'd known less than a day, who another man claimed was the enemy.

Levin nearly stumbled into the commander's blue T-shirt when Fra Boboy halted. "You can see it's volcano here." With his rifle butt he cleared away the leafy mulch cover. Levin saw a swell of gray pumice. From the disturbed vegetation rose a sweetish smell of mud and rot.

"Dormant?"

"The Jola don't have that word. A thing is alive or dead and this thing is alive."

Levin stared ahead into the verdant confusion.

"Do you know your way through here?"

"I take my constitutional every day this way."

They were passing through patches of light and shade, and the ground underfoot had begun to rise. The big teaks fell behind; the trees here were no more than fifty or sixty feet high, Malayan yews and twisted mountain gelam—names Levin had read but trees he'd never seen.

"Those peasants don't understand a man going into the forest without some business there," Fra Boboy said. "And they don't understand the need to be alone. Of course, it can be terrifying at first. Later, intoxicating."

"What do you think they make of you?"

"The Jola?"

"They don't seem . . . really in sync with your people."

"You may not believe it," Fra Boboy said, shaking his head free of something, "but do you remember that guy I told you went up to the crater during the Japanese occupation?"

Levin waited.

"They think the fellow has finally come down."

"Sort of a mythic presence."

"Modesty aside—that's it. On some level the association has been made."

"Isn't it embarrassing for you?"

"Dan, if I came up here preaching equality they would laugh me off the mountain. And rightly so. Equality is something to talk about later, but it has no place at this stage of the struggle."

"The Jola have quite a mythology."

"I tell you, in another life," Fra Boboy said with ironic wistfulness, "I'd have written a monograph. They are the thing itself." He had slowed so that Levin could walk alongside him. "Of course, monographs are for the birds."

"You don't explain the world now—you change it?"

"Not really. Marx missed that one too. We are given this finite human stuff in a finite world—trees, dirt. Any change happens on the level of perception, which is not finite but limitless. For example, you remember this morning the woman called you Ngot?"

Levin remembered.

"Ngot, as the professors would say, is the Jola's central mythic figure. Ngot is one reason they don't understand my walks. He is dangerous, hidden, tricky, violent. He has no pity in him because he comes from the forest where pity has no place. So there is no appeasing him. For Ngot there's nothing but struggle—defeat, victory."

The surrounding buzz of the forest absorbed Fra Boboy's words. Levin became aware of the absurdity of human speech— so many cicada abdomens chirping. Here in the wet scratching woods it was just pitch and tone. Yet Fra Boboy kept talking—and it seemed like hubris again, gross defiance. A man who could converse in the rain forest could blow up bridges, bring war to a large city, goad a nation into violent frenzy. If the woods said, You are nothing to us, then two human responses were possible: lie down and sleep under them, or take the chain saw to them. Defeat, victory. Fra Boboy was cutting down the woods.

"In the lucidity of midnight out here," the commander said, "I began to think about Ngot, this nasty fellow. And a little theory came to me. I believe Ngot is what makes history go."

They had come up into a clearing of the trees; the ground here was strewn with great rotting leaves and fallen timber aswarm with unseen creatures. Levin was sweating heavily into his shirt. Fra Boboy stopped and turned to him, looking almost grave.

"Even the Marxists, the ones left, think it all takes place reasonably. History as a sort of gentleman's agreement between thesis and antithesis. This is just one more oppression, another velvet fist from the Enlightenment. It certainly doesn't speak to the people on this mountain. But Ngot, the half man—he speaks to them. They feel his presence all the time. And now the country does, and everyone is reaching for a gun. Ngot is what creates the really big changes, what society hasn't understood about itself, what the foreign press doesn't write. And the individuals on this earth who have the clarity to grasp Ngot can make history."

Fra Boboy's fleshy features had relaxed as if the explanation itself were a kind of victory.

"Such as you?"

"Modesty aside."

"So violence, it's just—"

"Oh, violence is part of the human condition. Before I came to the mountains this was an itch, not a war. No one had the courage to see that the people required a certain level of it. The despair had reached a point where a release of violence would legitimize certain half-formed desires, and the people would turn our way."

"Something like . . . the 'impure' kind?"

Fra Boboy shrugged. "Dan, all this reminiscence is going to make me melancholy. I don't know that the language has any real application. But if you insist, sure."

"I wish I'd read the whole dissertation."

A rustling in the trees made both men look up. Thirty feet overhead a branch was violently shaking. Leaves and pods showered in and out of the filtered beams. Levin couldn't see anything, but Fra Boboy was raising his rifle, moving it right to left along the branch. His face twisted in the effort to sight along the barrel and his finger was clenched on the trigger, but for a long moment he didn't shoot. Levin followed his aim upward.

In the green and yellow leafiness something gray, something furry, had stopped moving and was lurking on the branch. Levin found himself confronted with the humanoid features of a monkey.

"See her?"

"Yeah."

Fra Boboy lowered his rifle. "She's yours."

The lips curled back over the teeth; the clownish eyes, ringed white, were wide in terror. She crouched on the branch, sideways toward them, looking over her shoulder—caught there. And she stared the men down with an intensity that was chilling and confusing. So unlike, and so like. Levin raised his rifle and sighted the creature within the small Vs of the Winchester's guides. He tensed for the blast.

Suddenly the monkey opened her jaws and howled—a staccato, honking, farcical, hair-raising howl, much louder than the little body seemed capable of. It was ferocious laughter. And then the howl got caught like a car horn and sank deeper into a sob of unearthly grief.

His gunshot cut it short. A light spray of blood flew from the head. The gray body rolled with absurd grace off the branch and crashed into the underbrush beyond the clearing. The fall was of dead weight and the ground shook with surprising force.

Levin lowered his gun. The air smelled strongly of smoke, burning. The blast rang in his ears as if his own head had been hit. He'd been expecting this sound from the hour he arrived in Direv Saraun, and now it mingled with the echo of the monkey's laugh and her sob. Every muscle in Levin's body seemed to be released from a cramp. He stood mute in the middle of the forest, stunned, dizzy with relief.

Fra Boboy waded into the underbrush. He poked about with the barrel of his rifle, then squatted and came up with the quarry. He carried it into the clearing in his arms, as if it were a child, the tail and a thin arm hanging lifeless. In death the monkey's face had turned wholly simian and strange. Part of the jaw had been torn away and the hair on that side of the face was wet and black. The eyes were shut so hard they seemed to have withdrawn into the white muzzle. The fingers were long and delicate.

"Good shot!" Fra Boboy cried. He was in high excitement. "Dusky langur. They can fly, almost. I don't know why she didn't jump."

"I—thought I would miss."

"You're a natural." Fra Boboy studied the corpse with a hunter's belated pity and interest. Then he dropped it into his canvas sack. "The Jola will take this as an omen. They'll cook her up this evening, before our Cultural Night. The spleen has magic in it." He didn't hide his satisfaction with Levin. "A dusky langur, really. So rare."

"What kind of omen?"

"Good," Fra Boboy laughed, as one who couldn't conceive defeat.

After the clearing the ground rose sharply. The canopy's height had hidden the approach of the cliff. Here the saddle where the village and the guerrilla camp were nestled ended, and Mount Kalanar made its last ascent to the dish of the volcanic peak.

The vegetation was changing, too. They were climbing into cloud forest: the trees became dwarf, stunted, writhing in gnarled shapes, but the leaves here grew to monstrous sizes like elephant ears, and great ferns fanned out of the earth. Trunks and branches were draped with moss and wrapped in tangled nests of bromeliads, whose flowers stood erect and carmine in the center of their spiked leaves. The path, under a cover of vines and ground roots, was uneven with igneous rock, and whole areas of the mountainside around them had been cleared by lava flow. The air was damp, fragrant—slightly bitter. A trace of sulfur dioxide was misting out of the volcano's severed head. The pumice soil nourished a garden of unimagined shapes and colors and smells.

Levin was struggling up a high step when he slipped. He grabbed at a fern, and the noise sent a bird fluttering out of a tree just overhead. There was a great flash of color—black, white, brown-red in the shade—and then it disappeared. Fra Boboy wheeled with his rifle but didn't shoot.

"Hornbill," he said.

It had flown from a fig tree—a strangling fig, coiled round another tree that was completely hidden and dying in its grip. At their feet lay dozens of green fruit.

"The big birds love these trees," said Fra Boboy. "Maybe that parrot from this morning. Wait for a while—get out of view, over there, in case he comes back. I am going up higher to look for more stranglers. Just wait—ten minutes. Take these." He gave Levin the binoculars. "Perhaps you can see down the mountain."

Fra Boboy left the loaded sack on the ground. And then, for the first time on the hunt, Levin lost sight of him in the elfin forest.

For a few moments, he clutched his rifle and didn't know which way to move. He was thinking about traps again: behind the fig, under that fern, that decaying log—solitude aroused the possibility of danger at every turn. But shortly, enough confidence returned for him to gather the sack and leave the trail under the strangling fig.

He walked sideways along the slope, about thirty feet through thin covering to a place where the sun hit the amber forest floor. There was a leafy seat of brown lava rock, fairly dry in the light. Levin set down the bag and rifle and looked out at the mountainside.

The forest here was low enough for him to see all the way down to the Jola village hundreds of feet below. He saw the clearing and the shaggy thatch rooftops, and when he lifted the binoculars he could make out, between shifting mists, the movement of human beings.

There was nothing to do now but sit and wait. From his lava seat he had a clear view to the trail. Behind him, sunlight and shade played through a mossy grove of twisted trees. But uphill, where Fra Boboy had disappeared, the forest had the advantage over him, closing off his view beyond twenty or thirty feet.

The smell of decaying figs and vegetation mingled with the faint rotten-egg odor of the volcano. A sharper smell was permeating the place, and he guessed it was the monkey. The mountain wetness had already begun to sour his prey.

He noticed flowers. Languid orchids and spiny shocks of bromeliad, hibiscus with their organs dangling, birds of paradise, were emerging from the green cover—a brilliance of orange and white and red. Soon he saw them everywhere, on all sides: they clung to the trees and hung overhead from clumps of swollen bulbs, sprouted out of rocks and logs. A blue hummingbird flitted among the orchid petals. Superabundance, movement and color, the heavy forest perfume and the great undifferentiated sound whirled around his head.

He had to look down. His left shoe had settled on a column of black ants, half an inch each; they continued under it with their freight of millipede. A thrust of his heel, and he could turn their universe into calamity.

If he had to find his own way back, he could not.

It had once been enough, the old self of moral sympathies and disinterested espionage in the world as it is. It had seemed like enough. His mother, for one, had never suggested there might be something else out there. His newspaper held on to a vision of the world at its fingertips. But this corner of it, this raw overgrown smothering mountainside, had not been considered. People had been wrong and he among them. Perhaps Melanie had tried to warn him. But he was far from Melanie—from all of them.

Even now, this moment, a hunter might have him lined up in a rifle sight like the monkey on the branch. In another moment, the report of the gun, and he would be the one howling.

He stiffened. Then he turned to look behind and had a vision of Ngot half slouching against a tree trunk.

There was no one, just greenery and sunlight. The only thinking, calculating, mindful thing in this place was him. Two minds in a world could find a way to survive, but one was a fatal number. Against these creepers and ants and monkeys and birds and figs and flowers it had no chance. They would all drive it crazy, or wait while the mind did the number on itself. One ticking mind in nature was madness.

The forest was like Feliz's coreless fruit, at the hollow of it a puny omnipotence.

The hunting sack had soaked through in one spot. He leaned forward and opened it. He saw coarse stiff gray hair, thin primate limbs. Under the twisted body, the dead little monkey head pressed against the side of the sack; the lips were drawn back from clenched teeth. A paw covered the eyes, as if in pain or shame or sleep. Levin closed it again.

You were the hunter, and also the prey. It was strictly a matter of positive thinking. What one wanted was air in the lungs.

He tried to wait. Simply to wait out the minutes alone before Fra Boboy returned. What he needed was a task. He could unload the shells from the rifle in his lap; but then he would have nothing to protect himself with. On the other hand, to sit with a loaded rifle in one's lap was asking for trouble. Because, who was one anyway? He tried to determine whether he was better off armed or disarmed, but the question so confused him that he had to wipe it away. Well, he could destroy this caravan of ants. But that would solve nothing. Or he could wait.

But he could not wait. He'd come halfway around the world to see a war, and he hadn't the ability to sit still with himself for fifteen minutes. It was no longer possible to sit in his Levin self, thinking his Levin thoughts. Now that he heard them—how strange and awful they were. It seemed unbearable to go on being that self and thinking those thoughts for another ten seconds.

He searched frantically with his eyes. The mountainside offered no help. There was nowhere in this forest where he could get outside his mind and stop being himself. No one to interrupt his thoughts, ask him a favor, and if he answered the monkey with a cry of his own no one would hear.

His hand gripped the Winchester's wooden stock. Just to turn the barrel this way, so the sights are reversed, in the mouth and out the forehead, like that dream . . . Now he became truly alarmed. He stood up and nearly blacked out and sought refuge in the sound of his own voice. His thin strangled human voice.

"You. Ding." The forest was spinning.

What you needed in Direv Saraun was an enemy. That was what Fra Boboy said; and everyone knew it was so. Only he'd imagined he could go without. Fatuous—impossible.

A buddy, and an enemy, and a gun. Well, here was the gun. He'd already found out what it was like to use it. It was all right; it seemed to help. And as for the other two things—they'd simply offered themselves. Who was he to refuse?

A rush of energy surged into his head, and it felt like strength. His lungs were filling with air. He'd never experienced anything like it. He sat down again, keeping his hand on the butt of the rifle, and now he felt that he could wait.

Somewhere on Mount Kalanar, Direv Saraun, Feb. 24—Excerpts from an interview with the Commander of the Army of Liberation's Southern Region:

"Thank you for coming."

"Thank you for inviting me."

"Is it what you hoped for?"

"What do you mean?"

"The war. The faces. The words. The whole feel of the place."

"Do you expect me to call myself a stupid romantic and admit my delusions?"

"Come on. I'd hoped we could be honest with each other, leaving recriminations aside."

"You can't blame me for being a little edgy. Suspicious."

"You've had a hard time, haven't you? Out of your depth?"

"I wouldn't say that. I still like the politics here, the intrigues."

"But you're always having to prove your goodwill. You get tired of having to be reasonable."

"What can one be but reasonable?"

"It makes you small and hollow. Your voice—such thinness. Don't you want to shout?"

"Sometimes I want nothing more in the world."

"Then why not do it? The whole world is shouting. All of us in Direv Saraun are."

"Not all of you. Feliz isn't."

"How many divisions has Feliz?"

"Is that all that matters?"

"At this stage—yes. And I'm not going to bother telling you that the sword is mightier than the pen. You already know that. What you

don't know is that sometimes the sword is better, too. Humanly speak-ing. Christ, the Christ of the Jesuits, said he wasn't bringing peace. Peace isn't what we need just now."

"What does that have to do with me?"

"You're the one who came here. To see. I'm telling you there's more than meets the eye. I feel moved to help you write the truth."

"You mean your propaganda."

"Propaganda is perhaps the only kind of truth we can hope to attain here. It nourishes and sustains. Its rightness corresponds to its inten-sity."

"And if it keeps us out of your war—"

"Then all the better. Ultimately, there's nothing that Americans can do about Direv Saraun. But it might be helpful for them to get a dose of clarity. It might help them resolve their own despair."

"Is that what ails us?"

"Of course. A lot of frantic behavior as a distraction from existential dread. The excess itself is despair."

"Sounds like grad-school philosophizing."

"I learned a great deal in grad school, and some of it I'm putting to use. Eventually, though, one outgrows it. But there you go again, changing the subject from yourself to the world."

"I'll bet I know what comes next. You're going to say the same goes for me."

"I'm afraid you'd call me presumptuous."

"No—I want you to speak freely."

"Well? Isn't it clear enough?"

"We all have our funks. Nothing new there."

"Is that what this is—a funk?"

"Why not?"

"Murder. Madness. Are these normal things for you?"

"They didn't start till I got here. Maybe they'll stop when I leave."

"Now you're not speaking freely. You don't really believe that?"

"Whether I do or not, it's no one else's business as long as I keep it to myself."

"That's what I mean by despair! You're going to go to pieces."

"What should I do?"

"Lay down the burden of your life. Just for a while."

"That's not so easily done. I can't seem to stop being me."

"Pernicious illusions! Of course you can. Not physically—we're trying to keep you from that. But remember the black sailor. And the

Army of Liberation, and the Cavaleiros de Aviz. Think of Connie. Think of Ding."

"Who's going to live it for me in the meantime?"

"I will."

"You?"

"Modesty aside."

"I know the game. There's always a quid pro quo."

"I only ask you to face things. Look at yourself with clarity and without reproach. Find out where your interests lie. Then stop wishing the world to be any different. And write accordingly."

"I don't accept the equivalence. That's sophistry."

"Is it? Are you sure it isn't arrogance on your part—hypocrisy? Isn't this journalism the ultimate fantasy of omnipotence?"

"No. And even if it is, it doesn't kill people. Why are you laughing?"

"Because you who talk that way don't even know you're going to die. There's no end to you, is there? In a dozen countries you could be a dozen people—and look! You're really not even one."

"I know enough about death. But I refuse to let it run my life. It has nothing to do with the living of my life."

"What you call the living of your life is just a million diversions from what the lowest Jola is born knowing."

"But he's not my brother. There's got to be other things—what about goodness, and love? Don't they have a role in this situation?"

"Spare me the preachments. In Direv Saraun those things amount to epiphytes, and Marapang Road. They're the world's wet dream of us and they won't get you anywhere at this stage."

"Then what are you fighting for?"

"You still don't know."

"You talk about the people, Saraunization. I don't know what these mean."

"They are what the professors call floating signifiers, set adrift by war. Because for them to mean any one thing would sink them, no? I'm fighting . . . call it my gesture against the sadness of limit and mortality. From a therapeutic point of view, violence has been consistently underrated. Why are you so glum all of a sudden?"

"I wasn't prepared for this. I didn't know it was going to be this way."

"You just forgot about yourself in the rush to get out here. You don't know how lucky you are that you found me."

"But it's hard to give up the old middle ground."

"Gone! It was never there. So isn't there anything I can do for you?"

A noise overhead made Levin start. Through a slow druggy gauze of sweat he saw that the hornbill had returned. The bird nibbled at a fig, its ruffled brown back and rufous skull exposed to him. Big and gaudy, a foot long, it perched there eating with its outsized beak as if the world held no dangers.

Levin was lifting his gun when the bird bolted. It flew off with astonishing speed and grace, toward the lower teak forest.

As his eye followed its flight down mountain, he had a glimpse of figures moving through the cloud forest. A couple of hundred feet down and to the west three men were walking in single file. He raised the binoculars and searched the elfin trees until he found the men again. Shock made him drop the glasses from his eyes.

With their weapons, they might have been guerrillas. But there was no mistaking the middle one—the purple streaks in the surprising hair, styled, almost *malaka*—and he was sure he recognized the others too. They were three of the soldiers in the jeep at the Fazenda Maria Luísa: Captain Bugan's elite scouts. They went without hats, two of them with bandannas tied around their heads; they wore camouflage trousers and T-shirts. On their backs they carried M-16s fitted with 40 mm. grenade launchers. Brown serious faces and the stealth of their stride suggested mission, a calm relentless seeking, a hunt. They moved like jungle cats whose purpose it was to be here and not be seen.

One of them stopped to survey the view of the village down mountain. Then the wind shifted, bitter mist blew over from the crater, and Levin couldn't see past the trees surrounding him.

He knew what these men were doing on this mountain. They could have no other business than the raid Dom Hipolito de Oliveira had brashly predicted to him. A sort of luck—journalist's luck—had come Levin's way. Yet even in the blood-rush of this discovery, he was aware of his own dissatisfaction.

He was flashing faces: Colonel Siriman's nod in the white glare of camera lights. The concierge at Las Encantadas, her desk-clerk smile when he'd made his slip. The lookout at the bamboo house fumbling with his two-way. The dyed hair of the man at the jeep's wheel. Captain Bugan whispering near the landlord's ear and Dom Hipolito's gaze going weak, his eyes on the terra-cotta tiles.

Everywhere Levin's mind went was the faint scent he himself had left. He was the marker, the bird with a transmitter fastened to its claw, the eagle flying unwittingly between sea and sky.

No matter how he figured, it came out this way: They were here because of him. They'd known where he was going and he'd led them to this place. They'd known because Fra Boboy was wrong, the infiltration hadn't been stopped, it fed on the infection of the guerrillas' paranoia. Deep-penetration agents. People Fra Boboy didn't want on Mount Kalanar had gotten in far enough to know about the invitation to an American reporter. But for the last step they'd needed someone to show them the way.

Ding could not have arranged things worse for him.

"Shit." He heard himself say it aloud and it made him think of the stolen notebook and how much trouble had come to him since then.

Gazing into the misted green that spread out below, Levin tried to see his situation with clarity. It might be craziness. It might be the paranoia of the forest. He might have spooked himself up here into a fantasy of omnipotence. But a coldness at the base of his spine told him to believe it, and he felt that he needed to trust the instincts more.

Slowly he began to imagine that he could turn it all to his advantage. He would have to be calmer and shrewder than he'd shown himself so far. He knew that he wouldn't tell Fra Boboy what he'd seen. There was no way of being sure that the commander wouldn't decide to turn against him, as Fra Timo and possibly others had already done. Fra Boboy wouldn't welcome the news and he wouldn't respond well to an ambiguous situation. If Levin had led the enemy here, why spare Levin? Why not believe Magkakanaw? Beyond these fears he recognized the instinct to let the story proceed, to place himself where it was happening. In some ways this instinct, smelling of ambition, was even stronger than fear. But strongest of all was the desire to preserve the moment he'd been afforded up here, alone in the strange cloud forest, the sense of powers restored, confidence renewed. The possibility of a new self.

And if a coincidence of wishes and instincts and fears had suddenly occurred, then that must be a sign. It happened seldom in one's life. He would have no right to refuse it. More and more he saw that this was what he had to do. He had no business working out moral responses; out here there was only victory and defeat. It was necessary to acknowledge the enemy, confront, act.

Then he remembered the captured American, and his spirit sank. Nobody in São Sebastião seemed to know what Bowers had been up to, whom Bowers had been working for. It could have been for Siriman. The colonel alone knew Bowers's location—then Bowers might have been part of the colonel's plan. Another marker, in case one failed. So Levin would have to find out what Bowers knew about him, what Bowers might already have told his captors and what he might yet tell. It wearied him to think that he would have to locate his journalistic tools and put them back to use. But nothing was going to be the same now, least of all himself.

He was standing in a barrage of memory and calculation, still clutching his weapon, when he heard a gunshot up mountain. Before long Fra Boboy came through the trees above him, holding up a bright green bird by the feet.

"You didn't see anything?"

"No. I mean, the hornbill came back but he flew off before I could take a shot."

Fra Boboy was shaking his large head. "Damn. That is a lucky bird."

"I told you hunting's not in my background."

"But you killed the dusky langur."

They started downhill. Fra Boboy carried the guns and Levin the sack that now contained a monkey and a vernal hanging parrot. On their left the sun was beginning to sink. The forest mist had lifted and a soft light slanted through the treetops, whose shadows were starting to cross the ground. Rustlings, birdcalls, odors of the twilight rose around them. Katydids had begun their crepuscular music, and somewhere in the distant trees a pair of gibbons was chattering.

Sun and exertions had taken a toll and Levin felt a headache gathering. Evening in the tropics had always come as a balm—it hid the day's ugliness and eased the tension of the day's discoveries, brought fantasy and the taste of his original adventure. But as he came down the mountain with Fra Boboy, he knew the darkness would be swift and feared what it would bring.

When they had descended into the gathering gloom of the teak forest, Levin said what he'd made up his mind to say; he spoke as casually as he could.

"I wonder if Ding has talked to you about staying up here."

Fra Boboy made a little noise—it almost sounded like a sigh of pleasure. After a pause, he asked, "Did he tell you?"

"I . . . heard from someone else. He doesn't confide in me. We've fallen out." Levin added, "Ding is not all that discreet."

"He told someone he was coming up here?"

"A bunch of journalists in Pulaya. He got pretty drunk. As I said, he's not very discreet."

Fra Boboy's large face tightened angrily. They walked in silence for a few moments.

Levin asked, "So why would he want to stay here?"

"He talked about taking pictures. Revolutionary images, he called them."

"Do you think that's what he wants to do?"

"I can't tell. A few of our people are worried. They don't know his intention."

Levin had somehow known he would hear something like this.

"Is that right?"

"I think," said Fra Boboy, "he perhaps is not good? Do you agree?"

Levin was moved to glance over the sack on his shoulder. "What do you mean?"

"Not reliable. Dangerous."

"Ah."

"What do you think?"

Levin thought about it. "I think you're right."

"Yes?"

"Yeah. On the trip here he stole a lot of money from me. I'm fairly certain of it. In general he acted suspiciously."

"So it's true!" The commander had allowed himself to become indignant. "As a matter of fact, he has something of mine—he stole something from me too. It's not an important thing, but he won't return it and that concerns me. And now you say he told others. . . . Between friends, Dan, we've had some occasional cases of infiltration by rightist elements in the past. Not serious, but a nuisance. So close to the command center—it wouldn't be good."

"Not at all."

"Then you see?"

"Of course."

"In our business we nip trouble in the bud."

"I'm beginning to appreciate that."

When they reached the fallow field and had the village in view, Fra Boboy asked, "What do you suggest?"

"About Ding? I think . . . it's up to you."

"Look, Dan. I value your advice. You traveled with this man. Can I trust him?"

Levin was breathing hard under the load of spoils. "I don't think so. But I don't know what he wants. Maybe keep an eye on him and see if anything develops."

"Yes, exactly." Fra Boboy seemed satisfied. "As you say, he's indiscreet. The future will tell."

"I imagine you'll find out pretty soon."

They had come to the edge of the village and wended their way through the alleys behind the market. The penned hogs were squealing for their evening feed. The air was gray with dusk and woodsmoke from cooking fires. In the middle of the village, where guerrillas were already rigging two makeshift poles with electric lights, Jola peasants milled about the open place, boys led buffalo from the day's labor to their posts. Levin didn't see the fellow who'd accosted him at noon.

He said, "You remember telling me I could talk to your prisoner before Cultural Night starts?"

"Of course. Just let Fra Timo know." Fra Boboy unburdened him of the canvas sack and jigged the corpses inside. "The headman's wife will prepare a roast. Everyone is going to enjoy themselves tonight." Levin started for his hut. "Dan—do you know what the Jola people say?"

Levin stopped and shook his head.

"When you hunt with a man, you trust him with your life. Then you become brothers."

Levin accepted the outstretched hand.

CHAPTER X

At sunset, as the fireball flared on the lip of the world, pinking the green edges of Mount Kalanar, Levin went in to find Gardner Bowers. The Army of Liberation had placed its prisoner at his disposal for the hour or so before the festivities of Cultural Night began.

As he ducked into the hut Levin was met by the smile of a young guerrilla in gym shorts who had the narrow, haunted, shrewd features of a Malay Al Pacino. He was standing over a chair in which Bowers was seated with his back to the door, his head lolling on an oddly long neck, eyes closed. The guerrilla appeared to be shaving him. Upside down, the eyes appeared sealed by swollen veiny pouches. Levin had counted on Bowers being a drinker. The lower face was lathered in watery soap. The guerrilla had the nose between two fingers and was scraping at the tender spot under Bowers's chin with what could well have been the same peach-colored disposable razor that Connie had used in the morning on Levin's groin.

In the beguiling light of a kerosene lamp hanging from a nail on the wall, they made a tableau of colonial leisure and native humility.

The guerrilla paused at his labor. Bowers's pouches opened and directly his eyes met Levin's; in the general dissipation of his face they stared out with a hard gray intensity. Levin's nod received no answer. The hoods dropped upside down.

The Saraunese gave a merry little shrug and returned to shaving. From somewhere in the soapy face a sigh escaped. And suddenly it came to Levin, outside the circle of light, that these weren't ministrations. Bowers was not a man of leisure under the care of a handsome minion, lifting a finger for a glass of Rum Direv. He was a captive creature being groomed and fatted for sacrifice, or prepared for feasting. A fish scraped of its scales.

Delicately, Levin introduced himself.

"I know who the hell you are," Bowers growled. The guerrilla clucked reprovingly at the motion of his jaw under the blade. "And I know what you're up to. I could smell it when you walked in."

Levin stood motionless. "What am I up to?"

"You're a goddamn snoop."

Levin glanced at the young guerrilla, and was met with a smile and a wink. He seemed to have understood nothing beyond the tone.

"Is that right?"

"You're a journalist, aren't you? You're with the *World Press,* aren't you?"

"You got it."

"I got it," Bowers said. "A goddamn snoop."

"If it's a bad time I could come back later."

"I could care less what you do. Stay, go. All the same."

Levin split the difference; he waited in the doorway.

"For Christ's sake," Bowers said. "Do you want an engraved invitation? Shut the door, you're letting the other bloodsuckers in with you."

Levin closed the door and went to sit on the only available piece of furniture, Bowers's cot, which still left him outside the light. From here he had a side view of Bowers's long pallid frame sprawled against the back of the rattan chair. He tried to imagine the prisoner being soothed by a friendly American voice from the darkness. Admittedly, Bowers was hard to see as a trusted intimate of the Armed Forces of Direv Saraun, sharing an imported cigarette with Colonel Siriman—but Levin had been proved wrong about everything else.

"What do you want?" said Bowers.

"Hey, Hartford!" the guerrilla barked. The razor was on Bowers's Adam's apple, which stuck out of the windpipe like a piece of broken bone.

"I just wanted to talk," Levin said.

"No you don't."

"What do I want, then?"

"Don't pull that psychology crap. You want a goddamn story, that's all any journalist wants. Doctors want pain, shrinks want fucked-up heads, whores want a sap with a hard-on he can't shake and journalists want a story. Preferably an unhappy one with an element of the bizarre and an angle the folks back home can relate to. That's why you've come to me. I don't hold it against you," Bowers said through his teeth. "We do what we can in this world. It just so happens that in a stinking world what we do usually stinks."

"Well, I'm sorry to hear that," Levin told him. "I thought you were brought up here by a noble cause."

A wrong move. Levin hadn't meant for it to come so soon. Bowers was eyeing him over the soapy, marred plane of his face.

"You want to know what brought me up here?"

Levin shrugged and answered indifferently, "Only if you want to tell me."

"I don't. Oh, I see through you, Levin. I know all about you."

"Really." Levin smiled thinly and leaned back a little deeper out of the light. "For example?"

"You're pretty fucking subtle."

"I'm not trying to be subtle."

"You got a recorder hidden on you?"

"Why would I do that?"

"I've had plenty of experience with journalists," Bowers told him. "I know my man."

"Where?"

"Here, there, and yon. The where doesn't matter. Same everywhere."

As the soap disappeared under the peach razor's quick strokes, Bowers's features were revealed. Lines plunged from eyes to chin on either side of a straight Roman nose that was raw with broken veins. A bit of scar under the lower lip created a fastidious overbite and a slight Hapsburg curl. The skin was dry-ash-gray and haggard, poised to slip off the skull. But most striking was the way the eyes pierced between distended lids. It was a face that hadn't done well by here, there, and yon.

"Vietnam," Bowers said unbidden. "Costa Rica. Hartford."

"Really."

"Hartford," the guerrilla repeated.

"That's my name up here," Bowers said. "They like it because it's where their guns are made. They read it on the stock. Gives them that tender feeling."

"You from there?"

"My dad was an exec in the insurance industry. None of your business anyway." The eyes shifted and caught Levin. "And what the hell are you doing here?"

"Well, as you pointed out, I'm a journalist. The Saraunese People's Party granted me an interview with Fra Boboy."

"That sounds pretty goddamn cozy to me," Bowers said.

"No. Not at all. It's not at all cozy." He hesitated. "Were you in the service in Vietnam?"

For an answer Levin got another narrowing of the pouchy eyes. It was meant to be threatening, but the effect was melodramatic and somewhat comical.

"It must be the atmosphere up here, but it's too bad there's so much suspicion going around. It's too bad as the only Americans up here we can't count on each other's good faith."

"Americans," Bowers said, "are some of the least reliable people I've had the pleasure of meeting."

"Well, as for Fra Boboy and me," Levin said after a pause, "we're on journalist-subject terms. We're using each other. Nothing untoward."

"He didn't send you here," Bowers asked darkly, "to look in on me?"

"Of course not."

"But you've been talking to him."

"I spent most of the day with him."

"So he must have mentioned me."

"Sure. He mentioned you."

Bowers was trying not to ask anything more, and Levin watched him wait for the blank to be filled in. By now Levin knew that he wasn't the type to hold out for long.

"And . . .?"

"Listen, we can't have this conversation without some degree of trust. If you've made up your mind not to believe what I tell you, then we've kind of come to a dead end." He started to stand up.

"Know what we used to say in Vietnam?" Shaking his head, Levin sat down again. "Wariness is next to godliness."

"I guess in some situations that may be accurate."

"Over there it was very goddamn accurate. And you didn't have to be a grunt to know it. I was with U.S.I.S., press officer in Saigon, then up in Ban Me Thuot, up in the Central Highlands—and hell, I knew it. I learned very fast."

Levin tried to conceal his smile. There was no need to, though, for Bowers was now steadfastly avoiding his gaze. The guerrilla was toweling Bowers's smooth face with a blue bandanna. Something in the face had turned unsound and the eyes gone liquid, as if a blood poisoning had reached his brain.

"So you do have an acquaintance with journalists."

"All types."

"I'm beginning to see why Fra Boboy finds you interesting."

"He said that?"

"Sure."

"Was that all?"

"That you've had experience of the world, you're not afraid to be in the thick of things. That's how he likes to see himself."

"So we're blood brothers, is that it?"

"I'd say he feels a certain amount of respect for you. He thinks of you as an example of U.S. power in the late stages of our world influence."

Bowers sat up in the chair and seemed to weigh this appraisal. The guerrilla was cleaning his instruments.

"I don't much care for being an example."

"Why not?"

"People like to make examples of examples."

"I don't think that necessarily follows."

"Levin, what the fuck else did he say to you?"

The guerrilla slapped him on the back of his head. "O.K., Hartford." He pulled Bowers's short-sleeve shirt at the shoulder, and Bowers sighed and dragged his elongated body off the chair. Hunching slightly, he unbuttoned his shirt while the guerrilla waited.

"You going to watch this charade?"

"What are you talking about?"

"Don't try to tell me you don't know what's going to happen tonight."

"Tonight?" Levin managed to shake his head; the blood was rushing to it. "No idea. Why don't you tell me."

The American stepped out of his pants, the lower half of a seersucker suit; he hadn't removed his loafers and he grunted and stumbled to clear the cloth over the heels. "Well how about that. Now what do you think about that. What lying fucks we send overseas these days."

Bowers stood in the middle of the hut, in his BVDs and loafers, smiling fiercely at Levin. In the lamplight his pallor was positively spectral.

"For a while, Hartford," the guerrilla said. "I go come back." And he went outside, where a vast chorus of frogs seemed to have taken up positions all around the hut and croaked in tremendous belches.

The gangly body covered the floor with remarkable swiftness. Bowers's hands were on Levin's shirt, padding furiously. "What have you got? A recorder? You got a recorder in here? You been taping me? What's this—what are you carrying, Levin? A piece? Huh?"

He was trying to identify the object he'd found in rapid gropes like a blind man, when all at once it dawned on him. His mouth opened and he removed his hands from Levin's waist.

"Now aren't you ashamed?" Levin reached inside his shirt and produced the flask so that Bowers could see the Rum Direv label. He'd brought it as a gift for Fra Boboy, but other needs had since arisen. At some point Ding had lowered the level an inch or two.

"That's a nice surprise," Bowers said, a little unsteadily. In fact he looked overcome, blessed. He sat next to Levin on the edge of the cot, the white tube of his belly sagging over the elastic of his BVDs.

"Suspicion is such a constraining thing," Levin told him.

"Suspicion," said Bowers, eyeing the flask, "is pure natural selection. It's man's response to a hostile environment. The survival of the suspiciousest. You notice that the jungle critters don't evolve characteristics of trust."

Levin saw the face of the dusky langur crushed against the sack. "All the same," he said as he unscrewed the cap, "one would like to think we had something on the critters. A spark of divinity. Something Platonic." He wiped the bottle mouth on his shirt and handed the flask to Bowers, who took a happy reverential breath and drank deeply, the Adam's apple disappearing into his shaven jaw. When he came up for air his lips were wet and his face had slackened.

"You believe that?" Bowers asked.

"Things are in flux. It's going to be very inconvenient if I'm wrong."

"You're wrong. You're young and you're wrong. This is the closest to Plato we get." Bowers raised the bottle in salute, swigged again, and returned it.

Levin knew it was now or never. "What were you doing up here?"

Bowers tried to hold him in a wary gaze but he'd weakened, and Levin saw that the compulsion to unburden and reveal was already spreading through his limbs with the alcohol. Fear and loneliness sped it on its way. Levin, feeling these things in himself, had anticipated them in Bowers. For all his stumbling, he wondered if in some ways they'd made him a better journalist.

Bowers asked, "What do the papers say?"

"They say you were looking for buried Japanese gold. They also say you were working for the A.F.D.S., or the C.I.A., or the A. of L. Some even say you were the tourist that broke the vibrator in that poor girl's vagina in Porto de Coral and you were on the run from local cops. As usual there were differing theories."

"As per goddamn usual." Bowers laughed harshly. "Something about this country—the truth has a half-life of about three minutes. And then it gets fouled into something fucking unspeakable. Over there at least the lies didn't take away every last shred of your claim to be a serious goddamn human being."

Levin was about to say that this sounded at least neo-Platonic but thought better of it and drank from the flask. Things had reached a delicate pass and he didn't want to derail them now with cleverness. "Then why don't you set the record straight. Look," he said, seeing the way, "I have the ear of the Southern regional commander. He's very image-conscious. I also have the attention of a million and a half readers in the U.S. The more people who know your story, the better for you. In terms of dignity but also survival-wise. But I can't write it if you won't tell me."

Bowers requested the flask. When he'd reduced the rum another half-inch, he said: "I was engaging in a little free-lance covert diplomacy."

For a few moments he enjoyed Levin's confusion.

"I was trying to make contact with the Jola Number One down mountain."

Levin swore in disbelief. It was a triumphant moment for Bowers and he allowed himself a faintly malicious grin.

"On whose behalf?"

"The U.S.G.'s."

"They knew about it?"

"Not really. Officially, they've lost their guts. Unofficially, at this stage they depend on initiative by persons of foresight and daring."

Bowers gave a dismissive little cough—hardly more than throat clearing. It was a nervous habit, signaling both toughness and retreat. Levin was contemplating a foreign policy dependent on men of Bowers's caliber. "Only my contact wasn't where he was supposed to be and I ran into these sonsofbitches instead."

"Bad luck."

"Goes with the territory. You do what you gotta do. Nobody leaves this life alive."

Levin stole a glance at Bowers's eyes. The pouches had reddened and above them his eyeballs were having trouble staying put.

"So you weren't in contact with either the embassy or Camp Pereira," Levin said. "Like you've never heard of a deep-penetration agent."

"Sounds like some sort of marital aid."

Levin laughed. "You don't know a Colonel Siriman. You're totally independent of A.F.D.S. operations."

" 'Down to Gehenna or up to the Throne,/He travels the fastest who travels alone,' Levin."

"Kipling, right?"

"Kipling."

"A very misunderstood poet. I'm a big Kipling fan myself." Levin sat back on the cot and breathed heavily. He took another swallow. It wasn't true, he hated Kipling. His relief threatened to make him garrulous. "So what's happening tonight? What's on the program?"

"You really don't know, do you? I'm playing the title role in a little skit they've arranged for the locals—Ngot the Half Man." Bowers sniffed. "It's an outrageous fucking way to treat a P.O.W."

"You're kidding."

"Why would I do a thing like that? Cockfights, burlesque, speechifying. Truth is stranger than fiction, Jack."

"I wonder what it's all about."

"Hell of a journalist you are. It's obviously a desperate move by a desperate man. It's conciliation, sweetener, diversion. Too much voluntary taxation and revolutionary justice and now there's a mountain full of peasants who've had it up to here. These Jola are ready to blow. That's what brought me up here in the first place. Until I ran into Uncle Trouble."

Levin remained silent for a long time. "So you don't think the Jola want the A. of L. here."

Bowers was still laughing when voices approached outside in the croaking darkness. As Levin hustled the flask into his shirt he felt Bowers's hand grip his forearm.

"What's Fra B. got planned for me?"

"Bowers, I haven't seen his order of battle."

"Levin!" The hand tightened.

"What?"

"I'd better be able to trust you."

"But that would be counter-evolutionary."

"Hey, Hartford!" The young guerrilla came in, all hurry and disapproval, toting a plastic bucket and a rag in one hand and waving Bowers into the rattan chair with the other.

He set to work. The bucket held several inches of a brown-black liquid paste. It was some crude mix of clay, charcoal, and water, probably a Jola concoction for painting the jars that ended up piled in pyramids at the Central Market in São Sebastião. The paint was applied to the left side of Bowers's face. From the height of his forehead where the hair was in silvery retreat, down the long nose from its thick bridge to its point, across one half of the gleaming raised skin of the shaven mustache, the sunken scarred skin under the lip, the left knob of the cleft chin, all around the puffy lids of the eye and the wasting cheek and the hard line of the jaw, half the American's features went dark. The guerrilla handled his rag with meticulous skill, drawing the line straight and clean down the middle of the face. And the effect was shocking. In the lamp's naked light, Bowers was transfigured. The blackened half had been erased of texture, shape, expression; it had gone primitive and blank.

Bowers sat out his humiliation with eyes closed. The untouched half of his face was clutched with strain, and the eyelid fluttered. His pallor grew, and as the other half went dun and dead what was left took on a quality of thick powder. It looked unnatural, diminished, lame.

The guerrilla moved to his neck and shoulder.

Without opening his eyes, Bowers began to talk. Though Levin was ten feet away, in the quiet and dark it was like a whispered intimacy.

"In Nam they had beriberi. In Nam they had brain malaria. In Nam they had leeches, tiger cages, B-52 raids, psy torture. O.K.? They had all that. That was tougher. But this . . . they didn't have to go through this. They got to keep their honor."

He coughed quickly; his voice had nearly broken on a sob. Levin knew now that he was going to get a story. He had tapped Bowers's fear and rattled his vanity and now he would get it. He was beginning to feel that he'd heard too many stories—too much information had come his way, in his neutrality, from all sides. He had always thought of information as a compact and useful thing, a notebook in his pocket; but now it was more like a look in his own eyes that he could neither see nor control. He knew all he wanted to about Bowers.

"I could leave if you don't want me to see this," Levin said, starting to rise. "I'd understand if you want to be alone."

"Oh, no." Bowers's eyes opened in a glare. "You're not going anywhere. You're going to see this thing through with me." And even the guerrilla shook his head and motioned for Levin to sit, as if his labors demanded an audience. Levin sat down again.

"It got weird very fast there." Bowers, eyes closed again, was already deep in memory. "Someone didn't like me from the start. They didn't have a house at first and I had to stay with the assistant director of the American Cultural Center, who was a very weird guy. He was queer, which would have been O.K. if he didn't have his Vietnamese boyfriends walking around the house in French silk drawers all the time. They were always getting my room mixed up with the linen closet, or trying to open the door to the john when I was there. It didn't have a lock and I had to sit with my foot holding the door shut.

"Levin, I found a way to go to Vietnam even though I was 4-Y on account of childhood T.B. I went over there to defend freedom against communist aggression. Instead I'm trying to keep queers out of the shitter while I'm on it."

"Did you leave a wife back home?"

Bowers didn't answer at once.

"Are you asking if I'm queer, Levin?"

"I'm trying to get an idea of your situation when you went, how you felt about leaving."

"No wife. No fiancée."

"I see."

"No girlfriend. Down to Gehenna—"

"O.K., I know. I'm thinking you must have been lonely."

"I wasn't. I'm all the company I need."

Levin had nothing to say to this.

"Anyway. I got out of that scene when USIS found me a place.

It was a nice house with hardwood floors, traditional style. It just happened coincidentally to be on a little street with no less than three all-night rock clubs. I like classical music, and I also like swing and bebop. But this was the Doors and Jefferson Airplane till dawn. I'd lie in bed furious. Petty-ass grunts and bar girls were smoking grass and rubbing each other up with coconut oil. Right then I knew the war was probably lost. You don't win a goddamn war when you've lost your honor.

"But I was doing my duty, like everyone else. I was at USIS every day handling press releases and slapping together a monthly dishrag called *Free World*. I did the cultural pages. Stuff on Annamite puppet shows, Thai classical dance tours, Bob Hope U.S.O. stuff, movie reviews. I gave *Patton* four stars, *Easy Rider* I tore to shreds. I never worked so hard in my life. You don't know what you're capable of till you're part of a larger cause, even if half your comrades are fools. The operating principle in Nam was no different than anywhere else—the average worldwide I.Q. is in the double digits."

The guerrilla was swabbing Bowers's hand, holding it in his own like a manicurist.

"One night USIS threw a dinner party for all its personnel. I had the great fortune to be seated next to the chief's wife. A real can-do American broad. She *loved* Vietnam, having the time of her life. She'd wangled something with A.I.D. to stay on when the dependents were sent home. This was just after the Calley thing came out and right away she asks me what I think. I'd had a little to drink and I told her I knew plenty of junior officers who'd managed to not commit mass murder in the hamlets. I said the sonofabitch should be put away for life, or strung up by his balls or forced to jerk off for the paparazzi, or some such nicety. I said we had to get rid of the Calleys if we were going to stand a chance of winning—the psychos who used the war as an excuse to be sadistic.

"Mrs. USIS didn't like hearing that. She started in on the booby-traps-laid-by-three-year-olds stuff. The grandma-sappers stuff. She said the war wasn't for the faint of heart and if I couldn't get on board maybe I should go back to Hartford. All this in her smoker's voice from Maryland somewhere, her face getting red. And the crazy thing was, the whole time she was flirting with me. Smoke in the face—the whole bit. I said to myself: Watch out for this broad. She'll strip you to the bones. I went home early.

"For a month I noticed something was different at work. People were making a point of ignoring me. I'm not a particularly social guy, but this was massive isolation. I started waking up nauseated. Funny things gave me nausea. Vietnamese faces, for one, and that nasal singsong language. And the color gray. Gray trucks gray ships gray tarmac gray buildings gray fish gray ditchwater gray rain. It rained every afternoon and the whole city looked gray. The whole conflict was out of hand. No one was in charge. There were no bearings. You start thinking: This is how the world is. And you feel sick to your stomach, because you're stuck with the world."

"Bowers, really, you don't have to tell me this. It sounds a little personal."

Levin, on the cot, was staring at the hard gray eye in the painted half of Bowers's face. He was experiencing a spell of nausea himself, and took it to be the rum; the Saraunese brand was very coarse.

"You're not walking, Levin. You wanted to know what I'm doing up here. Look, it's important to me at this point for someone to hear this stuff."

The guerrilla was swabbing around the sag of Bowers's belly. From the waist up, he was now bifurcated into light and dark: the border neatly cleaved his chest through the sunken patch of hair.

"And it's not that personal. It could have happened to anyone." Bowers lifted his chin. "It could easily have happened to you, Levin. It could easily be you sitting right here.

"So at the end of that month I got the word I was being posted to Ban Me Thuot in the Central Highlands to run a bureau there. I'd barely heard of the place.

"Two nights before I left Saigon I had dinner at a Shakey's. The waitress was this Khmer Krom girl with nice features, a very gentle girl who spoke good V.A.A. English. I asked her out after her shift. She was the only Vietnamese girl I ever touched. Su Ly. Isn't that a pretty name, Levin? Not like Mrs. USIS. The next night I asked her to marry me. And little Su Ly broke my heart when she told me she had a brain tumor that was giving her fainting spells and she didn't have money for medicine or the hospital and she might die in a few months. I held her and we cried till dawn.

"I told only one person about her, a junior Foreign Service guy at the embassy named Laroux. I ran into him at the Shakey's the day I left. He thought Su Ly was beautiful.

"From Ban Me Thuot I sent her money every week. And she wrote back these sweet broken-English letters telling me she needed more money for medicine and tests. I kept asking her for the doctor's bills—it wasn't that I didn't trust her, I just wanted to see what they said. She kept forgetting to send them.

"After a couple of weeks in the highlands I had the nausea again. Ban Me Thuot was just an isolated miserable godforsaken place. This place here reminds me of it a little. V.C. all over the mountains, but in town *nothing* was happening. Which was worse than if there'd been heavy action. I was organizing an American film series that nobody came to. I hardly ever saw Americans. For six weeks I didn't have a single visitor at my house.

"One night a car pulls up and it's an English journalist who needs a place to stay. A guy named Len Beer. The name made me somewhat suspicious."

Levin asked, "Why?"

"Len Beer? Does that sound like a normal name?"

"Maybe a little unusual, but—"

"Very fucking unusual. All evening the sonofabitch badmouths the U.S. war effort. In a don't-you-agree? way. I told him I did not agree. We made mistakes but our reasons for being there were justified. He also offered me opium, which I refused but let him smoke. Maybe that was an error. In the morning, before he left he said, 'See you again.' That was all. That night I get another visitor—a certain Captain Feuerbringer from MACV. You know what Feuerbringer is in German? Fire-bearer. They didn't know I studied German in school. The whole night I was trying to understand fire-bearer. What did it mean?"

"They?"

Bowers didn't hear. "Feuerbringer didn't say much, but sometimes I'd catch him looking at me. In the morning he goes. You know the last thing he says, Levin? 'I'll be in touch.' All day I kept hearing him say that. But there was no one I could run it by, give me a second opinion. That night, guess what?"

"Another visitor."

"Six weeks without a soul and then three straight nights I'm visited! The thing is, by this time I almost expected it. So when they showed up it was like a bad dream. Two French doctors doing a public health thing with the Montagnards. The tall guy spoke pretty good English, the other not much at all. They asked me about my family. They smiled a lot. And I'm thinking: Who are you guys? What are you here for? I don't know if you're the Agency, Interpol, maybe even from Hanoi. In the middle of the night I'm listening at their door and at one point I hear them switch to English. So that does it. The next morning over breakfast I ask where they live in France. I'm testing them, seeing if they trip up. I ask for the address so I can visit if I'm ever in Paree—and the tall one says, 'Don't worry, we will make contact.'

"That was enough for me. 'We will make contact' was enough. That's when I said, O.K., I'm out of here. Someone wants me gone and I'm going to oblige them. I called up USIS Saigon and said I wanted to be transferred out for medical reasons, and they said they'd send a plane up in the afternoon. Like they had one waiting for me.

"In the plane I sort of calmed down. We were flying over the mountains and all that green and then the Delta and the yellow water in the bomb craters and the rice paddies, and I could see the peasants and the buffalo, and thinking about how much they suffered, and I just felt this enormous love for the country and the people, beggars, prostitutes, farmers, even the V.C. symps, even the goddamn Arvins—I loved them all. And I knew I was there to help them, save them. And Su Ly—I loved her and wanted to save her more than anything. After Ban Me Thuot I was so damn happy to be having these nice feelings. By the time we reached Tan Son Nhut I was crying like a baby. I was ready to stay. I had nothing to go home to.

"Guess who's waiting at the airport? Mr. and Mrs. USIS. Smoking and smiling. They take me to their car, one on each arm. She offers me a Valium and I take it even though I don't take pills, because I'm a little wired. We drive to their house and I'm trying to tell them I've changed my mind but they don't listen. Once you've made the request, you're on the next plane home. They don't even let me leave the goddamn house, and I have to sneak to the phone to call Shakey's. The guy on the line sounds like the cook—he doesn't speak a word of English. Under my breath I'm screaming at him, 'Su Ly Thuong! Su Ly Thuong!' He doesn't know what the hell I'm talking about. A nightmare! Finally on about the fiftieth 'Su Ly!' he says— I'll never forget it—he says, 'Su Ly not work here, American.' Then there's some more whispering and cursing as I try to figure out if it's her night off or she's been fired or died of the tumor or if he's lying and if he's lying why the hell he is. But then I hear Mrs. USIS coming down the hall and I hang up on the sonofabitch. Back in my room I get an idea and sneak out again and find the phone book. There are two hundred goddamn Thuongs in the Saigon directory. So I didn't get to talk to her. I didn't get to talk to Su Ly again.

"Then the flight to Honolulu and D.C.—dead to the world. And dreaming about Vietnam, all gray and green, and Su Ly and the cook. I woke up at Dulles. Nothing seemed real. I didn't know how I let myself get back there. It was like I'd been acting without my consent. The State Department had me see one of its shrinks, and we had a nice little chat for half an hour, and then he writes a nice little letter for my file that says: paranoid schizophrenic tendency. Welcome home. What'd you say?"

"I didn't say anything."

Levin had sworn under his breath. The guerrilla, on one knee by the rattan chair, was rubbing and wiping and dabbing and blackening his way down Bowers's calf.

"So that's it—end of a career in public service. I have to live with that file for the rest of my life. If I wanted to run for Congress, I couldn't. As if cutting out wasn't a bad enough feeling. And Su Ly, not knowing how she is and whether she thinks I've abandoned her or she's been conning me all along or what. And my own parents, telling me they're worried because there's something different in my eyes. That's what they said—in my eyes. So I have to start from scratch. Nothing."

Bowers's eyes were open and he was gazing into the darkness where Levin sat on the cot. Feeling he could observe without being observed, Levin looked into his eyes to find whatever Bowers's parents must have seen there, back home in Hartford. The pupils had dilated almost to fill the gray iris.

"But you got back on your feet."

"Not really," Bowers told him. "No one likes to fail, but the worst thing is the way it shapes your conduct. I tried many things. Shrinkage, foreign travel, promiscuity. After the beauty and gentleness of Vietnamese women American broads looked gross to me, man-eaters. Every Vietnam article in the papers shot two bullets in my heart, one for Su Ly and the other for failing my country and hers in time of need."

Levin started to protest, but Bowers stopped him with a chop of the painted hand.

"You have to face these things, Levin. The only thing to do is face the enemy within and without. You don't rationalize—that's what the shrinks did and it was an expensive racket that gained me no good. You find the enemy within, and the enemy without. When I took a look around I saw America wasn't the country I'd left. She had a death wish. I wanted to help her. I tried going to Iran after the embassy takeover but I think State blocked my visa at the last minute. When I heard about Commander Zero down in Nicaragua I arranged to go to Costa Rica. I knew a guy who knew a guy who was supposedly with the Company there. My first night in San José my hotel room was robbed—everything. I didn't even have a change of clothes. I called the guy anyway—he wouldn't see me. I rented a car on my credit card and drove in my stinking clothes to the border, where this American rancher was training contras. They turned me away at the gate. I thought about flying to Tegucigalpa, but my credit was used up and I didn't like the sound of the northern front anyway. It sounded like the type of place Mrs. USIS would have been happy. So I had to go home again."

"Wouldn't it have been better," Levin asked, "to just settle down with a wife somewhere and get a boring job?"

"Well, I thought I did. The job part, anyway. Eventually AT&T employed me in New York selling cellular phone systems. I got pretty damn good at it, too, until last year they decided to send me overseas. Where's the first sales assignment? Jakarta. As soon as I heard the word I had the nausea again. I saw gray and green, I smelled warm rain and saffron. And I went. I sold the goddamn phones to the Indonesians, and I had a few days left to burn on the beach. In Bali I saw an article in the *Hong Kong Times* about the civil war in Direv Saraun. They quoted the D.C.M. at the U.S. embassy. The guy's name was Laroux. I went straight back to Jakarta and booked a flight to São Sebastião. Another strange city full of brown people. I phoned the guy at home—it was the same Laroux I'd met at Shakey's the day I left for Ban Me Thuot!

"We spent a long night drinking scotch and wallowing in Vietnam nostalgia. When I asked him if he'd ever heard about Su Ly, he told me he heard she ended up in Phnom Penh. Which means she's either dead or a refugee on the Thai border or a hooker in Bangkok. Either way, I allowed Mr. Dewars to change the subject for me.

"Laroux started telling me about the situation here. The Army of Liberation, the counterinsurgency. The Jola thing. He said he thought the situation could be turned without covert involvement if the Saraunese handled the problems up here right. The nausea suddenly came over me very strong—the strongest since back then. I knew I'd seen the last of Su Ly. I couldn't go home like this again. The best thing to do was face the enemy right up here in these mountains. So I came."

The makeup man was finished. With the loafer off, the last toe of Bowers's left foot was lost. He was ready for his role. The end of his story, with its familiar names, had pricked the guerrilla's attention, and he frowned and clucked and shook his head as he cleaned up and gathered his materials.

"And here you are."

"Here I am." Bowers surveyed his transformation with grim detachment. "I have done the state some service and they know it, Levin. But this could be the end of the road."

"You don't know that."

"Don't humor me. You have to look these things in the face. The one within is quiet now but the one without is closing in."

For a time the Americans didn't speak. Outside the hut the village had come alive, voices were converging in the open place and someone was blowing on a reed pipe.

"So you never married?"

Bowers shook his head. "Spared myself that disaster."

"It's a big scary world to be all alone, isn't it? In spite of Kipling."

"You think so?"

"Well, I don't know. I'm just thinking about your story."

"What's your story, Levin? Ever kill anyone?"

Levin understood that he was going to be punished for hearing the tale. He wished the guerrilla would leave the room so he could take a sip from the flask, though his nausea hadn't left him.

"Not to my knowledge."

"Ever marry anyone?"

"I've got a wife in Philadelphia. She's a lawyer."

"A real ball-buster."

"As a matter of fact, she's a very warm and levelheaded woman and I'm looking forward to seeing her again."

He was allowing himself to picture an airport on the other side of the world—the echoing P.A., Melanie's flushed expectant face in a crowd. Dangerously, he tried to imagine his own joy. Perhaps, once, it could have been this way. But the thing that had spawned in him had turned against her and against him too. He didn't belong with her now. He belonged here.

"Let me put it this way, Levin. The warmest, levelest-headed woman in the world never saved anybody from himself."

"Is that what everybody needs?"

"The enemies within and without can show up at any stage."

"No. It depends on the individual. If it happens, it happens for a reason."

The blackened hand was raised, the index finger pointing at him.

"There but for the grace of God go you, Levin."

From the darkness, Levin looked with hatred and dread into the half-darkness of the other's face.

"Can I ask you something, Bowers?" He cleared his throat to keep his voice from breaking. "Is it possible that State Department shrink knew something you don't?"

Bowers didn't answer, nor did he cease pointing.

The guerrilla left the room, passing Ding on his way in. Ding's face was aflame and his eyes were glazed with excitement. He stopped in the doorway with his mouth open, staring at the Americans. The Leica was slung around his neck.

"Things are starting to happen out there."

"I can hear," Levin said. "Why don't you join us."

For a moment it seemed that Ding was caught in the deference of the Saraunese who finds himself among whites. Levin withdrew the flask and waved him in; he was strangely glad to see him. Ding took a seat next to Levin on the cot, and he closed his eyes as he gulped the offered rum.

Finally he turned to Bowers. "What did they do to you, man?"

"None of your goddamn business, man. What did they do to you? Are you on drugs or something?"

Ding turned to Levin in bafflement and humor.

"It's a bad evening for him," Levin explained.

"Yeah, well, do unto others and you get your butt kicked."

He raised his camera and took aim at Bowers.

"Hey!"

Without shooting, Ding lowered the camera and grinned. "You make a hell of a pretty picture."

Levin asked, "Where have you been keeping yourself?"

"With them." Ding jerked his head toward the door and his vision seemed to shake loose. With black sprouts of mustache and goatee, his mouth ajar and his darkly blazing eyes searching the dim room, fingers lightly playing on his thighs as he waited for the flask to make its way back, Ding looked for all the world like a Chinese opium smuggler going bad on his own merchandise.

"What have you found out from them?"

"Amazing things." Ding turned to Levin with a tremendous secret on his lips. "They opened up to me. Fra Timo and some others. These guys have made the break, they've given up everything for the struggle. They live with death every day."

"So do we all," said Bowers, gazing on Ding as if he were a barely tolerated houseguest.

"This is different, boss. They *choose* it. And it makes them great. In ten years towns will be named after these guys. They'll go to death willingly."

"Know what's at the end of that road, Jack?" Bowers said. "A shit pond where a million billion deluded assholes have gone before them."

"To every man and every land," Levin intoned, "the task is always brave and new. Pass that over here."

"Death means freedom to the unfree," Ding said. "Power to the powerless. Their blood will make our country clean."

"Is this fool a friend of yours?"

Levin looked from Bowers to Ding. "Ding's no fool. He and I have seen a lot of water under the bridge. Sometimes the bridge is gone but there's still water. Not as thick as blood but it runs over and under and around everything."

"Dan's O.K. Not like your typical Joe." Ding turned to Levin. "You know that thing I was looking for?"

Levin waited.

"I found it."

"You did?" Ding nodded. "You must be relieved."

"I knew I had it somewhere."

Without touching his own pocket Levin could feel the film there.

"I gave it to Fra Boboy," Ding said. "Some things are more important than journalism."

"You're right there."

Outside, a beating of drums rose and with it the noise of numerous excited voices. Levin notified himself that he was drunk—just when wits were going to be needed of him. The same was true of Ding. Levin avoided looking at him. Tonight Ding seemed a bud of a man, a wood creature in the sight of a gun, a child crawling toward the fire, fearful on the edges of the known world. This feeling was not expected; it complicated things when he was trying to simplify. And he was not now in a position to alter the events that had been set in motion.

Bowers said, "I want to hear from our friend about this typical Joe. What's he look like?"

Ding threw Bowers a glance that was met with equal wariness. "You'd be surprised—he's a nice-looking guy. He's fun to be around. He knows how to be friendly when you beat him at cards because it doesn't matter in the long run because in the long run he owns you anyway. And he doesn't understand why you can't be friendly when he beats you. But the worst thing about him, the worst, is that when he's taken your last *coba* and you tell him you've had enough—the guy feels hurt. That's when you see red. You know there's no way to get through to him. Then you want to kill the guy, just so you can feel like a human being again. But you don't like yourself for wanting to kill him. So you wish he'd just leave you and your country alone." Ding passed the flask to Levin. "That's about it."

"Nice," Bowers said. "Very nice. Now for a sketch of your typical Saraunese. Actually it's a composite, because you see him all over—Vietnam, Indonesia, Costa Rica. But you always know him by the sneaky self-pitying look on his little brown face."

Ding laughed in loud vacant disbelief.

"Most of them are harmless. The ones to worry about have their eyes close together—that's the mark of a predator. People think sharks are predators, but they're not. They're scavengers; their eyes are on opposite sides of the head. Predators have eyes in front. Just like us. A man's eyes tell the whole story. And the most dangerous man is the composite typical Saraunese with the tight eyes."

"All right, all right." Levin raised his hands. "Let's keep the party polite." It reminded him of a song heard somewhere—in the family living room, a record his mother used to play. He couldn't place it; but he smelled the fur and dust of the white rug, coarse as sheepdog hair, under his chin as he lay listening.

"You were in Vietnam?" Ding asked.

"Who wants to know?"

"Just me, boss. Ding Magkakanaw. It's been just me for thirty years."

"That's some name you got. Listen, Jack, don't tell me to trash my country because I'm not going to. I love my country. Maybe more than she loved me. You're faithful for years and one day you start wondering if she's been faithful back. And then you get eaten up not knowing. But that doesn't change anything with me. If I have to die in this goddamn place for her, so be it."

"Something about the air up here," Levin said, "turns our thoughts to death. Personally, I'm skeptical. I've never been able to conceive of mine. I think it's mathematically impossible, a paradox."

"You better conceive it, Jack," Bowers told him. "Because it's out there. It conceives you."

"I don't give a shit if you were there or not," Ding said. "But it must have been some time. Like the whole U.S.A. just went crazy. Like here now. I wish I could have been there."

"It was a lousy goddamn time to be alive," Bowers said. "It was when she turned."

"Eve of Destruction!" Ding flung at him. "Hendrix! Detroit!"

Bowers put his painted face in his hands and muttered through his palms, "You don't know what the hell you're talking about."

Ding was laughing and his excitement rose. "Burning fragging white phosphorous Black Panthers off the pig up against the wall motherfucker! That was the time. The last best hope. And you blew it—like the guy said in that movie. And now you're nothing but a lot of dead money. Money and death. You're all wrapped up—it's over for you. That's the way I see it anyhow."

"You're misled. A very fucking confused soul. It was when she turned."

"Now all you can do is watch on TV while the rest of the world goes crazy." Ding's color was deepening with the rum to raw umber. "And if the world is going crazy, then I want to have a part."

Somewhere in the village the pariah dogs were barking.

"We all want action," Levin said. "As a journalist I require it. We're all here for the same reason. So let's put aside our differences."

He felt Ding's hand on his shoulder. "Thanks for the trip, partner."

Levin, holding the empty flask, didn't answer.

"Maybe we had some disagreements, but that makes it more real."

Levin turned to look in Ding's face but he had stood up, keeping balance on the shoulder.

"I'm going out there."

Levin stood too. He listened to the dogs, vigilant and warning—as if they barked especially at him. Goats and monkeys! he thought. They always found him out. The honking laugh and sob were inside his chest now, crowding out the air. There was nothing to do except breathe and wait. He'd had his reasons for acting and they had been good ones. An extreme situation required an extreme reply. But tonight predators and prey seemed to be exchanging eyes.

It was just the rum, a trick of feeling at the last hour. When two people try to destroy each other, Fra Boboy said, they're like lovers, they get each other's smell. It doesn't change what's really out there. Ding, any of them, would have done the same.

"Let the festivities begin," he said on the way out.

"It is outrageous," Bowers said. "It is criminal."

"What a crazy night," said Ding.

CHAPTER XI

The voice on the VCR was speaking in Saraunese, but the words were of no account. The meaning lay in their tone and in the pictures they accompanied. Emphatic, grave, stirring, hysterical, the voice was a voice for children. On the metallic, color-bleeding videotape, scenes flickered: of babies squatting in the filthy alleys along the Musa River, sugar workers toiling in fields just like those of Dom Hipolito, A.F.D.S. soldiers beating bound prisoners with rifle butts. Then snapshots of Saraunese dead: piled dead in ditches, bloated dead floating on the Musa, burned dead in bamboo huts, hanging dead in the yard of the old Portuguese prison in the Montes Xavieres, sun-drenched dead in Paranak the day Levin had gone there with Fraser; and the not yet dead, a furiously grimacing rebel pinned to the ground by the knee of a soldier about to cut his throat with a knife. The dead sped by faster and faster until it seemed there was nothing in the world but violent death. And still the voice ranted. And the music was music to weep by, the heavy, sea-like dirge of Albinoni's Adagio for Organ and Strings.

Suddenly the music switched midchord to the "Ode to Joy." Army of Liberation platoons were returning fire, rushing forward through flaming bushes, being greeted by villagers with open arms, raising the blue flag over huts, sharing bowls of rice. The voice soared with triumph. The piece ended on the silhouette of a lone guerrilla standing sentry duty on a hillside, against the full-sky sunset of the tropics of the mind. In the echo of the final exultant chord, the screen faded to black.

The VCR hookup stood on a makeshift mahogany platform. A few feet away, linked by wires, hummed a portable generator that also powered two low-wattage floodlights mounted high on poles at either end of the rectangular open place in the middle of the village. These cast a broad, weak, yellowish light on the assembled villagers. Some of the Jola had hiked here from outlying hamlets. A few of the children (dozens and dozens had materialized) crept close to the VCR and watched in silent awe or with shrieks of delight, but the adults lost interest somewhere before the tragic theme turned heroic. When the death montage appeared, a scattering of laughter broke out. The videotape left them restless and noisy, like a crowd during the lengthy introductions before a prizefight.

The guerrillas, Ding among them, stood casually armed at the end closest to the market and the animal pens. They watched the film attentively, and when it was over they clapped and cheered.

Closest to the ring of stones that marked the cockpit, a group of village men squatted, floodlit, arming their fighting cocks. They caressed the birds, stroked and goaded them, murmured near their heads, and from time to time squabbled with one another. They'd obviously drunk a great deal of rice liquor.

Fra Boboy sat among the village elders in wooden chairs; an automatic pistol was tucked into the waistband of his shorts. He paid careful courtesies to the old men in torn trousers at his side, and his compact energy vibrated amid their thin dark reticence. The others looked sated, a smell of roast meat hung in the air; apparently the dusky langur had already been consumed. Behind this group, Fra Boboy's hut stood indistinctly in darkness. Aside from the electric lights there was only the glow of a waning moon, big and low in the west. The pale light it spilled on the huts and the peasants set back from the floodlights dissolved from time to time as heavy unseasonable clouds blew across it. Last night's brilliant stars had mostly disappeared.

Bowers and his guard were nowhere to be seen.

Levin was standing with Connie in the middle of a crowd of peasants in front of the medical hut. He'd told her he wanted to hear Jola conversation during the revelry and asked her to stay with him. Their encounter of the morning lingered, smarted, and he found himself lapsing into edgy defensive banter.

"You look like you've had a long day."

"Thanks," she said. "Do you know what you look like?"

"I can't tell without a mirror. I suppose I look drunk."

"And very nervous. I told you to take care."

"I think," he told her, "you're projecting."

At their feet two small boys were prodding a crushed lizard with twigs. Nearby, village women sat with pyramids of sticky rice wrapped in banana leaves. In the air there was a sharp smell of cooking oil and raw rice liquor and human sweat.

Connie said, "Why don't we go over where Ding and the others are."

"You object to the company of peasants?"

"Of course not. I just thought—"

"I told you I wanted to be with the people."

"You're not listening to the people. You're talking to me."

"Only because your company is more delightful. And if we go where Ding and the others are, you and I won't be able to talk."

"But you can talk to them. And you'll be closer to the action."

"I don't want to talk to them. They don't like me anyway. Look at the way Fra Timo is blinking at me."

Connie cut a glance across the open place at her fellow cadres. "I should be with them."

"For God's sake, they're not going to court-martial you for standing with me and the Jola." She let out an abrupt staccato; this time it hardly sounded like a laugh. He took her lightly by the elbow. "Just stick around and give me a play by play."

She made no answer, but she didn't move.

Levin had summoned the presence of mind to decide that this was the evening's safest vantage point. It placed him as far as possible from Fra Boboy, the hut where the Toshiba blinked and hummed, and the fallow field that led darkly away to the mountain's ascent; and it gave him a direct view of these. Assuming Dom Hipolito knew what he was talking about. Assuming they were going to make their raid tonight at all. But he felt sure they were.

Beneath the anesthetic of the rum, he was vaguely aware of having grounds for fear. But tonight he felt terribly far from himself, fifty feet above the open place. When the sun had set he'd understood it was beautiful in the way he knew that a bullet in his head would kill him. He didn't feel it to be so. And knowing what no one else here knew, not even Fra Boboy, gave him an unexpected and complete clarity. He saw everything all at once, and everyone—not just individual faces but the larger geometry of the gathering. He was the proverbial camera. Yet he had never wanted to be this way; he'd always wanted to be involved, feeling it all for himself. He'd gotten so involved that he had stopped being a journalist altogether. Now, by some alchemy, he found himself on the other side, transformed into the omniscient eye. Tonight he was the perfect journalist. But it was a temporary state. Things were going to shake him, shake all of them. He was counting on it.

Levin saw so clearly that he spotted the smoking Jola before the youth managed to notice him. He was standing among peasants near the guerrillas, talking to no one, alone in the crowd. When their eyes met, Levin shook his head. As long as Connie was with him, there could be no talking. The Jola nodded in reply; Levin's recognition drew a smile. The face seemed less wild and menacing than it had in daylight.

"You must get tired of the village," he said to Connie. "It's not much fun for an educated city woman."

"They need me in both places. Wherever I can help, that's where I'll be."

"Where do you help the most?"

"In Impanang," she said, "we run out of antibiotics every week. Here we're lucky to get them ever. So I don't ask for results, such things."

"Don't you ever get discouraged?"

"It isn't a question whether I get discouraged, is it? It's not important. There's work to do, that's all."

She looked at him, and behind the glasses her eyes carried something like a plea. He thought for a moment she might cry—her eyes were shining. Perhaps it was only fatigue.

"Do you get discouraged?" she asked him.

"That's up in the air. I'm not a drunk," he said, "if that's what you're asking."

"It isn't."

"Does it matter if I do?"

"I think," she said, "it matters to you. I'm curious about the journalist's life. Going so far away all alone, asking questions so you can understand."

"I thought we weren't absolutely sure about me." It was a clumsy bit of provocation and he regretted it. She had to look away with a smile of embarrassment.

"Some things," Connie said, "we just decide to be sure of."

"Good."

"And if we find out we're wrong—then we consider the options. It happened to me once, you know. When I was eighteen I went to U.D.S. and I started thinking, Why am I a Catholic? And almost right away I knew I wasn't one at all. So for months I was ashamed of myself—my selfish ignorant little girlhood at the convent school. The nuns were spoiled and they spoiled us. And my selfish little life at home—doctor's daughter! My precious little body and my nice Portuguese-Chinese mestizo skin. I hated it."

She'd never spoken about herself at all, and Levin was surprised and thrilled by these revelations.

"That happened to a lot of people like you. I think Ding—"

"Ding . . . was different."

"How?"

"When I knew him at U.D.S. he was always a kind of loner. He wasn't in any of the radical student groups. He played his music. Ding is darker than most people at our socioeconomic level and you don't realize how much that means here. He has what they call ethnic looks. I had the feeling something bad was going to happen to him, drug overdose or . . . something. But nothing happened."

Across the floodlight Ding was standing with folded arms, his camera slung around his neck, engaging Fra Timo and another guerrilla in conversation. A stiff posture and grave face suggested an effort to simulate sobriety.

"I just didn't know him at all," Levin said.

"Well, you shouldn't have imagined you did."

He felt a little tempest rage in him and die.

"So, how did you learn to live with your nice mestizo skin? Which by the way is very lovely."

Connie forced a smile that materialized as a grimace. "I decided I would learn about the poor."

"Ah. Self-mortification, and the whole Santa Clara bit."

That touched her vanity, and she withdrew to compose herself. "Maybe—at the start. But I was humbled, really humbled by these people, and I really felt they were my only hope. So I quit U.D.S.

and went to work at the hospital in Impanang, and my father hasn't spoken to me since. He is a typical mestizo bourgeois, that way."

Levin thought that was a hell of a way to talk about one's father, and he didn't really believe she meant it either. Connie was holding her elbows, shoulders hunched; her glassy eyes were looking at him without appearing to see him. She seemed exhausted, yet wired, as if some tremendous invisible struggle held her motionless.

"Why did you ask whether I dreamed up here?" she said suddenly.

"Did I? Sorry."

"I was just surprised."

"I think it was a way of getting to know you. Since you make it so hard."

Abstracted, Connie didn't hear. She was hugging herself tighter. "Because last night I had a dream. Do you want to hear it?"

"I would very much like to."

"I was at a meeting in São Sebastião. There was a group of cadres and Fra Boboy was there. I think it was a room in the Hotel Pacifica and we all checked in under false names. Anyway—the whole time I was worried that someone had followed my car. So I wanted Fra Boboy to go back with me after the meeting—but also I was afraid he'd be angry that I let myself be followed. The whole time I was anxious, I couldn't pay attention. I was afraid they would burst in on us, but my own safety wasn't what I was worried about. It was the others' finding out it was my fault.

"When we finished, Fra Boboy had other business, so I had to go back alone. When I saw it—I was right. The car was just stripped, everything. The tires, seats, steering wheel, the engine—gone. Nothing was left but an empty shell, a—body."

After a pause, Levin asked who the thief was, though he imagined that it was Fra Boboy and that Connie would not be able to see this. She said she didn't know; a military, she supposed.

"So what does it mean?"

"The people here would say such and such is going to happen. Maybe that I'll be captured." She stared wide-eyed at the ground, where the boys had abandoned their lizard. "I . . . was going to ask your opinion. Since you're interested in dreams."

"You're stressed, as the psychiatrists say. That's the Western answer. My own opinion is that the movement doesn't want its cadres wondering about their dreams."

This seemed to make her even more anxious and he was sorry he had said it. The nakedness of her appeal had taken him aback, and moved him. He was beginning to be afraid for her.

"I don't know. Maybe you haven't completely stopped being your parents' child. Would that be so bad?"

"What do you mean?" She was staring at him, still without seeing him. "No, I know what you mean. That would be"—she fixed him with a look of the utmost desperation—"a terrible thing."

When the propaganda tape ended, a cadre came to turn off the VCR. The children at its feet let out small howls of disappointment. But immediately there rose a sound of drums and bells and wood flutes from a band of men next to the group who were readying the fighting cocks. The music brought a cheer from the villagers, rising with expectation. Their applause became a roar when two young guerrillas, skinny teenagers, spun into the ring. They wore body tights, plastic beaked masks, and floppy headdresses, one of them all in black, the other in blue. Wings of cloth draped from their arms. They were fighting cocks. On the wings of the black cock white letters said COUNTERINSURGENCY; on the wings of the blue were the bold initials SPP-AL.

In the ring of stones they tangled and kicked and flailed. The villagers shrieked, and the music rose. It had no melody; cued by the fight, it bodied forth frenetic rhythm, boisterous incitement. For a time the black cock had the upper claw and inflicted fierce blows, some in a kind of slow motion, wings flapping, to the legs and buttocks of the other. Then a cadre, wearing the short-billed camou-flage baseball cap favored by A.F.D.S. officers, ran into the ring, followed by a female cadre in a stovepipe hat striped red, white, and blue—Uncle Sam. They started calling bets with their fingers flash-ing; they had a line on the black cock. Another cadre bolted in, this one in the trousers and T-shirt and head rag of a Saraunese farmer. He had odds on the blue. The guerrillas and a handful of the more alert peasantry shouted bets to him. The black cock sneaked and gashed the blue from behind, whirling him to the dirt. The blue rolled away from a nasty finishing blow as the crowd screamed its outrage at the foul play. Filthy, he leaped up and let have at the other with a righteous flurry of kicks and flaps until COUNTERINSUR-GENCY collapsed in agony. The drums frenzied the audience; chil-dren were hysterical with glee. SPP-AL stood over his twitching opponent and seemed about to help him up. But with a final beating of the wings he landed a savage kick to the gut, and the black cock breathed out his last.

They left the ring, bettors trailing, to enthusiastic applause. Fra Boboy led the Jola headmen in a standing ovation.

"That was really something," Levin said.

"They don't hurt each other. It's like mime."

The explanation was an excuse; Connie seemed outside the applause.

"It reminds me of pro wrestling on TV. It's the best bit of agitprop I've ever seen. Uh-oh, look at this."

A pair of tough, venerable village men had come into the ring cradling their spurred cocks. The birds were astonishingly healthy things, like shiny puffed Rhode Island Reds, compared with the gamey village chickens that pecked about the dirt. Their ankles were fitted with bits of razor blades that glinted in the floodlights.

Levin said, "Those birds look like they're on speed."

"They put hot peppers in the throat and rectum."

"Christ. This is a very serious business."

"Do you know those cocks eat better than these kids here? And by the end of the night some of these people will lose the income of one harvest. They're like drug addicts. They call it cock-crazy."

In a calmer or more sober state Levin wouldn't have laughed; as things stood, he couldn't help it. A pair of stout women turned and shared his amusement. Their teeth were pleasantly browned from chewing tobacco; one had a grapefruit-sized goiter that trembled like a toad's throat when she laughed.

"I don't think you're in the spirit of things," he told Connie. "You've brought the bad city air, the convent air. This is just good P.R. Fra Boboy knows how to please."

"It's such a waste. It would be better not to encourage it."

From afar Levin tried to make out Fra Boboy's expression. He seemed to be relaxed and enjoying himself.

A clear bottle of rice liquor was making its way through the crowd. When it reached him Levin drank too fast. The moonshine was fire water, nearly raw alcohol, and his nauseated choking sprayed it through his sinuses, where it burned a path that seemed to reach his brain. He was afraid his high would turn against him now. Connie hesitated before accepting an experimental sip. A tiny old man beside her laughed and patted her on the back. She tried to smile through her distaste.

"That's it," Levin said. "It's a revolutionary duty to drink what the people drink."

The villagers they stood among had begun to press forward into the ring, in the unconscious, magnetic way of a rapt crowd. Bettors positioned along the edge were holding up fingers and twitching their hands; the gesture was enough to elicit frantic cries from the spectators. As the odds rose to nearly equal, the anxious jostling press of men and women with sharp deliberate elbows and shoulders, the throats competing for the bettors' ears, seemed to threaten a riot. The guerrillas looked on and did nothing. In the still center of the ring, the handlers sheltered and stroked their birds, cooing softly.

The cowbell was struck. In an instant everyone fell silent. The bettors disappeared into the crowd. The handlers moved apart, and then there were just the two cocks in the pit, with their gleaming claws. At once they flew at each other in a furious mass of kicking, beating, thrusting beaks and legs and wings. Razors flashed, feathers exploded. The Jola writhed silently to the struggle of the birds. The tiny old man was gripping the upper arm of the goitered woman as if he would tear her flesh. People bared their teeth and screamed without sound. A child, kneed and shoved, began to cry, but his parents were elsewhere or paid no heed. Somewhere a pair of crazed dogs were going after each other. The cocks and the village were locked together in the essence of a single will: hatred—refined, distilled, pure.

The fight seemed to go on endlessly. But within twenty seconds or so blood appeared on feathers and legs and the ground inside the circle. One bird, wounded, faltered, and the handlers rushed to separate the pair. The cock that had struck the blow was made to strut about, while the injured one was bound and cleaned and exhorted by its frantic handler, who soon had bright blood over his hands and shirt. Meanwhile, as if ungagged, the crowd had broken into shouts again.

When the birds were rejoined, the bloodied one gamely attacked as if nothing drove his petering existence but a residue of fury. The effort was plainly doomed. Within a few seconds the other landed the stab that finished him. Metal cut sickeningly into bone. The victim stumbled away and then collapsed in his own flow of blood, and with a few twitches of the damaged wings he expired.

From somewhere deep in the crowd a yell rose. And although it was an old man's hoarse, clotted voice, the sound was far more terrible than ordinary human suffering. Deeper than a moan, harsher than a snarl, it came out of some place of original pain and elemental rage—as if against the nature of life itself, which held such cruelties and such ends. The sound pushed its way to the front, and an ancient man, gray hair cropped close to the large skull, made his way into the ring. He seized his vanquished bird and tore fistfuls of feathers from its breast. The veins in his maddened face seemed about to burst his old skin. He ripped at the legs, twisted the head until it tore off, beat his fists on the tattered corpse and spread blood and feathers and flesh across the ground where he kneeled. And all the while, he howled—until something stopped his chest and throat. Gasping, he allowed himself to be led away.

In a short time money was changing hands on all sides.

"What do you think now?" Connie asked teasingly, but the sight of something in Levin's face softened her own.

"I don't know. I think Fra Boboy's a genius."

"You're a little pale, Dan."

The howl had reached him here, in the middle of the straining crowd, had found his chest like the sob of the dusky langur in the forest. And deeper than these, he heard his father's old cry. An answer surged strongly upward, and he pushed it down. *No!* he thought. *Down. Down! Or I would not be who I am. The little I am left.*

Now drums and bells and flutes began a tuneless, haunting number. It drifted out like the prologue to a play, mood-setting. In the open place, two villagers of about twenty, a man and a woman, strolled under the floodlights toward the center of the clearing. The young man wore a T-shirt and fraying Adidas sweat pants and sandals fashioned out of tire rubber, like a rice farmer. In one hand he carried a cutlass and over his shoulder he'd slung an empty burlap sack. His lithe companion, wrapped in a gold sarong, was clutching his arm and pleading with him. Her wifely concern was met with bravado, dismissive humor. She touched his face and said a final word before she disappeared beyond the VCR into darkness.

When the man was alone, the music dropped to a low, slow,

careful beat. And the audience, which had not yet settled down after the cockfight, went jittery. Old women murmured warnings and clucked and shook their heads. The children near the front grasped one another and strained forward, dead silent. A few plowed back into the crowd of legs in search of a parent. Somewhere in the village, the dogs were barking again at unseen enemies.

Someone seized Levin's arm, and his heart flew upward. But when he turned, there was Connie, smiling slyly.

"Scared? By a village play?"

In the receding quiver of rummy nerves his heart leaped at his chest, but it was mute.

"I just wish those dogs would cut it out."

Now the wayfaring villager was strolling farther out, and by his weaving and his soft-stepping and his glances the crowd knew he was in the forest. The music plucked him on his way. He rummaged about the ground, dug with the cutlass, and stuffed imaginary roots and herbs and mushrooms in his sack. Gradually he seemed to forget the forest dangers. Foraging absorbed him so that he no longer looked up as he approached the far end of the clearing, where the second floodlight hung on a pole.

The peasants in front of Levin were writhing again. Under his breath an old man delivered a furious tirade of warning.

And then the cowbell broke free of the drums, ringing out, and the flute shrilled.

Gardner Bowers jumped out from behind the pole. Or rather, he was pushed out by his guard. For a moment, lurching from the darkness, he was a terrifying sight. Half of him glowed brightly; the other half appeared to be missing. One leg moved, one arm twitched, half the face was incandescent with shock. The rest wasn't there. Only his thin silvery hair and the white BVDs outlined a whole head and body. As he stumbled into the light, the crowd erupted in panic. Women shrieked, men cursed, and the children in front scattered wailing. Wild screams broke out: "Ngot! Ngot!" Even the guerrillas were appalled. A camera—Ding's—flashed white.

Under the floodlights Bowers looked slightly more human. The children were comfortless, but the audience, still panic-stricken, tried the bravado of jeers and threats. In terror the forager had dropped his cutlass and sack and was backing away. Bowers, under a strange mechanical will, stalked him with curled fingers. The peasant saw there was no help, no escape. And so the two began a circling game, like wrestlers, the village man and the half man, crouched, hands poised.

When their limbs locked, the music rose to a cacophony and the crowd screamed. All at once the peasants snapped the slim band of restraint that had barely held them all night. They surged forward, and some of the men broke into a run toward the open place. Two hundred chaoses were loosed in a single urge to destroy, to tear the half man to pieces.

Levin's eyes were fixed on Fra Boboy. He wanted to see what the commander thought of the hell that was breaking loose.

The calm of Fra Boboy's face had vanished. He was rising from his chair. No, he hadn't counted on this. Things had escaped his control, and his expression, not yet panicked, showed a struggle to master surprise and unease. Something had happened for which he wasn't prepared. They were going to kill Bowers.

But something else was happening. As he rose, the commander started to turn. And Levin, seeing Fra Boboy react, realized that he'd heard it too—in the hut thirty feet behind the commander, a crash and a strangled cry. For a second the two of them waited, while between them the village continued its mad business. Levin felt a rush of shame at knowing what had started.

Then there were shouts from the dark field behind the hut. Fra Boboy reached for the pistol in his waistband.

Levin was starting to crouch and reach for Connie's hand when the computer hut exploded in a ball of flame. In the orange glare the headman and Fra Boboy tumbled from their chairs. The peasants, some of them halfway across the open place toward Bowers, scattered and ducked and fell. Through the echo of the grenade blast came a fusillade of automatic weapons fire, wild and aimless cracks. The guerrillas near the hut were shooting. Some of the spray flew overhead, and first one and then the other floodlight burst into a thousand fragments, electric smoke poured over the shower of glass, and the village was lost in darkness.

A silence descended upon the open place. Levin heard brief scuffling and the hum of the useless generator, and then the gunfire resumed. He found himself propped against the bamboo wall of the medical hut. He didn't know who was pressing against him; it might be Connie. From the darkened wastes of the field Captain Bugan's men seemed to be returning fire, thinner but more focused.

Now the shrieking began: the frenzy of villagers, their ceremony of rage turned horribly wrong, and the frightened anger of the guerrillas. Two men clutching rifles ran bent at the waist past the brilliant hut and disappeared in the dark. Bullets that found the burning thatch and bamboo and computer set off smaller bursts, like the jerking of a corpse that continues to be shot. Stray bullets sang about the open place, blowing into the dirt, ripping thatch or splintering wood. One hit the VCR, which exploded in a series of blue and red pops. Everywhere people lay flat or scuttled for cover behind huts. On the other side of the market, the pigs were squealing and some of them had broken their pen.

Levin huddled against the wall amid the smell of electric smoke and burned grass and powder. A few feet away Connie sat covering her face. She might have been crying.

Under fire, he experienced the pure terror of the bowel that he had dreaded. He did not run away—where was there to go?—but he was confirmed in being absolutely frightened. Yet there were other feelings as well—a kind of shock, not at the sound of guns, but at the flight of bullets in his direction. It seemed a gross mistake or terrible piece of injustice that men he'd done nothing to were shooting at him. It was almost unbelievable. You'd better believe it, he told himself. And he knew the years that had kept him from such knowledge for so long were a fluke. How absurd, he thought, to imagine I was anything but this small wriggling thing clinging to the earth—this crab! There are things to be afraid of, out there, in here, and even learning to be afraid might not be enough, the world might roll over me anyway. Burst me, burn me. And pressed there like a child against the bamboo slats, crashed from his perch fifty feet up, he had this thought too: *You'd better forgive.* That was all. And then it was gone, and he was separated from himself again. Within a few seconds he had forgotten.

The clamor was dwindling to ragged gunfire and dispersed cries.

By the light of the fire the guerrillas seemed to have gathered to confer. Their shooting had become experimental, and when the questions got no answer the sound of gunfire stopped altogether. Some of the villagers had gotten up and were walking around, dazed, in what had been the cockpit and the stage. The generator still went about its work, generating nothing. The pariah dogs had recovered their courage and were tentatively barking. With the floodlights out the sky had returned, a low blackness mixed with clouds. Wind was blowing up from the valley.

Levin stood and dusted himself off. He was about to ask Connie if she was all right when he saw through the darkness that she was looking at him. He couldn't make out her features, and so he decided to imagine in them fear, pardon, need.

A late-season rain from the valley had blown over the mountain and drenched the little village, quenching the fire and turning the open place into a field of mud littered with spent shell casings. It drove the peasants into their damaged huts and seemed to quell the last of the sufferers' shouts. The bodies of Captain Bugan's men lay out in the muck by the damp smoking ruins of the hut—only two corpses, because the third had been blown to pieces in the hut along with a Jola watchman.

One guerrilla had been shot up; another was hit in the back of the head, probably by one of his own. The assistant to the village headman had suffered a heart attack at the blast right behind him and died soon after. The bodies of the young fighters and the old peasant lay side by side on the wooden platform next to the shattered VCR. From time to time villagers and guerrillas came to pay respect to the dead. Captain Bugan's men were visited by the pariah dogs, whining and nervous. The raffish hair of the jeep driver was matted in mud where he lay.

Fra Boboy walked briskly through the rain in his flip-flops, the Tec-9 machine pistol stuck in his gym shorts, and spoke in a low voice, gesturing people here and there. He directed Connie to receive the wounded in the medical hut. He assembled half a dozen armed fighters and dispersed them to points surrounding the village as lookouts. None of the peasants from other hamlets was allowed to leave, and they took refuge with the local Jola in their huts. Outside, the figures of the guerrillas were half visible in the watery moonlight. Exigency had broken the illusion of hosts and guests. The village had turned into an armed camp.

Levin, sobered, remembered he was a reporter here and tried to waylay interviews with a few guerrillas who'd exchanged fire with the raiding party. But in these circumstances the getting of information needed more than usual energy and guile, and he found that his heart wasn't in it. Nor were the guerrillas in the mood to share their thoughts with an inquiring American. Mutual suspicion made a bad atmosphere for postmortem chatting, and after a few fatuous questions drew monosyllabic replies he ended the charade.

After tense discussion, the guerrillas began putting out a line that the A.F.D.S. had suffered a dramatic setback. Fra Timo announced to the other fras and suors and any villagers willing to listen that the goal had obviously been the assassination of Fra Boboy and a devastating blow to the headquarters of the Southern Regional Command. It was true that the Command had lost its data base, but destruction was far better than capture, and it could be built up again. The repercussions of this setback for the military would be felt all over Direv Saraun.

No one mentioned that the raiding party had had highly privileged information. That security this evening had been criminally lax. That the military had nearly achieved what no one had imagined they could even attempt. That there must have been help from infiltrators. When they weren't putting the best face on things, the guerrillas moved warily and stole glances at one another in the wet darkness.

As well as he could determine, Levin figured that the watchman had surprised a soldier in the computer hut. Realizing their cover was blown, his companions had decided to cut their losses and destroy what they'd meant to steal. A grenade attack had probably been part of the plan anyway (they had the 40 mm. launchers), a well-placed shot from far out in the field to let the guerrillas know as vividly as possible that they'd been found, triggering another round of reprisal killings within the ranks. But the interruption had hastened the attack and prevented their escape. Without cover in the fallow field, they had been cut down.

As for the assassination theory, Levin found himself unable to believe it.

The other newsman on the scene had apparently been instructed to put his camera away, or had done it unasked. Ding wandered from one guard post to another, sitting with each lookout and passing a cigarette. He was hushed and solemn, like someone doing double-duty mourning at the funeral of a dead man he didn't know well.

Levin had made up his mind to get out of the rain and look for Bowers when he saw Fra Boboy striding toward him from the remains of his hut.

"I have a few minutes," the commander said, "if you want to

talk." He was impatient and insistent, masking an embarrassment.

"We can always do it in the morning."

"No time like the present, hmm?"

They withdrew to the house of the village headman, who was being fed a bitter-smelling tea by his wife. Chairs were brought for the visitors and the peasant couple moved into an interior room, where two dirty children stared from the doorway.

Fra Boboy took out his pistol, removed the long clip, and set both on the floor. He fished a cigarette out of his shorts pocket and lit up. He made no offer to Levin.

"I assume you don't smoke. I know that educated Americans despise smoking."

Levin shrugged and said nothing.

"So. Everything is O.K. with you?"

"Unscathed. I was on the other side."

"With Suor Connie," Fra Boboy said. "I would be less than honest to tell you I wasn't surprised."

Levin decided to believe that the surprise had to do with the raid and not his whereabouts during it.

"But our fighters performed well. They are more used to being on the other side of the ambush. I plugged one myself." He gestured down at the automatic pistol, with its perforated barrel, then formed a gun with his hand and lowered his thumb with a soft mouthed pop.

"Really," Levin said.

So you could kill, then chat. Chat with killers and be no wiser; yourself kill, and be no wiser. But there was not much left of the good feeling in Fra Boboy's voice. His features had gone resolutely blank, Saraunese. The smoking made him seem uneasy, and diminished. Levin pictured Colonel Siriman smoking behind his desk; he thought that the colonel and the commander understood each other. They saw things eye to eye. So there would be no reason to kill Fra Boboy.

"The disks and laptop are a loss, but everything I had here the Northern Command has too, except for some recent writing. Perhaps you could buy a new computer for us in Singapore." Fra Boboy spoke without a trace of mirth. Suddenly he looked annoyed. "You still have no notebook?"

"I'll go by memory. This can be off the record."

"On the record. Everything is on the record. Off the record is for Saraunese who don't trust themselves or their own intentions. Whatever I want you to know I want the world to know."

"All right." Fra Boboy waited, and Levin plunged in. "How did those guys pinpoint here? How did they find you?"

"Clearly, with information. But from who?"

Levin waited for the commander to answer himself.

"Are you asking me?"

"Certainly you have thought about it."

"It's not my job to have opinions about these things."

"Oh, no. You have opinions that you don't tell me. Later, you give them to the well-known anonymous observer. That's O.K. I know how the game goes." He sat back. "In any case, we have already identified the traitors."

For a moment Levin was speechless.

"Are you sure?"

"One hundred ten percent. The integrity of the Southern Command can be restored."

As mildly as he could, Levin looked into Fra Boboy's black eyes. He wanted to see if the commander believed what he was saying. But blankness had descended, the gap of oceans and centuries, swallowing up the pretense of a common language and common irony. Levin was moved to wonder whether Fra Boboy could doubt the ultimate truth of even his lies, or their ultimate efficacy.

"So it's . . ."

"The cadres who brought you up here and the one who falsely accused that farmer you saw murdered. We have evidence they were in contact with the battalion headquarters in Pulaya. They confessed and will be executed tomorrow," he said offhandedly. "And our zealous Magkakanaw, as you know. He was the connection. But I'm sure he won't confess. I'm going to offer him a way out." Fra Boboy dragged on the cigarette and crushed it out against his chairback. "What do you think?"

"I . . . I don't think you're right."

Fra Boboy raised his eyebrows. "You've changed your mind?"

Levin's face was filling with blood. "I never said anything definite."

"You said he wasn't reliable. And that time would tell. Time has told."

"He's not reliable. He's misguided, twisted up, turned around. Maybe even crazy. But that's not being a 'traitor.'" The word sounded strange and melodramatic, a foreign order of discourse on the far side of the gap; it made him reel.

"I asked for some photographs he took—we developed what he gave me and they were not what he said they were. He hasn't been here twenty-four hours before we are attacked. Even if it was just the carelessness in Pulaya that you mentioned, it cost lives and we cannot excuse it."

"Look—you had a problem with infiltration long before we got here. Units wiped themselves out."

"I told you the problem was eliminated."

"But how can you *know* about a thing like that?"

"Can we afford ambiguity in this life?"

"I don't know what you can afford. I don't know how you can afford to be wrong about this."

Fra Boboy allowed himself to display anger for the first time in Levin's presence. "Levin, don't tell me what I can afford. I said I'm going to offer him a way out. In a thousand million years you will never understand what it is to have to fight. You have nothing but skepticism for us and it's aesthetically and morally unpleasant for you that we have none. But try to imagine a life where things matter too much for skepticism."

Shaken, Levin said, "Well—I am. Christ, I am trying. I'm just asking you to consider that you've got Ding wrong."

He had to look away. He was trying to find out what was left of him. He was asking himself how much he was capable of. In his mind he formed the words: *I'm the one, Fra Boboy. I'm your man.*

But he said, "You know what I'm thinking? I'm thinking of your dissertation—the attack on surrogate victims and all that. Maybe you'll have to revise your thesis."

Fra Boboy looked disgusted. "What bullshit," he muttered.

Recklessly, Levin pressed him. "Maybe there's something to 'pure sacrifice' after all. Because your impure kind gets out of hand, doesn't it? You were turning on yourselves, maybe even running out of cadres. You lost control. Nothing like a scapegoat to restore the social order. Right? And Ding qualifies. Bowers, too—wasn't that the idea? Feed the half man to these people and keep everyone happy?"

He stood up and walked to the door of the hut. The rain had tapered to an aimless drizzle, almost as light as fog. On the far side of the open place figures moved through the mist and mud like insubstantial souls in purgatory.

"And I'm thinking that it's really a shame, Dan," Fra Boboy said, controlling his voice. "You really led me to have hopes."

Levin put out his hands palm up. "Sorry to disappoint."

"There was something in you and I feel you've lost it. There was maybe a possibility of greatness. But I've seen these things die if we don't love them. Then we lose ourselves to the mob of anonymous observers."

"I don't know. It could be either of us. It could be cultural."

"Listen—we are very seriously fighting in behalf of people who have never been anything but poor and kicked around."

"That's what I thought."

"So don't come in here and talk about scapegoats to me! A revolution—is not—a dissertation topic."

Fra Boboy had become just another angry Saraunese. Standing in the doorway, Levin was overcome by sadness. Outside the world was only dark and fog and damp and debris; there was no reliability to be had of it anywhere, and he was in it and it went for him too. He had stared himself down long enough to know that an act of redemption wasn't within him. He had tried to make it be otherwise, but he couldn't offer himself in his enemy's stead. Nor would it matter in the end, since Fra Boboy had reasons for wanting to believe the things he had decided to believe.

So he would have to confront Ding and try to save him.

"It's too bad they ruined your party," he said. "Cultural Night."

"Oh, they didn't ruin it. You saw how the people enjoyed themselves. And then they found out who their friends are."

"You don't think they're demoralized?"

"Temporary. Tomorrow we begin the remoralizing process." Another surprise was coming. "I've already laid the ground for a counterattack. We're going to hit this buffalo where he'll feel it, in the balls."

Fra Boboy came to Levin's side. Something of the old intimacy had returned to his voice, but it was marred with motive and distraction.

"Can you guess?"

Levin tried to contemplate the inner life of Fra Boboy, and came up with an answer. "You're going to raid the milling central."

A hand clapped him on the upper arm. "That's pretty good. In fact we're planning diversionary actions there and at battalion headquarters. But the main action will be at the house itself. Symbolic."

"Do you think it's wise to go after the Fazenda Maria Luísa?"

"Why not?"

Levin shrugged, the only gesture he could think to make. He didn't want to go into an explanation of how he came to know the extent of Dom Hipolito de Oliveira's home security. But when he looked into Fra Boboy's powerful face, coloring, trembling with the drama of the plan, he saw that what he knew didn't matter anymore. The success of such a raid might not depend on anyone surviving it.

"Look, whatever there is to know, we know," Fra Boboy told him. "We have people in these Cavaleiros de Aviz. And this will fire spirits all over Salantin Province." He allowed himself a smile in his rising excitement. His grip on Levin's arm had tightened. "In Boston I learned a phrase—'Why not have it all?' There's some truth in that."

"I think this buffalo is going to kick and go on a rampage if you hit him there."

Fra Boboy nodded vigorously. "Then the people will know who their friends are. And with coordinated actions by the Capital and Northern commands, everyone in this country will have to choose. Because now is the time."

Amid this talk of apocalypse Fra Boboy's good humor was returning. Levin felt a chill touch his chest that might have been the wet mountain air.

"How am I going to get out of here with all this happening?"

"I was going to suggest you cover our operation tomorrow night. It would be a real scoop."

Levin allowed a few moments of consideration to pass before answering. "It's time to go back. I already have enough for five stories."

Fra Boboy released his arm and gave a pseudo bow. "Glad to be of service."

The headman's wife appeared from the other room with two enamel bowls of steaming tea. Levin accepted one gratefully and drank, feeling the liquid spread heat through his throat and chest. The tea tasted of the wild leafy smell of the forest.

"You can leave in the afternoon," Fra Boboy told him, "and be down the mountain by nightfall. Fra Simone will meet you with your car. From there you find your own way home. If you are lucky, our operation will distract Pulaya town. Because from now on, every-body is going to be less tolerant of anonymous observers."

Levin turned to face him. "How do you know Fra Simone wasn't responsible, or that girl Pin-Pin?" He hesitated. "Or me, for that matter?"

Fra Boboy was shaking his head. The gray of his hair bespoke weary resignation, a strong man blocked by a feeble and intractable world. "How is not a question. What is essential is to know and be seen to know." He shook his head again in some private disappoint-ment. "Really, Dan, these things are so basic."

Levin started to leave. "What about Ding's way out?"

"Magkakanaw," said Fra Boboy, "will be given the assignment of a lifetime."

"Dom Hipolito's."

"Do you think he would have it any other way?"

"And Connie stays here?"

"No. Suor Connie goes back to São Sebastião with you. She needs a rest—I'm afraid she's heading toward some sort of breakdown."

"But . . . "

"But?"

"São Sebastião won't be the place for her when . . . it goes."

"Then she'll have to decide where she stands. Once and for all. Everybody will. And the only neutralists left will be the acrobats in the foreign press."

"Fra Boboy, they're talking about the Indonesian solution. Any-one who works with the poor—"

Something in Fra Boboy's face shut down so completely that it was as though he'd put on a pair of dark glasses. The last of the lines between them was severed, and Levin experienced a sensation of falling. There was no ground beneath him now to break it.

"What about Bowers?"

"Bowers is a spy. He is also his own punishment. Take him back with you. Tell America the Army of Liberation is merciful as well as just."

Fra Boboy put out his hand, and for the second time that evening Levin shook it. In spite of the tea his chill deepened.

"I was just wondering about something you said before. You said 'love.' I don't know what you meant."

"Oh, that." Fra Boboy, slightly embarrassed, looked away. "It was just a word. It's the Saraunese in me—you know how sentimental we can be."

"It reminded me that Feliz had a question for you." Fra Boboy lifted his chin with interest. "He said to ask what you want."

"What I want? He asked that?" For a moment Fra Boboy looked at a loss; but then a smile spread across his face. "Tell Feliz . . . I want to be a brave soldier and an honest man."

"Shall I write that?"

"Dan, it no longer matters what you write."

Back in his own hut, Levin encountered Bowers. He was sitting on the floor, clutching his knees and shivering violently. He'd put on shirt and trousers but the paint beneath had not been washed off. Rainwater streaked black pigment across his white half-face, so that he looked more weirdly inhuman than ever. He seemed to be crying.

"Just get me out of here, Levin," he sobbed, rocking on his buttocks and heels. "Please just get me the fuck out of here."

"We're going."

Dawn came fogged and dripping. Levin woke with his heart forcing the stifled pressure in his chest. His pulse was in his throat. As the crust of sleep broke away a memory eluded him, a waking or dreaming fragment slipped; he grasped for it but had nothing; and he knew the day would pass in pursuit, under influence, with no stilling of the throat or chest.

As consciousness settled over him, he remembered that today was the day he was going back. He would see Melanie soon—and he realized she was somehow involved in the memory. He'd woken up with her laughter in his ear. It was the music of life lived fully elsewhere and it had nothing to do with him. He began to wonder how it would be when he was with her again.

He could see now that he'd never, in their time together and apart, allowed himself to be exposed to her, or changed by her, or ever tried to imagine what it was like to be her. In some terrible way he'd never given her a moment of real thought. And now, in his state, he didn't know what he could offer to the force of her feelings. He feared that she would overwhelm him, or leave him, and he would disintegrate.

Ding's sheet lay unused on his gear. In the corner, Bowers snored fiercely.

Levin went outside. Fires were lit and the heavy morning air had the flavor of woodsmoke. The peasantry looked bruised and wary, poised between cringing and snapping. With a minimum of greeting, fighter and peasant alike went about their daybreak business in the mire. But from the huts of the village elders, there rose occasionally a woman's wailing, thin and hopeless in the wet air, over the body of the old man whose heart had stopped with a grenade.

A Jola woman sold him hot tapioca flavored with raw sugar and a cup of the forest-herb tea. Three children swarmed about her legs and demanded more attention than she gave. Two were quarreling over a shell casing they'd found in the mud. The mother was young-ish, thick-bodied and full-breasted from continuous pregnancy (it was hard to tell if she was pregnant now or not). With a modicum of vanity she could have been a stunner—expressive mouth and fine chin line and clear, soft, amused brown eyes. Even her fleshiness and the prematurely deep lines of her face didn't entirely blot out the mild glow of beauty and inward delight that seemed to warm her.

He took a walk through the palm grove, under the eyes of one of the lookouts, and down to the stream, which had swollen from the storm. He kneeled on a rock near where the washerwoman had worked, and cupped half a dozen handfuls of water to his face. Cold and fresh—although he knew it to be full of bilharzia-bearing snails and transparent worms and little slips of leech. In the dancing sun-light it looked clean, anyway. There would be nothing like it in São Sebastião.

The smell of cigarette smoke made him look up. Above him on the bank stood the Jola youth, squinting in the face of the morning sun.

"Excuse me, sir."

Levin stood up and wiped his face.

"Marlboro?"

Levin didn't feel like smoking, but this time he took one anyway. The Jola helped him light it with his own.

"You probably shouldn't be seen with me," Levin said. "They're very paranoid right now." But the youth made no move to leave. "Did you want to talk to me?"

"Because the village asked of me. I alone have the English." His speech was different from that of the Saraunese, less fluent but more precise, as if self-taught from books. "But always you are refusing me, sir."

"I—didn't know what you wanted. But I think I know now."

The Jola features that had seemed so alien yesterday gathered in an intense question.

"You want me to write that your people aren't happy with these guerrillas."

The youth stared at Levin as the cigarette burned down to his fingers. And then, his mouth composed in a fierce oval, his eyes riveted on Levin's, he gave the briefest and firmest of nods. Without a word he disappeared up the bank into the palm grove.

Going back to the village, Levin reflected that he would retain little of Jola faces or the sounds of their words. As an anthropologist or a traveler it might have been different. In other circumstances, where everything said and done cost less, given the chance he might try to make a point of knowing them or people like them. But for now, with the Jola, it was too late.

Across the open place he saw them emerging from the headman's hut: Fra Boboy, Ding, Connie, Fra Timo blinking more rapidly than ever, and another cadre. They emerged stiffly, without looking at one another. Connie walked alone across the mud, which was strewn with leaves and glass, to her hut, where the wounded lay. Fra Boboy and his cadres disappeared into the mess of the market. Ding veered away from Connie toward his hut, and Levin pursued him.

"I want to talk to you," he said from the doorway. Ding was sorting through his bag; he barely looked up at Levin's entrance. Bowers showed no sign of waking.

"It's all going down," Ding said. "I've got to get ready."

"No, it's not. It's not going down."

"Don't come in here and tell me that." There was a strange determination in the narrow eyes. "You don't know. You're out of it and I'm in it." He lifted his chin. "He said so."

"I don't know what he said but he's lying to you."

"Why are you doing this to me, man?" The determination lifted from Ding's eyes to reveal once again the naked shine of desperation. "You always were trying to shanghai my things."

"Ding," Levin said gently, "I know certain things."

"No, you don't. You don't know what you think you know. But that's O.K. with me, I don't hold it against you now. Only don't get in my way. I'm in it and you're not. I'm going down there with them."

In the doorway Levin crouched so that they were eye level. "To the plantation." Ding didn't answer; he occupied himself in packing. "I've been there. You heard but you were too drunk to remember."

"I'm going to take pictures."

"I've seen the place, Ding, and I can tell you no one is going to get out of there. They've got machine guns on the walls, sandbags, dogs, crazy guys running around with Armalites—"

"Pictures," Ding insisted. "I can see them in my head. Blood and glory. The corpse of Dom Hipolito de Oliveira. I'm telling you, my country has never seen pictures like this."

He was caressing the Leica, shooting imaginary shots. He had nothing to fear from his camera anymore.

"My brother and sister are going to see these pictures somewhere and be proud. They'll see the Magkakanaws have a future in the new Direv Saraun. My father's killers are going to see them—they'll know their days are numbered. Poor mothers, hungry kids, they'll get courage from what I do, they'll stop being afraid. I'll take the pictures of the revolution. On the day of insurrection everyone in São Sebastião is going to be holding copies of my pictures."

Levin grabbed his wrist and forced the camera down. "He's setting you up! He told me so!"

Ding freed himself from Levin's grip. "Know what he called me?"

Levin thought he knew.

"Fra Ding."

His smile was triumphant, without malice. Of the blessed. Levin persisted. "I have a way to get you out of here. We can be in the capital by tomorrow morning, then you're on your own. Ding! Let me get you out."

"There's nothing there for me, just rot away all alone—Ding Magkakanaw." He spoke his own name with bitterness.

"Getting killed in Pulaya is better?"

"If that's what has to be—yes! Death can be better. That's what I figured out last night. If I choose it, if I have a purpose, it can be better than anything I've ever done. It's in your head, so you have the power. I already feel free. I'm telling you, I feel light as a feather. You can't touch me."

Levin stood up and watched absurdly as Ding went through his equipment, cameras and lenses and light meter and film, with his photographer's obsessive checking, breathing, rubbing.

"They're going to shoot people this morning," he told Ding.

"I know that." Ding swallowed and paused in his packing. "And I'm the one to do it."

Levin was looking down at the thick black ruffled crown of hair. There was a small part in the middle of the skull that he hadn't noticed before; it was like a trace of the elite schoolboy. Inexplicably, he wanted to kiss it.

"He asked Connie and she said she couldn't. Then he asked me."

"Ding, for God's sake."

"He said it would be a sign."

Ding went back to packing.

By midmorning the sun had seeped through the cover of spent clouds. Yellow light appeared over the mountainside and the mud and thatch steamed in the rising heat. Some farmers had been allowed out to their fields to inspect the storm's damage. The very old and young mostly kept indoors. Three teenage guerrillas were clearing the burnt wood of the computer hut; a knot of Jola women stood by, salvaging the less charred sticks for fuel.

Bowers's hut had been taken over by a group of senior cadres, and on the benches outside some of them were equipping themselves with cartridges and bandoliers and grenades (most of the latter, together with rifles and launchers, lifted off the corpses of Captain Bugan's men). They moved efficiently, saying little.

Connie was cleaning and packing her dispensary. Levin hadn't spoken with her since the first moments of the raid.

He was alone in his hut; Bowers had been taken down to the river to cleanse himself of Ngot. In the utter inertia of the village, Levin killed the time by listening to the tape of his first interview with Fra Boboy.

He didn't hear much of what was said. He was alive to tones: his own was flat, with a kind of strained reportorial authority that came off slightly pompous and fundamentally unsure; Fra Boboy's sounded natural in its range of inflections and always leavened with humor. He listened to the changes in his own mood, now defensive, now exhausted. Hearing the tape, even someone with no English would know that Fra Boboy had dominated him in every way, led him through his paces. For journalistic purposes it was worthless. He held the little Sanyo to his ear and was mesmerized by his own undoing. A whole personal debacle on ninety minutes of tape.

At the first shot he dropped the Sanyo and the tape fell out. There was a delay, then a second shot and a third, and after a longer pause a final one. They came from far beyond the market stalls, but he heard them clearly. He wondered which of the traitors Ding had needed two bullets to kill—if it was his sideburned, Rambo-capped guide, of the five-string guitar and "the liberation."

Levin didn't want to see Ding's face again. It would have become a face beyond rancor or longing, beyond the reach of any merely human hurt. He could not touch him. He would see in Ding's eyes the peace of a life's burden laid down. So he stayed in his hut and played out the tape, long past Bowers's return, and by the time he went out with his bag into the humid noon Ding and the squad of guerrillas were gone.

Connie was waiting outside the dispensary with a little blue duffel bag. Inside the hut, which smelled strongly of alcohol and putrefaction, bottles and bandages and small steel implements were stowed in boxes or on crude wooden shelves. Her wounded, cleaned and wrapped, had gone home. She had done her duty by them.

"Ready to go?" Levin asked.

She nodded. She had put on a pair of khakis and a blue workshirt, and over her shoulder-length hair she'd tied a cotton scarf, patterned with tiny red and yellow flowers. The scarf, and her wire-rimmed glasses, and the tense composure of her face, made him think of the convent girl. This impression was deepened by the way her drawn-back hair framed the roundness of her face, so that the mix of Asian and Iberian blood made her seem a light-skinned Latin. Pious and beautiful and fearful and sad, as she would have been on the day she said good-bye to the nuns.

From the headman's hut, which he seemed to have expropriated, Fra Boboy strolled across the drying mud alongside the headman himself. The commander was deep in explanation, gesticulating excitedly with his hands. The headman listened in apparent satisfaction.

"Time to go already?" Fra Boboy said upon reaching them. He squinted upward. "It's too bad to hike at this hour, but it's better than the rain."

He grinned all around for consensus, and the headman approximated a smile with his empty gums. Levin guessed that at least one of the dead had been a sacrifice to an unhappy mass base.

"The village feels empty," Levin said.

"It's a phenomenon of armed struggle," Fra Boboy said.

"Anyway, fresh recruits are on the way."

The shadow of a frown crossed Fra Boboy's face, but then it brightened and he gave a merry laugh, as if this were an old joke. "That's right. Fresh recruits."

Bowers showed up in his dirty seersucker suit, carrying the small vinyl Samsonite he'd packed for Asia and brought up here on his mission. Red-eyed and sleep-tortured, he was all apprehension and feigned contempt, like a compulsive talker trying not to say a word. At his elbows came two guerrillas, one of them the Counterinsurgency cock from last night. These were their escorts down the mountain.

Fra Boboy accompanied the band of travelers out of the village to the near edge of the rice paddy. With the sun overhead the clouds were burning off, and he held a hand to his eyes as he stood on the mound of dike where the farmer had knelt and met death two nights ago. The smile in place below the shade of his hand discouraged last-minute intimacies or parting summations.

"O.K., good-bye, don't let the night catch you in the forest."

He exchanged words in Saraunese with the guides.

"Those wounded men," Connie said, "their bandages—"

"O.K., they'll be changed." Fra Boboy was waving as if he were shooing mosquitoes.

Connie lingered; her hand went to her scarf in confusion. "Is there—"

"Go, Levin. Go."

Levin, starting to leave, looked at Connie. She was staring at Fra Boboy as if some final word was still to come from him. A touch, a gesture of recognition. But the steady hand guarded his eyes like a salute, and then he turned around and disappeared into the trees.

Walking in front of Connie, Levin heard the effort it took her to put one leg before the other. He knew she was mastering unshed tears.

CHAPTER XII

All the way down the mountain a song played in Levin's head:

> A lady wouldn't make little snake eyes at me
> When I bet my life on this roll
> So let's keep the party polite . . .
> Luck be a lady tonight

Somewhere on Mount Kalunur, Direv Saraun, Feb. 25—The eyes of the roll will always end up snake's because they are the eyes of the roller. The roller has predator eyes, and he is his own prey. He throws himself on every roll—in the end he has to lose. The roller is snake-bitten. An appropriate metaphor on this remote mountain, where several types of viper could appear underfoot at any moment, transforming a day's outing into a few seconds of richly deserved, agonizing death. As was made amply clear by last night's firefight. Leading this reporter to wonder if, having survived the news event of a lifetime, he has anything to tell you that you didn't already know.

But he soldiered on, toward the embrace of the world as it was. For two hours nobody said a word. The dripping green enveloped them; birds fluttered and sang in short afternoon bursts; the heat rose; insects buzzed and the forest pulsed, a mass of indistinct life. Sunbeams broke the canopy here and there and lit the gloomy floor in dusty shafts. In places the trail disappeared altogether. Whenever someone went down in the slippery mud, the guides paused in their descent. The village receded like a memory.

. . .

Just after dusk they reached the house on the dirt track where Levin and Ding had been met two nights ago and begun the last stage of the journey he was now repeating in reverse. In the forest, the dark came down with tropical speed. Lanterns were lit in the windows. A cadre with the same blue bandanna and two-way radio as before appeared on the porch and ran down the steps, but it was not the same cadre. A car was parked on the track—a Ford Escort.

It took the cadre several minutes of anxious explanation to get his story across to his comrades. Incredulous, they kept prodding him; everyone's eyebrows were in motion and everyone seemed upset. Finally Connie turned to Levin with an ironic smile on her lips and subdued panic in her eyes.

"They had an accident—Fra Simone and some of the Pulaya cadres. They wrecked your car and they've been arrested."

Bowers emitted an ostentatious groan. Like Levin, he was mudded and sweat-stung. "Fucking revolution."

"Shut up," Levin told him. "How? No, I know. I know how." He was thinking of the loose steering column. They would have lost control, Fra Simone high-spirited at the wheel speeding into one of Pulaya's hilly turns.

The cadre and their guides were talking things over.

"You might be in trouble," Connie told him. "They'll trace the car and want to know how it got into our hands."

"If I'm in trouble, you're in big trouble."

"I'm in trouble anyway. I always am."

She conferred with the other Saraunese. Levin noticed that they all treated her, even the guides, with a chilly reserve.

"They're wondering if you know anyone in Pulaya. You two could stay until we find a way to get you out."

"Sure, I've got lots of friends here." He was shaking his head. "I've run out of answers, Connie."

"We will think of a way."

"Pulaya must be hopping mad by now." Then he thought of Serge; the thought gave him a jolt of unreasonable hope. "Actually, there is a guy. Maybe he could find a way to get us out. He's a very cunning fellow."

It was agreed that they would drive under cover of night to the office of the *Pulaya Standard and Broadcasting,* dead in the middle of town.

"Maybe you should stay on the mountain a day or two," Levin suggested to Connie, "until things quiet down."

"I've been told to go back and wait until I hear." She tried to smile. "So I go back."

"Well, it doesn't matter. Things aren't going to quiet down."

The driver of the Escort, a burly, cheerful, older man who had been taking his dinner inside the house, maneuvered through the rain-filled holes along the track. Soon they gained the highway down into town, passing cinder-block houses with corrugated-iron roofs in overgrown lots, a chicken restaurant with outdoor tables, a truck yard, a closed bowling alley. A man stood with his back to the road, urinating into tall grass.

"Civilization," Levin said. Bowers summoned the courage to guffaw.

Electric lights sliced the darkness, and the mountain became a shadowy cone rising behind them against the blue-black sky. Their headlights caught a couple walking hand in hand along the shoulder: against brown skin the white sparkle of a skirt, a man's shirt. They had come out of one of the cinder-block houses and were probably on their way to a movie or nightclub. Levin thought of Fra Simone, assured in a way money made possible, driving through the revolution as boys like him in other places drove through early bachelorhood. Levin wondered how his idea of himself was holding up in one of Captain Bugan's interrogation cells. And he thought of the soldier with the dyed hair, dead in the mud with his companions, and the guerrilla with sideburns. And Ding. He tried to reverse the roles: imagine them college students, computer analysts, softball buddies; and his friends, his brothers, himself, forced to choose between fatuous luxury and war, or toil without end and war, or having no choice at all—thrown by some deadly mix of personality and circumstance into one or the other camp. It could as easily have been so. A cosmic dice roll, DNA and luck. But his effort was unsuccessful. White meant rowing machine, elevator music, remote control. And brown meant cooking oil, cinder block, pariah dog, click of the cartridge. He couldn't make it be otherwise.

The Escort passed through narrow town streets that were sparsely lit and almost deserted. But at the *Pulaya Standard and Broadcasting,* around the corner from the defaced mural, the windows were ablaze and the building was alive with human activity.

The watchman smoking behind the sandbags motioned the three

of them upstairs, as if they'd been expected. On the second floor journalists were perched on desks or standing close around a crackling radio held by someone sitting in the middle of the group. Serge.

He was the first to notice their arrival.

"I thought maybe you were killed!" Serge held the shortwave aloft. He was wearing his striped polo shirt and photographer's vest. "It's one of our guys—you met him, Siolao. He's outside the Fazenda Maria Luísa. There was a raid, really incredible. They got inside the walls, house badly damaged, Dom Hipolito lost his right hand. A big fire in the cane field, a bomb went off at the mill. Half a dozen Cavaleiros de Aviz dead. All the A. of L. boys killed—no prisoners."

One of the reporters hushed him. The voice on the radio was barely audible through rushes of static.

Levin whispered, "All of them?"

"That's what we heard. No, wait. He's saying some of the workers were part of it—two or three of them killed too. Really incredible. I did not think it was possible."

Apparently the radio was ham-operated because one of the reporters was asking questions of the man on the other end. Some of Serge's colleagues were giving whoops of surprise, not without a tinge of malicious delight. Others shook their heads in disbelief. One of them pointed to his right hand and said something mockingly.

"People here are upset with Dom Hipolito," Serge explained. "That girl we saw at his house—her head was left by our sandbags."

"Christ, that's terrible." *So much killing in this country!*—he could hardly take it all in. Unbidden, the image came of Dom Hipolito's severed hand, gloved in leather, working between the legs of a headless girl. He blotted it out. "Ding was with them," he told Serge.

"Magkakanaw? Ah. That's too bad. That's really too bad. Did he have a camera? We should find out at least if there are pictures." Serge took the radio and began speaking with Siolao in two languages at once. "You haven't seen the bodies? *Tadjo na lan* everyone reported killed? Ah. *Pansing na kamera?* Then ask. Keep looking." Serge turned to the others. "Magkakanaw—free-lance photographer. Killed in action, hey? But I don't think there are pictures."

The rest was lost in Saraunese. Everyone became extremely interested, mingling excitement with sympathetic clucks. Then the man in the jacket and tie called for quiet. One of the reporters went to a metal table where a microphone was mounted, sat down, and after a pause began speaking into it. The man in the jacket and tie flipped a switch on the radio, and suddenly the reporter's voice came over the airwave, absolutely clear. He spoke in rapid Saraunese, but Levin picked up the number fifteen and the names of Dom Hipolito, the Army of Liberation, Simkar Butang, and Ding Magkakanaw. The whole country was going to know Ding's name.

"It is big propaganda for the boys," Serge was whispering. "The house is hit, and then the military kill a journalist. And some of his own workers turn on him! This is really a story. And Siolao had the exclusive. He just happened to drive by and saw the fire."

Suddenly, understanding charged Serge's mild face. He drew Levin over to another desk. "It was retaliation? There was a raid, like Dom Hipolito told us?" Levin nodded. "You were there? Do you have pictures?"

"Ding has them all. Had. Ding's dead."

Serge had made Levin remember the canister of film in his trouser pocket. It was still there. He felt a spasm, just below his rib cage. But he thought: It wouldn't have mattered. It wouldn't have kept Ding from going to glory. He wondered if Ding had at last stopped waiting to live, there in the garden of the landlord's house, if the face lit by gunfire and his camera's flash had been aflame with its own exultation, the narrow eyes gleaming. And yet the canister chafed and nettled his thigh where it rested, and his diaphragm had hardened like a fist, cramping his breath. He found himself envying Ding's certitudes.

"No pictures—but you have the story. At least that."

"I have the story."

"So things didn't work out between you?"

"No."

"You decided to split up."

"Yes."

"Because he stole the money?"

"The money . . . no. Yes. He stole it. And my notebook. But it was just—guerrilla tactics. He felt under attack. We didn't know each other."

"Magkakanaw stole your notebook?" Serge smiled tightly. "I don't think so, Dan."

Keeping his eyes on Levin, he opened the drawer of his metal desk.

Inside, among shiny prints of the cane cutters, was a blue spiral notebook—the cover smudged, badly creased, pages folded back, but unmistakably Levin's. He stared at Serge for explanation.

"It was Dom Hipolito."

Levin must have registered disbelief.

"He told me himself. He was very unhappy that he let you know the military plans."

"Because he didn't know—"

"What?"

"Never mind." Levin was trying again to recall the names in it. He'd always been careful—Connie's real name wasn't there.

Serge seemed to read his face. "He wanted me to write an exposé, but he would not give it to me if it could be any use to him. He wanted to embarrass you as you embarrassed him. He told me to headline my article 'America's Book of Truth in Direv Saraun.' "

Levin flushed, remembering he had said something of the sort. "How could he have gotten it?"

"Who knows?" Serge said, raising his eyebrows, clearly knowing. "Maybe it was that girl you went with."

Levin could find nothing to say to this. He returned the little notebook to its place in his back pocket.

"So it was a misunderstanding between Magkakanaw and you."

"I think—" A spasm shot through Levin's chest and pushed into his throat, and for a second his voice escaped his control. The blood there beat violently. "We reached an understanding. At the end—we didn't, I think, hate each other."

"Oh, no." Serge attempted to be mollifying. "I don't think so. There would be no reason."

Connie and Bowers approached from the stairs.

"Serge, we need to get out of here," Levin said. As he explained their predicament Serge's color deepened and the humorous eyes began to calculate. Levin was relieved; he feared that Serge might have finally turned against him.

"Here's what we're going to do," Serge told them. "Because now is the best time to get out. You remember that couple—the Dutch? They are still here. I was going to tell them to leave, go back to São Sebastião. Because, you know, the military, Captain Bugan, already don't like them. They have a car. You can go with them."

Levin recalled the fair-haired couple with whom he'd drunk at the

Casa Amor. "I don't know if they'll want us. They didn't like me."

"My friend, this is not the time for like, not like. I'm going to tell them to take you. They owe me a favor."

"Everyone does, Serge."

They left the room full of journalists and the doubled voice of the man at the microphone, and walked the three blocks to Las Encantadas. On the way they were passed by a truckload of helmeted soldiers bristling with automatic rifles. Several of the troops in back saw them, but the truck sped on in the darkness.

The concierge was standing behind the front desk as if she'd never moved.

"Welcome back, Mr. Levin."

The Veeders were out by the swimming pool, in the company of a slight young Saraunese who turned out to be the head of a legal group that was organizing sugar worker cooperatives. The Dutch couple seemed more startled by Serge's urgent manner than by what he told them.

"I don't see in what way it concerns us," Erich Veeder said, pulling at his reddish patch of beard. At his side was a tall glass of soda water.

"It concerns, it concerns."

Renée said, "We are just beginning to make progress here. Do you wish us to break our promise to the people?"

Serge turned a fierce stream of Saraunese on the organizer. Apparently he was convincing.

"I think the work has to be put off," the man told the Veeders. "I have to—" He smiled apologetically and with a brush of the hand whisked himself out of existence. "And since you are known in Pulaya, Serge is accurate. Very accurate."

He had gone quite pale; the blood was leaving his lips. First Renée and then, slowly and with reluctance, her husband, seemed to consider the possibility that they were in some danger. Erich looked at Levin with hostility and bewilderment. But in an emergency, other alliances gave way and the deeper one of skin and eye drew near. Veeder forced himself to address Levin for confirmation, as if Serge or his colleague might be confused in their English. Levin said that everything he'd been told was true.

"We can leave, then, tomorrow," the Dutchman said.

"It would be better to go tonight. With the dark." Levin was conciliatory, though he couldn't deny to himself that he despised Veeder.

"Tonight, tonight," Serge almost shouted. "If you hurry you can go faster than this news. Once you get to São Sebastião . . ." He shrugged.

"Who are these two?"

Levin identified Connie vaguely as a member of the mass movement. Renée Veeder's tanned, desiccated face fixed on her a smile of radiant piety.

"And him?"

"Gardner Bowers," he introduced himself. "Let's just be on our way out of here, Jack."

"I know this name," Veeder told the others. "No, we do not take this one. He is I think from the World Anti-Communist League, or even C.I.A. This one can get his own way to São Sebastião."

It took another five minutes of explanation, exhortation, and finally indirect threat from Serge before the Veeders yielded. Their Saraunese friend and Connie stood apart, suddenly intimates, exchanging hushed words of counsel and solace. The organizer was constantly checking his watch.

Once persuaded, the Veeders packed and checked out with admirable dispatch. They clearly prided themselves on traveling light, just zippered and pouched backpacks—modern descendants of the Jesuits who gave up all to set sail for Goa, Quetzaltenango, Bissau, Manila.

Veeder brought the car around from the garage on the gravel drive. It was a rented VW Jetta, short on legroom, but with a full tank. His wife took the front seat; Levin squeezed in back between Connie and Bowers. The long night's drive was not going to be comfortable. He thought with alarm of his wrecked Toyota and then realized that it didn't matter. He wondered how long before he would hear from the military authorities.

Good-byes were awkward and brief. Through the window Serge grasped Levin's hand.

"Not good-bye," he said. "We shall meet in better times."

"I hope so," Levin said. "And I thank you. You know that, right?"

Serge dismissed it with a shake of the head. "Come back to Pulaya. Things happen here first. It is our social laboratory." He pronounced the final word in the English way; his tone suggested a promotional tour guide.

"You'd better mount a machine gun behind your sandbags."

"Oh, not really. Tomorrow I'll go out there—to get the story from his perspective. 'Terrorists Blamed in Cowardly Attack.' 'I have one hand left to kill communists.' " Serge laughed recklessly. As he moved away he touched Connie's arm on the windowsill. She looked up in surprise.

"Take care, sister."

"Thank you," she said, reaching for his hand. "You too."

As they pulled away Levin turned and saw through the rear windshield that the organizer had gone off in the other direction, his head down. Through the window of the lobby the concierge was just visible; she seemed to be on the telephone again. Levin wondered if they would be overtaken on the road. Serge was walking briskly back toward the *Pulaya Standard* building. Just before the car turned the corner, Levin stole a last glimpse of him in the rearview mirror. A shop's neon-light fixture, the color of jacaranda blossoms, caught his striped polo shirt. Then he was lost from view, and all Levin found in the mirror was his own face.

It startled him deeply, for he didn't know himself. The eyes encountered their own shock: sunken, underslept, darkly ringed. Where his jaw had been smooth, a thin rug of light brown beard grew. The mouth was partly open, seamed and tense. The black hair, matted to the forehead. The skin, sunburned from the day's walk; but beneath its reddish shine, pale with exhaustion.

When the instant was over and recognition came, he shuddered and his heart beat faster. He knew what would happen if he kept staring. He decided to keep his eyes off the rearview for the rest of the drive; but it required an effort, and he wasn't always equal to it.

"Take one of these," Connie told Bowers. She offered a bottle with the label of a German pharmaceutical. Bowers examined it in the interior darkness.

"You didn't know I read German, did you? What's this—I can't see a damn thing."

"It will calm you," Connie told him.

"I don't need calming. I'm no nut case, Fräulein. All I need is an airplane out of your fucked-up country."

"You are very nervous," she said. "Look at your fingers."

Around the ragged nails his flesh was bleeding.

"If it's a sleeping pill I'll take it. But I stay away from psychoactives."

Levin guessed that Bowers had some acquaintance with them. Connie was reassuring: the medication was very mild. Without water, Bowers grimaced and choked it dryly down.

"Anyone else?" she said. Renée Veeder was sleeping. "What about you, Dan?"

"You think I need calming?"

"Just to help you sleep a little."

Levin started to accept the pill, then changed his mind. He wasn't convinced that unconsciousness would be preferable. And he feared the numbing deception of the drug. It seemed important to stand stripped in the heat and cold of his nerves, endure them and know the worst they held for him. Although a few hours' sleep might do more good than this feverish waking brain.

"Veeder doesn't know the road. But feel free."

Connie hesitated before shaking her head.

Levin stared through the windshield and couldn't recognize this part of the highway. "Where are you going to go when we get there?"

"I haven't thought about it." Connie quickly added, "And you?"

"Before anything else I'm going to find out if my fiancée is still here."

"Your fiancée? She's in São Sebastião?"

"Arrived last week."

"You never discuss her."

"It didn't seem like a relevant subject, in the Blue Zone."

Connie clucked in disapproval. "You should be spending more time with her."

"Well, maybe that will happen."

"But why wouldn't she still be here?"

Connie was smiling unofficially, a soft smile of female amusement. It came from the same hidden place as the other thing he'd seen—her fear. She had become frail and interesting and affecting, and this too made Levin think of Melanie. Even love sometimes seemed like frailty. There were many reasons why he didn't want to answer Connie, some of them having to do with her fear, and others with her smile. So he said simply, "I'm hoping she will be."

Then he remembered the warm and levelheaded wife in Philadelphia he'd invented for Bowers. He glanced to his right. Bowers was already snoring lightly against the window.

. . .

They drove and drove. They crossed the foothills, the central highlands where coffee grew, the Musa River gorge and then the endless darkened villages in the valley along the North-South Highway. The return seemed faster than the journey out, though Veeder slowed to a crawl in the bad stretches. He wouldn't allow Levin to take the wheel, and Connie said she didn't drive well.

How long, Levin wondered, since I covered this very ground? Just four nights. That first time as if into adventure, limitless mystery in a limitless world. Now, the second time, like a defeat, and what lay unseen or half seen beyond the car offered only menace, an opacity that nevertheless had somehow to do with him. The return trip always returned you to yourself.

Staring ahead into the darkness, he had hints, half risings, of the mood in which he'd awakened. A glint of the same feeling had come when Connie stood on the paddy dike before Fra Boboy, expecting something. It was surely neither justice nor assurance—maybe a simple affirmation of who she was and what she was enduring. Forgiveness, for being human. He wasn't going to have it from Ding now, but it might still come from Melanie.

"What did you mean," Connie asked, "by 'fresh recruits'?"

He had thought she was asleep; but she was only gazing, forehead pressed to the window, out at the night. Renée and Bowers dozed on.

"When did I say that?"

"To him—just before we left."

"Ah. That was something we talked about before."

"What was it?"

"Just that everyone keeps telling me the neutral space is closing. So it would seem to mean the ranks will swell."

She turned to the window again. He saw that she was dissatisfied.

"Do you think it's true?" she asked.

"I think he meant it in maybe more than one sense. That there's a metaphysical neutrality that is probably already impossible. You can't imagine a place for yourself outside the two camps if in fact the place doesn't exist. Even if you imagine it, your instincts, your will are doing something else. So you're just a fool who doesn't know what he's doing while he's doing it. That's his whole idea of America, in fact."

Connie laughed, so suddenly and richly that it was like the accidental intrusion of another self. Of Sylvia Moktil, perhaps. She herself seemed startled by it.

"I've never heard you laugh like that."

Before the words were out he knew this was a mistake. The round yellow scarf-framed face flushed and her eyes flashed wetly.

"I wish you didn't say that."

For a few moments they neither spoke nor looked at each other.

"Anyway," Levin said, "my guess is that he wants to make this abstract, this metaphysical level, come down to the real level of actions. Where it's physically not possible to be outside the two camps. Or at least to make that spot so difficult that no one will want it for himself. And I think—I think he's going to have his way. That's all I meant."

He hadn't intended to go this far, but she waited for more, the color disappearing from her cheeks.

"Things might change soon. Something could come, a declaration of martial law? I could be wrong. I probably am."

"I think you are." Her eyes were filming. "Why do you say this?"

"Connie, when I went to the mountains I was acting as a kind of courier. I didn't know it—I didn't know what the hell I was doing. But someone in the A.F.D.S. wanted Fra Boboy to know that they're this close to staging a coup followed by civilian killings. On a very large scale. And tonight there's raids like the one in Pulaya happening all over the country. So I don't think there's much doubt."

Her mouth fell open as though she'd received a soft blow.

"I don't believe it."

He could see that she very nearly did.

"Maybe it's just games," he said. "Someone setting a trap for someone else. But I don't think so. I think everyone knows exactly what they're doing, and for now a faction in the military and Fra—a faction in the A. of L. want the same thing. And they're just about acting as tactical allies to make sure it happens."

He stopped, wanting to let her challenge, protest, refute. Behind her glasses the irises fluttered like birds madly resisting some force spreading over them. He watched her try to make it come out her way, and he hoped that she could. But it wouldn't.

"So you say he wants this," she said quietly. "He knows this."

"Knows, because I told him."

"But wants?"

"He hasn't done anything to show he doesn't want."

"Yes! He's sent me back!"

Her mouth hung open. A soft cry rose. And then for a long time she was silent, looking out the window at the speeding darkness. At last he heard her mutter, "I should have taken one."

She meant the pills.

When she showed him her face again it was tear-stained.

"Can I ask you something? Does anyone have the right to lose their faith twice?" Her eyes were desperate for an answer.

"If the thing turns out to be wrong."

"You see, Dan. I don't know if I have a right to feel betrayed. Or angry, or even disenchanted. I don't even know if I have that right. You don't decide to give yourself because you're enchanted. You're not in it because it meets your needs. The people don't benefit from my needs. Why should my faith make any difference? But I can't help it. So I'm just spoiled, like a convent girl, the whole—damn time I was really only thinking of myself. Isn't that shameful? He was right to do it!"

"You're being much too hard on yourself. Things are already tough enough without your help."

"What am I going to do?"

Connie was crying openly now, the tears spilled under her glasses and her mouth twisted and her shoulders shook with childish sobs. This too was a defeat for her, this flight she had to share with four white people. And although Levin longed to touch her crumpled face, he forced himself to look away.

The road became familiar. He knew these turns, these trees, these potholes. And then the headlights identified three metal barrels up ahead, and a wooden shack off the road. It was the checkpoint where the soldier had stopped him and Ding. They were closer to the capital than he'd thought. And here were soldiers coming out onto the road, four, five of them. They wore mesh helmets and fresh-looking combat fatigues, and they carried their Armalites at the ready. From the backseat he looked for the bean-eating soldier but didn't see him.

Veeder had braked abruptly at the first sight of them. Now he crawled toward the roadblock, and the slowness seemed to convey an admission of guilt.

Three soldiers approached the car; they were purposeful, in charge. One of them planted a shiny boot on the bumper to signal Veeder to stop. Then he kicked it, hard. The Jetta jerked to a halt. Renée and Bowers were stirring out of sleep.

"Get out," the soldier ordered. When Veeder hesitated the soldier flung the door open.

"Veeder," Levin warned, "do it!"

"Officer, why are you—" Veeder was paralyzed by fright and outrage. The soldier grabbed his wrist and yanked him with great force from his seat. Stumbling through the door, Veeder let out a cry of pain and shouted in Dutch.

His wife, slow to realize what was happening, began to scream. "Don't do that!" Levin told her. "Nobody say anything." And he reached over Connie to open the door, pushing her out of the car. His legs, cramped for hours, nearly buckled under him when he stood.

Veeder was kneeling on the asphalt, cradling his wrist. The soldier seemed at a loss what to do next. Levin scanned the others and approached the one who looked most senior. "What's the trouble—Lieutenant?"

Reasonably, with quiet authority. As if they'd been stopped on the New Jersey Turnpike.

"Why are you on the road tonight?"

"We're going back to the capital."

"A dusk-to-dawn curfew has been declared. You don't know that?"

Levin said that he didn't.

"There is a new government in São Sebastião. The Armed Forces is the sole authority."

"We didn't hear. I'm sorry, Lieutenant."

"You have no radio in the car?"

"It was off."

The lieutenant grunted at their carelessness, but he was temporarily stymied.

"I want to see identification."

Levin took the keys from the ignition and brought the soldier around to the trunk.

"We're missionaries," he told the lieutenant. The lie alarmed him, and in the adrenaline rush he groped for the appropriate denomination. Evangelical, millenarian and staunchly anti-communist, churches built like Sunbelt condominiums and shady business dealings in the Philippines, South Korea. They owned a tenth of Direv Saraun. "Church of Christ the King. My Dutch colleagues and I and our American colleague Reverend Bowers are coming from Karoep. To set up a mission there. With our Saraunese colleague, the young lady, Miss—Moktil."

The lieutenant had their bags on the road and was going through them for papers; the soldier who had sprained Veeder's wrist came to help. Levin hoped that the others' passports gave nothing but name and date of entry like his. He lied some more, with no idea what effect he was having. The soldiers were all business and gave nothing away: they seemed more severe, aggressive, assured than he'd ever seen the A.F.D.S., as if for the first time they had a job to do. Connie joined them and spoke in Saraunese, dry-eyed and amiable, falling back on long habit. Neither soldier answered. Renée Veeder knelt maternally over her husband, hugging his shoulders. Bowers, drugged in the backseat, was glancing through the windows one by one.

The lieutenant stood up. Without a word, he motioned for Levin to put the bags back in the trunk. When it was closed he nodded, a slight lift of the chin, toward the road ahead.

Levin got into the driver's seat. Veeder, held by his wife, retreated to the back. He looked aggrieved, unhappy, and in real pain.

A soldier who had stayed by the shack was moving the barrels aside. The lieutenant came to lean on the driver's windowsill.

"Direv Saraun has no need for missionaries," he told Levin.

"We'll be leaving soon."

"Not missionaries, not foreigners. No more."

Levin nodded. They started again for São Sebastião.

Dawn was breaking over the southern suburbs. Washes of pink and azure and gold spread over the slum lots, the highway overpasses, the garbage mounds along the river beside squatter shacks. On a mild breeze the salt smell from the bay mingled with the fresh dawn air and the clean light, in the half hour before haze and smoke and exhaust would rise.

The day dawned on a nearly empty city. The traffic was sparse and the few vehicles on the roads hustled from block to block in an uncustomary silence of horns. There were a few slum dwellers about, women vendors crouched by doorways and solitary men walking hurriedly with their heads down. But the Jetta passed no newsboys, no women in government skirts and blouses, no public taxis. Every shop was shuttered.

The streets were given over to the Armed Forces of Direv Saraun. After the roadblock Levin had turned on the radio, which emitted an endless stream of martial music and military speechifying that reminded him of the Cultural Night videotape. In the seat next to him, Connie was too disconsolate to translate. They had encountered three more roadblocks, and they had managed to get through all of them. But with each one the number of soldiers was greater and the weaponry heavier. Files of soldiers waited at the roadside next to pickup trucks carrying artillery. At one roadblock, a dozen men stripped down to shorts sat in a cluster under guard. They were poor men, sullen with fright. Some of them had been beaten.

In the city they passed a tank, and then a column of tanks. Troops began to appear at the intersections, some with machine-gun setups. An army vehicle with a loudspeaker mounted on the roof overtook the Jetta: the voice blared the same dozen words over and over. As it drew alongside, an officer in the passenger seat peered out his window. Levin pointed ahead and shouted, "Going home." With the loudspeaker and the noise of two cars he didn't know if he had been heard. The officer neither spoke nor changed expression but continued staring as his vehicle moved ahead.

In front of the Hotel Pacifica the shirtless corpse of a heavyset man lay on the sidewalk in its own dried blood. Two young soldiers were hauling another body into the back of a pickup truck. A group of street kids stood a little ways off, watching with large serious eyes.

Levin at the wheel, trying to drive steadily, glanced at Connie. Her face was in her hands, and he had nothing of comfort to say.

"O.K.," he told his companions. "Let's do this very fast." He looked to the rearview mirror and was met with the three faces behind him. Veeder was ashen, crumpled. "I'm going to take you all to the airport. It's probably the best bet. If it's already closed, maybe it'll open later today."

He waited for a quarrel from the Veeders, from Bowers. But they were simply white people in flight now, and the two men sat stonily silent while Renée nodded in a kind of trance.

"Connie."

She removed her hands from her face. "Sylvia," she told him. "It's Sylvia."

"Sylvia. Where should I take you?"

She gazed out on the city of her birth and seemed not to recognize it. She barely shook her head; her lips moved around words no one else heard. Then the lips flickered with a smile and she turned her face in quarter-profile toward Levin.

"Impanang. Take me to work."

"The hospital isn't safe. They might come for you. Lie low for a while and see what happens."

"But I'll be needed. Look." She pointed through the windshield at a small crowd gathered near three more bodies. One was a woman's. "They are killing the people."

The highway east to the airport was jammed with every vehicle that wasn't on the city streets. And the airport itself, small, flat, as befitted a country of little consequence, with its name written across the top of the control tower, was a madhouse. Cars swinging toward the front of the main entrance actually collided for space. A knot of people crowded with their luggage at the glass doors among ornamental palm trees and jacarandas, while a cordon of soldiers, rifles unslung, blocked the entrance, demanding documents. A pack of Japanese men, probably sex tourists, was bulling forward as one. There were whole families of Saraunese, overdressed, burdened with suitcases and boxes and trunks; there were single men without any luggage at all. Some waved fistfuls of *cobas* at the guards. A European man pushed a Saraunese child to the pavement. On the other side of the glass, the terminal was alive with spectral figures in jerky, confused haste.

Behind the building, two Air Saraun jets and several military aircraft were parked on the tarmac.

Away from traffic Levin pulled up alongside a grass island that divided the entrance road from the parking lot and highway. When the bags were spread out on the grass he said, "You've got as good a chance as anyone else. No polite stuff, just hurry."

"The car was rented at AutoDirev," Veeder said.

"That's fine."

Veeder was pulling himself together. "This isn't the way one likes to leave."

"No. Things aren't going to happen on our terms."

"It's a tragedy for their country. Don't you think?"

"I suppose so."

Bowers drew Levin up onto the island. He was struggling to will clarity into his bloodshot, narcotized eyes.

"Tell me straight, Levin. Can I trust these people?"

Levin told him that it appeared he would have to.

"They hate me. See the way that Dutchman's looking at me. As soon as we're inside he'll tell the cops I was doing illegal stuff."

"I don't think so. Right now you have common interests. You'll make it—you're a lucky man."

"Levin." Bowers seized his arm, and Levin felt a shiver of the ghostly face of the half man. "Those bastards creeped the hell out of me up there—I can't face going home like this again."

"You don't have any business here."

"What about you? You're staying. I could do legwork for you."

"You asked me to get you out of here." A pair of underfed Saraunese youths was crossing the road toward them, smiling solicitously. "Find the courage to go back and sell telephones. Write a book, Bowers—tell your story. End it up on that mountain. There could be a market for it. They say we're looking for heroes."

One of the youths called to Veeder, "Boss, you need porter?"

"I'm not anyone's boss," Veeder said. "Don't name me by that."

The boy started relaying flight information. It was reassuring, then alarming, then reassuring again.

Bowers's grip on Levin tightened. "Don't make me beg."

"No!" Desperately Levin twisted his arm free. You won't drag me down there, he thought. If I'm going down there, it will be my own business. "Good-bye, Bowers. Really, write a book."

Levin and Connie drove away into the chaotic hustle of cars. As they rounded the entrance to the highway he caught a final glimpse of the tableau across the grass: Bowers in his seersucker suit was holding the boxy Samsonite and staring askance at his new companions; the Veeders were saddling themselves and fending off the would-be porters, who were trying to grab the packs off their very backs; and beyond them, the mob at the doors stamped and surged, looking for all the world like the Jola villagers in the maddening presence of Ngot.

. . .

They avoided Camp Pereira in the Montes Xavieres, taking the long way back on Avenue U Thant past the Central Market. The market itself was closed, but on the other side of the broad empty avenue a few of the shops edging the downtown district had raised shutters. In front of one, Levin saw a public telephone. He pulled over.

"I'm just going to call someone."

Inside the booth, he dialed his own number. His heart raced as he waited for the familiar ring. Two, three, four times, and then the answering machine clicked on. No one! Before he could hear his own voice on the tape he hung up.

He stood in the tight box, his hand on the dirty metal phone cage where other users had scrawled numbers. Even in the narrow heat, instinctively he had shut the bifold doors behind him—on a coupless day the noise of the street would have made it impossible to hear. Sweating, he kicked the doors open, fed the machine again and again dialed his own number. She might be screening calls—who wouldn't in these circumstances. This time he waited out his little message, enraged by the complacency of his tone, and when the beep came he said, "Melanie? Are you there? It's me, it's Dan. I'm back—I just got back just now . . . I guess you're not there. Where—well, I'll find out. I hope you're still here—I hope everything's O.K. I'll be home in a few minutes—at nine o'clock or so. Hope I see you."

And he hung up.

On his way out of the booth he heard a rattle and noticed a small shop at the corner whose shutter was being raised by an elderly man wearing glasses. The sign above said ANTONIO'S ONE HOUR FILM PROCESSING.

He glanced across the street. Connie seemed to be thinking her own thoughts, unaware of him.

In the shop, breathless, he surprised the old proprietor, whose iron-gray hair and bony nose looked wholly Mediterranean.

"What can I do for you, my frien'?" On the wall there were full-color Kodak posters and a map of Spain and Portugal.

"I've got one roll—just five shots."

Over his reading spectacles the proprietor surveyed Levin with shrewd humorless eyes.

"And you got to have these five shot right away, my frien'?" His smile was sour. Levin wondered if he assumed the pictures to be pornographic.

"That's right."

"Pickup or delivery?"

"Can you deliver it?"

"Just write your address here and the boy deliver one hour."

He paid and started to leave. The owner caught his eye: Levin waited, knowing he was about to be taken into manly confidence, the way strangers in bars or at ball games swap looks and presume a common opinion.

"They fuck it up good this time," the old man said.

"Yes, they certainly have."

"I come from Lisboa fifteen year ago, open store, make some money, and then business start to go bad. Now, everything—" He gave the thumbs-down sign. "Fuck up. The rebel, the army—they all crazy."

Beneath his disgust the old man seemed to be truly grieving.

"They probably are."

"You think I should to stay? Or go."

Levin was touched that he should be asked. "Would you go back to Portugal?"

"Portugal fuck up too. Philippines, fuck up. Indonesia, same. Hong Kong, going communist. America—too old for America. You American?"

"That's right."

"You lucky. Oh, I get. You taking eleven o'clock flight to Hong Kong—you need picture."

"There's a flight out at eleven?"

"That what the radio say. You not going on it, my frien'?"

Levin thought about it for a long moment. "I don't think so."

"You stay, my frien'," the old man told him, cheering up a little, "I stay. Maybe this military do good."

"The eleven—is that the first flight today?"

"Seven-thirty gone to Sydney already."

"Ah. Is that so. Well, thanks."

That he should have come back to a city she might have already fled brought Levin a jolt of panic. His pulse racing, he rushed from the shop into the deserted street.

He was going to tell Connie what he'd heard, but when he reached

the car she was slumped against the door, shut entirely within herself. Connie. Her nom de guerre had been so sadly wrong. War had
given her none of her namesake's fulfillment and now even constancy
eluded her. Sylvia evoked the woman who was haunted by bad
dreams of empty bodies, and for this name and her burden he had
nothing but tenderness. But whatever it cost her, the pride of the
bourgeoise mestizo, the convent girl, the revolutionary was not going
to leave any of it for him to carry. So he drove her in silence to the
hospital.

At Impanang a crowd had gathered, but not like the airport
crowd. The people here were uniformly brown, poor, and—except
for babies and a few mothers or wives or sisters just given bad
news—quiet in their anxiety. These expected little and feared much.
Blood was smeared on the hospital's concrete steps, where bodies
were being carried up. The wounded lay on the terrace outside the
front doors—some attended by nurses, others still being interrogated
by police. In the surrounding streets, they had passed dozens of men
being herded along the gutters by soldiers. Levin had wondered if
Mrs. Balatang's husband was among them.

He walked Connie inside the gate. "This country could use a
revolution," he said.

"I'm glad you think so."

"Too bad you've got the one you do."

"It's not a thing you or I can pick."

They were passing under a stunted flamboyant; its orange blossoms littered the ground. In this setting, the colors were almost
heartbreaking. Levin made her turn to face him.

"Do you think you could stop being a good cadre for two minutes?"

"You don't like it—I'm sorry. Understand my situation."

"I wish there was some other way of being with you."

"I don't know any other way. This is the only way I have left."

"It doesn't have to be like that, Sylvia." He sounded foolish in his
own ears and his cheeks burned but he heard himself persist. "Why
does it? For either of us. I liked it better when you were crying. Why
can't we—be more than the situation."

It had been a long time since he'd spoken so tenderly to anyone.
It was a reckless gesture, certainly futile, even cruel. He couldn't
stand, though, to let the feelings go unsaid that this woman, passion-

ate, self-mortifying, and doomed, had disturbed. The pressure seemed almost to expand his rib cage. He feared more for himself if he didn't speak.

He had surprised and embarrassed her. As he watched her round face color the blush seemed to carry a trace of pleasure.

"The situation is everything," she told him. "Without it . . . who knows what we would be like. We could be friends. Perhaps someday we will be friends."

She put out her hand; she was leaving. He trembled to touch her. Over her shoulder, outside Impanang Hospital khaki-uniformed police with leather holsters at their belts were stepping among the wounded. He told her to be careful, to let him know if she needed help. She neither nodded nor shook her head, but smiled with such abstraction, seeming to see straight through him again, that he felt the chill return to his heart. And then she was gone.

Alone, for the first time since he'd stood alone on the mountain, Levin drove home.

His building seemed empty. And in his apartment there was no sign of Melanie. Her clothes, her bags, were gone from the bedroom; even her toothbrush was missing.

He went to the telephone in the living room, having no idea whom to call. It was there he found her note, taped to the answering machine whose red light blinked in sequences of four.

> I don't know when or if you will get this but I have gone to stay with John and Rose. I didn't feel safe here alone with all this weirdness happening. There are all kinds of rumors. You picked a hell of a time to leave me.
> Re lollipops—I don't know what you mean but the act itself makes me think we're even further apart than I thought. We must talk about this.
>
> M.

Clumsily he folded it into his shirt pocket, then pressed the rewind button of the answering machine.

The first voice, female, sounded obscurely familiar. It told him that Colonel Siriman of the Armed Forces Press Office desired to speak with him at his convenience and would he call the office immediately? It was the Chinese secretary, with the tissued fingertips. The second was from his editor in Philadelphia, on the verge of losing his cool and wanting to know what the hell was going on in Direv Saraun and whether the wire report from Singapore was accurate. Then he heard his own frantic message.

The last was Melanie's.

"Dan, it's me. I doubt you're there or you would have called. There's supposed to be an eleven o'clock plane out of here and I'm going to try to make it. John and Rose are driving me to the airport. This is no place for me. Or you, I don't think. But that's . . . We're going to stop by the apartment and see if you're there. But then I'm going to leave. Try anyway." There was a pause. "I may not see you again." Another pause. " 'Bye."

He sat for a moment at the table where she'd given her dinner party, by the picture window looking out on the bay, while the tape rewound. Her voice lingered: so familiar, so known, after all the Saraunese voices out there. But it frightened him, with its decisive strength and its assumption of intimacy. It made him think that the unknown thing was himself—the inescapable I he'd been left alone with. If she hadn't come by already (and she couldn't, couldn't have, there would be a note, something), he would barely have time to prepare for her. It struck him as an impossible task, to gather the fragments of the past days and in five minutes assemble them into some satisfactory version of himself that he could present to her. He tried to recover the moment of waking up, but what he located was so slight and remote that he had to give up. The wait was going to be unbearable. It was going to dissolve whatever coherence was left.

He knew he smelled bad, but he didn't want her to surprise him in the shower.

He called Fraser's apartment. He waited seven rings but nobody answered. He went into the kitchen, opened the refrigerator door, stared in its naked light at an unopened carton of milk, an orange on the shelf, a container of Australian yogurt, and a foil-wrapped plate that was the pula-pula left from dinner five nights ago. He shut the door again and returned to the living room; there he phoned Feliz.

"Who is it?"

"It's Daniel Levin."

He'd reached Frankie Young, Feliz's companion. Frankie sounded out of breath, at once wary and confidential.

"Oh, Daniel! He's gone. He hasn't slept here for two nights. He won't even tell me where to reach him. He says—" The voice dropped to a whisper slurry with lithium and husky with feeling. "Maybe the phone is tapped. I don't know what to do. I haven't gone outside since he left. Oh, Daniel!"

Frankie Young burst into tears.

"No, Frankie, don't do that. He's all right, he just took a precaution. It was the right thing for him to do. Have they come looking?" In spite of all, Levin found himself able to think on behalf of someone else.

"Oh God! Not yet. I keep hearing footsteps, then a knock. I open the door a bit, I wait for the gun to go off. But nobody's there! Yesterday I cut myself opening a can of peaches, now I can't use the bloody opener. What am I going to do?"

It was the universal voice—this one Chinese in tone, the music flattened by acquired Londonese English—of sheer human need. It also came in Portuguese, Saraunese, and American; and sometimes it sounded without any accent or articulation on the inner ear. Hearing it stabbed at Levin's heart.

"Have you been taking your medication? Frankie, I'm sure he'll get in touch once it's safe. But if you really feel—" He hesitated. Foolish, meddlesome, duped! he told himself. All cannot be made well! "You could come over here when the streets are busy again."

"What's that? Someone's knocking."

This time Frankie Young was right, but the knock was at Levin's own door.

"I have to hang up now," he said. "I'll call you later. Be calm."

The knocking came steadily, light but insistent. Not at all calm, Levin went to the door and opened it. There stood a shoeless youth—underslung jaw, bangs cut straight across; benign, almost imbecilic expression. He held up a white envelope stamped "Antonio's One Hour Film Processing."

"Fast," Levin said.

"One hour."

But the boy was in no hurry. He looked at Levin and gave the envelope a provocative little wave he might have picked up at one of the American action-film ripoffs.

"What's this about?"

"I see the pictures, boss."

In his distraction Levin was slow to understand.

"You looked at them?"

"I think you no want somebody see them?"

The ruse suddenly broke over Levin like a hot dirty rain.

"You sneaking little sonofabitch."

He grabbed for the envelope but the courier snatched it deftly away.

"If you fuck with me, kid—" Then what? Then kill kill kill! Insane rage flooded his throat and in a second Levin had seized the boy's square head in an armlock. He clenched until he felt the contour of skull through hair. Oh, it would be easy to grind his knuckles into this nose or forehead! To smash this face—smash!

The boy was shouting and dropped the envelope to the floor. Without releasing him—he was slight, bony, stunned into easy capture—Levin grabbed it and tore it open.

"Where are the negatives?"

The boy struggled to pull them out of his back pocket. When Levin had them along with the envelope, he relaxed his hold. The courier sprang away and glared: hair disordered, face reddened with friction and fear, there was still something clownish about him.

"That was a sorry piece of extortion," Levin told him. And because he'd already lost heart for the fight and couldn't stand the sight of this barefoot blackmailer, hurt, delinquent, dopey, and confused, Levin turned away and shut the door.

He leaned against it, exhausted, as footsteps retreated down the hall. He could not stop his knees from their absurd trembling— shaken, as after altercations with strangers in Philadelphia, shouts from car windows. But not like this. So . . . extreme; so much. Everything here was so much. This was it, what he had left to offer her. A simpleton knocked on the door and was greeted by Ngot.

Hearing his heart beat like a noise somewhere in the room, he made his way to the *nara* table and sat down with the envelope. He knew that there would be a better time to look at its contents. When he had not been walking and driving a day and a night. When he did not find himself showerless and alone in a city under martial law, everyone he knew dead or desperate or departed or about to depart. When his heart had receded from his stopped throat, and his chest had ended this business of bending his ribs. When he had his breath again. When all had been made well again.

But—he turned the envelope over and Ding's photographs fell out.

They were black-and-white, and of the five, one—the one of him—had come out as a blur. The other four were clear enough.

The Jola farmer stood shirtless by a tree, in his dandy's white cap pulled to a jaunty angle. The taller guerrillas were talking to him, explaining something, not angry. His head was turned, and in another second he would see, thirty feet away, the camera and Ding. It was the white-eyed Jola face, within the tangle of bushy Jola hair. This face looked uneasy, cognizant, ashamed, preparing. Hands clasped behind his back, like a child admonished, shifting his weight. In the next picture the farmer dully stared into the camera. His hand was at the crotch of his trousers, tugging or scratching.

In the third, one of the guerrillas held an automatic pistol. The farmer knelt, neither tense nor slack, head neither down nor up—waiting, his cap still dashingly cocked. And then he was the body sprawled in the grass and mud of the paddy dike, capless and shoeless, awkward, grimacing with clenched teeth, that Levin had seen with his own eyes that night.

He looked from the living man to the dead and back again. He searched in the face for a shadow of the corpse, in the corpse for a flicker of the face. But there was nothing. Here was a man; here, he was dead. Levin knew; he had seen. This moment, as he sat at his *nara* table, the farmer lay in the earth like a stone. As dead as earth or stone, for reasons that perhaps did not bear thinking about. But here he was again, a man in a ridiculous cap at a ridiculous angle in a Jola mountain village—scratching his crotch. Levin's hand went down to his own and he remembered the hair he had lost for his sins. Naked I came into the world. I wonder what happens to the hair of the dead. The guy with the gun was dead, too. And the one who took the photos. Ding was dead.

Putting the pictures down, Levin began to cry. The tears came unannounced. They startled him and he tried to stifle them but found he could not. They flowed heavier than he could keep them down, blurred and burned his eyes, fused the lashes, dampened his cheeks and filled his mouth with salt. He straightened in the chair, fought for breath, and he muttered, "Jesus, it's ridiculous." But it was no good. Although it was only a Jola farmer among millions, he couldn't help himself. He pressed his hands to his eyes and wept through his fingers. The tears poured upward from a place deeper than his hot face—from his chest, that locked box, which was at last giving way and breaking down and bursting free. Everything knotted in him had come loose, and as his shoulders shook his throat filled to overflowing.

Soon a noise reached his ears, and he knew it was his own sobbing. It was terrible to hear. He'd dreaded it for so long, heard it in so many places, but the sobs were torn from him now without warning or coherence, long, heavy, pained, meaningless—the moaning of a dumb beast. But even this no longer mattered. He lost the last of his grip on himself, and when it was gone he let the sobs pour out of him, a great complicated single surge. And his heart, released, cried out what it had whispered the night of the firefight: *You'd better forgive, you'd better forgive.*

A long time passed before Levin became aware of the knocking. Unable to speak, he looked up and saw the door open. Melanie! She stood in the doorway in skirt and blouse, beautiful, exhausted, astonished.

She cried, "You're here!"

He rose to go to her, but she ran across the floor and seized and held him. He sank into her embrace.

"Danny, thank God you're here."

Indiscriminately, he was dampening her sleeve and shoulder. The hold of her arms and the sound of her soft words made him cry with all his heart.

"Sweetheart." She was stroking his hair. "You came back to me."

He couldn't speak. She moved her head aside because he was weeping on her neck.

"Everything went through my mind," she said, "but the worst was I wouldn't see you. I couldn't stand it."

"I'm here." He was breathing in the fragrance of her hair. His senses were wide open and everything about her poured in—the moisture of her back, her fingers through his hair, her veined neck, her breath. He remembered it all. There had been nothing to fear; so he wept.

"Danny. We're together now." Her arms had stiffened around his shoulders. "Sweetheart, what, what is it?"

She held him a little away and looked into his distorted face. Apprehension shaded hers.

"Why are you crying? I heard a noise—was it you?"

He managed to say, "I was just looking at these."

Her eyes fell to the photographs. She released him and picked them up off the table and flipped through them.

"They're awful." She threw them down. "Why are you looking at them?"

"Ding took them."

"Well, for God's sake, give them back to him."

"He—went and died."

She stared, utterly dismayed. "My God. This country is—so full of death." Her arms were at her sides now. "Danny, I can't stay here. I can't."

"I partly killed him. At least, *I* can say I did."

"Daniel!" She actually took a step away. Her eyes widened in horror, but when she spoke it was with reproach. "What do you mean? What are you talking about?"

"It seemed like I had to. I was really at the limit. There is a limit out there."

"This is making zero sense. Danny, please get hold of yourself. I need you to be with me and get out of here."

"I am with you," he told her. "I need you too."

She said, "I've always wanted to hear you say that." But her voice was still high with anxious reproval. "But I can't make any sense of these things you're saying."

"Try to understand, Melanie."

"I don't! I've never seen you like this and it scares me. You're not *like* this. Corpses and killing Ding and that noise you made and the—look in your face. It's not the face I know."

Although he fought it, at this his heart sank and began to harden and the open spring dried.

"Don't say that."

"You're like a stranger."

"No. I'm not. I'm myself."

"You don't see!"

Down on the street a car horn sounded.

"They're waiting," she told him. "John and Rose. They're taking me to the airport to get a plane out of here. Come with me. Don't even pack."

In spite of the invitation, he saw that she was gathering herself, preparing to leave him. It was taking an immense effort, heavy with disappointment, and he felt a pang of admiration and nostalgia.

Already he'd begun to mourn their single instant of acceptance, as ephemeral as a mistake. He tried to cast his heart out to the way he knew she wanted it, but each time he fell short. He took her slender hand and held it. She squeezed his hand, but she avoided his eyes.

"I bought you a native basket," he told her. "About the right size for fruit. But I lost the car and it was in the car."

"That was nice," she said uncertainly.

"I want to be with you."

"You know I want to be with you. I need your strength."

"Look, I can't say everything now except don't go. Melanie, look at me!" She did, and then away again. "It is me. And what you heard was me, and I don't know how to tell you what it's like but it's—not awful. Not completely awful. And about the situation, things are going to settle down and you and I will be O.K. So just—stay here, and we'll talk, we'll learn to be together."

"It's like a war out there and you talk this way! Why are you doing this to me? How could you go off like that?"

The horn again. Melanie dropped his hand and checked her watch.

"Danny, I'm not going to miss this plane. Come with me and we'll fly home and try to get back where we were before all this—craziness started. Or don't. But you have to decide."

"We can't."

Now she looked at him: her blue eyes filled with panic. She thought he meant there was no way to leave.

Levin walked to the picture window and gazed down at the boulevard. In the passenger's seat Rose was squinting up; Fraser stood halfway out his door, a hand on the horn. On the grass island, the mother with her children in the lean-to was trying to start a fire of leaves and magazine pages. Beyond them, the sea glittered in the morning sunlight.

Fraser gazed up at the picture window and he and Levin locked eyes. Fraser's mouth curled in a half smile of frosty triumph. Levin turned back to Melanie.

She was avoiding his eyes again. Something had been severed and they both knew it. He felt the tension that had always held them fade. It astonished and pained him how quickly it went.

"So Direv Saraun wins," she said. "I lose."

"No. It's not that way."

Fraser honked a third time.

"O.K.," she said. "I'm leaving." Her voice was loud with decision.

"I can't go back, Melanie, the way you said. I ask you again to stay with me."

She was going to the door. "This is your decision," she told him. "Remember that."

She reached the doorway and he waited for her to pause, to give a last glance backward. But she went through it and then she was gone. In a minute he saw her come out on the sidewalk and disappear into the car. Pulling away from the curb, Fraser gave one more long honk.

Levin stood alone in the middle of the room. Slowly he became aware of the electric hum of the refrigerator. He was breathing steadily, waiting for everything to fly. In a moment his fingers would be on his wrist. He would register the spasm, the last centrifugal whirl.

But he remained standing, and it seemed that he was calm. The rush of things outward to chaos was poised with a pull from the blind center and he stood held in equilibrium, suddenly a point of stillness. His face was wet but he no longer heard his heartbeat in the room. It quivered quietly in his chest.

After a while he walked into the bedroom. There was his computer, on the desk; in his black bag, the tape recorder, and the notebook in his pocket again.

He was a journalist. His editor had called and now he had things to write.

He took out the tape recorder and notebook and sat down with them before the computer screen. The machine started up with its familiar grunt and zing. He watched the letters fade on in green.

São Sebastião, Direv Saraun, Feb. 26—How can one person carry the load of a life without being crushed?

Are you asking me?

Who else is left to ask? She's gone, he's dead, even Fra Boboy has written you off.

It was his question, wasn't it?

You remember. Are you satisfied with his answer?

I guess I have to be.

Why does that follow? Have you made the leap from omnipotence to abdication? Are you leaving the world as it is to Fra Boboy?

Having successfully explained it and me, isn't he entitled to both?

To the interpreter go the spoils.

That was the name of the game in his last job and in a way it still is. Yes. Because the world turned out to be a trap for all those guys out there. And Ding. At any moment. I didn't know about that. Then imagine expecting something like humanist justice. Fatuous! The world doesn't compose itself in that way. Its chemicals, gases, minerals aren't structured to make such allowances. Even this I, this face, shambling through its little life, could find itself changed in a moment to something else entirely. For example, a goat. Fra Boboy knows it, and he's putting it to use.

Well? Lay down the burden of your life.

But I can't. Can't.

Prideful. Skeptic.

No. There are—things.

Like what?

I don't know how to explain them. I don't know if they have any real existence. But what should I think about this feeling in my chest? For Connie, Sylvia, expelled from paradise with a carload of whites. And that guy who said "the liberation." And Ding my enemy. And Melanie who wants me but not the things I know. What about that moment when the bullets were singing death and I felt something? And the same thing when I woke up, and again half an hour ago?

Well?

A recognition of—myself.

What of it?

That I am me. The same constituency of hair and eyes and limbs I've always been. Without a mirror, there I was right before me.

That's a pretty small thing.

Very small. A living thread, pulled. In fact, hardly able to stand the force of things out there. Or in here—this pulse, this heart, this voice that goes on and on, until one day it stops.

Everyone else knew all this a long time ago.

That's just the thing. I thought of everything and somehow I overlooked it. Ding knew and it killed him. And Bowers—trying to outrun his shadow. It seems to be more than we can possibly stand.

So is that all? A rudimentary tautology that you are you? Do you think this little feeling does Ding any good, or the rest of them? Is there any reason why Direv Saraun should care?

Not at all. It's useless. Even if Ding were alive—bigger things would always prevail. Fra Boboy was right on that. Though I saw eyes in him that he doesn't see.

So you're left with yourself again. With your ticking self. What if you find out this one is snake-eyed too? Bullshit? Pernicious illusion?

It may be. Then, I don't know. But this thing in my chest, face, hands—this feeling, a quickening. That I know, now, on this spot. So I have to pay attention. There'll be plenty of time later to be sorry.

In the other room the phone rang. He wouldn't go to it; he would stay where he was. He started a new file and named it "Boboy." After four rings the answering machine turned on—and then came the chopped Saraunese cadence of Colonel Siriman.

"Mr. Levin, if you have returned, as I think you have, please call my office. There are some few things I would like to discuss as per our last conversation. I hope we can be helpful to each other. Please call me."

But he didn't move. He listened to the tape turn itself off and placed his fingers on the keys of the machine before him. At the top of the screen the cursor light pulsed, waiting for words. He set about to write them but had none.

ABOUT THE AUTHOR

GEORGE PACKER was born in 1960 in the San Francisco Bay Area. He graduated from Yale and has worked as a Peace Corps volunteer in Togo, West Africa, a carpenter in Boston, and a freshman English instructor at Harvard. He is the author of *The Village of Waiting* (1988).